SUMMARY

"I dreem [sic] of kneeling...for her."

It's a simple sentence carved on a school maintenance shed wall, but it's a message a Domme can't ignore. Especially when Veracity Morgan meets the man who wrote it, and he's nothing like any submissive she's encountered.

Rev Leone is a janitor at a middle school and possesses a singing voice that "calls the soul home" in his family's church. He's the most spiritually mature and intuitive person Vera has met, a man good at caring for others; the school kids, his congregation, and his family. But the relationship he yearns for with a woman is a challenge to his family's understanding, and their control over his life's path.

While only a Mistress with a strong spiritual compass herself can help him reconcile the two, only he can bring her the love Vera feels like she's waited two lifetimes to have.

AT HER WILL

A Mistresses of the Board Room Novel

JOEY W. HILL

At Her Will

A Mistresses of the Board Room series novel #5

Copyright © 2025 Joey W. Hill

ALL RIGHTS RESERVED

Cover design by Scott Hill

SWP Digital & Print Edition publication February 15, 2025

Digital ISBN: 978-1-951544-31-7

Print ISBN: 978-1-951544-32-4

ACKNOWLEDGMENTS

To La Crimson Femme, for the lovely videos and information on doing aerial performance with chains instead of silks. *Wow*.

My thanks to a friend for her painful description of ending a marriage. It helped put form to Vera's struggle with this difficult experience.

To Rachel, for her interpretation of Jesus's sacrifice.

To Lisa L, for her insight as to why she loved the Dominant female/strong male sub dynamic in *Natural Law* so much. It helped Vera speak to her own desires that way.

To *The Chosen 40 Days with Jesus, Book Two* by Amanda Jenkins, Kristen Hendricks and Dallas Jenkins, for the structure of a prayer, which led to a lovely scene between Vera and Rev. And to *The Chosen* series, for its many inspirations, particularly the fabulous 5 & 2 concept.

To Stefanie, for an illuminating insight into how to forgive what seems unforgivable.

To Tim Emerson from the JWHMembersOnly Facebook fan group, for providing a great quote at the Club Progeny entrance – something we should all remember.

To Cassandra Lorius, author of *The Tantric Pillow Book*. Her detailed descriptions were very helpful.

To Gabriela W, who was a member of my editing team since 2018. She left this life this past summer, and I will miss her dearly, not just for her excellent help as a detail-oriented proofer, but for her sense of humor, and her example of strength and optimism as she dealt with her own challenges, including the loss of her husband. I like to imagine them reunited as I write this.

She was always pinging me on waiting *for* versus waiting *on* (very easy to mix up when writing BDSM stories, lol). Well, Gabriela, I wait *for* the day when I'll get to see you again, and give you the face-to-face hug we didn't get to have in this life.

Thank you to Kath P for your continued, equally invaluable proofing help, and Dotty W, for stepping in on this manuscript to be the second set of eyes it needed.

Now, before we get to Vera and Rev's story, let's address the elephant in the room. A Christian/Wiccan BDSM romance? Joey, have you gone over the edge?

The sacred and spiritual have always been in my stories; love IS spiritual, the example and gift of the Divine. Sex isn't the same as love, yet sex in the service of love? That's a very different, very powerful and transformative thing.

As a result, I've never been hesitant to integrate faith with a BDSM romance, because it belongs there. It belongs in any love story, in my opinion. Faith in the Dom, faith in the sub, people having faith in one another and the love they offer? That's a vital part of any relationship.

Not long ago, a fellow author posted on social media, asking why genre authors (romance, fantasy, et cetera) are afraid to include spirituality and faith in their fiction. The obvious (and valid) reason is to prevent our using the story to browbeat our readers with *our* beliefs, rather than letting our characters lead the way.

I agree with that. Since Vera and Rev are both spiritual leaders in their New Orleans community, it played a vital role because *they* made that choice on the story direction. I loved the results, and I hope you do, too.

CHAPTER ONE

I dreem of kneeling.

Vera traced the misspelled word on the maintenance shed wall, following the curves and spikes with her manicured nails. The depth of the carved letters had kept them defined, the weathering increasing their contrast with the pine siding.

"Kids can't resist a forbidden canvas." The female voice, trained by necessity to fire no-nonsense directives at juvenile targets, matched the look of the woman who joined her at the school maintenance shed.

Middle school principal Mavis Petunia Martin wore brown slacks, matching rubber-soled flats and a gold blouse. A slim chain, strung with a cross and a man's wedding ring, was around her neck. Mavis's husband had died of a heart attack a few years ago.

The female principal had broad shoulders and a square torso with impressive breasts. To the student causing trouble, she looked like an oncoming war ship. To one who needed help, she was a Coast Guard rescue vessel.

"Yet this canvas seems devoid of profanity and super-sized male anatomy." Vera's attention passed over cartoon doodles, poems, movie and book quotes, as well as declarations of love, so keenly felt at this young age. None of the carvings had the precision of the one she'd been examining, which was how she'd noticed it. The "ng" had been

1

visible beside the bench placed against the shed wall. A bucket beneath the bench had concealed the rest until she'd shifted it.

"That's a shame," the other woman said. "Who doesn't appreciate super-sized male anatomy? It's so rarely seen in real life."

Vera shot her an amused look. "Why Principal Martin, don't make me blush."

"The only blush you've experienced comes in a compact, some fancy brand that costs a week of my salary."

"Oh, that's ridiculous. Your salary is pitiful. It's at least a month's worth."

Mavis elbowed her. "We have expression boards throughout the school grounds. Students can't put any obscene or hateful messages on them. We get the occasional smartass who breaks the rule, but having to spend a couple Saturdays as a slave to our custodial staff cures them of repeat offenses."

Vera noted no cameras mounted on the shed. "How do you figure out who did it? Waterboarding until someone rats?"

"Sadly, the school board frowns on that tactic. Rev usually knows who's done it."

"Rev?"

"Right hand to our head custodian, Beau. Rev's got an eagle eye for mischief. For other things, too. Every teacher and admin is trained to catch what you're here for today, and he still manages to recognize it twice as often as we do."

"Sounds like a man who needs a raise."

"Won't take one. Been working here for years, but says what we pay him is more than he needs."

From her own well-in-the-past school days, Vera imagined a grizzled worker with kind eyes, pot belly, rough hands, a ponderous gait, and a belt jangling with keys. A man who considered the kids his to safeguard, same as any other adult who worked in an "official" childcare capacity.

"They're coming out now." Mavis drew her attention to the playing fields on the slope below them. "Janis is wearing a plain blue T-shirt and black jeans. He'll stand out because he keeps himself apart from the others."

Based on the separate streams of students that emerged, and the teacher head count, Vera determined it was PE time for four classes.

2

Most students made beelines for the basketball courts, baseball or football fields.

"They're required to do some kind of physical activity for most of the period," Mavis told her. She pointed to the track, where less sports-oriented students had chosen to walk the loop, in pairs or chatting groups. Mavis had a cell-free school, all phones left in lockers or at home. With a nostalgic half-smile, Vera noted groups of girls giggling and gossiping, or seeking sympathy for a personal drama.

Janis had chosen to walk as well, but not on the paved track. He walked along the edge of the soccer field, dragging his hand across the chain link fence or scuffing his toe through the dirt. When he reached a live oak at the far end, he leaned against the broad trunk. A teacher would have to expend effort to get his attention and tell him to keep exercising. Vera didn't think any would, because Mavis had told his teachers what kind of day Janis was about to have.

His head was down, brown arms crossed against his narrow chest. His hair was shaved to a thin layer over his scalp, probably his own work. Barbers cost money.

"His mother was processed into the rehab facility this morning." Vera checked her phone to ensure there'd been no updates. "The DSF worker said three school breakfasts were at the apartment, untouched, though it looked like he was trying to get her to eat them."

"Shit." Mavis's jaw tightened. "We don't let them take food out of the cafeteria, so we can make sure they eat, but they have their ways. We should have gotten DSF involved sooner."

"It's going to be a rough road for her."

"Junkie prostitutes already know what a rough road is. I'm too old and jaded to ask this question, but what are her chances? I taught her when she was here, sixteen years ago. Damn it all."

"She loves her son. If anything can get her on a better path, it's that." Vera put her hand on Mavis's arm. "The important thing is we're getting him the help he needs, so he doesn't have to keep doing what even an adult would have a hard time handling."

She looked at the boy again, the boniness of the shoulders under the shirt, evident even at this distance. "He has a room at Laurel Grove now. DSF signed off on it."

Vera was a veteran at navigating family services paperwork and bureaucracy to make that kind of thing happen. But she gave credit to those inside the system, the overworked social workers who wanted these kids to land in a good place. Laurel Grove, the domestic shelter started by Vera's bosses at Thomas Rose Associates, was the right kind of sanctuary. The adult caretakers there would watch out for Janis until his mom cleaned herself up. Or find him a good foster home if she didn't.

"Good." Mavis sighed. "I'm talking to him at the end of this period. Will Serena be the one picking him up?"

"Yes."

"Excellent. She's good with the boys." Mavis glanced at Vera. "So why'd you drop off the paperwork yourself?"

"I had a meet with a nearby client. I also wanted to go over Career Day with your admin, so my team will know where we are on the speaker schedule, and how big our booth will be."

"Big as you need it. I love how the girls respond to five accomplished women." Mavis winked. "You all being smoking hot means the boys pay attention, too."

"Breasts are well known for being able to open a boy's ears to his opportunities," Vera chuckled. "And once he's halfway listening, Ros's laser gaze will get his mind out of his pants. At least for a few moments."

Mavis's attention swept over her. Vera wore a black fitted skirt with a satin ribbon stripe on the sides to define her hips, plus seamed stockings and black high heels to accentuate her legs. A purple beaded flower sewn on the shoes complemented the amethyst earrings and sleeveless silk blouse she wore. Her silver pentacle was suspended on a short chain just above her Maat and Isis pendant.

With her chestnut-colored smooth skin and thick black hair, a fluffy, gleaming mane that drew attention to her silver-gray eyes, sharp cheekbones and full lips, Vera knew she could hold a man's attention —or a boy's. It was an advantage she didn't oversell, though. The heart and mind behind it, her intentions, mattered more. She touched the pentacle, her personal reminder of that.

"Security could have driven you here in the golf cart to save those heels," Mavis noted.

Vera shook her head. "Cyn brought her way-too-tempting cinnamon rolls this morning. I wanted the walk."

"Has having a man softened that crazy bitch at all?"

"Not physically." Vera laughed at the description of TRA's account manager. "She can eat two of those rolls and not gain an ounce on her skinny, toned ass. But emotionally...yes. She's in a better place. Still Type A and volatile, but that connection to Mick, the commitment to one another, has made the edges a little less sharp."

She squelched the pang of envy and yearning. She was the member of their five-woman group who'd most wanted commitment and a family. Yet here she was, the only one who'd yet to find the right male with whom to share that desire. In pathetic moments, the past crept in and whispered her mistakes were to blame for it.

But things happened as they were meant to happen. At the lowest point of Vera's divorce, Rosalinda Thomas and Abigail Rose had asked her to move to New Orleans and handle the legal and HR demands of their growing marketing company. Vera had walked away from her job as a corporate lawyer, and she'd never regretted it. She, Cyn and Skye helped Ros and Abby run the company, which was fulfilling on its own merits, but the four women had become Vera's chosen family. Being all Dommes only increased the bond between them.

Mavis's phone buzzed. The principal sighed. "I told Cherry to give me ten minutes to meet with you before the next crisis. She was able to hold off the wolves for nine minutes and thirty seconds, a personal best."

"Give that woman a raise, too."

Mavis offered Vera a firm and fond handshake. "Watch the kids as long as you like. I don't get to do it myself too often, but it puts me in a better mood. No matter how the adult world tries to fuck them up, the little assholes are so damn resilient, God bless and protect them."

Vera grinned. "I'll pick you up for our usual lunch at the end of the month."

"Just make sure you're taking me somewhere I can't afford, and you pick up the check."

"Don't I always? And I don't even ask you to put out."

"That's because you're 100% lady, Veracity Morgan." Mavis's amused gaze coursed over her again. "I'm loving those shoes, girl-friend. Give my thanks to Ros and the whole team. I have to deal with so much bullshit, and you cut through it and help my kids. It means a lot."

5

"With what you do for them, it's the least we can do. When do you sleep?"

"When you all do. Never."

With a parting salute, Mavis turned and strode back toward the main building. A far easier accomplishment with rubber soles, Vera admitted, but as she glanced down at her purple and black heels, she was okay with appreciating Mavis's practicality but sticking with her own style.

Mavis deserved indulgences, though. Vera already knew which foundation and blush would work best with the principal's skin tone. A prettily packaged box of that makeup she'd teased Vera about would be part of this year's Christmas gift for her from TRA.

The bench was worn smooth, and clean, so Vera sat down to watch the kids play. Janis had slipped down to a seated position against the tree. Arms still wrapped over himself, eyes closed. Probably taking a needed nap, thinking at the end of the day he'd be back at that ratty apartment, cleaning up after his mom and watching over her. Trying to get her to eat the free school meal he himself needed.

Today was a good turning point for Janis, but he wouldn't see it that way. He'd believe he was abandoning her. Relief that someone else was taking the load was something he'd reject, punishing himself with guilt when it managed to penetrate anyway. But the counselors at Laurel Grove were top notch. They'd help him.

That kind of boy grew into a good man. A service-oriented one. Perhaps among the giggling girls was one who would notice that. She'd grow into her desire for it, wanting to draw that propensity for service toward her, to honor and cherish it, nurture it into a loving submission.

Vera knew firsthand the power of a Dominant and submissive relationship, the spiritual and erotic depths it could reach. A fantasy *and* reality that never grew old.

She needed to get going, but she wanted one last look. Shifting onto her hip, she reached down and traced the letters. When she rose, the feeling lingered in her skin.

She didn't mind attaching those words to a fantasy of a male of legal age. Maybe she'd stop in at Club Progeny tonight and see if any of her favorite regulars were there, and in the mood to play.

Following the current of erotic energy between her and a male submissive, she'd let his needs and desires draw the river's path. She'd put in the curves, rocks and white water, to create a more complex and intense experience for them both.

It required her absolute attention, and she loved that full absorption. It quieted the crazy that tried to rise up too often of late and take bites out of her soul.

She scanned the contributions on the adjacent wall, looking for more evidence of the *I dreem of kneeling* author.

Nothing.

But she might as well check all sides, right? Bags of topsoil and play sand were stacked against the back wall, along with ladders, more buckets and a roll of chain link for fence repairs. This area obviously wasn't part of the "expression board."

It had been an overcast morning, but the sun peeked through the clouds, throwing sunlight against the aluminum ladder. As her gaze was drawn downward because of that flash, she saw an "er" in that same careful lettering.

"Gotcha," she said softly.

She dropped to her heels, smoothing her skirt under her hips. She couldn't see what the rest of it said, because it disappeared into the gloom behind the bags of play sand. But a couple inches of space were between it and the wall.

Fishing out her phone, she scooched closer, wincing at the scrape of the gravel against her expensive shoes. When she turned on the flashlight app, she managed not to fall on her ass when gleaming eyes reflected the light. A dark brown toad stared at her.

"My apologies, good sir," she said with dignity. "This will only take a moment. Thank you for not being a giant spider."

What the light showed her caught her breath in her throat, her heart tilting in a not-unpleasant way. Though it made the toad adjust backwards, she put her hand in that narrow opening to touch the words, the way she had the ones on the front of the building.

I dreem of kneeling.

For her.

～

She took a picture of the words. Then she followed Mavis's path through the back entrance of the building and navigated the maze of halls that would bring her to the front door and parking lot where she'd left her car. The click of her heels punctuated the sounds of learning happening behind closed wooden doors. The divided light windows on the upper half showed grease paint graphics, some of them hinting at what class it was. Algebraic symbols for math class, sketches of tall ships for history.

Blending with the teacher's voices was occasional laughter and overlapping responses, as more than one student came up with an answer. One class was watching a film. Through the window, she glimpsed single-celled organisms swimming around on the screen and heard the drone of a deep male voice. The narrator sounded like the one from her own middle school biology class. The man must be a hundred years old. Or it was the same film.

The wall clock in that class reminded her that she was behind schedule, so she quickened her steps. She had another meeting this afternoon, and needed to get some lunch before returning to the office.

Unfortunately, she accelerated at the wrong moment. As she turned a corner, her high heel hit a puddle of water.

Her leg shot forward, the rest of her body in a pre-fall flail, but she didn't try to stop the descent. Her cushioned ass was far better equipped for the fall than her wrist or fingers.

"Whoa, hold on now."

She didn't land on her backside. Big hands caught her, her own flying up to grab the rough fabric of blue coveralls. She inhaled disinfectant and bleach, blooming pittosporum, the sharp tang of pine sap, and earthy oak. Plus heated candle wax.

Her gaze lifted to meet eyes the color of baked gingerbread. Eyebrows were straight slashes below a furrowed brow, and his cheekbones drew her attention right to plum-brown lips with a seam of pink between them. His hair was a crop with corners at the temples and a straight line over the creased forehead. Bronze skin made his eyes more vivid.

He drew her upright, hands at her waist for the proper yet-too-brief amount of time before he stepped back. Chagrin was on his handsome face. "So sorry, ma'am. Didn't get around the corner fast

8

enough to warn you about the mopping. I heard you coming, but you was moving faster than I thought possible in heels."

His voice... As he spoke, it pulled forth memories and hopes. It brought together the missed and the wished for, and created a bridge she could trust to hold her as she followed them toward the unknown, toward something fantastic that she couldn't resist.

Holy Goddess. Or as Cyn would say, *What the holy fuck?*

The timbre wasn't exactly like a DJ, or a movie star, or a news commentator, but it had those compelling elements. A person would turn toward that voice, curious about the owner, and interested in what it could offer.

Vera was a student of Tantra, tapping into sacred levels of sexual connection and expression. His voice lit up the chakra at the base of her spine, a signal fire that ignited the others from genitals to her throat, holding her in that pleasurable energy channel that only strengthened as she took in everything about him.

His Southern accent suggested Louisiana native. Not Cajun, which wasn't a surprise. Only a small percentage of the city's current population had that accent, no matter what movies and TV suggested.

When he'd talked about her shoes, his gaze had moved that way. He took a good look at her legs, and when he pulled his eyes up, he took in the terrain between them and her face, but he wasn't disrespectful about it. She felt the weight of that look, enough that she maybe wanted him to linger a bit more. Until she told him he *couldn't* look, that she wanted his gaze on the ground.

Even after he took his touch away, she felt the tingling pressure of his hands at her waist, the heat of his thumbs over her hip bones. His grip, strong yet gentle, offered a support she'd never doubt, even as the strength could lift any weight off of her heart and soul.

Wow. Okay, Vera. Easy, girl.

Perhaps because of her silence, he still looked concerned. "I finished this section, and it'll be dry enough for the kids and their sneakers when the bell rings, but it's too slick for your kind of shoes, ma'am. If you can forgive the need for a longer walk, you can backtrack to Hall A."

She gauged the length of the damp hallway. "If you lend me your arm, I think I can get safely through."

When their gazes met, and neither of them said anything for a few heartbeats, she realized something unsettling.

Her cheeks were burning. She was *blushing*.

Thank Goddess Mavis wasn't here to see.

"It'd be my honor, ma'am," he said. "Just stay right there one second, if you don't mind."

"I don't mind."

He pushed the mop and bucket closer to the wall, and set cones around the slippery spot.

A good submissive anticipated his Mistress's needs. Her protection. He was obviously upset with himself for her near spill. If he inhabited her world, she'd punish him to help him handle that. The thought stirred her libido, like her kitchen mixer creating a smooth cake batter out of multiple ingredients. She could taste the sweetness of it, inhale it.

She wasn't in the habit of letting herself fantasize when she needed to be fully present, but it didn't feel like she was absenting herself from this moment. Just the opposite.

He closed the distance between them and offered an arm. The courtly gesture was strangely familiar. "Here you go," he said. "I can move at your pace, so don't hurry none."

"I should hurry some. You'll want to get your mop and bucket out of the hallway before the teen army emerges."

His lips curved. The coveralls were long-sleeved, and he had them buttoned at the wrist, but she could feel his forearm beneath it, the hint of firm biceps as she tucked her fingers into the crook of his elbow. He kept his bent arm still, like the arm of a chair. He was there for stability, and didn't take liberties, and he matched her pace as he'd promised.

"You right about that," he said conversationally. "It's an awkward age. 'Specially boys. All arms and legs, and not good at watching where they going. Eyes too full of pretty girls. Girls know they the ones being watched, so they tend to be more careful of where their feet are."

"Present company excepted," she interjected.

"That was my fault, ma'am," he said. "But a woman has different things on her mind, far more serious than whether a boy is watching her and thinking she's the most astounding and beautiful thing God's ever created."

She paused, and he gave her a sidelong glance. She noticed a stain of color in *his* cheeks, but as she started moving again, he continued in the same casual tone. "Which would be blasphemy, except the most astounding thing God created was love, and that's what that boy's feeling, even if it's just a passing thing. Love at that age can sometimes only take up a minute of your time, but it's mighty powerful. It can carry you for awhile."

Ros, I'm so sorry I was late. I had to kidnap an irresistible man and lock him in my basement. At least until he agrees that I'm keeping him.

When her heel wobbled on the slick surface, he shifted so her hand rested in his opposite one, his other now at her waist. She wouldn't have minded being close enough their hips bumped and thighs brushed, but the formal way he continued to hold himself apart, while interest wafted off him like the scent of that heated candle wax, was too enchanting to disrupt.

"And here I was, thinking the most astounding thing God ever created was the possum," she said.

He grinned. The light that flashed through his eyes had her heart leaping like that toad she'd encountered.

He might be younger than she'd first thought. The boyish smile dropped off about five years, but thankfully the legal drinking age was well in his rearview mirror. While she'd enjoyed sessions with men a decade younger than her, things were more structured in a BDSM club. For a relationship outside of it, she wanted a male settled enough that he could consider commitment. One whose hormones didn't replace good sense—most of the time.

She wished he'd mopped a mile-long stretch of hall. Not just a handful of feet between here and the spacious front foyer, approaching too quickly.

"When I'm here near dark, in the wintertime, I'll see possums scavenging on the grounds," he said. "One time it was a momma and her babies, clinging to her back. She hissed at me. Mean critters when you mess with them. But just scared, like most of us when we act mean. Here we go."

Her feet were on the dry tile. Cases for sports trophies lined the wall on her left, while the front doors were to her right, across a checkered expanse of blue and gold tile, the school colors. Her car was parked where she could see it, her bronze DBS V12 Aston Martin.

She had to look up at him, since he was over six feet, and her heels only took her to five-seven. He was studying her, yes, as a man did, but it was more than that. He felt it, the same as she did, and that he recognized it enough to stay silent, to try and make sense of it the way she was doing, told her more about him.

It also made her heart pound higher in her chest. Sometimes wishful thinking made a woman do foolish things, like lead her to ridiculous conclusions better kept behind closed lips. His gaze had fallen there, and when she moistened them, heat flickered through his eyes and his hand tightened on her. He hadn't let her go. She'd punish him for that, too. If he was part of her world.

"What's your name?" she asked.

"My given name is Karman Leone," he said. "But everyone calls me Rev."

"Rev." Surprise filled her, and she wryly recalled her earlier imaginings about his appearance. "I'm Veracity Morgan. Most of my friends call me Vera."

"Most? Not all?"

"No. I have other friends, a small group, who have a different name for me."

Before she filled in that blank, her gaze moved down to his strong hand, clasping hers. Could it carve upon a shed wall with precision, the pressure driven by desire and need? Had he put out that call to the universe, and the Universe had answered?

Her belief in such things had diminished, and she was tired of her moroseness over it. It was time to take the risk.

"Do you dream of kneeling, Rev?"

The shock in his gaze confirmed her shot in the dark. Fierce joy vibrated through those energy channels and down to the soles of her feet, nestled in the precarious heels that had landed her on a collision course with him.

Now on firm footing, in more ways than one, she inclined her head with stately reserve. Without waiting for an answer, she moved away from him, feeling his hands slip away from her sensitive skin.

At the front doors, she paused and turned. He stood in the same place, staring at her. His jaw was firm, his lips pressed together, his eyes lit with the same kind of fire she was feeling. Which made her own spread upward and out, through and against her breasts, shoulders and throat.

It was going to be a pleasurable journey, figuring out what this would be and where it would go.

"What do those other friends call you?" he asked.

She held his gaze. "Mistress. See you later, Rev."

~

On that intriguing and perplexing note, Veracity Morgan slid out the double doors. Rev moved closer to them to watch her go to the low and sleek sportscar. She folded herself into it without looking back, making his point. Girls didn't have to look. Particularly one like that.

When he'd righted her and gotten a good eyeful, Lord God above, she'd sucked all of his breath into her. He hadn't felt like he could talk until she was in the mood to hand it back to him.

She had high, good-sized breasts and a trim waist, and wore seamed stockings on her attention-grabbing legs. Women didn't often wear stockings in New Orleans, not even in offices. Too hot, and it was a casual kind of town. Her thick hair formed a dark fluff of curls around her face, and reached her shoulder blades in the back. Her lips were a wet silver pink color. He'd gotten a real close look at those when he caught her.

Her skirt, that satin ribbon along the side, made him want to trace it over her round hip. The sheerness of her blouse offered a hint of the lace-edged bra beneath. He'd also glimpsed it from the shift of her neckline, as well as the swell of her breast, though he'd turned his gaze away from that and kept it on her feet. Helping her regain her balance was his first job, keeping her upright and in control. But the image had stayed in his mind, and he went back to it now.

Two silver necklaces had rested in that area, one of them a pentacle. It gave him a start, since he mostly saw that symbol on rock band posters kids put up in their lockers to shock the adults. Adults who, when they were teens, had followed the heavy metal bands for the same reasons.

She wore hers with the single point at the top, instead of the two "goat horns," so he wasn't sure what it meant to her. The other necklace had a winged Egyptian goddess instructing another woman. That one held a goblet, like a gift to a thirsty man.

Veracity's weight in his arms, her hands on him, seeking balance, the surprise in her eyes but no real alarm, would stick with him. She hadn't been afraid of falling, of the unexpected. She hadn't seemed flustered except when he'd stared at her, and she didn't seem like a woman who got flustered by a man's stare.

Maybe a man had never looked at her with the feelings in his eyes that he'd felt.

I think I might be yours. If you want me to be.

"A woman like that is definitely worth a second look." The comment, preceded by a wolf whistle, heralded the arrival of Beauregard Williams, the head custodian.

Rev didn't know that Beau was a closer match to Vera's school memories. Fifties, bald, with a paunch and mostly good humor, depending on the day and how much the kids were testing him.

"But looking's the beginning and end of it," Beau added. "Fancy corporate type."

"She sees with true eyes," Rev said absently. "She looking for a spark in the soul."

"So I have a chance with her, then." Beau executed a stylish spin and jangled his keys. "I got plenty of fire in me."

Rev chuckled. "No doubt. Ladies at the church all want me to introduce you. I put 'em off. I know how shy you is."

Beau's thick lips split into a grin, showing off the gold tooth in front. He had a scar under his left eye from a knife fight in his teens. "Only one I care about is Theresa James. Not that I can get anything out of her other than a polite nod and 'Thank you, Mr. Williams, I'm not interested in seeing anyone right now.'"

Rev hummed a note. "I can tell you what I heard her say to the other ladies when they were canning for the food drive. You man enough to hear it?"

"Boy, I'm man enough for anything. Lay it on me."

"She say she put in her time, caring for a man and getting their children off on their own lives. She don't want to be saddled with another man who wants a maid, a nurse and someone to 'stroke his ego.'"

"Ouch." Beau winced.

"Yeah." Rev shrugged. "So prove her different. She running the church luncheon this Sunday and two volunteers bailed on her. Step in and prove you a man who's interested in taking care of a woman, not just finding one who'll do for you. Do what she needs."

Beau eyed Rev. "Sounds like a lot of work for my day off."

"If it not worth doing one Sunday, it not worth doing for a lifetime, is it?"

"But the heart wants what the heart wants."

"If that's how you feel about it, ain't the heart we're talking about."

Rev gave his boss an even look. He liked Beau, but he'd already gone through two marriages. Rev had faith Beau would figure it out, and maybe Theresa could be that woman, but Rev wasn't going to let her be trifled with.

Beau pursed his lips. "You always tell it straight to me, Rev. You're a good boy. Okay, I'll think about it. I'm going to go check the east bathrooms. You got the west ones?"

"You know it. Yes sir."

Beau moved on, his comfortable rolling gait and the squeak of his rubber-soled shoes a contrast to the brisk get-it-done stride and tap-tap of Veracity Morgan's heels. She'd had rings on her elegant fingers, a bracelet that jangled with some delicate charms. It was nice, being able to call up so many details after the fact, especially when he thought he'd lost a lot of them, the moment he looked at her face.

Rev glanced back at the parking lot. His mind was full of that last thing she'd said. He didn't think she was the type of woman who said stuff casual, without meaning.

I'll see you later, Rev.

He didn't question his thoughts much. They were pretty clear on most things. Mostly he waited for things to reveal themselves to him, show him the path. Right now, he had a feeling he'd arrived at an important fork in the road. So he'd wait. But he had a feeling he wouldn't be waiting for long.

CHAPTER TWO

*V*era's route from the school to work took her through the business and industrial districts of New Orleans, and to the heart of the city. Mardi Gras World passed on her right, followed by Harrah's Casino. A freighter was heading down the Mississippi, and had just passed the Aquarium. Tourists strolling the parallel sidewalk headed for the Jackson Square overlook.

When she ended up behind a horse-drawn carriage, traffic was too congested to allow her to pass, but she enjoyed the people-watching around the French Market.

She pushed the preset for Mavis's number on her dash mounted cell phone.

"Hey, girl," the principal greeted her. "I have about three minutes."

"Two more than I expected. So in sixty seconds, tell me about Rev. Don't ask me why I'm asking, because I really don't know how to answer that. Yet."

Mavis's chuckle held no note of surprise. "He's something else, isn't he? He has that effect on women."

"So he's a player." But even as she said it, Vera knew he wasn't. Mavis confirmed it.

"I've never even heard him talk about dating. Beau says Rev spends his time at our school or the church his aunt founded. God's Light and Voice, just outside of the town limits. She raised him, but passed away about a year ago."

A different emotion touched her voice. "It was a tough loss for him. He's smiled a lot less since, but bless the kids. When they found out, they were so good to him. Brought him cards. He keeps the whole stack of them in his locker, a couple of the homemade ones taped to the outside."

Vera remembered his gaze lingering on her pentacle and Isis pendant, but she hadn't seen any disapproval. Only curiosity, about every detail he saw. Just recalling it speared heat through her.

"What does he do at the church?"

"Beau says he's got a hell of a singing voice, and does a little preaching, when the spirit moves him."

An edge entered Mavis's tone. "Rev moved out of the aunt's house when her sister and her son Witford, Rev's cousin, sold it. They run the church now. Rev lives in a rented room near the school. I don't always know that they have Rev's best interests at heart."

"Do they have too much control over him?"

"It's a peculiar relationship, but no," Mavis admitted. "I had my concerns when I interviewed him, but Rev's autonomy was out front and strong. When he told me he wanted the job, his interest was whole-hearted. Witford visited me face-to-face before that, to get Rev the interview. He wanted to warn me that Rev's reading and writing skills weren't great, but that shouldn't count against him."

"Learning disability?"

"According to Witford, no. I've tried to get deeper into it, but Rev just thanks me for my concern and tells me if he's not worried about it, I shouldn't be, either. He doesn't volunteer much on his thoughts about himself. When you talk to Rev, he always manages to get the conversation back to you, or someone he's concerned about. In a school our size, there's always someone.

"Witford told me Rev was a hard worker, and I'd never regret hiring him. Both things are an understatement, but it doesn't really cover it. Some things... It's better to get to know him. It's too difficult to describe, what it is about Rev."

Vera frowned. "There's more you're not telling me. You're holding back."

"I'm telling you more than I'd tell anyone else. I want to respect the man's privacy." Her tone became lighter. "He handles himself well enough around women, always very courteous, but if they get forward, he backs off fast, like they're a salesperson who showed up at his door with an offer that doesn't interest him. He politely declines, steps back in and shuts the door. He has an remarkable level of self-possession."

Vera heard a voice in the background, probably Mavis's secretary. "Yes, I'll handle it," Mavis said. "I better go, Vera. I'll expect an answer to that question during our lunch. About why you're interested."

"I might have one by then," Vera said. "Talk to you later."

The carriage turned off, and the Aston Martin purred onward, into the Garden District, where Thomas Rose Associates had their offices.

After she parked in the back lot of the former antebellum home, she took the side stairwell entrance. It allowed her to walk the path through the landscaping, under the wide arms of live oaks that had stood for several centuries. The everblooming azaleas were thick with deep red and clean white blooms. Statues and fountains were bordered by beds of flowers that thrived in the humid Southern environment, and benches scattered throughout the area allowed employees the option of taking their lunch or working on their laptops outside.

The discovery of an intriguing man had given Vera a sense of anticipation. The beauty and comfort of familiar surroundings fed it.

She paused at the statue of a dancing girl, placed on a pedestal in one of the fountains. The water splashed off her flowing skirt, long hair and arched back, elegant hands lifted to the sky. It was a newer piece, one Vera had found and added to the garden. She'd discovered it soon after Cyn and Mick had gotten together.

It was a reminder of what she'd told herself earlier today. Though the years were passing, her soul was still dancing. The important things in life would happen as were meant to happen.

Even if they were never meant to happen at all.

Damn it all, wisdom had taught her the cruel irony of human nature; the more a person had, the more room there was for such baseless melancholy, if one allowed it to creep inside and become a squatter there.

She would never be alone and unloved. Never. The women who managed TRA—Ros, Abby, Skye, Cyn and herself—cared for one another, and the men they'd bonded with felt the same way. If Ros wasn't available, Lawrence would be just as quick to come to Vera's aid, for whatever she needed. Same with Neil, Tiger and Mick, very capable males with a remarkable range of skills to offer, emotionally as well as physically. They were dedicated to serving their Mistresses. Even Neil, who was a Dom himself, but took care of Abby's Domme-side needs in the way unique to them.

Vera knew she also shouldn't let her wishes assign too much significance to a potentially short-term attraction. She was almost certain Rev was brand new to actively pursuing a submissive orienta-tion. There was an innocence to that side of him, mixed with a curious maturity and level-headedness that Mavis had confirmed with the clues to his background. Self-possession. That was a good term for it.

Sometimes solving the puzzle was the peak for a Dominant and submissive relationship. Once it was fully explored, the interest waned, and they moved on. Him to the next step in his journey, as she moved on to her own.

She carried those thoughts up the stairs and into her office. After tucking her purse into the bottom drawer of her desk, she turned on her computer, and considered the day's to-do list.

She had a lunch interview with a candidate for Cyn's department, a marketing executive from Florida who was interested in joining the busy firm. His credentials looked good, and they'd already had several phone interviews. The face-to-face impression was the final step. After lunch, she needed to turn her attention to some client contracts.

But instead of getting right to her email and phone messages, she moved to the windows and looked at the grounds from this side. A couple of employees were working on their laptops in the shade of the oaks. Bastion, their indomitable office manager, was pacing along the iron fence, handling a phone call on his earpiece.

Courtesy was the reason he was as far from anyone else in the garden as he could get. He was smoking a cigarette. They all wanted him to quit, and he would do so, for short periods, but if something stressed him out, he'd pick up a pack again.

"Keeps me away from the beignets, Vera," he'd told her, smacking his drum-tight ass. "Gotta keep this looking good for my pets."

"Oh yeah," Cyn had said, coming into the executive coffee room to get her fifth cup of the morning. She'd pulled an all- nighter for an account presentation. "Lung cancer is soooo sexy. That hacking cough gets me going."

"That's just an excuse," Bastion told her. "You know I'm too much man for you."

Cyn had scoffed. "No such thing."

Vera studied Bastion as he pivoted and wrapped one large hand around the pineapple finial on the gate. He cocked a hip when he hooked one ankle over the other.

The man had discipline *and* drive, a Dom who preferred two subs at once, one male and one female. And he was a muscular god, so he had the discipline to routinely win the war with his emotionally-driven sweet tooth. He didn't like to talk much about the things that stressed him out, and whatever it was usually passed in a day or two, but she'd keep an eye on him.

She thought about Cyn's comment again. *No such thing.* But that had been before she'd met Mick, the man who *was* too much for her... in the exact right ways.

Vera knew so much about how love worked. She'd been there to see it grow, crest and die, and suck the joy out of her soul. She knew how hard the road back from that loss was.

She hadn't let it make her bitter, or unwilling to take that road again. Mostly. But this morning she'd been reminded that when a woman met a man who unbalanced her, it could take over everything. All good sense was swept away in a tide of feeling, beyond her reach.

"You're not working."

Abby was standing in Vera's doorway. Her catlike hazel eyes were clear and sharp, and she was making eye contact. That, and her presence in the office, said it was a good day for their CFO, who suffered from paranoid schizophrenia.

Neil was also home right now, which helped. The active SEAL could be called away for missions that spanned a few days or a few weeks, but when they'd gotten together, Abby had insisted he keep his job. Between an amazing psychiatrist who helped her manage her medications, and the support network in this building, her foundation was strong. She was determined that Neil would be able to serve out his twenty-year stint.

Neil had agreed, with one caveat; that he'd make his own decision about when and if she needed him to be here full time. She was the most important thing in his life, and nothing would undermine that, even his life's calling.

Abby's long red hair and body of a Hollywood starlet upset the stereotype of the bespectacled and bookish-looking accountant. Her aptitude for finances was exceptional, but since her diagnosis, she had her work double-checked by her team, just in case. She accepted her limitations without often letting them dismay her. When they did, the women and Neil helped her over the rough patches.

"Yes, I'm such a slacker," Vera told her. "I took five minutes to look out the window before I dive into the contracts Cyn's far-too-successful account teams have created. Darn overachievers."

"Well, working for Cyn, they're not likely to under achieve. They live in fear and awe of her."

"As do we all. Her and Ros."

Abby chuckled. "You look like you have something on your mind that isn't about this. Something good?"

"Maybe. I ran into someone intriguing at the school."

"Intriguing enough to pull two of my essential staff away from their work?"

Ros had arrived behind Abby, her jewel blue eyes sparkling as she teased them. Her gaze also touched Vera's purple and black heels. "Told you those would look great on you. Skye said, 'They add a subtle punctuation to Vera's already fascinating personality.'"

People who went shoe-shopping with Ros never looked at a pair the same way again.

"What voice did she use?" Vera asked.

"Mine," Ros said. "Little wiseass."

Their I/T and communications director could sign fluently, but for a speaking world, she employed the latest in digital voice technology. While she liked using celebrity voices, her coworkers and friends' voices weren't off limits.

"I keep telling you we shouldn't use voice recognition as a security measure here," Vera said. "If we ever tick her off, she'll empty our accounts and head for the islands."

"She won't go without Tiger, and he's not leaving his garage unless he's being carried away by a funeral home. I think he plans to have his precious motorcycle collection cremated with him, like a Viking funeral pyre."

"Plus Skye gets paid more than all the rest of us," Abby added. "She has more reason to stay."

"Except for Bastion," Ros corrected. "His skillset is the most indispensable."

They were joking, but all of the staff were paid generously. Ros and Abby believed in rewarding success, and their employees were paid commensurate with their efforts.

As Abby moved further inside Vera's office, Ros stepped up to her desk to lay a folder on it. "We got the contract with the Bullington Group."

"I had no doubts," Abby said dryly. "Especially after he told you he'd never trust his sizeable marketing budget to a female-led firm."

"I'll probably regret it, since we'll have to handhold him through the ups and downs for the long-term gain." Ros nodded at Vera. "If the senior marketing candidate you're meeting today gets hired, tell Cyn I recommend she give him and his team that account. Bullington will be able to self-manage those ups and downs if the point man *is* a man. I don't mind taking the short cut."

"Because you've single-handedly scored the account, vagina and all."

"There's that." Ros showed her white teeth in a cutthroat smile and brushed back the dark streak in her white-blonde hair. "Plus, we'll take such good care of him, he'll revise his whole life view and moral structure."

"She loves to fantasize," Vera noted to Abby.

"What happened to the moratorium on acquiring major accounts?" Abby arched a brow.

"He made that asinine comment at the Kensington and Associates cocktail party, and Matt Kensington bet me a five-thousand-dollar donation for Laurel Grove that I couldn't change his mind."

"He knew you would," Vera said, with satisfaction.

"Yes, he did." Ros's smile flashed again. "Speaking of which, is Janis all squared away?"

"Yes. I saw him. He's in rough shape, but he's strong. Serena and the counselors will be able to help him, whatever the outcome for his mother."

"Good."

Vera returned to her desk, sitting down and placing her fingers in a

AT HER WILL

fan shape on either side of her laptop. As she considered them, she remembered gripping Rev's arms, the rough coveralls and firm shape of the man beneath.

With a sigh, she pushed back from the desk and crossed her legs. "Have you ever met the custodial staff at Mavis's school?"

Ros and Abby exchanged a look. Abby sat down in her guest chair while Ros leaned a shapely hip against the desk. Ros was all sharp, sophisticated edges, her Upper East Side New York background never completely absent. She had a sleek shoulder length bob. Her stylish skirt and blouse ensemble were paired with today's unforgettable shoes. Bold red, blue and green colors were checkered on the uppers of the stilettos. Her makeup enhanced the thickness of her lashes, the precise brows and curve of her jaw.

"I haven't met any of the custodians," she said. "What's his name? Whoever he is, he's unsettled you, and very little does."

"He goes by Rev. He's younger than me. Not much younger, and he's handsome, which is beside the point."

"But worth mentioning," Abby put in.

"Yes." Vera traced the colorful mandala sticker on the top of her laptop. "He has a submissive orientation, I suspect unexplored."

Ros raised a brow. "You told me you weren't interested in breaking in any more BDSM virgins."

"Yes."

The path submissives followed at the beginning, those initial steps, had a sameness to them. Though it was still a pleasure to watch other Dommes handle it, she'd taken that journey enough. Vera preferred to get them later, when they better understood what they wanted. Exploration at that level could go deeper, and wider.

"I believe his spiritual and emotional development is already there. The rest...that's just mechanics. You know what Mick, Neil and Lawrence say about being a cop or SEAL? How despite all the training involved, there has to be an aptitude for the job already built into their makeup? That's what I mean. I know I'm not making a lot of sense."

"But you know what you feel," Abby said.

"Yes. But I also feel nervous," she admitted. "Like there's a lot there, and what I find...it might alter important things I believe about myself. And what I want from a man."

"Is that bad?"

"I've been in a relationship with a man who changed the core of who I was, who I thought I was. It wasn't a good thing."

"All of the men we are with now transformed us," Ros noted. "But because they were the right men, it was an augmentation to what we already are, the things we liked. Whatever they altered, wasn't altered in a bad way. Because it was love that changed us. Not fear, ego or insecurity."

"I said that to you, didn't I? When you met Lawrence." At Ros's amused look, Vera drummed her fingers on her desk. "Skye's not the only wiseass around here."

"Boss Wiseass, if you don't mind."

Vera sighed. "I'm going to think it over before I do anything with it."

"Okay." Ros rose with Abby. "But what's the plan after you do?"

"Mavis said when he's not in school, he's usually at his family's church. I may go there Sunday, see him in that environment, to learn more about him. Maybe invite him to Progeny with me next week, as my guest."

"Well, far be it from me to give advice," Ros ignored Abby's exaggerated shock, "But I assume you'll use a more nuanced approach than sidling up to him at church and saying, 'Hey, come with me to a kink club and have your mind blown.'"

"In addition to other parts."

Vera saw Bastion leaning in the doorway, his arms crossed over his wide chest. He'd obviously picked up the conversation on his approach to her office.

"How a man your size moves like a field mouse is beyond me," Ros informed him.

"I beg your pardon, oh Queen of All. I move like a ninja."

Vera rolled her eyes. "I'm surprised Cyn and Skye aren't in here." They all had a knack for knowing when a conversation of import was happening. This seemed like a casual discussion, but it wasn't. Something significant had happened between her and Rev.

A perverse part of her wanted to do just what Ros had intimated. Shove Rev in the deep end and let him prove to her that she was wrong about that moment of deep connection. Which would give her an excuse to avoid going down what seemed like a new path, only to face the disappointment of it leading where she'd been before.

Was she really throwing down a gauntlet before Fate, just to shield herself from that kind of hurt? She knew better than that. What was it her mother used to say?

When you get to the gates of Heaven, you don't want to say, "I took no risks."

Life was full of ironies. That was before she told Vera she could never come home again, because Vera had chosen a path her mother abhorred.

"Skye is ass-deep in debugging that database for Birdwell and Sons," Bastion said, "and Cyn is at their offices, testing the interface."

"Anything I need to do?" Ros asked.

"Nope." Bastion shook his head. "Skye said it's just the typical bullshit involved in integrating current tech with a decade's worth of crappy software. Or something like that. She was speaking geek. I got the important part—she and Cyn have it handled."

"I'll get started on Bullington's paperwork," Vera told Ros. "The sooner we shoot the contract over to him, the less time he has to reconsider."

"Prioritize it, but wait until tomorrow to send," Ros told her. "He needs to think we're not all that eager to have his business. I told him we had a major client freeze right now to give our current roster our best efforts, but because we were bringing in a new experienced marketing rep, we had space for one more. I also heavily implied I was doing this as a favor for Matt, since they're boxing buddies."

"The hard-to-get plus exclusivity approach."

"For a personality like his, it was the closer." Ros had Abby precede her to the door, her hand brushing Abby's hip. Ros wasn't the touchy-feely type, but not only was Abby her closest friend, they'd had some close calls at the beginning, when her diagnosis had threatened to take her away from them. Even now, managed as well as it could be, there were rough patches. With schizophrenia's unpredictable effect on the brain and limited effectiveness of medications on Abby's system, there always would be.

On top of that, the two women had once been a trinity. Their closest mutual friend, Laurel, had been killed by a drunken, abusive husband—hence the Laurel Grove shelter Ros and Abby had started. The impact on Ros had been deep and lasting.

So when she touched Abby, it was reinforcement their usually invincible boss needed. It also conveyed to Abby that Ros was there in every way she needed. She'd have her back, always.

Ros was like that with all of them. As she proved when she glanced over her shoulder at Vera. "Are you all right?"

Vera met her piercing gaze. Ros's intuition made her a successful CEO, and a formidable Mistress. The latter role was only for Lawrence now, for the transformative reasons Ros had stated. The former SEAL had Ros's heart cupped in his strong hands like a bird's egg. No force in the world could make him crush it.

That ache in Vera's heart was back.

How a chance meeting with a school janitor had her emotions kicked up this way, raising issues from her past, as well as goading her longings in the present, was a mystery. Maybe she was having an off day. Maybe it was mere chance, nothing significant about any of it.

Sure. He'd caught her in his arms at just the right moment, and he'd written that message, which seemed to be just for her.

For her.

"Yes. Thanks for asking. An interesting man isn't a bad thing." She managed a half smile. "I just don't want to go to the same old theme park."

"The theme park is always the same. It's about someone who can make you see it through new eyes." Ros paused. "*You* told me that, too. Not long before I met Lawrence."

"Damn, I sound crazy smart."

"It's why I hired you. Do you have plans this weekend?"

Vera took a breath. "I think I'm going to church."

CHAPTER THREE

*G*od's Light and Voice Church was a long rectangular building with beige vinyl siding, and a few tall narrow windows edged with white trim. It was the type of structure that could be erected with limited funds.

The marquee by the road, with the usual interchangeable messages one saw in front of many churches, said "Find God Here." Behind it were three tall and rough-hewn wooden crosses. The purple sash draped on the middle one fluttered in the breeze. Two big apple trees near them had benches to enjoy their shade and contemplate the crosses.

Vera found a space in a mostly full parking lot. The landscaping that flanked either side of the wide front walkway made up for the plainness of the building. The lush flowers and ornamental grasses said the church had an accomplished garden club. The concrete pedestals of two bird baths, one on either side, were angels with lifted hands and arched wings.

At the door another angel held up a boat. Inside the boat were multi-colored smooth stones shaped like tiny fish. When she touched them, she detected an energy that suggested they were prayed over, as she often did to her own talismans, like her pentacle. She expected the congregation could take and use them like worry stones. Choosing a blue one, she slipped it into her coat pocket.

Someone inside was speaking in a muffled but sonorous voice, backed by trills of organ music. She'd changed her mind about coming, then changed it again, so it was thirty minutes after the service had started. Even so, as she stepped into the foyer, an usher met her, a middle-aged black man in a gray suit, a purple flower in the lapel. "Welcome to God's house," he murmured and opened the nave door. "May He be with you, sister."

"And with you."

When he offered her his arm to escort her to a pew, she knew why Rev's gesture at the school, to keep her from falling on the wet floor, had seemed familiar. She thanked the usher quietly and slipped into the back row.

The church was two-thirds full. Potted plants set in the narrow windows dressed up the surroundings. A carved and polished cross was mounted in the transept. To the left side of it was an area for the choir, dressed in purple and silver robes. The pulpit was on the right side.

She had the pew to herself, except for the usher who took a seat at the other end of it. From her glimpse of the phone now balanced on his knee, she saw he had a view of the parking lot to know when any stragglers had arrived, so they could be greeted as she had been. A customer-oriented marketing technique Ros would approve.

The minister, a tall and compelling man with a clipped beard, single gold ear stud and shaved head was finishing up a rousing call to serve Jesus. The price of his tailored suit didn't mesh with the plainer setting, but his message was passionate, even if a little overly scripted.

In dealing with the rejection of her family, she'd explored a lot of Christian denominations, as well as the paths of other faiths. She'd eventually found her home in Wicca, and was now a spiritual leader in NOLA's pagan community. She routinely led Sabbat rituals and officiated at handfasting and crossing over ceremonies.

Wicca wasn't a conversion faith—it respected other forms of worship, so she was comfortable attending most churches. She ignored the tenets that harped on being the only right path, and focused on what connected it to hers.

Do no harm. Love one another. Give more than you take.

No matter how humans managed to twist and fuck up those messages, the common thread endured. Religion didn't trump faith, which in her mind was always about cherishing life through compassion, kindness and service.

The oil paintings mounted on the walls between the windows were done in bright, bold colors and looked like the work of local artists. Most depicted the Gospels, Jesus's journey and teachings. In one of them, Jesus was healing the leper.

He'd understood what faith was, too, and had loved humanity, despite their thickheadedness.

She reminded herself of that when she thought of her ex-husband. Or the family she'd had to leave behind, but remembered daily in her prayers before she quietly shut the door on that heartache and got on with her day.

And while it might startle some people, she also felt closest to what spirituality and faith were about when she was in a session with a submissive. Raising that sacred sexual energy connected them to the Lord and Lady, the male and female divine principals.

"Let's hear Brother Rev's take on what I just told you."

The preacher's announcement pulled her out of her head and into the present. From the expectant shifting in the audience, the highlight of the service was about to happen. Calls of "Amen" and "Blessed Jesus" confirmed it.

Then they stilled. And remained still.

Vera glanced at the usher. His smile at her seemed to say, "Get ready for this."

A single note filled the air of the church. Not from an instrument. From a human throat.

No words. Not initially. Just that note, drawing out, filling the room, touching down, touching her, touching everyone. The energy in it turned all souls toward it, like sunlight after six days of clouds.

Vera's fingers were in a knot in her lap as the note expanded into harmony. Still no words. None were needed. She shut her eyes to get closer to it. The male voice reached for the heavens, the earth, and everything in between. Gathered it up. Then the words evolved from the notes.

"Gather the wheat. Gather the souls. Show them light. Show them hope. Show them truth."

A voice so fluid and strong, she could have listened to it forever.

She'd already heard that voice speak words. Now it sang them, moving closer. She opened her eyes.

Rev was coming down the steps from the small balcony over the chancel and transept. She expected he'd been listening to the sermon, waiting for his cue. While acoustically the elevated position would have helped the power of his voice, she had no doubt it would have felt the same from ground level. Even from a cellar. He wasn't using any sound enhancement, not even a mic in his lapel.

His brown suit, white shirt and plain brown tie weren't expensive, maybe secondhand off a rack, but it had been altered well for the body she'd felt beneath the coveralls. Shoes shiny. Short crop oiled and gleaming. As he sang, he reached out toward the congregation.

The calls to "Praise Jesus" and "Bless the Lord" rose and fell as he moved down the two steps from the transept and into the nave. Half of the congregation were on their feet, their hands in the air. From the profiles she could see, many had their eyes half closed as they swayed like that wheat he was singing about.

He kept singing, but his gaze was moving, left, right, left, right. It wasn't the passing eye contact of a performer, but a purposeful scan. A seeking. When Rev came to a stop, his attention was on a woman in the middle of that row. Her shoulders were bowed, and from the way they were shaking, she was weeping.

Though no obvious direction was given, the standing members settled back into their pews, though quite a few were energized enough they perched on the edge, ready to surge to their feet again when the spirit moved them.

Vera noticed a faint tightening on the preacher's face. He shot a glance toward an older woman, sitting on a short bench perpendicular to the pulpit. She made a slight quelling motion.

"Sister, come sit here," Rev was saying to the woman. "Help her come. She needs all y'all's help." Rev pointed to the aisle seat. Obligingly, the eight people between him and her shifted, the one closest to the woman encouraging her to rise. She seemed to lack the strength to do it on her own, and multiple hands helped support and get her there. Including the man on her opposite side, whose face held pain. Her husband, from how he touched her waist, his simple wedding band gleaming.

When the woman at last sank down in the aisle seat, her head was still bowed, and she wrapped her arms around herself.

Vera's heart tilted as Rev went to one knee beside her. He touched her knee, the silky stuff of her skirt. Her dress had flowers on it, a bright pattern she'd likely bought on a far better day.

"You gonna sing with me, sister," Rev said gently. "Sing this line. 'Show me hope. Help me, Lord.'"

He sang it, low, easy, a plea set to music.

She shook her head and began to rock, but he brought her hand to his face. He sang the words again as that intimate contact drew her attention to him. He did it without hesitancy. Confident. Vera was leaning forward herself, hand gripping the edge of the pew in front of her.

"You sing that first bar, and I'll come in behind. Just like the Lord, holding you up, standing behind you, helping you through anything. He going to catch you, sister. He's holding you in His Hand right now...can't you feel it? Just like my hand on you..."

His grip tightened, and her fingers slowly curled around it. Her voice was thin and quavered as she haltingly sang the words. "Show me hope... Help me, Lord."

"Help her," Rev said, and the room was swept with "Go on, sister... Let the Lord help... Bless his name... He loves you..."

Rev picked up those same words and put them to that music in his voice, a whole orchestra in it, every note clear. As she repeated the line he suggested, her voice began to strengthen. The power of the effort tingled against Vera's skin and sank into it.

Each time the woman sang the line, Rev came in behind her, doing in song form exactly what he'd described, a subtle but strong presence echoing her own plea, lifting it up, carrying it forward.

Then something broke and she was crying out different words. "Forgive me, Lord, I've been so afraid, I've been so afraid...and that was wrong. I should have known You were there."

"He's with you sister... We don't need to be afraid..."

People rose, more hands lifted. Since Vera was on the aisle seat of her pew, she could still see Rev and the woman.

"It's scary to let go of what we know." Though spoken lower, a conversational tone, Rev's voice resonated through the church like the preacher's had. There was still that hum to it, on the cusp of becoming music again. "Because we don't know God, not face-to-face like you and me now. We don't know His face. We know our bodies, and it's scary to let go of our bodies. We know all about them, and when they get sick and they letting us go, they're freeing our soul, cutting it loose. That's new and scary.

"We wonder, can we get that coffee we like anymore? How will we do without that? How will my husband manage? The poor man don't even know how to wash his own clothes."

His tone had changed, creating a ripple of laughter, the most powerful kin to hope.

The woman lifted a tear-stained face to Rev, smiling. Vera could see the evidence of poor health there, a woman struggling with serious illness. She'd likely been sitting in church, feeling overwhelmed by her fear, isolated by it, but Rev had brought her back to them.

As he rose, and gestured to the others in the row, the woman was helped back to her seat. Her husband put his arm around her, and she clung to him in a way Vera expected she hadn't done in a while. She'd been holding herself apart, caught alone with her fear, needing to be brave, thinking she needed to do it all by herself.

Vera had led energy raisings for people with emotional or physical afflictions. The person was put in the center of the circle, a symbolic as well as literal focus, the coven participants putting hands upon them to channel healing energy and intent toward them. To give them whatever they needed to help connect them to the Divine, for healing, acceptance and strength.

It was a beautiful, intimate thing, like this. It brought tears to her eyes, but she also noticed the subtle motion of the preacher. In response, the ushers rose and began passing collection plates.

Learning how marketing worked from some of the best—Ros, Cyn, Abby—she knew their timing was excellent. Churches often provided resources that helped people in need of jobs, food, clothing, housing. If the money was put to good use, she had no objection to it. But something about this...it felt a little off.

It wasn't a calculated coordination with Rev. He seemed as oblivious to it as Skye was when she was deep in a programming issue, and Bastion left her favorite soda at her elbow for her to hydrate when she surfaced.

Rev was working his way back to the transept. He'd also moved on to Michael Jackson's "Man in the Mirror," with lyrics that lent itself to a religious setting. His voice made the transition easily, pulling them into a song they could sing with him. The choir joined him in leading it.

When they concluded, there was a general call to praise. Rev gave the impassive preacher a respectful nod and skimmed his fingers along the wood molding of the pulpit. As he did, he shot a smile toward the older woman. Despite her cryptic exchange with the preacher, she gave Rev an approving look, her expression poignant.

It was obvious he did it as an acknowledgement, a silent nod to the one who'd once occupied that pulpit. Probably the aunt who'd raised him, that Mavis had mentioned had died a year ago. The older woman was likely her sister, and Vera was guessing the preacher was Witford, Rev's cousin. Some similarities in his and Rev's features suggested it.

An alcove behind the pulpit had a door to other parts of the church, but it also held a chair. Rev was mostly concealed by the shadows as he took a seat in it, but his head lowered, and his shoulders slumped, as if the energy to do what he'd just done had taken a toll. Maybe the emotion he put into it had overwhelmed him.

She wanted to go to him, and would have, if she was formally his Mistress. However, she continued to watch him as the preacher handled the last half hour of the service. The choir offered a mix of traditional and contemporary hymns. They were excellent, but her body was still humming from the music that came from Rev.

At length, he left, slipping out that door. In case he was departing, she considered leaving to see if she could catch him in the parking lot. Before she could make a decision, the side door to the nave whispered open and he was there. The usher was no longer in her pew, so he moved toward her unimpeded. As he took his seat next to her, his slacks brushed her sheer stockings and the hem of her skirt.

Her breath caught from him being so close to her, so unexpectedly. His gaze met hers, and it was alive and fierce and wondering, to see her here. The energy between them was like a sewing needle flashing back and forth, stitching together two pieces of cloth.

She had her hand on the small expanse of cushion between them. Rev's eyes were on it when he reached out, but he didn't touch her. With his fingertip, he traced the shadow her braced arm was casting.

It might be the most intimate thing she'd ever seen a man do. She wasn't breathing as he did it. When he put his palm down on that shadow, she wanted to touch him, but it would dilute the potency of the act, so she didn't.

The service was concluding. "I need to help my cousin," Rev murmured. "Can you wait a few moments so I can talk to you afterward?"

"Yes."

He rose. To exit the pew this time, he moved in front of her, his gaze on her lifted face. She touched the crease of his slacks over his knee, just a glancing brush. His eyes went there, those gingerbread eyes heating, and then he was past her and slipping out of the door.

As she brought her attention back to the front, she noticed the aunt staring at her. So was the preacher. And their looks weren't friendly.

~

Leaning against her car door, Vera could see the front of the church. As the remaining parishioners came out, Witford and Rev's aunt shook hands and thanked them for attending.

Rev had joined them, but he was quiet, standing back, only engaging if someone spoke to him. Since the preacher took the lead in almost every instance, very few did, though Rev was touched often. His forearm, his shoulder, a hand pressed. A grateful smile sent his way. Like he was a sacred relic they needed to touch, or connect with in some way.

When the church was empty, Witford spoke to him. Rev shook his head and gestured toward Vera. The aunt responded with a note of urgency. Interestingly, Vera saw Rev's expression harden, though his tone with her was patient. She couldn't hear most of the exchange, but she heard his parting words. "I'll be by later, Tisha."

As Rev went down the steps, their worried eyes followed him. While Mavis might suspect their motives, which meant Vera did, too, at least some of the worry she saw in them was for Rev, which mystified her. He was a grown man, after all.

As he reached her, he extended his hand. She placed hers in it, curious, and he pulled a folded paper from his pocket and transferred

34

it into her palm. It was the hundred-dollar bill she'd put in the collection plate.

"How did you know it was mine?" She kept her fingers curled over his, so he'd know she didn't want to break the contact.

"It smelled like your perfume. And Ray told Witford the 'new lady in the back' offered it. You aren't here for that. It's not necessary."

She turned their hands over, closed his fingers over the money and grasped his wrist. His gaze flickered at her grip. "First lesson, Rev. Don't second guess my intentions. Understand?"

His pulse accelerated under her touch. "I'll be back," he said.

He crossed the parking lot, intercepting the usher she now knew was Ray. When he handed the money back to him, Ray gave him a curious look, then a grin and a light punch to his shoulder. Rev smiled wryly.

As he returned, she reminded herself she was standing in a church parking lot. She shouldn't obviously ogle him, no matter how good the man looked and moved in a suit. But it was a view worth appreciating.

"Couldn't give it to him later?"

"I don't like handling money much." Rev paused, waited. She arched a brow.

"You said I shouldn't second guess your intentions. I'm waiting to hear them before I tell you mine."

"I'd like to take you to lunch. Or a coffee. Whatever you prefer this time of day."

Those light brown eyes held hers with an unsettling expression. He still didn't say anything.

"Problem?"

"I just want to be the one doing the asking."

"Fine, then." She produced a card from her purse. "This is my cell and email. Reach out to me when the spirit moves you and we'll see what works out."

She pivoted on her heel. Yet when she reached the driver's side of the car, he had followed her and was standing close. He held the card carefully, but he didn't seem to have taken his eyes off of her.

"Miss Morgan? Veracity?"

"Yes?"

"May I take you somewhere?" At her look, he added, "Didn't say I wanted to wait to ask. Unless you prefer that."

Her brief irritation was overruled by a larger desire to smile. Rev took a step, bringing himself closer. Not too close, not really, but his sexual appeal was a strong, pressing energy. His easy indifference to it only increased the effect.

Sunday church goers looked forward to lunch, so the parking lot had emptied fast, leaving them mostly alone and unobserved.

"There's a place I like to go, near here," he told her. "It's quiet and pretty. That's what I prefer after church. I eat later, at my aunt's. She do a full Sunday dinner, and if I don't leave room for every dish, I hurt her feelings. You welcome to join me for that, if you have that kind of time."

"Not today. But the pretty place sounds good."

"I usually walk. It about a half mile down the road, but there's parking, if you want to drive it."

She dipped her head toward her car. "Hop in. Unless you'd like to meet me there."

His eyes holding hers, he opened her door. "I don't want to make you wait for me."

～

Rev's destination was a turnout area with a short walk to a scenic marsh overlook, a good rest stop for a vacationer using the rural highways route to get to Texas. In addition to three parking spaces, there was a picnic table, a trash can and a marker that said some historic person had once camped overnight there.

The boardwalk to the scenic overlook posed no challenge to her heels, but Rev provided his arm as they walked together. They had the place to themselves, so when they reached the rectangular deck with its bench seating, she turned toward him, tall and looking down at her. Waiting. Not passively, though. She didn't think Rev did anything passively. "Did your parents like astronomy?"

He blinked. "I didn't know my daddy. But my momma liked reading to me from a book about stars and planets, and one of the few things she told me about him was that he liked the sky and everything in it. I still have the book. Why you ask?"

"Your name, Karman Leone. Leone is a version of Lion. Lion

sounds like Line. The Karman Line is the line between earth's atmosphere and space. The known, the unknown. Home and other."

"I didn't know that. Thank you." That, and a flash of wonder in his eyes, told her he welcomed a glimpse of something he didn't know about his mother. "She died when I was three."

"So you remember her."

"Yes."

A simple answer to emotions that weren't simple at all.

She sat down on a bench, her knees together, her feet aligned, back straight and hands resting on either side of her, because she wasn't inviting him to sit with her. "Kneel in front of me, Rev."

His hands curled at his sides. Energy wrapped around his whole body, holding it rigid for a beat. She half closed her eyes, lifting her chin to feel it touch her, the heat of that anticipation.

He dropped to a knee.

Firsts could be indescribable, but everybody knew that, so "first" usually covered it. First kiss, first love. First time to experience this, with this man. Each move he made under her command would build the feeling between them, as well as guide her own reactions. When he obeyed her, it introduced him to her every erogenous zone, as well as knocked on the door to her heart.

"Take a moment to look at me however you wish," she said. "But do not touch me."

He started with her face. He studied her brow, his attention vibrating through her third eye and crown chakra. With a stomach-hollowing breath, she pulled more energy through her core to expand that feeling, widen her sensitivity to him, feel what was going on with him.

She looked, too. At his mouth, the curve and shape of his lips, their dimensions and capabilities. She thought of how sensitive and responsive her skin would be to their touch. As his gaze slid to her throat, she lifted her hands to the purple blouse she'd worn beneath the lavender skirt and jacket. She slipped the button at the V, then the one below that. It revealed the black lace of her bra, the satin cups that covered the nipples. Though she kept her breath controlled, the slow in and out to match the heavy thud of her heart made the ample C-sized curves quiver.

His own breath drew in at the sight. "Look, but do not touch," she said. A reminder.

He honored the gift with avid appreciation, but the gaze that moved back to her face showed he was in command of himself, while acknowledging her command over him.

"You told me once. You never have to repeat yourself, Mistr— Veracity."

He'd naturally wanted to call her Mistress, but she'd said only a select number of people had permission to call her that. He'd remembered.

"You may call me Mistress," she said.

His eyes lowered again. Moved over her breasts, the folds of her blouse framing them. He moistened his lips.

"What would you do, if I said you could do anything?" she asked. Her body was tight, ready. Wanting him.

"I'd put my mouth and hands there. I'd peel back the lace and suckle you, feel you quiver under my touch. Taste your perfume, your skin. You. Hold your waist in my hands, press my fingers into your hips."

That energy coursing through her widened and intensified. "Keep looking."

His attention slid to the skirt smoothed over her thighs.

"Do you like to use your mouth between a woman's legs, Rev?"

"Yes ma'am." His voice was husky. "I like that taste, too. I like having my mouth there when she find her joy."

A lovely word for orgasm. She slipped the tiny buttons along the right side of her skirt to reveal her leg, the loosened fabric sliding away from it. Reaching up, she curled her fingers around his tie. When she tugged him forward, his eyes held fire. "Put your hands on my knees."

She parted them beneath his touch. She also took her hands away to brace her arms on the bench again. As she leaned back, she flexed her foot, dropping the shoe from it so she could put her stockinged sole on his thigh. The other foot, still in its stylish heel, was planted beside his opposite knee. "Bring your mouth as close between my legs as it can get without touching my panties. Then be still, until I tell you otherwise."

He'd left his suit coat in her car, so when his back curved, she watched the dress shirt stretch over muscle and his shoulders. As his hair, jaw and ears brushed her inner thighs, sheer lust tightened her nipples and gave her gooseflesh on her arms, the small of her back, her neck. When he was so close a twitch from her might have pressed her cunt against his lips, he stilled.

The moist heat of his breath made her want to close that miniscule distance, but she didn't. Lifting one hand, she smoothed it over his curved back. The shirt had a softness to it that added to its fit. At his collar, she trailed her nails along his nape. As she inhaled the masculine scent of his aftershave, the light touch of oil in his hair, she detected some rosemary in it.

"Think about your breath. Draw it in, draw me in. Then exhale, knowing the heat of your breath is stroking me. Making me wetter and making me want you even more."

"I right here, Mistress." His voice was muffled, slightly hoarse.

"Yes, but the wanting is part of the pleasure. Isn't it?"

The puff of his breath as he spoke made her inner muscles contract and her lower belly flutter. She bit back a moan as he followed her direction, and his breath's stroke became more rhythmic. She noticed his grip on her knees had constricted and suspected he'd recognized the order to keep them there served as a restraint. His shoulders lifted and lowered with each breath. Her body wanted to move in that same dance. She'd lift her hips and rub her damp pussy against his wet, so close mouth.

But this was a blissful test of the possibilities. She reined herself back, though her arousal was intense enough she might have to pull off the road and finish herself before she arrived at the privacy of her own home.

"Are you aroused, Rev?"

"Yes ma'am." A half chuckle, strained.

"Sit back, stand up and show me. It's my turn to look."

He did so with reluctance. She was taking him away from where he wanted to be, but it also might be the first time he'd displayed himself to a woman this way. She liked the thought of that, enjoyed seeing the internal battle to meet her desires without self-consciousness, and settle into it.

Yes, Lord and Lady, the man had been blessed. The generous evidence of his cock against the slacks made her ache to put her hands on his thighs and play. Knead, squeeze, stroke, all while requiring him to stay still, until his body started to tremble with the effort.

Instead, she lifted an approving gaze to his. "You did well. How do you feel?

She saw heat and strong male desire. "Like I hoped to feel."

"And how is that?"

"I've pleased you. Created desire in you."

"And in you."

His lips creased in a smile. "They the same thing."

The honest answer rocked her. When she shifted, intending to reclaim her shoe and get up, he lifted a hand.

"May I help you?"

At her assent, he knelt—with some effort, given his erection—and guided her foot into the shoe. His touch was strong on her ankle and heel. When he stood, offering her a hand to rise, she could tell he'd recognized it was the end of the moment, and she wanted to move to the next. He showed no attitude about that, even while that strain to the fabric of his slacks told her he was ready to serve her.

The man was acing the test for her preferences.

"The doing is new to you. But not the thinking about it." She touched his cheekbone, straight as a sword under the smooth skin. Her thumb followed his nose to the curve of the nostril, the rougher skin above his lip, along his jaw. Shaved, but the hint of the beard was there. "'I dream of kneeling. For her.' Tell me about that."

The tiny muscles around his eyes creased. The irises showed sparks from his emotion, like moving water when the sun's light struck it through tree branches. Giving him time with his answer, she started them walking again, her hand curved in the crook of his elbow, their bodies brushing.

"For a long time," he said at last, "maybe since I became a teenager, I'd think of the Virgin Mary when I kneel. Or sometime an angel with a face like lightning, and wings so strong, but hands so delicate, resting on my bowed head."

Rev looked at her. "Always female. I feel the power of God in it, but the power of earthly desire, too. Like it something right, that desire to kneel to a female spirit that's another face of God. Of Love. I want her to tell me what I can do for Her, how I can serve Her."

"How does that gel with your family? The preacher is your cousin, right? Witford? And your aunt Tisha was sitting on that bench near him."

He nodded. "I never told anyone about it. Seemed too private, and didn't affect what they need from me. I didn't even tell Teena Joy. She the aunt that raised me, Tisha's sister."

Grief vibrated from him, still strong when called to the surface. Vera turned toward him, resting her hand against his neck.

Under her touch, his eyes closed, but then opened, his gaze meeting hers. "I know you not God, Veracity. It not like that. I see you as a woman, and desire you like that. I won't put you up on the wrong kind of pedestal."

Most men new to a relationship, trying to secure the affections of a woman, would go the opposite way to build her up. He understood the mistake that would be. A woman needed to be seen as human and fallible, to know the love she was being offered was real and true.

Though he'd moved her, she kept her tone light. "Good. Because that would be a lot to live up to, and while pleasure can be sacred, I also like the kind that keeps us close to the earth." She curled her fingers around his tie to tug on it again. "Primal and needy, the heat of the storm."

He gripped her wrist, telegraphing the need she was spurring. When she gave the hand a significant glance, he let her go, fingers slipping away reluctantly. She propelled them into a walk again.

"Rev, are you familiar with BDSM? Dominant, submissive? You called me Mistress without prompting."

His lips tugged. "When I was a boy, other boys showed me things. Magazines and videos on their computers, but most of it just worried me. So, yes ma'am, I know some of it. I feel the words, in the way you say them. And there's a lot about surrender in the Bible. Submission and surrender."

So he recognized it when it was in front of him. The magazine and video reaction made sense. Porn didn't usually offer the spiritual side of the relationship, and he'd made it clear that he needed that.

"There's a place here in New Orleans, Progeny. It's a club for people who embrace domination and submission in their relationships. I'd like you to join me there one night, as my guest, if you're interested in going. What do you think?"

She walked with him without saying anything further, letting him have time to make his decision. Even so, she was amused to discover she'd been holding her breath until he did.

"I think I'd like that. But may I take you out first, and then you can ask me again, if you still want that?"

He wanted to get to know her before they went down that road. She had mixed feelings about it. He was asking up front for their relationship to be more than that. She would have preferred to start them inside that boundary. But it was a fair request. And, since she could tell how much their talk about the club intrigued him, it said good things, that he wasn't rushing toward more intense levels of Dom/sub play without getting to know her better.

"Where will we go?"

"Wherever you want. Where do you want to go?"

"Surprise me, based on what you know of me so far. I'm not trying to trip you up, Rev. What you choose will tell me more about you." She flashed him a half-smile. "Dommes love information."

"Like if I tried to take you somewhere expensive and fancy, thinking that's what you want, I'd be sticking to your surface. Not seeing you."

"I already knew you wouldn't do that." She cocked her head, considering him. "Your confidence is tied to a curious lack of ego. Ego is what causes that kind of mistake."

"I might make other mistakes." He looked down at her. "I want to please you, Mistress. It unsettles me."

"I'm glad to hear it." Deciding she wanted another taste of that desire, she turned toward him, bringing them to a halt again. She loosened his tie, slid it free and unhooked the top button of his shirt so she could caress the valley between his collar bones. A deliberate and proprietary act, saying she could handle him as she wished.

His reaction to it was another unforgettable first. The heat and pulsing life against her fingertips was a match for what she could sense lower down, for both of them. She wanted to press herself against him, but restricted herself to this one intimate contact. The earthy scent of his aftershave would linger on her fingers. She liked knowing that.

He wore a silver cross on a slim chain under his shirt, and she remembered she'd seen the hint of it under the collar of his coveralls. She was surprised he didn't wear it over his tie for the service, but sometimes a faith talisman was a personal message to oneself. She lifted her gaze to him.

"That's the good kind of unsettled, Rev. A Mistress likes to have her man off balance sometimes, so he learns he can rely on her to right his world. What should I wear for my surprise date?"

With his eyes holding hers, her body resisted her brain's order to step back. But she managed it. "Rev," she prompted, with a smile for both of them. He cleared his throat.

"Wear shoes good for walking. I know you'll need to drive, since I don't, but I'll come to you. Is Thursday afternoon okay? I have a half day off."

"Yes. Pick me up at work. We can go from there." She removed her cell from her purse. "Let's exchange numbers in case anything changes."

"I don't carry one, but I usually here or at school. If you call either place, they'll find me. Can you tell me where you work, what it near?"

"Thomas Rose Associates, in the Garden District, near Coliseum Square Park. The address is on the card I gave you."

"Okay. I know the area."

She studied him. "Part of being with a Mistress includes telling her what might inhibit your ability to serve her needs and desires. Do you understand that?"

His gaze remained steady on hers. "You asking me something, but you haven't gotten to it yet."

"You don't read well, do you?"

"I didn't have a lot of book learning, but I can read. And do the math a man needs to take care of himself."

"Did you have problems in school?"

"No ma'am."

She was reminded of what Mavis had said, about how he'd politely dismissed her concerns and firmly moved off the topic. "Honesty and trust are vital to determining where you and I can go together, Rev. If you aren't ready to tell me the full story about it, that's an acceptable answer. But at some point, I'll need to know."

"It not that I can't tell you. People don't understand. They judge, based on what the world is." His mouth tightened and he sighed. "I don't want to know you going to judge me like that, and I know that's the wrong reason not to tell you. I'm enjoying this right now, where we are together."

"Me too." She took a breath. "I can't promise I'll react the way you wish, but I will try to understand."

"Okay." They started walking again. "When I was little, my momma would read to me, like I say. The day after she died, that was the first time I sung. Teena Joy was listening to a hymn on the radio, and I started to sing with it. She said I sang as good as the singer, got every word right, but also gave the song a power that told her my voice came from God. Told me my momma had sent me a gift to comfort me, to help me get by without her."

He'd tucked her arm further under his, so instead of her holding onto his elbow, he could hold her hand, fingers interlaced. His grip was light, cognizant of her rings, though his thumb was worrying the onyx stone on one of them.

"Teena Joy took up the reading to me, like my momma did. When she thought I old enough, she started to teach me my letters. I did well enough on that, but then...I started to zone out for a couple minutes at a time. Usually when I was trying to read stuff back to her."

Childhood epilepsy, she thought, and Rev confirmed it.

"The family doctor said he thought it was seizures, but he wanted her to take me to a specialist. There weren't no money for that, so he gave us some medicine and said it usually worked itself out with age. But every time I did much more than basic reading and figures, it'd get worse.

"Since I loved being read to, she did that to help me learn what was in books that I needed to know. I liked fixing and building things, too. Beau says I have mechanical aptitude."

He was measuring her reaction so far. She wasn't sure what to think, since the story wasn't done, so she kept her expression neutral.

They'd reached her car. He opened her door so she could sit in the driver's seat while he leaned against the side. "First day of kindergarten, when I woke up, I had really bad laryngitis, even though I was fine the day before. Teena Joy said God had decided I shouldn't go to school, so she taught me at home. One of our neighbors was home-schooling her kids, so I joined them sometimes, but mostly it was Teena Joy."

The discomfort from him hit a different note. Because he *was* an honest man. "She made sure my schooling was considered enough for anyone checking. I wasn't sure she was truthful with them about it, which never sat quite right with me, but it over and done with, and back then I wouldn't disrespect her by going against her on it."

He crossed his arms over his chest, rubbing at his chin with his thumb. "So that's it."

The story was one of a poor family trying to take care of a special child, the best way they knew how. But it only added to the mystery of the man before her.

"Do you believe your voice came from God, and that it's dependent on you not being formally educated?"

"I think Teena Joy thought that. I just serve God, and respect the people in my life I love. I don't go against them unless they put something in my path I know ain't right."

An intriguing response. He wanted to talk about something else, she could tell, and truthfully, she needed to think about what he'd told her. She decided to take them out of those waters for now. "Did you have friends your age growing up?"

That appealing boyish smile crossed his face. "Plenty. I have more relatives than corn on a cob, plus there was the kids in Sunday school."

He touched her hand, resting on the window frame. "You got a furrow in your pretty forehead, but it don't need to be there. I never lacked for the things that mattered growing up, and I get along fine now. I have people who watch after me, same as I watch after them. That what a family do."

I have people who watch after me. Her mind returned to his aunt and cousin. Whether it was good or bad depended a lot on why they were watching.

She gazed at their fingers, resting together, and then withdrew her hand and put her keys in the ignition. "Want a ride back?"

He shook his head and shut her door once she'd tucked her legs back in. "I'll be staying here a while. But I see you Thursday."

"Okay." But she didn't turn over the engine. She looked up at him through the open window and he met her gaze for one of those prolonged pauses. She thought about kissing him, giving him that option, but it was too soon.

"Veracity." When he touched her face, she saw resolve. "I not an educated man. But I not a stupid one. You mind me?"

It was an old turn of phrase, with a variety of meanings, but this one was clear enough. *Respect what I'm telling you.*

She'd asked him not to second guess her as a woman and as a Mistress. The same was required in return.

He'd used the phrase well. Rev gave mixed signals, both beta and alpha. This moment was an alpha one. She liked a sub with an extra helping of that.

"I mind you," she said.

CHAPTER FOUR

$\mathcal{I}$n preparation for her "first date" with Rev, Vera had brought a change of clothes to work. As she finished putting them on, she gave herself a once-over in the mirror behind her office door.

Black jeans with a studded pewter belt, and a dove gray sleeveless V-neck knit shirt that clung to her curves. Silver snake bracelets wound around her wrists, slim matching squiggles dangling from her ears. The comb that pulled her hair back on one side showed the four gleaming rings along the shell of that ear.

Normally she would have donned square heeled and silver trimmed boots, but mindful of Rev's warning, she chose athletic shoes she kept for walks in the Garden District at lunchtime when she needed the extra exercise.

She leaned in to ensure her makeup didn't need touching up. Yes, it was fine. She looked the way she desired to look. There was a leashed energy to Rev, and she wanted to be handed that leash. Wanted him to trust her with all the explosive power and need she could sense behind it.

"Miss Veracity Morgan?"

The formal address on the other side of the door had her brow raising. As she pulled it open, Bastion's dark eyes were dancing, his firm mouth in a mischievous curl. "There is a very polite and exceedingly attractive man in the lobby saying he's here for you. He brought lemon bars for the office, homemade I believe, and I've already tasted one. If he made them, you're out of luck, girlfriend. I'm kidnapping his ass and keeping him chained in my kitchen."

"Wait, lemon bars?" Cyn's office was across the hall, and she appeared in her door. "Brought by a hot male?"

"Very hot," Bastion confirmed. "And so sweetly polite. He can call me 'sir' all day long."

"Down," Vera told him, and tossed Cyn an equally severe look. "You have your own hot guy. Go back to work."

"Yeah, right." Cyn was already headed for the stairs. Her lean body moved like the trained fighter she was. She had abundant and untamed brown curls around foxlike features, and her big brown eyes could draw a man like bait on a bear trap. If that man had the right appreciation for it, Cyn could teach him that fear, pleasure and pain were all the same under her command.

Despite her admonishment, Vera had no worries about Cyn poaching. First, none of the five women would ever think of crossing that line. Second, their resident sadist had discovered her match in Mick, a former cop and special agent. He gave her everything she needed as a Mistress, while she inflicted everything he needed on his overtaxed soul.

"Do *not* scare him," Vera called after her, then shot Bastion a look.

"Yep, on it. I'll keep her from devouring him." Bastion pivoted toward the back stairs, since he could beat Cyn to the lobby that way. "And while I'm not suggesting you cut short the anticipation of your arrival in that mouthwatering outfit, he's attracting attention. You never bring boys home. Everyone's all a-flutter."

Vera chuckled, but when she returned to her desk to get her purse, she realized she was tense, and wondering if she should have had Rev meet her elsewhere.

She examined the unexpected reaction. She wasn't worried about Cyn intimidating Rev. She was worried about what Cyn might think about her choice, and what it revealed about Vera. Which was crazy. These women knew everything about her.

No. They knew everything she wanted to share, plus a few additional things that had shaken loose over the years as trust in their friendship grew. She wasn't insecure, but her soul was well-guarded. She surrounded herself with the people who would protect and care for it in the way she did herself. But like everyone, she had a vulnerable underbelly. Her attraction to Rev, so new and unexpected, meant that underbelly was exposed, and it might show things to herself, and to them, that she hadn't had to handle before.

Okay, well, so be it. She accepted the raw emotions and took a few cleansing breaths. A handsome man was waiting for her. He had that delightful mix of patience—knowing what was worth waiting for—and impatience—a man's desire, rising in proportion and proximity to what he wanted—that the best male submissives had.

When he'd held her hand during their stroll at the roadside overlook, his grasp had a comforting, caressing weight. As if he was holding her, through everything she was doing, thinking and feeling.

During the initial infatuation, it was easy to have such idealistic thoughts. Much as she didn't want to compare anything about this to that, she'd done the same with her ex-husband. It was true until it proved itself untrue, until his attention had been replaced by resentment, restlessness, and a readiness to break the bond already broken.

After it had happened, she'd felt tapped out, like she had nothing left worth having. And she didn't want anything, other than to feel nothing.

When it came to love, there were checkpoints of honesty and trust that had to be navigated to reach the deeper levels of the heart, to create the bond that could last through a lifetime journey together. Donovan hadn't been ready for that. At least not with her.

Initially, she'd judged him for it, and the words "shallow" and "lazy" still came too easily, because the scar he'd left was deep. However, she knew now the failure of their relationship wasn't a failure of her life. They'd had their time together, learned what they needed to learn, and then the journey continued separately. That was all.

It was human to want to have a more complicated explanation for a pain that large, but the soul's path was the soul's path.

Skye appeared at her door with her inquisitive dark eyes and spiky blond hair, shaved on one side. Her moon-shaped face gave her a fairy child look. With her brilliant mind, she navigated TRA's tech and communication needs. With her strong will, she'd won the heart of Tiger, a sexy and dangerous biker. Who also happened to be a volatile alpha submissive.

"Okay?" she signed. Because the four other women were fluent in

ASL, Skye could use it with them when she chose, instead of her library of recorded voices.

Ten minutes had passed, Vera saw. Chagrin kicked in. There was a line between playing the Mistress card to tease a man's desires, and being rude.

"I'm okay," she confirmed. "He's something new to me. It's putting me deeper in my head."

Skye stuck out an elbow, as if offering Vera an escort. Vera gave the arm a playful squeeze. Though not overweight, Skye was far softer than Cyn, since she preferred spending time with her screens instead of working out. But just like with the rest of the women, Cyn had harassed Skye into learning basic defensive skills to give herself an edge in sticky situations.

Vera smiled, remembering Cyn's caustic response to Skye's attempt to avoid their sessions. "Yes, I know being the 'old lady' of a former member of the Fallen Angels MC keeps you off the strike list of most petty criminals. But there's always the chance someone hasn't gotten the memo. Or is too stupid to realize that if he touches a spiky hair on your adorable head, Tiger will remove his internal organs and eat them in front of him."

Each woman was protective of the others in her own unique way. Skye had installed top-end security systems on their personal and work devices. Abby did their taxes and guided their investment decisions. Ros looked after everyone however they needed it. With a listening ear, with financial help and a wide network of seemingly never-ending contacts and resources.

The women watched after their employees in much the same way. TRA was a family company. You didn't get kicked out of it unless you didn't respect or value it the way you should. Ros didn't tolerate fools.

Once they reached the second floor, Skye stayed there. She understood the importance of a Mistress's entrance. The staircase continued along the curved wall, down into the spacious foyer, where Bastion manned the reception desk. Still out of sight, Vera paused, listening to Rev respond to Bastion's question about where he worked.

"I'm a janitor at the middle school," he said. "When I not doing that, I help out at God's Light and Voice Church."

"You work around teenagers?" Bastion tossed his next teasing comment toward Cyn. "I thought Mick held the top masochist award."

"Maso...masochist?" Rev felt his way around the word. "What does that mean?"

He asked without self-consciousness. As Vera continued down the steps, Bastion and Cyn were exchanging a look. Probably a *what is Vera doing with a male this inexperienced?* expression.

"In that context, it's a person who enjoys suffering," Vera said. "Who derives sexual pleasure from it."

She kept her volume at the level where it wouldn't be overheard through the open French doors on either side of the foyer. On one side was the bullpen for a dozen junior and senior account executives, the overflow from Cyn's department, who took up the second floor. Abby's accounting staff and Vera's HR and legal team were in the opposite wing.

Rev's gaze was on her, which meant he'd been watching the stairs for her while he spoke to them. As she came into view, one stair at a time, she saw his appreciation grow. She didn't wear jeans often, but she could make them work for her. His expression said they were performing above expectations.

She could say the same for his. He wore belted dark blue jeans and a forest green, short-sleeved shirt with brown buttons. Casual wear, but nice enough to say he'd taken care with his appearance for her.

When he recalled himself enough to absorb what she'd said, he looked startled. "Oh." His gaze moved to Cyn. "Mick...your man," he said cautiously. "You mean...he likes you to hurt him."

"Prodigiously."

"Which means a lot." Bastion shot Cyn a *don't-be-a-bitch* glance.

It wasn't like Cyn to be cruel, not like that. But pushing past the kneejerk surge of anger, Vera realized her friend was testing how Rev handled the needling. If he didn't have the confidence to hold his own on that, he wouldn't do so on other things that would serve Vera the way she needed. From Cyn's viewpoint.

As she'd said, they were all protective of one another, but she needed to remind Cyn about the things that were her call, not anyone else's.

"That one I know." Rev offered Cyn and Bastion an unabashed smile. "Teena Joy, the aunt who raised me, told me a 'prodigious amount of worry does nothing but make us miss the good the day brings us.' She liked to say that, whenever I got too caught up in my head."

He nodded to them politely, and when Vera reached the bottom stair, resting her hand on the polished wooden finial, as round as the moon, he was there. He held a small box tied with a black ribbon. A purple paper flower dusted with glitter was attached to it. It was like the one on the shoes she'd been wearing.

"Did you do that, or did you resort to child labor?"

"The girls in Miss Sweeney's art class dressed this up for me." His eyes twinkled. "I expect you don't usually wear sneakers. I thought you'd like to make them more you."

Aware of Cyn and Bastion's fascinated stares, she took the box and untied the ribbon. Rev relieved her of it and the paper flower, so she had a free hand to pluck off the top of the box. Inside were two sneaker charms, purple rhinestones with silver edging, to thread onto her laces.

"May I?" With her standing on the bottom step, they were face-to-face, and his gaze roved over every feature. "I thought a lot about you this week," he told her.

"Same," she answered. "And yes. But let's do that in the parking lot. I think we're disrupting the workflow here."

"Oh no, not at all," Bastion said, tucking the handset to the office phone under his ear and riffling through a folder. "We're not paying any attention to the bunny-level cuteness that is the two of you."

Vera rolled her eyes, though the teasing filed down the edges of her baffling anxiety. Glancing up, she saw Skye leaning against the second-floor railing. Ros was beside her, her boss's gaze speculative but reassuring. Abby was on her other side, her red hair falling forward over her shoulder. She was smiling at Bastion's comment.

"I'll see you all tomorrow," Vera said, giving Rev the cue to follow her to the front door.

"Call us if you need us," Cyn said. Not casually, her pointed glance at Rev a direct warning. *Goddess.* They were acting as if Vera hadn't ever had a relationship outside the safe boundaries of the club.

Okay, maybe she hadn't. At least nothing like this, and these women were smart enough to know the difference.

Rev had opened the door for Vera, but he turned at Cyn's

comment. "She'll be safe with me," he told her. His attention lifted, taking in the women on the upper level. "I promise."

"You'll be held to that promise," Cyn said.

A familiar hardness crossed his expression, the resolve she'd seen when his cousin and aunt hadn't wanted him to go off with Vera after church.

"I wouldn't make it, unless I was going to hold myself to it," he said.

～

When they reached her car, she leaned against it, watching him drop to a knee to thread the charms onto the laces of her sneakers. They sparkled in the sunlight. It was a thoughtful gift from a lover.

"So why would a man get pleasure out of being hurt by a woman?" he asked, his head bowed over the task.

"There are a lot of reasons, on the emotional side. But flogging or spanking, impact play, it can also stimulate the body, arouse it."

He lifted his head, his attention sliding over her thighs, waist and breasts. When he reached her face, he had to take a breath, and his hand had curled over her foot. "Is that something you like doing to a man?"

"If it fits the man." She cocked her head. "You don't get embarrassed when you don't know something."

At his curious look, she clarified. "Not knowing what 'masochist' meant."

A trace of a smile went through his gold-touched eyes. "Lots of things people don't know, every one of us. I'd rather ask and learn, rather than pretend I know. The teachers at the school tell the kids they should be like that."

He returned his attention to the lace adjustments. "Moses couldn't string two sentences together without God's help, and he fought God's Will over it. He thought God was making a mistake. Some of it was the natural kind of worry, not wanting to be thrust out in front like that. Not wanting people to think he was dumb, and God chose wrong. But that the wrong kind of pride, thinking he knew better than God what kind of person is right for the job."

Finished, he left his large hand on the top of her foot, and looked back up at her. "You came across my path for a reason. I just glad for it. Don't need to think more about it than that."

When he rose, she laid her hand on his biceps, holding him in front of her. "I have a very strong desire to kiss you, Rev. Full body against body, mouth taking over yours, and letting you inside mine. I'm not going to do it yet, but I just wanted you to know."

Putting his hands on her waist, he gripped firmly. Though he didn't draw her to him, she felt the desire there. "Good thing I don't drive. You putting that in my head might end us up in a ditch."

She smiled. "Where are we going?"

As he opened her car door so she could settle into the driver's seat, he plucked out her seat belt and got it started. She took it from his hand and threaded it across herself, watching his gaze following its track between her breasts. She could feel the ready tension in his muscles, that erotic promise, so close with him leaning over her.

They might end up in a ditch after all.

When he saw she'd noticed his gaze, he shifted it. She touched his jaw. "You can look, Rev. I want you to look. I'll tell you when you can't. Same with touching. Understand?"

"Yes. When you use that tone, I want to call you Mistress, if that still okay."

"That sounds fine with me. Why do you use Veracity instead of Vera, when you speak my name?"

"It bother you?"

"No. But I'd like to know."

"Veracity means truth. I like that reminder. I like calling you that." A faint shadow crossed his eyes. "And hoping what this is, between us, is a true and lasting path."

Only time could confirm that, so she didn't think he expected her to respond. Proving it, the shadows cleared with the next blink of his long-lashed eyes and he left her to get into the car's passenger side. She hadn't adjusted it since he'd been in it, so it still accommodated his long legs. He gave her the address for one of the state parks outside of New Orleans. The man liked his natural areas.

As she navigated through the congested inner-city traffic, he touched the car's dashboard. "First car like this I seen in New Orleans. What made you choose it?"

"I like James Bond. Aston Martin is one of his preferred rides. Do you have a favorite Bond?"

"My aunt didn't let me watch too much TV. It makes me...unsettled. But I watch movies in the player at school after hours. I seen the one that had the actor from *Cowboys and Aliens*. And Scrooge."

"Daniel Craig and Albert Finney. You saw *Skyfall*."

"Yeah, that was the name of it." They were at a stoplight, and Rev had been studying her profile. He reached out, pausing over her ear, waiting for her nod. When he had it, he touched the rings along the shell, a caress that sent sensation rippling down her neck and over her breasts. "Who your favorite Bond?" he asked.

"My favorite hasn't been cast yet. If they heed my barrage of social media posts, it will be Idris Elba."

"*Concrete Cowboy*."

She shot him a surprised look. "Not the movie most people think of for him, but yes."

"They showed it in one of the current event classes. I was cleaning the windows, and Mr. Dillon saw I was interested. He loaned it to me. It reminded me of here, with the horses and the carriages, only this was cowboys in Chicago. I like the unexpected."

His gaze lingered along her ear and neck, moving down to her arm and the swell of her breast, curve of her hip. "You unexpected, Veracity. It hurt to look at you, in the right ways."

"You like trying to make me blush."

"No ma'am. But that's also unexpected." His knuckle grazed her warm cheek. I guess men are always saying how beautiful you are."

"Have you been in a long-term relationship, Rev? Or married?"

"Now, or in the past?"

"If you say now, it's a long walk back."

He grinned. "No. Not now. I had relationships, but mostly with women I met through the church. Nothing that took for long. About a year was the longest, and she off to college most of it, so it was more phone calls than anything else."

"Why 'relationships, *but*,' like they didn't really count if they started at church?"

He didn't immediately respond. At the next light, she glanced his way. Rev pressed his lips together. "People see a storm, they might like how it light up the sky, the thunder making the ground shake. It's a show. But most don't want to stand out in the rain, feel what a storm really all about."

At her expression, he shook his head. "It not something that hurts me, Veracity. Not no more. My aunt say that's why I need to be a janitor, don't need to be more than that. There's a balance to it. Some women hear my voice, see that I ain't too hard on the eyes, she a fly to honey. Then she finds out more, and I become a mud fence. She don't want to get too dirty with it."

While that statement didn't sit well with her, he'd made it clear from their last trip down this road he wasn't seeking an opinion other than his own on it. But she did have to ask. "Do you think I'll be that way?"

His eyes sharpened. "You saw me at the school. Saw my writing. Then you came to find me at the church. You interested in more. I'm interested in you, so I'm glad."

She put her hand on his thigh, and he curled his hand over hers. They stayed that way until they reached the state park. The winding drive took them past camping spots and hiking trail markers. He had her stop at the one that said, "Wishes Mailbox, 3 miles."

"Can you walk three miles?" he asked. "If you can, it's worth it."

"I can, if we stop for ice cream on our way back to town."

He tapped the small backpack he'd placed at his feet. "I brought us some lunch and drinks."

"A prepared man. I like that. But I'm still stopping for ice cream. What's the Wishes mailbox?"

"It just a mailbox in a thinking kind of place. They leave pens and notebooks in it, so people can write down their thoughts to share with others. It has a good feel to it, like those kinds of places can have. There's one up in North Carolina, at Sunset Beach, the Kindred mailbox. The person who put his one up wanted something like it down here."

He exited his side and came around to open her door. "What your favorite flavor of ice cream?"

"Lately I've been in a salted caramel fudge vanilla mode. You?"

"They have ice cream sandwiches in the cafeteria. I like them."

He guided her to a wide, well-tended trail. As they walked, she could see creeks and marsh land through the trees. They shared the scenery in silence, occasionally broken by relaxed conversation about their surroundings, stories about him working at the school or church, or her at TRA. What two people talked about who were testing the fit for the pieces of their lives.

Rev put a hand on her arm, stopping her in place. He also stepped forward, so she was partly behind him.

Now hearing the crackling of leaves that he'd heard, she saw an alligator emerge and ponderously cross the trail ahead of them. The pendulum swing of his head matched the sinuous movement of his body, the flat eyes, set so wide apart, capturing them in his view. He kept coming, at least fifteen feet from nose to tail. Then he was across, tail swishing through the fallen leaves on the other side of the trail. He slid into the shallows that led into deeper marsh waters and disappeared.

Rev shifted to her side, and they started walking again. "Good to give a big feller like that a wide berth when you know he coming. You okay?"

"Yes." She chuckled at her nerves. "I was born and bred a city girl, so seeing wildlife like that so close can still take me by surprise. But thanks to Abby, who's a Louisiana native, I know they don't tend to bother humans unless someone has been stupid enough to feed them. What would you have done if he'd charged?"

"I would have told you to run and made sure you stayed ahead of me, so if he got anyone, it would be me. I'd hope I could stomp on him...dissuade him from dragging me off into the water, without hurting him too bad."

Their bodies brushed as they walked. In the outside world, an intimate gesture might be interpreted as a chance to press for more. In a club, boundaries were well-defined. Subs asked permission for almost any liberty that hadn't been pre-approved by a Master or Mistress. He walked the line between the two without much instruction.

"You hesitated over the word 'dissuade.' Why?"

"You don't miss much."

"I don't. Keep that in mind. You didn't answer the question."

He lifted a shoulder. "Liked the way it sounded for this moment, but it's a new-to-me word. Witford used it in his sermon the other day. I looked it up in the school dictionary, the big one on the pedestal in the library. Been there for twenty-five years."

A faint smile touched his mouth. "Under the Ps there's a paper flower glued to a card. It say, 'I'll love you perennially, March 2003.'"

"Is it signed?"

"No. But the flower is the kind of pink that Miss Wilhelm, our head librarian, wear a lot. She was in love with an assistant principal, Perry Walters. He was killed by a drunk driver years ago. Beau, my boss, was around back then, so we think she put it in there. She's kind of reserved, strict with the kids, but fair."

"You like her."

"I do."

"Because she's reserved and strict." She nudged him, and his smile deepened.

"It don't hurt. She has nice hair, too. Smells good, and her eyes are a pretty brown. She don't miss much, either."

He pointed out a root jutting across the trail to keep Vera from tripping over it, though his grip was secure enough on hers she doubted he'd let that happen. "Neither do you," she noted. "Why no phone?"

"Gets in the way. You miss too much stuff. If they need me at school, they use the intercom system. 'Rev, come to the West boys' bathroom for a Code 15.'"

She shuddered. "Do I want to know what a Code 15 is?"

He chuckled. "It mean a child in the bathroom during class and they upset about something."

She glanced up at him, intrigued. "Okay, explain what that's about."

"When a student ask to go to the bathroom during the class, the teacher can tell if it just to do their business, or because something has upset them enough they need to go somewhere quiet to think on it some. Or cry over it. Teacher can't leave the class, so they send up the call for me to go check on them. I come by, pretending to be cleaning."

He winked. "The Code 15 happen more often for the girls' bathroom. Girls got a lot of drama at that age."

"I daresay. And you don't ever worry..." Vera paused, concerned that the practical consideration might offend him, but he filled in the blank.

"Beau's thoughts were like yours, at first. He told me never to be alone with the kids. Said they too messed up these days and will accuse me of doing things."

He lifted a shoulder. "But I just busy myself cleaning outside the restroom and start singing in a low voice. Whatever God tell me to sing. They always come out."

"Church hymns?"

"Every once in a while, but God do know his audience. Might be a boy band or Taylor Swift. Some R&B for the boys. That work pretty good." His lips curved, a wry half-smile. "We sit on a couple of my buckets and talk it out. They good kids. Just a hard road for a lot of them, because of how confused they can be about the world. Plenty of times, they just need to hear what the kids do at Sunday school. We all get caught up in stuff, but we a village, all together. All they gotta do is reach out for help and kindness. No need to be afraid of doing that."

He returned to her original question. "Village breaks down when all we talking to is screens, not looking each other in the eye to share what's in the heart. That's when we find that quiet and calm we all need, and when we realize we never alone.'

He paused. "Sorry. Sometimes I sermonize when I don't mean to. I just feel it through me, and I have to say it."

"It's good stuff." Listening to the rise and fall of his voice, Vera thought its gentle, appealing authority reached down into the well of what male strength was supposed to be. In Rev's case, it pulled up an overflowing vessel. "You should write it down for your next singing sermon."

He blinked. "Singing sermon?"

"Your cousin does the pulpit sermon. You do a singing sermon."

He tapped his head. "It here. God give it to me when it ready to come, and I say it the way He makes me feel it."

The trail had taken them to an open view of the water. As Vera drew in the heavy marsh scents, she saw a knoll up ahead, populated by a grove of wind-shaped junipers. The mailbox was planted inside their shelter.

A tidy border of smooth rocks and shells was around the base, a bougainvillea vine climbing the post. Two anchored benches were nearby. Small concrete animals had been tucked into the foliage. Vera suspected the whimsical pieces had been left by visitors, along with oyster shells tied to the juniper branches. They made a clinking noise in the light breeze. Many had messages written on them. It reminded her of the expression boards at the school. Proof that adults needed such things, just as children did.

The palpable energy here was laced with the poignant air of wishes voiced, dreams left to linger. As well as grief, celebration, deep thought.

"Why don't you sit there, Mistress?" Rev pointed her to a bench as he went to the mailbox. He removed a spiral notebook and brought it to her, along with a pen. "You can look through this one while I set up our picnic."

The purple cardboard cover was stamped with a silver fleur-de-lis. Vera opened the book in the middle, and began to read what had been left on the pages, in various handwriting styles and ink colors. Because of the humidity, the pages were a silken weight against her fingertips.

The first entry was from a girl who'd just graduated high school. She spoke of her hopes for her future, her enthusiasm for the North Carolina college she would be attending. Another page was claimed by a man grieving his father's loss, followed by a woman dealing with cancer. Many entries expressed gratitude and pleasure for the serene space the mailbox offered.

She heard their voices in her head, people she might have passed on the streets in New Orleans—natives, transplants, tourists. Several entries were written in foreign languages.

While reading, she'd stayed aware of Rev's movements, but when she realized there was more than lunch in the sizeable pack, she lifted her head. Next to a soft-sided cooler bag, he'd set up a half-shell sun shelter, like people used on the beach. A fabric screen attached to the front could be pulled down to keep out bugs. He'd spread a blanket on the ground inside it.

When he sat back on his heels and saw her watching, he explained. "Sometime when I come out here, I stay awhile. We stay as long as you like, but I didn't want too much sun or the bugs to make that decision for you."

He rose and came to her, sitting down on the ground by the bench instead of on it, one leg bent beneath him, one knee propped up. He laid his arm on the bench, in a curve that followed her hip, coiling around her without touching her, without imposing on her space.

Wanting to be closer, but waiting for her to make the decision of how much closer.

"Would you read me some of the entries?" he asked.

She read him the ones she'd scanned, then several more. He looked pleased by the elated tone of those with milestones to celebrate, compassionate or sad over entries of longing and need. Like the one she read now.

"'I don't think I'll ever find someone to love me.' Just that one line," she noted, showing it to him. "Signed by Z. Can't tell if it's a man or woman, or a young person. But the ink looks smeared, as if they were crying when they wrote it."

"Maybe if we look through them other books, or come back in a few years, we'll find another entry. Maybe they won't be alone no more."

"And maybe they'll have gotten over themselves and on with their lives."

His brow creased. "It bothers you."

"No. Not if it's a teenager..." The entry had kicked her in a vulnerable spot, but she would tell him what was in her mind. "There are people who get stuck on that, and waste so much energy on it. I learned a long time ago the best cure for loneliness or staying away from that abyss in human nature is giving. Helping others. It's presumptuous to second guess the Universe's plan for you. Like what you were saying about Moses."

"Sometimes we ask more of life than we need to ask of it." He nodded slowly. "We turn our back on the table that's already laden up with food and drink, looking for what's not there. But we can't say if this person like that. They may be out there giving, doing all you say."

Rev put his fingers on the text, his hand brushing the tips of her fingers clasping the book. "This a place to say something deep in your heart. No judgment. Have you ever felt like that? That you have so much love you want to give someone, a special kind of love just between you and him, that will be treated as special as it should be? And you been waiting and waiting to do it...what seem like forever."

As he stared at her, her bitterness went away, taken like sand carried by the salty wind touching her lips.

"I guilty of turning away from that table," he admitted. "I was looking for something not there, something I needed and wanted. But

I think the same God that provided what's on that table put our paths together. Because now, I thinking if that table had half as much, or nothing on it, as long as I had this one thing I've been wanting, I'll be okay."

She didn't say anything right away. He continued to stare at her, waiting her out. Waiting for whatever she wanted.

"How private is it here?" she asked.

His fingers curled next to her hip. "We didn't see anyone in the parking lot, so we the only ones here for a while. But I can hear people coming, and see them at that lower point in the trail." He gestured in that direction. "Gives us a few minutes before they see us, unless they know where to look."

"Will you serve me as I desire, Rev?"

She gazed at the shelter when she asked, not at him. There were too many things inside her right now, and she wasn't sure if she wanted to see her face reflected in his eyes.

"Yes ma'am. Yes, Mistress."

She turned her mind away from herself, and let it rest on him. In him. She could almost hear the sound of his heart thudding against his chest. When she put her hand there, a jolt went through her, especially when he put his hand over hers.

She rose, and he did too. Once she reached the shelter, she put her hand on his ready forearm to remove her socks and shoes. When she stretched out on the blanket, she lifted her hands above her. It made her body lengthen and arch under his intent gaze. He ducked into the shelter with her, letting the screen fall against his back. One knee pressed into the blanket next to her hips.

"Take off my jeans and shirt, Rev."

Watching her, he unbuckled her belt and slid it free. Every movement slow, reverent, but not too reverent. His gaze dropped to study the skin he was revealing, his fingers trailing along it without taking more liberties than she'd given him. She lifted her hips to help him get the jeans off. As she arched her back further so he could remove her shirt, his breath drew in. He took it carefully over her hair, then set her clothes aside in a folded stack.

"Sit back and look at me, Rev. Everything below the neck. You don't have permission to look at my face, and though you can take as long as you like, you only get one look, from neck to feet. When you get to my feet, close your eyes and keep them that way, until I say otherwise."

"Yes ma'am."

She tracked his gaze's passage over the column of her throat, her collar bones and curves of her shoulders, her upper arms, her breasts. She'd worn a black satin bra with a tiny white bow and black pearls between the cups. It had a front fastener, and his eyes rested there an additional second. She could imagine him slipping that clasp, opening up the cups to reveal her aching nipples and full curves to the hunger in his expression. But she stayed still, waiting to see how he followed her direction. The flood of sexual energy felt too good to rush.

He moved to the slope of her abdomen, the flare of her hips, the fit of her matching panties. When his attention passed over her covered mound, heat washed through her there. On to the columns of her thighs, and all the way to her painted toenails. Once he reached the same place, his eyes fell shut. His hand, braced on the ground next to him, had become a fist. Though he had physically maintained the position she'd dictated, his aura, that force field around him, felt as if he'd braced a hand on her opposite side, and he was curved over her like the shelter he'd set up. Only much, much closer.

She breathed slow, pulling that sexual fire from her core to her chest. The power of what was happening took over and drove the next command.

"Breathe deep, Rev. Think about what's going on in your cock, your thighs." Her eyes swept over that pleasurable terrain. "Draw that energy up into your chest. Keep drawing it up with every inhale. On the exhale, think about what you've seen. Repaint me against the inside of your eyelids. Did you like what you saw?"

"Lord, yes, Mistress. Good God above, yes."

The emphatic response was underscored by male need. His voice was a rumble of heat. He'd described a storm, its thunder and lightning, as a mesmerizing show. Watching him follow her direction was every bit of one. She watched his shoulders rise, his chest expand, and knew what she wanted next.

"Take off your shirt, Rev. Keep your eyes closed."

He complied, and she held her breath, then let it spiral back down through her chest, feeling the impact in every erogenous zone. Beautifully sculpted muscle, as she'd expected. Tiny dark whorls of chest hair. His dark skin gleamed from the filtered light coming through the screen. The silver cross was now fully revealed, engraved with a flowing script. She spoke the words aloud.

"We walk by faith, not by sight."

Since his eyes were closed, a smile touched his mouth, and the coincidence gave her one as well.

"Did Teena Joy give that to you?"

"For my thirteenth birthday."

Propping herself on an elbow, she reached out. "Lean forward, Rev, and put your cheek on my thigh. Facing my voice."

She guided him down, her hand moving from forearm to biceps to shoulder, then to his nape, caressing him there, hooking the chain over her fingers and then letting it go again.

He laid his cheek where she directed it, his mouth only a few inches from her damp cunt, just like at the overlook.

"Do you smell me, Rev? Smell my need?"

"Yes, Mistress. I want…" He cut himself off fast, his body jerking with the effort.

"It's not wrong to ask me for what you want, Rev." She bit back a tight smile. "Only to demand it."

"It feels like demand, inside. But I want to ask for permission to use that…forcefulness. Does that make sense?"

"Yes. I like knowing it will be there, for me to call for it when I'm ready. Understand?"

"Yes, Mistress." His response, touched with that same forcefulness, sent a tingle up her thigh muscles.

"Good. Now sit up again and remove your shoes and the rest of your clothes. Stay on your knees."

It took some skill to do that and not look awkward, but he was a patient man, not rushing what didn't need to be rushed. She savored the reveal, the bare hips, the stiff shaft of his cock that emerged as he pushed down his jeans and boxers. When she hummed her approval, he paused to absorb the sound, though he didn't stop long enough to disrespect her order.

He wore white cotton boxers, pale against his brown skin. After he was done removing all of it, his clothes in a folded stack next to hers, she gave him another order. "Spread your knees to shoulder width, Rev, and put your hands on them."

He complied, eyes still closed, lashes fanning his cheeks. She put her hand on herself, stroking, lifting into her touch. When she let out a breathy sound of pleasure, his mouth tightened along with the rest of his body, responding to what he could imagine.

"I'm looking at you while I touch myself, Rev. Would you like to hear me climax while I do that? Knowing it's because I'm looking at you, wanting you? Making you sit next to me with your eyes closed, only able to look at that painted picture in your head?"

His voice came out even deeper than usual, vibrating through the lowest, most aware parts of her. "I can barely breathe, Mistress. I want you so much, but I want... I want to hear that desire in your voice. Know I doing what pleases you. It hurts and make me want to thank God a hundred times, that I'm worthy of that kind of gift."

Goddess, she loved hearing what was going through a sub's mind when he didn't edit it, didn't change a thing about the flow, straight from mind and cock to mouth.

"You said earlier what you're feeling is like a demand. Tell me about that. In detail."

A pause as he digested her meaning. Just as she'd hoped, he picked up on it, his voice getting deliciously rougher. "I want to press myself upon you, all your curves against me, feeling the way they fit, the way your hands might grip my shoulders, hold onto me. That plea in your voice as your pleasure rises, knowing that plea is for me too, as much as the command."

She half-closed her eyes. His words ignited every nerve ending. "Breathe with me, Rev, that deep breath I talked about. Pull it from your testicles, through your cock, to the top of your head."

Taking his hand, she guided it between her legs, pressing his fingers against the dampness of her underwear, holding them still there, letting him feel her swollen sex shift under his hand as she drew in matching breaths. His cock and testicles convulsed, the tip of his cock glistening.

"You don't use rougher words, do you, Rev? Cock. Cunt. Ass."

"No ma'am. But if those words mean something different to you, special or sacred, then that's what they'll mean to me."

"In Tantra, the man's sex is called a lingam, the woman's a yoni. They're just words, and they mean the same thing. It's how you say them that makes them special or sacred."

Under his touch, she stroked herself some more. His expression, even with closed eyes, was intent. "Tell me what you're thinking," she said.

"I'm following what you doing, so I know what you like."

"That's good. But a man's hand can give a woman different sensations, even doing the same things." She changed the position of their fingers. "Take off my panties and put your fingers inside me, Rev. Gently."

"Always, Mistress." The resolute note in his voice was the same as had been there when he told Cyn he promised to care for her. It made her tremble.

He slid the garment off, then found his way back up her thighs with lingering touches, strokes with a yearning pressure. Her legs parted for him. As he eased in two fingers, he used a careful skill that told her it wasn't his first time, but it wasn't something he did often enough to get careless with the privilege. She let out a pleased moan, and a strong desire gripped his expression.

"That breathing you have me doing...everything in me is on fire, but it so still, too. Vibrating."

"Yes. Move your fingers like you'd move your cock inside me, Rev. Go slow."

He started to thrust, and she rolled her hips with the movement, lifting her body with the rhythm. She clasped his biceps, drawing him down toward her. "I want your mouth on my breast, Rev. Put it to good use."

He touched his lips to the upper curve, exploring it like he had with his eyes. An inch at a time, making his way to her nipple without rushing. His body quivered, showing he was doing everything he could to go slow, to take his time. When he finally covered the nipple, the slow draw that led to a tender suckling pulled more low, harsh moans from her. She moved in a dance with his efforts.

His fingers moved in her, lips suckling her. She had to fight to get words out, but she'd win that fight because the Mistress in her wanted even more from him.

"Can you deny yourself for me, Rev? No climax for you, not until I say?"

He lifted his head enough to answer. "I want you to find your joy at my touch. From my touch. From looking at me."

"Open your eyes and tell me more about what you want."

Their faces were close, so when he obeyed, she saw the alpha lurking in those depths, able to partner with the beta, changing leads as the moment called for it, as experience and intuition had taught him. The gingerbread color had deepened to the darkness of fertile soil.

"Let it happen now, please. Mistress. For me."

The orgasm gripped her, that red fire spiraling tight out of her core and adding to what was already rushing through her, hardening her nipple under his tongue as he put his head down and recaptured it. While he suckled more forcefully, he passed his thumb over her clit in featherlike brushes. He thrust his fingers in and out, in and out, curling them up against her G-spot. She gripped his shoulders, clawing at the flexing muscle as her head tipped back, throat arching, pressing her breast deeper into his mouth.

His free arm slid under her, palm flattening against her back, fingers spread to hold her up. He helped her work through every blissful spasm as she cried out her pleasure to the marsh and to all those wishes written on the notebook pages.

When the climax finally ebbed, she dropped a hand from his shoulder to the back of his head, over the short crop of his hair, pressing into the firm skull beneath it as he kept slowly teasing and sucking on her nipple.

"Oh Goddess..." When his fingers slid out of her, one last shudder of reaction followed the withdrawal from her slick flesh. She had him raise his head, his cock steel against her thigh, the wet tip leaving a kiss of reminder against her skin.

"There's a song," he said. His voice held the urgency of a man with a raging hard-on and no relief in sight. The sound caused one last ripple through her cunt, a tiny spasm of reaction. "One they play on the radio, that remind me of the songs they sing in church. One lyric of it go something like, "'I'll rise up a thousand times to do it all again... No matter the ache...'"

"I think I know that one. Sing it to me."

His eyes glinted at the challenge she gave him, but he managed it, the uneven notes adding to the erotic pool immersing all her senses.

"'Rise Up,' Andra Day. Rev...you are an interesting man."

"You a fascinating woman, Mistress."

"I want you on top of me and inside me, Rev. No climax, no release. I want to feel you inside me."

His nostrils flared. She loved seeing all the muscles tighten in his throat. "Sure you don't torture people in that club you been talking about? Because you sure good at it."

"A Mistress only tortures the sub who wants and needs that." She flashed teeth at him. "Do you need to use anything? I'm on birth control, and I always use protection with my partners."

His expression flickered. "It been over a year, and when I was with her, we used protection the whole time."

Over a year. It made his control even more impressive. "Rev." The urgency in her voice increased.

He slid between her legs as she parted them for him. He paused to stare down at her. "Do you trust all men like this? This fast?"

She could claim that sex could be a casual thing that two adults could indulge on the first date if they wished. But she didn't do casual sex, and this didn't feel casual. She wouldn't lie to him to protect herself.

"I only let a man get this close if I do trust him. And I find myself trusting you more than most."

Emotions crowded into the small space, and then he slowly slid into her. She was still wet, but he showed tender respect for how sensitive post-climactic tissues could be as he worked himself inside. Watching his face as he did it, him in the throes of unreleased pleasure, and her on the sated side of it, was always an incomparable experience, knowing her sub was fighting his natural need to thrust and climax, just to serve her desires.

When he was hilt deep, she felt full and stretched. His muscles were rigid under her hands. She let them glide down his back, to his ass. A marvelous, muscular ass. She traced and teased the seam as she locked her legs over it.

"Mother Mary," he muttered, his eyes starting to close.

"No. Look at me, Rev. Look at what I'm demanding of you and show me your willingness to submit to those demands. To serve my will with every ounce of your own."

His face was still and tight, eyes showing the fire they were channeling. She passed her fingers over his lips, and he nipped her, unable to stop the reaction. Her cunt squeezed down on their joining point.

She wasn't above consciously stroking a man's cock with her inner muscles, but the experience he'd given her meant her body was doing it for her, caught up in those lovely tiny aftershocks.

Eventually, she would have him withdraw, watch him get dressed, working around that impressive erection. She would tell him not to give himself relief between now and the next time they saw one another. She wanted him on the edge of that desire, feeling it, letting it expand to the full scope of the power it could carry. She would keep testing what he wanted to give her as a submissive.

Not just because it connected to who the man was, the elements that formed the shape of that part of himself, but because it was the kind of Mistress she was, that wanted that kind of response.

But for now, she let her awareness go beyond the two of them to the chirp of birds, the wind through the marsh, the oyster shell ornaments clinking in the juniper. Maybe she'd leave one herself, a memory of this. And because he'd told her there was no judgment here, she'd leave her own sentence in the book.

Would she be back later to see if it was still true, or just a wistful hope that departed with the passage of time, like the sun that always ultimately dropped behind the horizon?

I think I've found him. The one I want to keep.

CHAPTER FIVE

"I have what we need to get you started," Vera told Ren Borgata. For the past half hour, she and the new senior account manager had been parked in her office, handling the forms required for every new hire.

Ren was attractive, as most people on the front lines of marketing were, and projected his experience in the field with an appealing confidence. He'd be supervising the project team that had been led by Grenadine. Last New Year's Eve, Dina had announced her resolution, to save up and sail around the world with her husband. Since she'd left three weeks ago, she'd been posting regular pictures on her social media pages and sending love to her former coworkers.

Usually TRA promoted from within, but they didn't have a team member seasoned enough to take over Dina's accounts as lead, so an external hire had been recruited.

"Good deal," Ren said, sitting back and putting his ankle on his knee. He wore a tropical weight suit that fit his body well. While the office's daily dress code was casual professional, he was showing respect for the final steps of the hiring process. She appreciated that in a man. "Gotta say, I didn't expect to get the job," he added.

"Why is that?"

"Scuttlebutt in the industry was that you only hire women or..." he paused. "Well, women."

"Women or beta males," she said. "John Turner?"

His brows rose. "Dead center."

"John has applied here before. He didn't have the qualifications we were seeking."

"Let me guess." He gave her a wry smile. "You were looking for someone who isn't an egomaniac with impulse control problems?"

"There's only room for one egomaniac here. I refuse to share the limelight."

Vera's gaze shifted to Cyn, leaning in her door frame. "You're no egomaniac. But as far as impulse control problems..."

"Uptight people often think *normal* people have impulse control issues." Cyn crossed her eyes at Vera, then turned her attention to a grinning Ren. "I know you don't start for a couple weeks, but before you head back to your hotel, I thought we'd do lunch with your team."

"I'd planned on it. If you have other things to do, I can take them solo. We can get to know one another before I'm formally their boss."

"That would work." Cyn tossed Vera an approving glance. This was going to be a good choice.

Ren rose and shook Vera's hand with a firm but not overcompensating grip. "I'll shoot the copies of your benefits paperwork and contract to your email," she said.

"Great. I'm looking forward to working with you all."

Cyn stepped aside. "I'll meet you at Bastion's desk in a few minutes to do the hand off, so they know I okayed it."

"You got it, boss."

"Supreme Bitch in Charge is sufficient."

Vera sighed as Ren took his leave of them with another chuckle. "The bad thing is he thinks you're joking."

"Not at all. My winning personality came through loud and clear during our interview. Bastion took a decided interest in him, by the way. Nothing inappropriate, HR nazi," she added. "I could just tell. Hard to say if Ren's bread is buttered on the bisexual side, though. Sexual preference really should be part of the hiring process. Stupid EOE guidelines."

"Said no smart HR rep for a company, *ever*," Vera responded. "Using the workplace as a dating pool isn't wise. Just ask Watt."

"Wisdom and sex have nothing to do with one another." Cyn grinned. "You want to be my date at Progeny this weekend? Mick won't be back from Quantico until Monday."

Vera straightened the two pens on her desk. "I may bring Rev. He's not ready to be thrown into the deep end, but he can take a stroll around the pool."

"And you're going to be his lifeguard to keep him from falling in."

"Or to keep him from being pushed." Vera did the watching you gesture at her friend.

"No pushing." Cyn glanced over her shoulder, confirming no employees from the lower levels were visiting Skye, Ros or Abby's offices. "But if he decides he wants to be slathered in oil and strapped to a fucking machine, I'll help choose the right sized rubber dick to put up his ass. Because the right size is everything. How's his, by the way? Dick, I mean, because his ass looks superb."

"Cynbad Marigold...you are in a forever, until the end of time relationship, with a male whose stamina has to compete with a racehorse's to keep up with you."

"Just because I've chosen the cake I want doesn't mean I don't notice how good the others in the case look. And Mick hasn't lost a race yet."

Vera eyed her. "Get out of my office. Your tender smile creeps me out."

Cyn's sexy laugh trailed over her shoulder as she headed for the stairs. "See you later, HR nazi."

Two days later, Vera had a meeting with the client near Rev's middle school again. She'd called the school that morning to verify Rev was working today, and that he usually took his lunch break around one-thirty. She could have left a "call me back" message for him, but for certain things, she was on the same page as he was about the phone. Asking him if he was ready to join her at Club Progeny, now that they'd had their first date, was a face-to-face thing.

She let Bastion know she was taking a long personal lunch hour. When she told him it was none of his business who she was meeting, he smugly informed her she'd told him exactly who it was. She didn't confirm. Or deny.

When she arrived, she went to the admin offices for her visitor pass. "I can page Rev for you," Cherry, the school secretary, told her. Mavis was at a school board meeting.

"If you know where he takes his lunch, I'll go there, so he doesn't waste any of it coming up here to fetch me."

"Where you met Mavis on your last visit, the shed by the playing fields? You'll probably find him with one or more of the kids. They like to talk to him during their lunch breaks."

"Mavis said he's the kid whisperer."

"Not just with kids. He has this knack..." Cherry stopped. "Anyway. He's good with people."

"I went to his church this past Sunday." Vera turned as if starting for the office door, but casually threw that out. "I saw him help a sick woman, just by holding her hand and talking to her. Singing to her."

"Yes. That's just like him." Cherry's more open expression told Vera she'd knocked on the right door to find out what the admin had been going to say. Her voice dropped a little. "My husband and I, we were going through a rough patch about a year ago."

"I'm so sorry." Vera's sympathy was genuine. She came back to the desk. "I hope that means you're okay now."

"We are. Much better." Cherry offered a grateful smile. "Thank you. Anyway, Rev happened to come by my car when I was feeling low about it. He took my hand and told me it was going to be okay. He asked to pray with me. For me."

She waved a hand. "I'm not really into that, but he said I wouldn't have to do anything. He put his hand on my shoulder, and prayed, and I did feel better.

"Later that day, I felt like my husband and I had just been looking at the problem in the wrong way, drawing battle lines instead of working together. I was about to call him when he called me, and we both said how sorry we were..."

She shook her head. "That all sounds just like common sense, stepping back from the problem, giving it time to breathe. Maybe that's all it was, but honestly, that day before I saw Rev, I was reaching my wit's end. I was considering whether we needed to separate. I don't know what it is about him, but it's something special."

Her blue eyes fastened on Vera. "He's important to all of us here."

"Is that a warning?"

Cherry's cheeks warmed. "I apologize. I wasn't trying..."

"Watching out for a friend isn't anything to apologize for. Not in my book. I'm asking if I've given you reason to think I need the warning."

"Not at all." Cherry tapped her pencil on her desk. "Rev doesn't need anyone's protection. Most people, if they have the wrong intentions, they won't make any headway with him. He's not a pushover."

Vera agreed with the assessment, but still... "Most?"

"Just a general qualifier," Cherry said.

She was covering the slip, and Vera could let it go, but Rev's well-being was becoming important to Vera as well.

I am a Mistress. Don't fuck with my toys.

A T-shirt message Vera had seen on Lace M. Tight, a Mistress/switch who did whip demos, as well as bondage performance art. Her real name was Laci Montague, and when she'd shared a drink with them at the BDSM conference they'd all been attending, she'd told the TRA women she liked being a rope bunny for the Zen of it all, and using the whip to exercise her inner warrior. She refused to be classified and changed her preferences all the time. Whatever served her art, she would follow.

Vera thought Rev would like her. Lace would like him, far too much. But she'd also fully understand what drove Vera's surge of protective feelings now. "When I was at the church, I noticed some not-so-friendly vibes from his cousin and aunt," Vera said. "I expect that's who you mean by 'most'?"

Vera spoke plainly, so the woman could decide how she wanted to answer. And if she wanted to answer.

Cherry's gaze flickered. "When they come to the school to pick him up for church events, they don't seem to like how much we appreciate Rev. Truthfully, it seems to bug them, like they'd rather him not work here at all."

"I thought Witford got him the job."

"He helped him apply, because Rev insisted he needed a job outside of the church, but they really want him to come back to work fulltime with them."

A teacher entered the office with a folder in hand and an expectant look for Cherry, so the secretary handed Vera her visitor pass. "I may have spoken out of turn," she said, "but Mavis trusts you, and if you and Rev are becoming...closer, I wanted you to know."

"What you told me is nothing Mavis wouldn't have told me if I asked the same questions. You can verify that with her."

The slight tension in her expression eased. "Thank you. And by the way," her eyes danced, "Mavis loves knowing you're interested in him. She says he deserves a good woman who'll treat him right."

"Tell her if she's not going to pick up the slack and handle it, someone's got to."

Cherry's laughter followed her to the door. Vera smiled at the incoming male student who held it for her. Under her approving smile, he nearly tripped over his own feet. He watched her head down the hall, something she noted in her peripheral vision, but his act of courtesy had earned him the look. It was never too early to teach boys the rewards for service to a Dominant woman.

The playing fields were overrun by kids on their lunch period. As Cherry had warned, Rev had company, but Vera wanted to watch him a few minutes before announcing herself, so she leaned against a post by the back entrance.

He sat on the bench that hid the first part of the intriguing quote. An open container with a half-eaten sandwich was on his right, his lunch companion on his left.

She had a blond ponytail, expressive eyes and even more expressive hands. She was signing to him. And he was signing back.

He wasn't fluent, but he was learning. The girl giggled when he got it wrong and showed him the proper way to do the word he'd attempted. Then she gestured to the sky. Rev tilted his head, and they looked together before the girl said something and brought his attention back down to her.

That was when he saw Vera. He pointed toward her, and the girl turned. The teen mouthed a *woo-hoo* taunt and Rev executed a mock swat at her head. She ducked, lips parted in laughter.

Vera started moving toward him. The flat sound of the laughter confirmed the girl had been born deaf, or lost her hearing before her speech skills developed. By the time Vera reached Rev, she'd run down the hill to rejoin her friends. Rev rose, an act of deference that pleased Vera. She took his outstretched hand in a squeeze that locked and held.

"I wanted to reissue my earlier invite to the club I frequent," she told him. "And I wanted to do it in person."

75

His gaze flickered but swept over her, warm and very welcoming, taking in her heels, sheer hose, fitted skirt and silk blouse. "You a really nice surprise, Mistress."

Between them was the shimmering memory of when they'd last been together, skin to skin, him inside her body. She reminded herself Mavis might frown on her ravishing him against the shed. She'd totally understand, but she'd frown on it.

"You're learning sign language?"

"Yeah. She spends some of her lunch period teaching me, and she brought me a few picture books so I could learn more when she's not around."

"Your idea or hers?"

"Some of both. Kids have a lot of ways of talking. I like learning them, because it help me know when something's not right with them. Also gives her someone else who can understand her in the way that's easiest for her. Most of her life is the harder way, though she handles it good. She can speak, so she can say the words as she signs them."

Vera glanced at the sky. "What was she pointing at?"

"She said that yesterday, right before sunset, there was two layers of cloud, one above and one right below the sun. The sun looked like the eye of an alligator, and the bottom clouds were split, so it looked like his mouth." He pointed to his eye, then made a gesture that looked like an alligator's jaw clapping together, straight up and down. "That's alligator."

"Yes, it is." She made the same sign back. "Our information systems and graphic design VP, Skye, is mute, so we've all learned. You saw her the other day. The one on the second level, with the spiky hair?"

"That good to know. I'll have another couple teachers to help me learn more, and impress Debbie when I see her here. Skye isn't deaf?"

"No. But she's told us the same thing you just did. It's nice to find people who can sign. She communicates with electronic voices for others."

"That rare, a person being mute but not deaf. Something happen to her throat?" Rev gestured to the bench. "Will you sit with me?"

At her agreement, he ducked into the shed, returning with a clean towel. He laid it on the bench. "It not dirty, but it's outdoors and you wearing nice clothes." His gaze slid over her again. Today it was a purple skirt and green and purple striped blouse, with amethyst and silver jewelry.

It was a short bench, so their legs and hips touched when she sat down. She glanced down at her slim and delicate heel, aligned with his work shoe.

"They don't know," she said, returning to his question about Skye. "She was in a car accident with her father when she was very young. It was fatal for him, and they think it was a neurological injury of some sort." Vera recalled the times their group had touched on that story, with care, when Skye wanted to talk about it. "She has this odd memory, that her father told her he was taking her voice with him to Heaven, to remember her by. She thinks he'd give it back if she asked, but she wants him to have it."

Though Skye had never said it was a secret, it was one of those things Vera wouldn't say casually to someone, but she didn't feel like she was.

Rev gave her a solemn look. "She loved her daddy. It makes her still feel connected to him."

"Yes. Skye also feels she's lucky, because learning to talk a whole different way is a lot easier when you're a child than when you're an adult."

"Yeah. Debbie was born deaf. It was harder for her to learn how to talk with her vocal cords, not being able to hear the sounds she was making, but her parents wanted her to know how to do both things."

"Smart parents." Vera considered if she was about to put her foot into something she shouldn't, but decided to go there anyway. "Have you ever thought of going back to school? Formally?"

"Why you ask?" His expression remained open, but she detected a guarded tone.

It was a legitimate question. Was she asking for herself? Or for him? Could it be for both?

"You like learning. There are opportunities that come with more formal education. Just looking at these kids, we all know that. Why not for adults, too?"

"I never been moved in that direction, Veracity. But maybe one day I will be. I respect your opinion and will keep it in mind." He fished in his lunch tote and brought out a package of Oreo Cakesters. "Want half?"

The switch from odd formality to the offer made her blink. Noting it, he smiled. "Be easy with it, Mistress. You didn't offend me. Just made me think. I liked visiting your office. I like the dancing woman statue in your gardens."

"I picked that one out." She took the sweet and bit into it. "I'll need to walk a few miles to work this off."

"You look good. Them clothes are lucky to have a body like yours to show them off."

She nudged him, and he gave her that boyish smile. "You've used that line before."

"No," he said, with dignity. "Mrs. Everett Meriweather says that to me at church. She about ninety and likes to flirt."

"You learn any other moves from her?"

"I best hold them as a surprise." He grinned and his gaze went down past the hem of the skirt. "You have beautiful legs."

"That your studied opinion, is it?"

"It's a school. Right place for lots of studying."

Somehow, they seemed to be sitting even closer now. She delicately brushed a bit of cream off her bottom lip, and enjoyed watching his attention rest there.

"So this club, it's a place where people, Mistresses, go to...play."

"Mistresses and Masters, and those who want to serve them." She gave him a serious look. "Do you feel ready to go with me, now that we've had our date?"

"You feel ready to go with me?"

"Would I be asking if I wasn't?"

He lifted a shoulder. Vera wiped her fingers on the napkin he'd provided. "Tell me what's in your head, Rev."

"Thinking of what's ahead. What's changing, what's about to change. How that's going to touch the people I care about. My family. Weighing what I should do."

"Anything I can do to help with that?"

"No. But thank you," he added with grave courtesy. "Some things a man has to think through. But yes, I would like to go with you. When?"

"Friday night. This time, let me pick you up, if you don't mind. Do you have other questions?"

"Probably a hundred of them, but I'm guessing the best thing to do is to trust it will make sense once I'm there with you. Learning some of it up front might make me more nervous about it than I am already."

"You don't look nervous."

He closed a hand on hers and squeezed, a little tighter than expected. "It's that thing I told you about. Feeling a lot of mixed-up things inside, wanting and needing you so much, but also wanting and needing to do what makes you happy."

He glanced at his watch and grimaced. "I got to get some things done before the end of the workday, because I have to be at the church tonight. I not meaning to cut this short…"

"I have a little time. Can I tag along? I promise not to get in the way."

The skin alongside his eyes crinkled. "Never known a woman that didn't get in a man's way, but it not a bad thing. Sure. You get bored, I can walk you back out to the parking lot."

"I can find my way."

"It's not about that. I like walking with you." He sent a meaningful glance toward her legs, his gaze sliding over her hips in a far-too-appealing way. "And I like watching you walk, Mistress."

His tasks were in an empty classroom, one used to teach math. The bulletin board was pinned with equations and amusing math puns. She asked Rev if she could help him. He was appalled by the idea, but when she pressed, he told her she could erase the board, something he did on certain days because Mr. Jones was a single father who had to "high tail" it at the end of his last class to pick up his two kids from the elementary school.

After Rev replaced two rusted window locks, he cleaned the blinds, glass and sills. Erasing the board had given her some interesting ideas, so after she used a handwipe from Mr. Jones' desk to wipe her fingers and took a seat at a student desk, she percolated on those thoughts. All while watching Rev do the windows, which involved plenty of backside and shoulder flexing.

"There's a Progeny member, Whistler, who operates a cleaning service," she said. "If you ever need extra work or decide on a job change, he'd be delighted to have someone with your work ethic." *And your great ass.*

Rev glanced over his shoulder. "He like to be the one in charge, or is he on the other side?"

"Dominant or submissive," she said. "Those are two of the terms we often use. As well as Master or Mistress, top and bottom, slave." At his troubled look, she clarified. "In the BDSM world, it doesn't mean what it does outside of it. Even inside our world, the terms have various meanings, depending on the desires of the person using them.

"A person with a Dominant sexual orientation may not be an alpha in the outside world, or in a position of power at all. And a sexually submissive male doesn't mean a weak or docile personality. Far from it. Whistler enjoys submission, and he's also a business owner."

A driven overachiever, Whistler needed the break that surrendering to a Mistress in session gave him, but it had also spawned a creative twist to his successful cleaning operation.

"He hires submissives for his cleaning business, those with a strong service bent, and many of his clients come from the club. They can get a regular cleaning, but his staff also offers BDSM perks upon request. Role playing and wearing certain kinds of clothing while cleaning. Or..."

The sound of sneakers squeaking down the hallway stopped her. The last period bell had rung, but kids who'd remained for after school activities were still around, as well as other faculty members. Rising, Vera went to the door and closed it. Rev had turned from the windows, wiping his squeegee with a towel as he watched her.

"Wearing restraints," she finished. "Or having devices strapped to them, or inside them, that stimulate them as they work, so they have to put extra effort into doing the job right. Vibrators, sex toys..."

His eyes widened. "It would be mighty hard to get a window clean with all that going on."

"Some Doms hope for that. So they can find a missed spot and then punish the sub to 'improve' their focus."

"Does the sub ever mess up on purpose?"

She laughed. "You catch on quick. Sure you haven't been doing a little Internet surfing?"

He shook his head, but she suspected he didn't seem more shocked because his own fantasies had wandered down some of those roads. History had proven the human mind didn't need visual aids to spawn Dominant or submissive cravings—they were already there, and the human mind was more than capable of pursuing them in creative ways.

"Sometimes the Master or Mistress just wants to watch them clean the house. The sub might do additional things if they've negotiated that, and both find pleasure in it."

"Like taking care of the Master or Mistress, too?"

"Yes."

The cleaning cloth was twisted in his fingers. He'd put the vinegar solution to the side and was studying her.

She laced her hands on the top of the desk. Her legs were folded at an attractive slant, her ankles crossed. "Are you thinking about kissing me, Rev?"

"I am. I also thinking about how you taste." His gaze drifted down, then back up. "And the way you felt against me. How much you are, how much you might offer me. What I might be able to ask for. It overtakes me, how much I want to ask for."

It took effort, but she managed not to betray her own "overtaken" reaction, and focus on what he needed to know.

"You'll see a lot of things at Progeny that can make you feel that way. Some of them may make you uncomfortable." She tapped her nails on the desk. "What's important to remember is that everything that happens there is consensual. If something goes over the line, there are monitors, we call them DMs, for dungeon monitors, who are always circling, watching. If they think somebody has gotten so lost in it they're missing a safety issue, or their sub is in distress and hasn't been able to voice it, they step in to help."

"That's good." When his expression relaxed, she appreciated the reminder of his guardian instincts.

"You'll see things you like, that speak to the fantasies you've had about a Mistress. But don't be surprised if you're intrigued by things you didn't think you'd find appealing. You might feel uncomfortable with that reaction, but we can talk about any of it, and see if they're things you would like me to do to you."

"Or have me do for you?"

"I like that you think of how to serve me first, Rev. But taking you places in your head you don't expect, and having you discover the bliss in deeper levels of pleasure and service, that's where I like to go with a sub, though it takes the right connection for it to happen."

Those windows might never get finished if she kept distracting him like this. But she wasn't likely to cut the conversation short, not with his full attention on her and his eyes telling her he was tasting every word the way he wanted to taste her.

"The men you find that with...you aren't with them right now?" When he asked the question, his tone was neutral, but that warned of what lay behind it.

"Sometimes a Dom and sub are only seeking an outlet for those desires in a controlled environment," she said. "Like at the club, in a scheduled play session. They don't desire a relationship outside of that. I have several male submissives with whom I share that kind of relationship, though I also consider them my friends. Whistler is one of them."

She paused, holding his gaze. "It's something you figure out as you get deeper into that world, the difference between play and friendship, and what happens between a Dom and sub looking for something deeper together."

"Is play and friendship what you looking for with me? To be another one of them kinds of subs?" He met her gaze. "Cause that don't interest me."

Yes, Cherry was right. Rev had no trouble speaking his mind when necessary. She appreciated and respected that, even as she had no problem asserting herself in kind.

"I can't tell you what the parameters of our relationship will be right now. I don't think either of us can." She pushed down the wall that her fear of the past told her to put up. "But wherever we end up going together, I think this is different from what I've known before."

His expression relaxed again, but his eyes still held a measured look. "You asked me if I'd been married," he said. "Have you?"

"Yes. We divorced some years ago. He's not part of my life, and we didn't have any children."

"Was he...a submissive?"

"No," she said shortly. "We never got there together. Not in any lasting or real way. We were just young, and Donovan was the right choice for my family, but not for me. I confused the two, because I loved my family and wanted to honor their wishes for me. I didn't realize then that to truly honor my family, I had to know and be true to myself, and love and respect them from that place of strength."

She realized her hands on the desk had tightened into a knot, matching what was in her stomach. "I'd rather talk about something else."

"Okay." He was studying her in that penetrating way he had, but it didn't feel like an invasion, someone outside her door she didn't want there. More like he was the house itself, who understood what kind of haven she needed from what had happened outside that sanctuary. "But I sorry it didn't work out. It's hard, for love to end that way."

"Yes. Rev...really. Ask me something else."

He set aside his cleaning tools and came to her, dropping to a knee and putting his hand on the arm of the chair. A few seconds of silence ensued between them, him looking at her, eye to eye. "I here for you, Mistress. Will you tell me something you imagining doing to me, from that world you know?"

The pain around her heart loosened, a sensual warmth replacing it. "The list is long, Rev."

Sparks of light flickered in his eyes. "One thing, then?"

Rising, making sure her hip and thigh brushed his shoulder, her hand following that track, she moved back to the board. Aware of him turning to watch her, she lifted the eraser.

She patted it across the surface, creating layered rectangles of chalk. Then she picked up a piece of chalk and printed words in block lettering.

I dreem of kneeling. For Her.

Beneath that, she wrote in her own flowing cursive.

I dream of You kneeling.

With a quiet rap, she dropped the chalk in the tray and turned. "Come here, Rev."

She loved these moments, when she issued a command, and a man responded to it, a million reactions in his muscles, in his expression, behind his eyes. That vitality reached out and wrapped her up, so that when she closed her hand over Rev's wrist, the connection felt blessed by whatever power was behind it, and meant to be, this incredible intimacy. Waves of power shifted between them, carried them.

Lifting his palm to the dusted area, she had him press it there. She kept her hand on his forearm.

"I imagine having you stripped, Rev," she murmured. "Both hands on the board like this. I'll pick up that wooden pointer," she nodded at the cane-like item, "and mark your beautiful ass and thighs. Not enough to cause real pain. Just enough to let you know I like punishing you."

"Why?"

"Because you let me. Because you want me to."

His reactions confirmed it. Shortened breath, pupils getting darker and larger, body more tense, closer to her, the energy drawing them together.

"When I tell you that you can remove your hands, your prints will remain on the board, evidence of what I did to you there." Her gaze shifted. "I might use the eraser on your backside, because I'll like seeing the chalk mark there, too. When I'm done, I'll have you stay naked while you write these two lines, over and over, until the board is covered."

He lifted his other hand and touched her cursive. "Do you really dream of that?"

From the moment I met you. From the moment I felt your hands on me.

But she only said, "Yes."

Then, lightening the mood, she added, "School scenes are a role-playing favorite in BDSM. Plenty of useful props."

He looked amused, though his gaze returned to the board. "Why did you capitalize *Her* and *You* that way?"

She hadn't intended to introduce the subject now, worried it could drive a wedge between them before they knew one another well enough to navigate those waters. But her subconscious had had other ideas, and it was right. They'd swim together, or not.

"Because in Tantric terms, we're reaching out to the divine in ourselves. Shiva to Shakti. Shakti to Shiva. For my faith, Wicca, it's Lord to Lady, Lady to Lord."

"You're not Christian." His gaze moved to her pentacle.

She stiffened, but his tone and body language held no censure.

"There are beautiful truths in that faith," she said. "But Wicca was the path where I felt the Divine's presence the most strongly, where it spoke to me in a way I wanted to answer. You can straighten."

The breath he drew in was unsteady. When he turned, and she stepped up to him, her breasts brushing his chest, her hand dropping, she knew she'd find the erection beneath his work clothes. She stroked it, enjoying a Mistress's right.

"Veracity," he said low, but he didn't stop her. One hand gripped the chalk tray.

"I have the right to touch what's mine when I want to do so. Is this mine?"

His expression was tight with self-restraint. "Yes. I want it to be."

A little unsettled by how strong the desire to voice that had felt, she reined herself in and stepped back. The heat of him through his clothes seared her empty palm.

He read her intent to take a breath, and as he pulled himself back in line with it, he touched her pentacle. "This is a symbol of your faith. Like the cross is for mine."

"Yes. The four points represent the elements, the top point the divine in all. The circle around it symbolizes the cycles of the seasons. It's also a reminder of how life and death itself is a never-ending circle." She closed her hand over it, and he brushed his fingers over her knuckles.

"What is the most important rule in it? Wicca." He pronounced the new term carefully.

"And it harm none, do as you will. Which I interpret as love one another and respect all life."

"Like do unto others, the golden rule."

"Yes. A lot like that. It also believes that any harm we do will be visited upon us, three times over. Not just as a punishment, but as a lesson and a balance, to bring us closer to the Lord and Lady's path."

He glanced at the windows. "I better finish that."

"You'd better. Yes."

He ran a hand down her arm, then returned to his task. When she sat back down at the student desk, she checked her phone for work messages, and once again enjoyed the view as he worked. The vinegar cleaner smell was sharp but not unpleasant. When he finally spoke again, his mind had returned to their upcoming plans. "What should I wear?"

"There's no dress code, but any excessively revealing clothing has to be covered outside the club. Inside the club, people wear everything from suits and fancy nightclub dresses to jeans and T-shirts or fetish wear. Leather, latex, costumes. Some may be naked, if that's what their Masters and Mistresses desire."

"In front of everyone?"

"In front of everyone."

"And they don't have no say in it?"

"They have a say in everything. Everything is consensual," she reminded him. "The relationship is negotiated up front, altered by mutual agreement as they grow together. That can include what's called consensual non-consent, where a submissive has agreed to turn over all choices to the Dom, unless there's a medical emergency.

"They have a way of signaling that, if the Domme doesn't catch it herself, which she should, but it's always good to know your sub is looking out for himself as much as you are. Even if you're also hoping they'll trust you to move outside their comfort zone into an area you both might enjoy more."

"All this is tumbling through my head like a dryer full of warm socks." He finished the last window and turned to her. "I didn't say it right. What would *you* like me to wear?"

Her eyes wandered downward, taking her time. "Jeans that fit the right way."

"What's the right way?"

"Not too tight, but I want to be able to see your backside, and get a good reminder of how much cock you're carrying." She liked the stain of color the words brought to his cheeks, the spark of fire in his eyes, but continued in a casual tone. "Choose a shirt you think I'd like, but I might have you take it off while we're there."

"So you can...show me off?"

As soon as he spoke the words, she detected the resistance in them. Rising, she came to him and rested her fingertips on his chest. "So I can touch your bare skin whenever I wish. But if you're uncomfortable with being exposed like that, I'll reserve that as a private pleasure."

He shifted. "I'm sorry. I shouldn't have—"

"You absolutely should have," she said. "I told you how I feel about honesty, Rev. The only rule I have about you expressing it to me is that you be respectful. Creativity earns extra credit. I'll give you an example. 'Mistress, may I ask that you have me undress only for you, in private?'"

The appreciation in his chuckle made it even sexier. She could tell he was internalizing everything, a man used to taking notes in his head. "The only way you can disappoint me is if I demand something that makes you uncomfortable in the wrong ways, and you don't let me know."

Her piercing Mistress look stilled him, pulling his focus to her. "If I'm paying attention the way I should," she said, "I'll know. But I don't recommend having me find out that way. As I said, I want to feel like you are mine. You asking me if it's okay to do something or not do something honors that, while protecting our pleasure, the beauty and power of our time together. Do you understand?"

So many things could change that gingerbread color in his irises, creating intriguing lights and shadows. "Yes, Mistress. I think I do." He let out another breath. "I'm smack in the middle of things I dreamed about, but there's more there than I understand. I want to, though."

"You'll understand more as we go along, just as you suspected. But you have the right and ability to protect yourself at all times, to let me know your desires, and to ask questions. If you keep that in mind, we'll have a good time. That said, if the club isn't your scene, if you find you really don't like it there, you can tell me and we'll go."

He frowned. "But won't that mean you won't want to see me no more?"

"If it does, then that's what's meant to be." She tapped his chest. "But it won't necessarily mean that. There are plenty of ways to explore domination and submission that don't involve a formal venue at all." Her gaze slid around the classroom. "As I think I just demonstrated."

His tense expression morphed into a rueful half smile.

"Yes ma'am. You sure did."

CHAPTER SIX

"*V*era? You have visitors."

Visitors? She was expecting Rev for lunch, but it was a little too early for his arrival. He was picking up a part at a hardware store and would take the bus from there to the Garden District.

"Witford and Tisha Butterford," Bastion continued. "They said they don't have an appointment"—which Bastion knew, because he kept Vera's calendar—"but they said they hope you have a few minutes for them."

That confirmed Rev hadn't turned lunch into a family affair. Something she wouldn't have expected anyway, not without some kind of heads-up to her first.

"Certainly. Show them up." She considered asking Bastion to call her in ten minutes with an excuse to cut the meeting short, but then she rejected the idea. This was Rev's family, and she would offer warmth and courtesy. Unless something in their behavior said she shouldn't.

A cold ball in her lower belly said that might happen, and it wasn't unwarranted. If Rev had known about the visit, he would have let her know. She couldn't think of an acceptable reason they would be meeting with her alone, without his knowledge. But she also might be letting her personal history assume the worst.

Having them brought up instead of coming down to escort them herself wasn't what she did for a friend or someone she wanted to feel particularly welcome. But she would obey her intuition, which told her to stay where she was and appear busy, even if she was in danger of putting a hole in the page where her pen was tracing the same word. She made herself stop doing that and opened an app on her computer instead. She finished activating it just as they reached the top floor. Bastion was doing the courteous small talk thing, explaining the origins of the house. There was a lift elevator, but they'd apparently preferred the stairs.

Bastion's tone was friendly but formal. When he arrived at the door, his watchful expression said he was picking up an odd vibe, too.

Vera came around the desk with a polite smile, her hand outstretched. Witford was a step ahead of Rev's aunt, and shook with a firm, dry grasp. Tisha had her purse clasped against her body with both hands, and nodded.

"Would you like to sit down?" Vera asked, pointing to her two guest chairs.

Witford gestured to his mother to take the inside chair while he took the one closer to the door. Vera met Bastion's gaze. "Thank you, Bastion."

Bastion nodded. "Sure I can't bring you something to drink? We have water, sodas, coffee and tea, plus some fresh lemonade."

"We won't be here long," Tisha said stiffly, though she looked at Bastion with perplexed fascination. Even in New Orleans, a six-foot four office manager with long locs, the build of a graceful NFL quarterback, and a fashion sense that kept pace with Ros's taste in shoes, was a puzzle.

Bastion touched the door with a questioning look. *Open or closed?* Vera shook her head. She wanted it open.

She returned to her seat behind her desk. "Is Rev all right?"

"Yes, of course," Tisha said, seeming surprised she would ask.

Lacing her fingers together on her desk, Vera leveled a gaze on Witford. "Then can you explain why you're here without his knowledge?"

Witford's brow rose. "How do you know we are?"

"Because he would have told me."

"You know him that well, do you?" Witford said mildly.

"I know he's a respectful and kind person. Would you disagree?"

"No," Witford said. "My aunt raised him with a simple, loving view of the world, a faith in its goodness. Which can lead him to trust those who are perhaps not trustworthy."

His tone had built in volume, an orator used to being heard. But she wasn't going to play this game, a passive aggressive attack veiled by false courtesy. "Please indicate the purpose of your visit, and dispense with the subtle digs."

His face tightened, but he gave her a cold nod. "Fine. You are college-educated and wealthy. He doesn't have a high school diploma, and lives paycheck to paycheck. His life is dedicated to his church. You are not a Christian. We see no good reason for you to be interested in him."

"So you're worried about his well-being."

Tisha's gaze rested on Vera's pentacle with obvious distaste. "We have to look out for Rev. He's God's special gift to the world."

"Then don't you think God would look out for him?" Vera didn't intend mockery, but since she couldn't keep the edge out of her voice, Tisha's annoyed expression said she'd interpreted it that way.

"God works through others," Witford said, touching his aunt's arm, a counsel for restraint. "Like his family. What do you know of God, Miss Morgan?"

"As much as anyone," Vera said evenly. "What I feel in my heart, the path I seek to be a good person, loving and helping others, it's all connected to my spiritual path. Every faith worth something has that focus."

"A witch can have the devil's silver tongue. I expect she can even quote scripture." The gaze Tisha lifted to Vera held venom. "Yes, we know you practice witchcraft and worship Satan."

Past and present slammed together like a car crash. *If a choice comes before you, between God and family, God must prevail. If they will not hear the Word, shake the dust from your feet and leave them behind. Do not risk losing your faith and devotion to the Lord.*

Her family had interpreted God's word according to the church and preacher they followed, and acted upon it accordingly.

"Mother." With the same mild warning in his tone, Witford let Vera know he'd preferred to keep the discussion on a different footing to achieve their objective.

"She said she wanted us to be direct," Tisha said.

"I do. Though courtesy and respect would be appreciated as part of that." A visceral reaction had gripped Vera, but she was getting a handle on it. Ignorance was the primary driver of hate and fear. And Wicca was not a conversion faith, but as a spiritual leader, just as Witford was, she had a duty to educate.

This is Rev's family. Be patient.

"There is no devil in the Wiccan faith," she told Tisha, including Witford in her glance. "There's no need for one when humans are capable of evil all on their own. The guiding tenets of my faith are do no harm, and honor and revere all the life."

Tisha sucked in a breath through her nose, her knuckles white on her purse straps. "You think you know him. You think you know everything, and judge my motives from a worldly view. He's a simple soul with a pure heart. You will corrupt him and make his soul wither. My sister saw God in that boy, and told me to protect him, not how the world thinks I should, but how God wills it."

Witford's jaw was tight, but he'd laced his fingers against the vest of his well-cut suit as he let his mother have her say. "Is that it?" Vera asked her. "You've convinced yourself he's an uneducated simpleton, a singing savant, to justify how you're disrespecting him now?"

"You're not hearing me," Tisha snapped.

"Just because I don't agree with you, doesn't mean I don't hear you." Vera locked down any emotion that wouldn't serve her and addressed Witford. "You're the preacher, but you don't feel God the way he does. That can breed resentment, can't it?"

Witford's face went cold and still. She saw it then, the sickness twisted by his ambitions. He wasn't all the way lost, but darkness was around his heart.

Somewhere along the way, he'd probably rationalized it. Rev was able to feel such a deep connection to God because he didn't have to worry about the realities of the world. His cousin would make the sacrifice and take care of those things, watch after him. Even as he also reaped the benefits of that connection.

"He loves that job at the school, you know," Witford said. "It would be difficult for him to keep it, if parents found out he was involved with someone like you."

"New Orleans is home to a lot of faiths, including voodoo. I don't think—"

"That's not what I'm talking about. I didn't come here unprepared,

Miss Morgan. I'm aware of the rumors about you and the other women who run this place. The deviant lifestyle you pursue. The school would let him go to protect the students. After all, at the end of the day, he's just a janitor."

Boy, you just barked up the wrong tree.

If she'd had any doubt about where her feelings for Rev were at this point in their relationship, a territorial surge drowned that doubt, never to be heard from again. He was hers, to care for and protect.

Vera turned her laptop toward Witford, showing him the red button glowing at the bottom. "That's a recording app. It's useful for remembering meeting and interview details. Or for things like this."

"You're not supposed to record someone without their permission. I was a lawyer, before the Lord called me to His path."

"You're way the hell off of it, if you're here doing this to your cousin."

"If you share that tape with Rev, he'll find out what you are."

She met his dark gaze. He had a straight nose and Rev's mouth. He was a handsome man, but what she saw behind the mask repelled her.

"Rev is fully aware I'm a sexual Dominant. I'm not ashamed of my preferences, and I'm fortunate nothing important in my life depends on me hiding what so many people don't attempt to understand."

Tisha had flinched when Witford brought up the subject, but the revulsion in her face, unmarked by shock, said Witford had shared this with her before this meeting. Shock would set in when she really thought about why Rev might want to be around a sexually Dominant woman. But Vera wasn't going to be the one to point that out. Rev deserved his privacy.

"Did you even think of how your doing this would make Rev feel?" she demanded of Witford. "What he'd think?"

"I expect he'd wonder if his cousin had lost his damned mind," Rev said.

He stood in her doorway. Bastion had sent him up unannounced. Vera was glad for that, but she wished she could have spared him the far-too-familiar emotions he was feeling as he stepped into her office. She could see them in his face, in the tension in his shoulders.

Tisha came out of the chair like a jack-in-the-box. "Rev, Witford wouldn't have done it. We were testing her. If she'd been fine with it, it would have told us she didn't value you."

Witford stood to face Rev. "She's telling the truth. You know I'd never do anything like that to you. We just wanted to discourage her from seeing you. A woman like this...you're out of your depth, cousin."

Rev's gaze shifted to Vera. "Are you all right?" he asked.

Even with what they'd just done, he sensed the turmoil in her, and was concerned about that. The pain in her heart doubled, but she managed to keep it out of her voice.

"I'm fine, Rev. I'm sorry."

"Don't seem like you have much to be sorry for. You didn't ask them to come here and do this."

He was holding his bill cap in his hand, and he glanced down at it, rotating it meditatively.

"Rev," Witford began. "Let's go get some lunch and we can talk about this. I—"

"No."

Vera was sure Rev hadn't raised his voice. Yet somehow that one syllable filled her office and bounced echoes off every corner of the top floor.

Two seconds later, Cyn and Skye were outside her door. Vera shook her head, the lift of her hand holding them off.

"Please, Rev. Come home with us." Tisha pressed her fist to her chest, above the purse. "I feel it in my heart. We've prayed about it, Witford and I. Put this woman behind you. She's not in God's fold."

Cyn stepped forward, but Skye gripped her arm, holding her back. Vera's gaze sharpened on her coworker, reinforcing the message. She could handle this. Plus, no matter how Rev was feeling about it, he wouldn't be okay with Cyn body slamming his aunt to the floor.

"Perhaps you should have thought to talk to *me*. Pray with *me* about it," Rev said. "You had no call to come talk to Miss Veracity this way."

"Rev, we *are* worried about you," Witford said forcefully. "Maybe we went about this the wrong way, but Tisha loves you. She's sick with worry."

Rev stared at the hat in his hand again. "I hearing you, Witford. But I got nothing for you right now. The anger in me isn't letting me see this clear. I come see you when I ready to do that." He looked up and met Witford's gaze, man-to-man. "But right now, you take Tisha home."

Tisha placed her hand on Witford's arm. "We didn't mean to hurt you, Rev. I just told Teena Joy I'd look after you, and this situation," her gaze flicked toward Vera, "makes me very worried for you."

Rev's gaze softened perceptibly, but his voice remained implacable. "Teena Joy asked you to look after me when I was a child. I not no child anymore. I respect your love, wisdom and guidance. But I also respect what God tells my heart." His expression hardened again. "This isn't a 'situation.' I care about this woman, and you will respect her and respect what's my business. You understand?" His gaze shifted to Witford. "Both of you."

Witford gave him a tight nod. "You're still welcome to join us for lunch. We can talk."

"Not today. Mind what I said." Rev shifted out of the doorway and glanced toward it meaningfully. "You owe Veracity an apology, but if you don't think you done anything needing forgiving, just go."

Witford looked Vera's way and gave her a cold nod that conveyed nothing resembling an apology. Tisha didn't look toward her at all.

Tisha tried to pause when she was parallel with Rev, but Witford met his cousin's gaze and ushered her past him with a firm hand on her lower back.

Vera heard Bastion meet them at the stairs, still cordial but definitely cooler. He'd make sure they took a direct route to the parking lot and off the grounds.

Rev moved behind the chair his aunt had been using, his eyes on it. That cap was still going in circles. "We'll be nearby if you need us," Skye signed to Vera.

Vera nodded. She gestured to Cyn to close the door.

Silence reigned in her office for ten seconds. Then he lifted his head and met her eyes. "Erase it," he said.

Her HR and legal background told her it was the last thing she should do, to protect his interests. She could fight with him about it, or respect his wishes.

But he'd just chastised them for treating him like a child. She erased the file and closed down the app.

"I'm sorry, Rev. If I'd known why they were here, I never would have let them come up at all. You can stay with me for a few days, if you want."

"I have my own place," he snapped. Rev sighed, and tapped the hat on the top of the chair. "I'm sorry. You didn't deserve that."

"I get it. I wasn't trying to imply you don't take care of yourself. I just know how deeply a family can hurt you."

His harsh chuckle made her throat ache. "Your family treat you like an idiot who don't have the sense to know what's good for you?"

"I chose a faith and a path they disagreed with. Strongly enough they told me to get out and not come back. I could afford a hotel, but at the time I remember wishing I had a friend to stay with who understood."

His eyes narrowed, his mouth tightening. The man could look intriguingly dangerous when he chose to do so, but she held up a hand. "I didn't say that to turn the subject to me. I just wanted to explain that I'm speaking from a place of understanding."

Rev ran his hand over his face. "I appreciate that, Veracity, but I need to go think this through."

It hurt, but the reaction was attached to her own need to make sure that his aunt and cousin's actions, or anything Vera had done, hadn't alienated him. She had to let that go and focus on the most important thing—if he was okay.

"All right. Reach out if you need anything, Rev. I mean it."

He'd turned toward the door, but he startled her with an about face and purposeful stride that brought him around the desk. He dropped to a knee and kissed her hand, holding his cheek to it. "Your family shouldn't have done that to you," he said gruffly.

And yours shouldn't have done what they just did.

She'd wanted to comfort him, and he'd managed to comfort her. She gripped his shoulder, trying to convey everything she wanted to do to make this better.

Nobody could fuck you up like family.

"When I was little, if I was unhappy about something, I'd sit under Teena Joy's desk while she was writing sermons. I'd sing to her. Take a nap. Listen to her think aloud. It brought me peace." Rev looked under Vera's desk. "Think I'm too big for that now."

"I wouldn't mind having you under my desk all day." She knew some stimulating toys, restraints and positions that would make the Mistress in her pleased to have him there.

Not the time to share that thought, but something in her voice must have conveyed it, because the gaze he flicked up to her showed intrigued heat. Erotic humor slid away, though, as he rose, drawing her up with him. He brushed his knuckles over her cheek.

"You made a good impression on Cyn and Skye just now," she noted.

"I'd prefer them to get that through how I treat you, not how I set my family straight."

"They took it as one and the same."

His lips thinned. "Witford...he having some problems in his relationship with God, but I didn't think it was bad as all that. And Tisha, she get too carried away with things that don't matter."

"It's okay. I'm just worried about you."

"I all right." He put his forehead to hers, his hands on either side of her face, then stepped back abruptly. "I'll come find you, when my head in the right place."

He didn't tell her what he'd told Witford, not to come looking for him until he was ready. She could decide it was implied, or do what the Mistress in her told her to do.

She'd give him a little time. Then she'd find him.

CHAPTER SEVEN

A couple days later, she acted on that decision. How much she missed him might have compelled her as much as her worry for him, but since both were true, she had no problem with that.

When she called the school, Cherry said he was working at the church in the afternoon.

The thought of encountering Witford or Tisha upset her stomach, which pissed her off, so Vera put her ass in her car and headed that way after lunch.

Only one car was in the parking lot, a red Toyota four-door. Bastion had reported Witford drove a Lincoln Continental. His presence or absence shouldn't matter either way. She wasn't here to see Witford.

The doors leading into the nave were propped open, but it was empty. The clacking sound of a computer keyboard in use came from the hallway to her right. The sign posted at the corner said *Church Office*.

But before she headed in that direction, she stepped into the nave and moved down the aisle until she stood before the large cross. How did Rev feel up here? Or when he walked along the aisles, singing? Reaching out toward the souls that needed him.

Most people she could figure out. She understood what drove them, what fears and insecurities, the needs they had. Often it didn't change anything, to know and understand. But sometimes it did.

Rev had brought forth things in her she thought she'd made peace with. She hadn't. She'd just buried them, because with that kind of loss, she could only bury the body and move on, missing the soul of what was, and the connection that had been.

He wasn't a preacher. He was a soul minister.

She left the nave and went to the office, finding a woman in her forties, with bouncy curled hair and well applied makeup. Her navy-blue dress was printed with white polka dots, and her gold name plate said she was Mrs. Byrd.

"Hello. I'm Vera Morgan, a friend of Rev's. Can you tell me where I can find him?"

The woman looked up from her screen, the welcoming warmth in her brown eyes releasing Vera's tension like air from a balloon, sending it sputtering away. In some corner of her subconscious, she'd absurdly imagined Witford putting her on a blacklist to keep her off the church grounds.

That cold look in his eyes, the venom in Tisha's words, had rattled her more than she realized. It wasn't like her.

"Well, lucky Rev. He's doing his Garden of Gethsemane right now."

"Pardon me?"

"It's what he calls it. He goes into the contemplation garden behind the church to pray and think. He seemed like he had a lot on his mind."

The secretary's concerned expression was replaced by a speculative one. "You know, Rev doesn't pay attention to what most of us find important. I've seen him hand two twenties to a convenience store clerk for an eight dollar purchase."

The segue took her off guard, but since it was a story about Rev, Vera rolled with it. "Did the clerk take advantage?"

"He thought about it. You can see that kind of thing in the eyes. I was about to step in—we were on a church trip, and getting some snacks. But Rev was gazing at the boy as he waited, and humming to himself. That voice..." Mrs. Byrd shook her head. "Even under his breath, you want to listen close, because it brings on a feeling you want to have."

"That's a perfect way to put it," Vera murmured.

"You've heard it." Mrs. Byrd's smile deepened. "Good. When the clerk gave him the right change *and* the extra twenty, Rev told him that being able to look in the mirror and see no tarnish made every day a good one. Then Rev gave him back the twenty and said he'd meant for him to take that for his mother. She apparently had a cold and needed some medicine. When that boy smiled, it looked like the first real one he'd had in a long time."

Vera saw the scene in her head, as clear as if she'd been there. "Why'd you tell me that?"

"You looked like you expected me to tell you Rev couldn't see anyone right now. But I've learned people come looking for him, at the right time, for the right reasons. And not just because he's a pleasing man to look at."

"I've noticed that."

"You're not blind, so I expect so." Mrs. Byrd winked. "He's not much on book learning. Says it doesn't take hold in his mind. But between you and me, he may be the smartest man I've ever met."

Mrs. Byrd waved a hand toward her door. "Take the exit at the end of my hall. Turn left and cut through the cemetery. You'll see the garden entrance. If he's deep into it when you find him, take a seat nearby and do your own prayer until it's over. There are plenty of places to sit."

"Thank you." Vera turned toward the door, then paused. "Mrs. Byrd, what was the significance of the Garden of Gethsemane? I know it had to do with Jesus."

"It certainly did. The Garden of Gethsemane is where our Lord spent His hours before His arrest, dealing with His fear and sadness about the trial ahead of Him. I think it was also where He let Himself really feel the sadness and pain for all of us. Are you familiar with John 11:35?"

Vera shook her head.

"'Jesus wept.' Shortest verse in the Bible, and possibly the most powerful. I think about it whenever it rains."

Vera met the woman's gaze. What she detected there suggested Mrs. Byrd had come upon Rev in the garden before, and knew first-hand what he sought there.

Perhaps she should leave him be. If he was talking to Higher Powers, nothing Vera could offer would top that. But the compulsion she felt to see him had grown overwhelming. Maybe it was being driven by reasons beyond her own desires.

Or she was just telling herself that.

Fuck it, as Cyn might say. Vera wanted to see him, needed to see him. She wasn't dealing with another sleepless night.

"Thank you, Mrs. Byrd. It's a genuine pleasure to meet a true friend of Rev's."

The woman's shrewd eyes registered the word choice, and she nodded. "I hope I've done the same, Miss Morgan. Sure feels like it."

As Vera headed down the hallway, she noted it looked freshly painted. The building wasn't fancy, but everything was clean and well maintained. Even the base boards gleamed, no accumulation of dust or scuff marks.

Once outside, that trend continued. No pollen on the siding, no bug residue or abandoned webs. In a coastal city where everyone struggled against the effects of a sticky, humid environment, the keepers of this building were on the ball. They cared about their church. She had no doubt Rev was part of that effort.

In the cemetery, she saw a recent grave, surrounded by fresh flowers. The polished tombstone said Betty Miller had passed at the seasoned age of ninety-four. Beloved wife, mother, friend and teacher. A line of pretty stones was on the uneven marble top, twenty-eight of them. She wondered if they'd been left by her students.

Even beyond the grave, people always had more stories to tell. Sometimes that was when the best stories came out to be noticed.

A hedge separated the cemetery from the garden, but a powder coated black metal archway woven with bougainvillea provided an entrance. A plaque above it read, *Give your worries to the Lord. Offer Him your hope and faith, to give both strength.*

Nested in a cluster of rugosa roses to her left was a replica of the Weeping Angel statue in New Orleans' Metairie Cemetery, her head resting on a pedestal, body and wings stretched out nearly straight behind her. At the base of the pedestal was a planter holding the fish shaped worry stones.

The garden was a mix of wild azaleas, tended flower plots, potted plants and more religious statuary. A large cross marked the garden's center. As she worked her way through the maze-like plantings to reach it, she kept an eye out for Rev.

Then she heard a deep, guttural moan, a swallowed sob. It was coming from the left side of the garden, so she changed direction, heading for it. Every few steps, she heard it again, so she'd stop. Such a sound required stillness to absorb it. Yet when it became a cry, torn from the soul of the one uttering it, she quickened her step.

The lance through her heart told her it was him.

He was kneeling beside a stone bench, his back to her. In front of him, on a hill of mulch and surrounded by azaleas, was another angel statue, this one standing tall and strong, wings spread and robes billowing, as if she was in a strong wind. Her face was kind but stern, a finger raised in gentle admonishment to counsel silence, to listen to what was being offered.

Rev had his head down, his elbows on the bench, face cupped in his hands, his broad shoulders shuddering. He wore jeans and a T-shirt, his knees on the concrete pad around the bench. His back was rounded, as if what gripped him held on tight and hard, curling him in on himself. As she drew closer, she realized that between the sobs and cries, he was singing in a broken, rough voice.

"Judge not lest ye be judged...

"All things are possible through He who gives me strength...

"Let go... Just let go... Just gotta let go..."

Even now, in the throes of such personal anguish, the pitch of his voice, its ability to compel and mesmerize as he put random words to music, was not diminished. If anything, it held more power. His pain took strength from her body, making her sit down on another nearby bench, but it pulled her spirit right to him. The notes rang through the garden, keeping even the birds silent.

He raised his head, his eyes closed. When she saw his tears, she could feel his worry and agony. Only love could create a wound that deep.

Her strength came rushing back. She couldn't refuse the compulsion that told her he needed a Mistress's care as much as he needed God's.

She took off her shoes and stockings. Having the pathway under her bare soles felt right, as if she were on holy ground. She came closer, until she could put her hand on his shoulder.

He didn't start at her touch. He went still, until another shudder passed through him. Lifting a hand, he covered hers and held it tight.

She went to her knees next to him, her arm across his back, her cheek pressing against it.

She'd been angry, wanting to strike out at Witford and his aunt, for the wrong they'd done him, wanting to make them suffer for hurting a man she already deeply cared about. But here, she was pulled into what mattered to him about it, and tears rose and spilled down her cheeks.

She wasn't just crying for what his family had done, but what hers had, and how lost they all were, every one of them.

He turned, and suddenly he was holding her. Every fear and worry she had bubbled up and, in his arms, were washed away. She was safe and cared for, in a way she rarely let herself know she wished for. He knew, and understood. He saw and felt her, down to the soul.

She was a Mistress, a woman who could care for herself and others. She could care for him, which was why she was here. Whether she'd wanted to be here or had been called here, it didn't matter. It was all the same.

She was also a child, wondering at the world, sometimes afraid and hurting over it. Just like him.

She understood why he was here, not just to seek guidance for his own pain, but for the suffering of others. He saw their isolation, pushed past and through it, took that feeling of being lost, alone and desolate, and tossed it aside for the lie it was.

But it could overwhelm him, as it would anyone. When he raised his head and she looked up at him, she touched his face. He gazed at her through wet eyes, his mouth firm and soft at once under her fingertips.

"Money and power, they not evil," he said. "But a man's soul can get sick and let them become a poison. Don't have to be a lot of money or a lot of power, just a lot in his world."

His mind was on his aunt and cousin, she knew, but she stayed silent, listening.

Rev looked down at her hand, clasped between his. "We lost a kid last year because he had twenty dollars in his pocket from mowing a yard. Another group of kids beat him to death for it, but that wasn't why they did it. They beat him for not joining their gang, for showing them they didn't have to be that, didn't have to take what wasn't earned. They wrote $20 on his forehead."

She closed her eyes. She knew the kind of helplessness he was feeling. She and the other TRA women felt it whenever they couldn't get someone in desperate circumstances to come to Laurel Grove or one of its sister shelters.

"Witford...he's a good preacher," Rev said. "He want to be a great one, but he don't realize that's not what they need. He just needs to care about the people and let God guide him to the lessons He needs to talk to them about.

"He's gotten to be about Witford, standing over them on that pulpit, having people shake his hand consider him important. We're only important as God's instrument, and He gives us the gift of being important to those we love."

Rev sighed. "Guess that can be one of my singing sermons, but how do I sing it to Witford so he hear? I don't know, but hopefully God will know and tell me."

She pressed her head to his shoulder, gripped his arms, a silent wish for the same. "Is it okay that I'm here?" she asked at length, lifting her head.

His beautiful lips curved and he touched her cheek, rubbing the tear track there. "I'd like to kiss this, hold onto it in my mouth, Mistress. Is that all right?"

At her assent, he leaned in, touched his lips there. Her fingers tightened on his biceps. "You're going to give me impure thoughts," she said.

He drew back and looked at her seriously. "Nothing impure about the way you make me feel, or the way I make you feel. Our bodies linked to our heart and soul. Can't you feel it? I kiss your skin, and think about kissing more of it, all over, being inside you like I was the other day, and my heart hurts wanting to be that close to you again. You made it...sacred, that energy you were talking about. The way it's meant to be."

Rev was a devout, loving, balanced soul. He was also a powerful male who desired a woman and had no shame in the way he felt that desire. It made her all the more determined to be his Mistress. And thank the Lord and Lady, God, the Powers-that-Be, for the gift.

"Yes. Sacred." Her lips tipped up. "Yet it feels so good it almost feels indulgent. What your people might call sin."

"My people?" His eyes glinted at her teasing, then he sobered. "Sin don't feel good. Not really. Not if your heart's open to what's right. Everything about touching you feels good, Mistress. Why'd you come to me here?"

"Something you said. About needing to get your head in the right place." She held onto him tighter. "I've been thinking...have you ever thought I can be the person you can come find when you feel that way?

"I'm not trying to compete with a Power that knows way more than me," she added, looking around them. "This is a way to get your head right with God. I just...you can have an earthly version of getting your head right with yourself. Someone to lean on when you need it. A Mistress can be that."

"For a submissive like me."

Because the typical interpretation of the word implied bad things about manhood or strength, the ability to protect and care for others, most men with a submissive orientation avoided the direct characterization, at least at first. But she wasn't surprised that Rev had accepted it. He understood what surrendering control meant, and knew it wasn't weak at all, not when done willingly, with that open heart.

"Teena Joy said nothing gives the Lord as much joy as giving Him your trust." Rev appeared to have read her mind. "She said she thought that might be the source of His strength, our trust in Him."

He helped her onto the bench, and slid his hands over her knees, removing tiny bits of gravel. "You could have scraped your pretty knees on that concrete." He leaned in and kissed each one, his fingers lingering.

"Rev."

He chuckled. His face still showed signs of weeping, but the contrast with his sensual teasing made her heart tilt. He glanced at the angel. "You two have the same look on your face, like you about to scold me."

She pressed her lips against a smile and clasped his hands. He put his head on her knuckles, his wide shoulders a platform she could rest her free palm on. It wasn't enough. She leaned forward to put her cheek on the back of his head, and then he turned it so her hair brushed his face and he could inhale her scent, his back expanding from the deep breath.

"What you said earlier, about inviting me to your home," he said. "Is that invitation still open?"

"It is." She straightened, and he did the same, looking at her.

"Then I'd like to take you up on it. Just for a night," he added. "I won't take advantage of you."

"It never crossed my mind that you would." She leaned back in. "But I intend to take full advantage of you."

CHAPTER EIGHT

*T*he Italian architecture of her house in the Irish Channel section of New Orleans reflected the many things the city was. The house was blue with cream shutters and trim, the small front yard bound with black wrought iron fencing. Flared shelf molding embellished the tops of the tall windows. A welcoming front porch spanned the width of her home.

She parked the car in her detached garage in back and led him to the cozy screened porch that overlooked her backyard. It had just enough room for her vegetable and herb garden, plus a meditation bench under the sprawling oak. The tree draped its arms companionably over the backyards of her neighbors.

As she took him up the steps past her potted flowers and unlocked the back door, he held the screen, his body close behind her. She turned to gesture him inside.

She'd loved the historic house from her first walk through. It was narrow but long, following the typical footprint of houses built in this area during the early 1900s. The floor-to-ceiling windows were in the master bedroom, as well as the front living room and dining areas.

It smelled like well-loved historic houses did. Old wood, plaster, and a mix of new materials to keep it maintained over the decades. The polished floors in the narrow rooms were mostly the original wood, but when needed, replacement boards were matched. She'd had the walls painted in the vibrant colors she preferred, a different color for each room, embellished with white crown molding.

She liked furniture crafted before 1930. Or looked like it had been. The avocado green velvet sofa with diamond tufted seat, cushions and arms could convert into a full sleeper sofa, and she had cream-colored pillows on it, printed with New Orleans street scenes. The sofa and two matching side chairs were grouped around one of the six fireplaces the house had.

A large watercolor of Ella Fitzgerald singing in a smoky club was over the couch.

Plenty of daylight streamed through the tall front windows, flanked by shimmering green and gold striped curtains. When she closed them so the living room became more intimate, light from the room's tear-drop chandelier made the velvet of the couch and the gold in the painting's frame gleam.

She wanted what she had planned to stay private, and her front porch was only a few feet from the street.

She turned to find him still within a step of her. Perhaps thinking he was crowding her, he started to step back, but she put a hand on his forearm. His ended up at her waist, fingers curling in. Energy vibrated from him, but he was waiting to see what she wanted.

"Kneel to me, Rev."

The relief that swept him was so strong it rocked them both. He sank to one knee, but kept gazing up at her, a curious mix of submission and expectation, hope and demand, that made curbing her anticipation difficult. She wanted to unspool it in slow ribbons of pleasure.

"This is my home, Rev, and I've invited you into it. Would you hurt me here?"

Shock gripped his face. "No, Mistress. Not here, not anywhere." Then he did that inner reflection thing, and added to it. "Never, Veracity. You're safe with me. No matter what."

"What changed there? When you chose to tell me both as a Mistress and by my given name?"

"I want you to know that I ache to be on my knees to you, but that change nothing about my promise to respect and protect you, as a woman trusting a man should expect. As you should expect, when you trust me."

Vera took a steadying breath. "Thank you for that, Rev. You have the same promise from me, because when you willingly hand me control, I *can* hurt you, physically and mentally. The more you open yourself to me, the more that risk increases. So I promise to care for everything you entrust to me about yourself."

She gestured. "On that note, take a seat on the sofa. We need to talk about some things first."

When they moved there, he waited until she sat before he did, one cushion-width between them. "Before a Dominant and submissive engage in anything too involved," she said, "we talk about limits first."

Not just to bring him up to speed, but to gauge his reactions to the information she gave him now. Hard and soft limits, and examples of both. Impact play, sting versus thud, fire play, electric play. Suspension, restraints, toys.

She didn't bother with the ones that didn't appeal to her. As his knowledge of this world grew, if he found something that interested him in those areas, she could help him explore them with other Dommes.

She wasn't thrilled with that thought, but under her supervision... she might be all right with it. A discussion for another day, if it became an issue. She'd shared subs before, usually with the other TRA women, but unless they were regular playmates, it was only for the occasional session.

It was rare she brought a man home to play. But Rev needed to explore this side of himself in a private environment, without the sensory overload that Progeny could be to those new to this.

She recognized when she needed to further explain a term or type of play. Not because Rev pretended to know something when he didn't, but he'd get lost in thought over it, enough that she'd inject more information until that puzzled expression cleared, to be replaced by interest, indifference or amusing horror.

He showed interest in impact play and restraints. Full recoil on anal play. She enjoyed fucking a male, but him proving his devotion by worshipping and pleasuring her body usually took the lead in her sessions. The psychological elements of Dominance and submission were her favorite areas to explore, and if she was with a sub who embraced that as she did, they found what worked for both of them. So far, Rev had earned straight As in that.

An example she gave him: A male standing at her back, waiting for her—waiting on her—with endless patience, to prove his service, even as he also exhibited those titillating signs of effort to leash his drives and desires.

Sometimes she coiled that leash around her hand and drew it taut, proving in more stringent ways how much in charge of his responses she was, especially when the sub needed that, too.

But she also liked to be the kind of owner who let the leash trail next to her sub, knowing his attention and focus never really left her. He wanted the leash there, and so did she, but she had no need to hold it.

"Play seem a strange word for some of this, Mistress," Rev noted. "Electric *play*, fire play."

"Yes. But many submissives start in the shallow end of the pool and eventually are only happy in the places where they can't touch bottom at all. Or get well over their head."

"They drown."

"Depending on what you're drowning in, it's not always a bad thing."

His gaze moved around the room. "Your house match the clothes you like to wear. Sophisticated, from a different time."

It might seem like he'd changed subjects, but this phase included a meshing between what the Mistress or sub wanted, and who they were. Rev was looking at that for her, as much as she was for him.

"In the church I attended growing up, you looked your best there, supposedly to please the Lord, though I'm sure there was some vanity involved, a little competition in the hats and gloves, the type of shoes, the pin just so on the lapel. The color of your man's tie, his cuff links."

She smiled as his lips tugged, showing his understanding and familiarity with it. Mostly black congregations hadn't changed much on that, no matter the "casual dress" approach some churches now took.

"It still serves that primary purpose, I think. Deliberate care with appearance reflects attention to action, thought and words. So as an adult, I decided to do it every day of the week, a reminder that it's important on all days, not just Sunday."

"Deliberate care," he repeated. "Teena Joy taught me that, too. In the way to dress, stay clean and care for your body."

"I've noticed. I'll send her a prayer of thanks."

He grinned. "I gotta stay on my toes with you, Mistress. You telling me a lot of things, finding out what I like or might like. Will you tell me what you like?"

She put her hand on the cushion between them, and his gaze fell to it, to the sparkle of her rings. Today she wore three silver ones. One with a sparkling elephant head, one with a pentacle surrounded by a chain of flowers, and one simple band, engraved with the word Love.

"I'll tell you eventually, but I don't offer that up front. It's automatic to say you want to do what I like, but that doesn't help me know what's driving your desire to submit. Whatever I do in my sessions with submissives comes from understanding what my sub needs. If those needs overlap with mine, then we both find what we need."

"And if they don't?"

She tapped a finger on the cushion. "It's like we talked about before. If I have to have something from a sub he can't provide, it's incompatibility, not failure. I'll steer him toward someone who's a better fit for him."

A frown appeared, and he put his hand over hers. "I want you. I want you to be happy. That means I'd do that thing to make you happy."

"Unfortunately, it doesn't work that way. Because your happiness and what you need is just as important to me. I think no matter what, we'll be friends."

His lips tightened.

"You don't want to be my friend."

He gave her a half-amused look. "I do, Mistress. But I want to be a lot more than that, enough that the idea of being just your friend isn't all that appealing right now."

"The feeling is quite mutual."

The intensity of those gingerbread-colored eyes, the set of his mouth, his closeness to her on the couch, was distracting enough to make her want to leave it alone for now. After all, it was anticipating something that might not happen. But though it had been a while since she'd initiated a newbie, Vera hadn't forgotten her responsibility. No matter how much he'd captured her interest, it couldn't be avoided.

"If something is meant to be, it happens. That's how I approach the opportunities and disappointments in my life. There's a path and a plan I may not understand, but I trust the Lord and Lady as I walk it."

"I submit to God's will," he said.

"Yes, exactly. Though I'm not always gracious about it. Especially when I really want something."

She looked down at his large, chapped hand and cupped it in hers. As he watched her, she felt like the emotions they were feeling were shared, nothing unknown or held back. A strange feeling with someone she'd barely met.

Focus. Do your most important job first. Care for him.

"A lot of things happen when you enter this world. Your defenses get stripped away, and things boil up you may not expect. Just because you have a bad reaction to something doesn't mean we've hit the 'time to go our separate ways' point. So as I said from the very beginning, don't lie to me, and don't be dishonest with yourself. 'I don't know' or 'I don't know how I'm feeling,' are acceptable answers to any scenario we explore. As long as it's the truth."

She lifted her gaze. "I'll take care of you, Rev, in the ways I know that you don't, and I'll look forward to discovering how you want to take care of me."

Though he still looked tense about it, his shoulders eased enough to tell her that he'd heard her. They'd covered enough preliminaries. She pointed to the rug in front of the fireplace. "Go stand there, and take off your shoes and socks."

His attention held her for a measured second, his hand squeezing hers briefly, before he rose to comply with her order. As he did, she moved to her antique cherry corner cabinet and withdrew several candles, infused with scents she wanted for this. She placed them on the metal tray on the top of the cabinet.

Before she lit them, she scooped a heart-shaped polished rose quartz out of the Swarovski bowl beside the tray. She held it in her closed hand, feeling the texture, absorbing the properties. Then she put it down and did the same with a rough cut one. Relationships were like that, going back and forth, rough to smooth, smooth to rough.

This was a beginning. Or was it? She suspected it wasn't the first life where her and Rev's paths had crossed. She sent a thankful blessing to the Lord and Lady that they were allowing it to happen again, in this way.

"Does it bother you that I'm not book smart?"

The question startled her so much the flame from the match singed her fingertips. She dropped it into the tray with a stifled oath and turned around. Before she completed the motion, he was in front of her, his eyes on her hand. When he gripped her wrist and blew on the injured area, he held her with that distractingly gentle strength.

"Does it bother you, Rev?"

His countenance was troubled. "I never thought it mattered, long as I doing what I'm supposed to do, for those in need of what I can do for them. Seemed wrong to get too caught up in it."

"So why ask now?"

He gave her a rueful smile. "Fear of losing something I need and want bad. Wanting you not to look at me and see something less than what you need. I heard what you said, Mistress, and so I hope you know this isn't that. I just need to be what you need. I want that. I want to be able to take care of you."

As he spoke, his gaze was moving. Over her eyes and mouth, the pulse in her throat, the neckline of her blouse, the swell of her breast. A physical perusal backed by a powerful emotional hunger. Her skin heated from the concentration of it. She gripped his forearm and used his hold to step out of her shoes. She wanted ground contact, preparing to be a lightning rod. The carpet was cool through the stockings she'd put back on in the church restroom before they left there.

He wasn't looking for reassurance. He was asking if he had the skills to do the job before him.

"All right. Go back to the fireplace and take off all of your clothes. You can take the cross off or leave it on, whichever you prefer. Stand there, feet shoulder width apart."

He didn't argue. He returned to the fireplace and removed his clothing. He left the cross in place, which she liked, because it said he didn't think anything they were about to do would be in conflict with its presence.

He was already erect. God and Goddess, the man was beautiful, and she wouldn't deny how much that beauty was intensified for her by his obedience. He stood, waiting respectfully for her next command. Her next wish and desire.

"Close your eyes. You need my permission to open them. To look at me again."

His lashes fanned his cheeks. When she turned on the gas logs, the flame flickered over his bronze skin, tempting her to touch.

"Do you know some believe that looking is an act of possession? That's why we read passages like we 'capture' someone in our gaze. Hold them, lock them into it. It's why I'm telling you that you need permission to look at me. And it's why I'm looking at you now. As much as I wish."

His body tightened at the implication. His throat worked as he swallowed, and his heavy cock twitched against his thighs.

"Do you want that?" she asked. "To possess me, or be possessed by me? Do you want to consider yourself mine? I don't want you to answer the question, Rev. Even if I ask you a question, stay silent until I tell you specifically to talk. Say 'Yes, Mistress,' if you understand."

"Yes, Mistress."

The two words echoed inside her head, swirling down into her chest, her stomach and between her thighs. She drew them back up with her breath and held them under her ribs. She spun the energy they created from the base of her spine and took it up to her third eye, that sensitive center between her brows. All of its meanings tingled over her face, lips, throat and beating pulse.

In Tantra, a man and woman were opening themselves up to the Lord and Lady, channeling their energy. They each became a representative of those entities, him the Lord, her the Lady. God and Goddess, revering the sacred energy of their bond. Their joining.

She removed all of her clothes, and then moved closer. When she dipped down to graze his toes with her fingertips, he started, the touch unexpected, but then he stilled, a column of electrical vibration. Lightning gathering.

She followed the energy channels up to his knee, the muscles of his thigh, then across, circling the base of his rigid cock and brushing the soft hair around it. She lingered, stroking the shaft with her nails, her thumb pressed against his lower abdomen, before stepping around him, letting her fingers trail over his hip. She stroked his fine, taut buttocks and teased the seam.

Continuing a spiraling touch, she came back to his front, to his stomach, the navel—another connection to the female Divine. Up from there to the middle of his chest, the depth and breadth of it a physical manifestation of the heart beneath, the man that he was.

Her own heart was beating as strongly as his when she flattened her palm against him, her fingertips brushing his cross. She channeled the energy coming from her through her palm and imagined it spreading through his body.

She created another spiral around his arm. After she gripped his fingers, a brief hold, she was back to his corded neck, that strong throat. She made sure her touch passed over his lower lip, right cheek, eye and forehead, and let it rest on his third eye in his forehead before stroking over the crown, over his skull, and his hair. He dipped his head, so she didn't have to lift on her toes. Seeking any way to show his desire to serve her.

As she drew deep on the power she was raising, his skin was reacting to her touch, the nerves answering it. Whether he was aware of it or not, his body was swaying in a slight spiral motion, following the energy flow.

She did the same route from the opposite side. Tracing solar channels, which were His energy. The lunar channels, which were Hers. Their energy.

Every part of her felt alive, caught in this moment. "How are you doing, Rev? You may answer me."

"I'm...it's like bliss, but there's...I want to touch you, Mistress. Hold you. Have you under me. Over me."

"The desire to worship and devour, to elevate and possess. They're not inconsistent desires."

"Your voice...it's gotten deeper, throatier. I like it. Like it's that way just for me."

"Yes," she said. "It's the energy you're willingly letting me touch and share. Take for my own."

When she did this in the club, channeling elemental energy, she let it take over her voice, her body, and guide her down the right path. Plenty of nights she didn't go this deep, though. It was more of a meditative exercise at the beginning, to get her in the right mindset to play. When she flogged her sub's handsome shoulders, his tight ass, that energy spiral tightened into an arrow she directed toward his need to release, even as she immersed herself in the visceral pleasure of making him fight to hold back, for her.

But this was her home, her hearth, and she wanted more from Rev. There was a danger of wanting too much from a sub, especially one that answered the darker needs, the yearning emptiness, the disappointments and pain of betrayed and confused relationships. There was also the right path to take past that quagmire, letting the energy heal it, not letting it take over in the wrong ways and taint it.

She pulled her breath into her heart chakra, and leaned toward him. As she let the breath out, she caressed his chest and the base of his throat with that heart energy. She gave it light and color, watching it drift like a mist into the intimate pockets of his collar bones and float over the curve of his shoulder. The terrain of his body was like a planet, like the moon, a new universe and yet home, all at the same time.

The quiver of response told her he felt the impact of the breath energy. His cock was getting ever harder, thicker. She wanted to touch and taste the meat of him, the glistening fluid at the tip, tease the slit, grip and work him. She wanted to lay him on her floor, arms outstretched, legs together, his pelvis the center of him, rising and responding to her touch.

"Let's see how well you've done your homework. Without opening your eyes, can you recall my face, Rev? Every detail."

She moved so her hip was against his upper thigh, her hand on his biceps. She felt the energy rush of his reaction as he realized she'd removed all her clothes. Her bare skin brushed his as her breath rippled over his shoulder, cheek almost touching it. While she leaned into the solid support of his body, she laid her head there and looked at the fire. He steadied himself to support her.

"I been doing that since you showed up at the school," he said. "Each time I see you, I look some more, because when we apart, I want to call it up in my head, strong enough it's like you there with me."

"I do that, too."

"You do?"

"You sound surprised I've been thinking of you as much as you've been thinking of me."

"I don't think that's possible." Humor mixed with desire in his voice. "You couldn't do all those complicated things you do if you was thinking of me that much. Easier for me when I cleaning up after the kids or keeping things fixed."

"I'm a very good multi-tasker. Just ask my boss."

She lifted her head to lay a finger on his beautiful mouth, stroking the cushion of his lips. "Sing for me, Rev. No words. Just whatever music is in your heart. Keep doing it until I say stop."

She laid her head back on his shoulder and waited as he sent the command wherever it needed to go to respond as she wanted. When it came, the notes were slow and powerful, like drums calling others from their homes to dance in the darkness, risk whatever was there, because it was too sensual to resist.

It was a different sound from what she'd heard from him before. As he continued to stand as she'd ordered, feet shoulder width apart, hands at his sides, twitching with the desire to touch, she drew back so she could take her fingers on a journey down his chest, scrape his nipples with her nails. A zigzag motion over the stomach muscles took her even lower.

The notes went up, down, erratic, as she circled his cock. When she dropped to a knee, flattening her palms on his thighs, she bathed his shaft in that caressing, heart-energy-filled breath. There was also a good mix of sexual energy she pulled from the base of her spine.

He shuddered. With his eyes shut, the notes would spin in the darkness in his head, getting wilder and less predictable. The deepness of his voice became a growl, a call to mate.

She touched her tongue to the tip of his cock, rolled it around the ridge of the head. She closed her whole mouth over it, sliding halfway down, as much as she could take without pushing him into her throat. As she came back up, she did it slow, tasting and experiencing that part of him, the strength and power of it.

Yoni and lingam. Lingam was a good word. It made her think of *linger*, and she liked lingering on this part of him while she tracked his reactions. She gripped his buttocks, the muscles flexing as she drew him deeper. When she increased her hold, it was a non-verbal cue to tell him to remain still, to not push into her mouth, no matter how much the animal need in him wanted that.

She liked feeling his struggle to obey, to rein back his primal need to prove his power and strength. She could command it, call it

to her, but a part of him would want her to know it could overwhelm her. Which only increased the dangerous pleasure in testing it.

She intensified her sucking and stroking, and released one buttock
so she could cup his balls, roll them in her palm, squeeze them. His
song was changing, the drum-like notes punctuated by the passion
behind them. Like men dancing around a fire, crouching low, bran-
dishing their spears at the flames as they shouted out short, sharp
notes that matched the thrusts.

She slid her mouth off of him and rose. As she straddled his cock,
gripping him between her thighs, she rubbed her wetness over him. A
breathless oath broke through the wordless song before it stumbled
forward again. She laid her hands on his chest, lifting onto her toes to
put her mouth on his and take the song inside her, a vibration of
notes.

The power of the contact escalated what was already spiraling
around them. She held his neck so she could draw him into her mouth
and play with his tongue. That growl was back, his violent need. His
hands were still at his sides, but he wanted to use them so much it
made her dizzy with anticipation.

She drew back, biting his lip. He had his eyes screwed shut,
showing her how difficult it was to keep them that way.

"Lie down, Rev."

She had her hand on his shoulder and, as he went down, that touch
slid to his arm. He captured her fingers, impulsively bringing them to
his mouth when he paused on one knee. She cupped his head as she
leaned over him. "You earned a punishment for that, Rev. That pleases
me."

A huff of half breath, maybe a chuckle, and then he stretched out
before her, a glorious sight, his thigh muscles drawn tight, cock erect.
"Arms out to your sides. Keep them there. Feet together."

When he complied, she straddled him, stood over him. "Open
your eyes."

His irises were melted copper, the centers black as the primeval
darkness his song had evoked. He stared at all of her, her thighs, the
triangle of her sex, the tilt of her breasts and her mane of hair, tangled
over her shoulders.

"Blessed Lady," he murmured. "Thank you, sweet Jesus."

Her chest was tight with painful, pleasurable need. "What do you want, Rev?"

"You upon me, Mistress. Me inside you. Serving you."

"Ask for it."

"Please, Mistress. Let me serve you. Give you pleasure. Give you joy."

She lowered herself, gripping his cock to guide him into her. His attention latched onto her mouth as she bit her lip. She was slick with need, but he was engorged enough to make it an effort to take him, a balance she appreciated with pure feminine ecstasy, the right fit between their two bodies.

His arm muscles flexed, fingers curling. She wanted his hands on her, but she was exploring how well he respected the boundaries she set. She told herself her aching need to toss them out the window wouldn't serve them going forward, even as a truer voice told her she was protecting herself from how much she was feeling for him.

She accepted that. She rocked her pelvis on him, drawing that ecstasy closer, but holding her own leash on it as his body tightened. She was making it tough on him, and that gave her joy, too. He groaned as she dropped her head back on her shoulders, arching her back, tilting her breasts. The air movement made the nipples more sensitive as she rose and fell, the friction of him within her only stoking that fire.

"Mistress...please...I need to..."

"Not yet," she breathed. "Not yet... Move with me, Rev."

He did, hips thrusting up, trying to match her rhythm even as his breath grew more ragged. Her chin came back down as she gazed upon him. His face held granite strength. He was dedicating himself to her need, to her commands. Fighting his own will. It caught her on fire, and it spread all over her.

Let's see just how good you can be...

She let her orgasm roll forth and take her, a strong wave that rocked her body, locked all her muscles and turned a hum of pleasure into a cry. Every nerve involved, the energy she'd channeled throughout this session turning the release into a long wave that held her the way she wanted him to hold her. A thrilling embrace, experienced on an eternal journey together.

She wanted him to see it, to want to be within it with her, enough to deny himself whatever she demanded inside this intimate circle, a circle about the two of them and their connection to things far bigger than the mundane world.

Then, pinnacle reached, those thoughts were swept away. The strength of it bucked her upon him, so much it made her lose her balance. His hands were there at once, one on her waist, one at the side of her throat, holding her steady, his eyes upon her, still fierce with the desire to release, but it hadn't overwhelmed his desire to serve.

Everything she could want in a sub.

She put her hands over his and gripped, their fingers lacing as she rocked and shuddered, convulsing from the power of the climax.

When it finally ebbed, that hold was still there, and he was a taut cord beneath her, his cock pulsing inside her cunt, her quivering, sensitive tissues gripping him.

"What do you want, Rev?" she asked again, her voice trembling.

He stared up at her. "To stay like this forever, Mistress."

"Without releasing, finding your own...joy?"

She liked how that wry look found a place amid the urgent need, its darker side. "I afraid...if I do that...it like a storm. The more powerful it is, the more it can take away what you don't want to lose."

Her mind was swirling and chaotic, body trembling. And yet his words created a still point that made her find her balance. And her answer for him.

"Your grip is strong, Rev," she whispered. "I know you won't let go. Draw a deep, slow breath."

When he struggled to comply, she slid up his length, and started to come down. "Let it out," she murmured. "And come for me now."

He conceded the battle but disengaged his fingers, gripping her hips with such bruising strength she knew he'd done it to protect her fingers. The gesture made the song inside her rise to a greater pitch.

Vera moved with him, gripping, stroking, and crying out at the jet of his seed. Her hands fell to his chest, digging in as they rocked together, caught in a boat on a turbulent ocean. It took them up higher and plunged them down over the crests, only to bring them up again.

Her second orgasm wasn't as powerful, but it didn't need to be. Joy had many different ways of expressing itself. She gasped at his guttural cry and how forcefully he brought her back down on him, again and again, the animal in him as fully unleashed as she'd commanded it to be.

She reveled in feeling that power answering her call. And when he finally stopped, chest expanding and contracting, the veins in his throat still throbbing, his strong face was contorted in wonder from the depth of it all. She stroked his jaw, his cheeks and temple, her hair falling around her face in a dark, soft cloud as she gazed down on him.

She came lower, her nipples brushing his chest as she kissed his forehead, that third eye. She held there as his hands passed over her back and hips, the dimple above her buttocks, then reverently molded over the curves.

Right after, though, he stopped, a slight tension passing through him.

"It's all right," she whispered. "You may touch me, Rev."

"I thought I had to ask first."

"There are ways of asking and answering that have nothing to do with a voice. You asked with them."

She took him to her bedroom. On the way, his fingertips brushed her hair, a curtain he was adjusting to see what was beneath it. She stopped, glancing up at him as he discovered the tattoo on the back of her shoulder, a whimsical black cat curled around a pentacle. Her skin shivered under his touch, especially when it moved back up from there to her nape, to close on a handful of her hair.

She put her hand on his chest and lifted on her toes to meet his lips, their bodies pressed against one another. His grip tightened, an intriguing pull against her scalp before he recalled himself and eased the touch. She broke the kiss.

"If you want the guest bathroom to clean up, you can meet me in my room at the end of the hall."

He nodded, his mouth wet from hers. When she turned to leave him, she felt him watch her until she disappeared into her bedroom.

By the time he arrived in the doorway, she'd taken care of her own needs and slipped under the covers, her arm bent under her head. He paused at the threshold, a handsome nude male.

The bed was a sturdy antique with spiral posts, a ribbon design carved into the headboard. A couch faced the fireplace at the opposite end of the room. On the wall near it was a framed 1900s photo of a coven doing a circle ritual by a harvested field, their willowy bodies bent backward toward the moon, their pale hands joined in its light. Over her bed was an erotic painting, a naked man and woman, artistic shadowing giving hints of hip, buttock and breast, as well as clasped hands. The painted words, *As above, so below,* followed the curves of their joined bodies. Sculpted pieces on her dresser and side tables reflected similar spiritual and erotic themes.

Mounted around her antique wardrobe were five rare vintage BDSM photos, where a black woman in petticoats and chemise dominated a man in his small clothes, his cropped hair slicked back, eyes fixed on her as he served her on his knees.

Rev took in all that before his focus came back to her. "Can you spend the night?" she asked.

"Yes. I have to be at work by seven. I'll get myself up about five-thirty and slip out quiet."

It was earlier than she rose, but not by much. She would send him on his way with a cup of coffee, and some almond coffee cake she'd baked a couple days ago.

"You got an interesting picture in your guest bathroom," he said.

It was a caricature drawn by an artist in the Square. Vera in a claw-foot tub, one shapely leg dangling out of a froth of soap. Fairies rode floating bubbles while a three-legged black cat, perched on the sink, peered at them.

"Do you have a cat?"

"Ros does." She smiled. "Me or Skye are his sitters when Ros has to travel. Freak likes to go to Skye's loft, and sometimes to her and Tiger's place out in the sticks, though he got banished from the barn when he decided to take a nap on Tiger's beloved Harley and sharpened his claws on the seat. He's missing one leg in front."

During their visit to the Wishes mailbox, she'd told him some details about all the women, and their husbands or significant others. "Come lie down next to me," she said.

As Rev did, she turned on her hip to face him. His gaze touched the painting above her. "That one's interesting, too."

"It's a study from a bigger photograph, one that depicts the Great

Rite. That's a ritual drawing down of the male and female faces of the Divine, the Lord and Lady, into a man and woman while they make love. A circle is cast, and the energy they raise between them...it's a strong thing."

"That something you do in your faith?"

"There's a symbolic way to do it. But I've watched the real thing, done by a married priest and priestess. It's beautiful. Maybe you could incorporate it in your next church revival."

He gave her an amused look. "Sometimes you like to misbehave, Mistress."

"I do."

He reached out to twine a lock of her hair around his finger. "You are beautiful to me, Veracity."

She knew she was attractive. Compelling. Striking. She liked decorating what she had, and changing that look with her moods. Her master bedroom closet was for her hats and jewelry. Her clothes and shoes required the square footage of her smallest guest room, though the shoes were Ros's fault. She'd taught Vera to be overly appreciative of footwear.

The word beautiful, as he meant it, felt different. He saw the vulnerability beneath the strength, and his words said he wouldn't abuse the knowledge. She'd just unraveled him, and he had responded by doing some of the same.

"I like knowing that, Rev." She touched the lids of his eyes, one at a time, making his lips curve. "Sleep," she said, and shut her eyes to give the impression that she was doing the same. Yet when she opened them, his were still open.

"I can sleep anytime," he said. "What you said, about memorizing your face? I'd like to keep doing that instead. I keep seeing new things in it."

She didn't mind the idea of doing that with him as well. "There's an exercise in Tantra. Studying one another's faces, gazing into one another's eyes. Saying nothing. Just looking your fill. It connects to that thing I said, about possessing one another through your gazes."

She touched the area between his brows, "Sometimes, as you do it, you find your gaze moving here, because that's the spiritual center of the soul. You can feel it, if you put your fingers there."

With that thoughtful look, he did so, but then he put his hand back down and gripped hers, between them, his knuckles resting on the upper rise of her breast. "I like the idea of looking at you without having to say anything."

"Me too."

So they did that. And in time, their breathing aligned, their lids grew heavy, and they both slept.

She woke a while later. Because she was in the mood to indulge herself, she slipped down to her kitchen for a glass of wine and a bite of cake. This room was for cheerful moods and brighter colors. Ceramic voodoo dolls sat on the sink windowsill with glass bottles holding cut greens from her yard. Her mixer was blue, as was her toaster, while her fridge was covered with magnets collected from her travels.

On the wall behind her eight-setting oak table was a painting of a woman stirring a cauldron at a fireplace, watched by a half dozen cats and two children, one boy and one girl. The boy sat on the hearth petting one of the cats while the girl pressed against her side, the woman's hand on her hair. A man stood by the hearth, drinking coffee, his hand on the woman's shoulder in a way that suggested he was caressing her neck with his thumb under her hair.

The title of it was "The Kitchen Witch and Her Family."

When she moved in, she'd bought the picture from a Royal Street gallery. Knowing it represented a wish that hadn't come true, she'd lately been thinking about replacing it. It made her melancholy, and she didn't hold onto things that encouraged wallowing in self-pity.

Tonight, the picture didn't make her feel melancholy.

Vera closed her eyes as she ate the cake, not only to savor the sugar and almond flavors, but the picture of Rev's face. Of his long and powerful body beneath her, between her thighs. Of how he had responded to her.

She didn't stay in the kitchen long. When she returned to the bedroom, he was still sleeping, his fingers curled in the sheet that held her warmth and scent.

Teena Joy had believed he was called by God to serve a purpose. She'd held him out of school, taking childhood epilepsy, laryngitis and reading difficulties as proof.

Through her work at Laurel Grove, Vera had seen abuse spawned by ignorance, instead of deliberate cruelty. But while Vera questioned

Tisha or Witford's motives, Tisha wasn't entirely wrong. A worldly interpretation of Rev's circumstances could cause its own problems.

Rev had told her what his aunt believed, but not necessarily his thoughts on it. Yet he'd made it clear that when he sang and channeled that energy, he was content, feeling he was doing what he was supposed to be doing.

He wasn't victimized. He'd served his aunt as he was serving Vera, with no sense of subjugation. He didn't perceive his relationship and service to God as at odds with what Rev needed and wanted to do. In his devotion toward the Virgin Mary and other representations of divine female energy, he'd recognized his yearning for the Goddess in his life, and how that connected to his desire for an earthly Mistress.

Yes, maybe some opportunities had been taken from him, but as he matured, rather than getting hung up on what ifs, he'd focused on his blessings and the will of forces bigger than himself, to take him where he needed to go.

Tisha and his cousin's recent behavior weighed heavily on him, though. The relief he'd shown when Vera told him to kneel on her carpet, willing to give him a port in that storm, told her that. She had no doubts now that she'd made the right choice, coming to find him.

She'd seen glimpses of the alpha will that had made the decisions that led him to her bed tonight. He minded none of the obligations in his life—his family, his congregation, his job at the school—but he wanted something for himself. And it looked like that something was her.

Unlike Witford and Tisha, she had no intention of standing in the way of that.

CHAPTER NINE

*W*hen Rev thought about what he'd wear to Club Progeny, he'd thought about the clothes Veracity wore. So when she pulled up to their agreed rendezvous, the coffee shop on the corner near his place, he watched her face to see how he'd done.

He wore an ivory-colored suit with a slim black tie. The jacket nipped in at the waist, and his pants were hemmed to brush the tops of his polished shoes. The cuffs of his blue dress shirt were visible under the sleeves of the jacket, and had silver button cuff links. He'd shaved twice to make his jaw smooth, and his hair gleamed from the light touch of a scented oil he thought she'd like.

Every stitch of clothing was smooth, pressed, and fit him the way it should. He could have worn one of his church suits, but instead had decided to spend some of his money on a suit from a consignment shop.

Mrs. Levitt, who taught the home economics class, had altered it for him. She wouldn't take payment, saying she was thanking him for her tires. She'd been driving on bald ones, and he'd gotten her a good discount on a new set at a local tire company. The owner was a man Rev had helped, through late night companionship and prayer, to stick with his twelve-step program at AA. When he got his one-year chip, his wife had let him come back home and given him a second chance with her and their two kids.

After finishing the last adjustment, Mrs. Levitt had given Rev an approving nod. "You'll please your lady, Rev, never fear."

She must know what she was talking about, because Veracity's thorough look woke up every part of him.

Though he didn't respond just to that. As he approached the car, he saw her skirt was snug and black and came up high on her thighs, the way she was sitting behind the wheel. A flirty transparent hem added a few inches to it. He expected she was wearing her preferred seamed stockings, those straight lines up the back of her legs teasing a man's imagination as they disappeared beneath the skirt.

Her apple green fitted coat over a black lace top had a belted waist. It made her breasts look even more blessedly generous. She also wore black gloves, an emerald ring on one finger and a matching bracelet around the wrist. An emerald necklace rested on her high and full bosom.

The black pillbox hat with a gleaming green net on the brim veiled her eyes, but drew attention to her mouth and the slim line of her nose. Emerald teardrop earrings completed the look.

Her thickly lashed eyes blinked at him through the veil. When she smiled, his heart restarted with a jolt.

"Need a ride?" she asked in a sensual purr.

She had her hand resting on his seat, and when he got in, she moved that hand to his thigh, arresting him there as she looked him up and down, then leaned in.

"Stay still," she murmured, when he would have turned his head to kiss her.

Sometimes what he couldn't anticipate was worth even more than what he thought she wanted. She'd told him she'd take care of him in the ways she knew that he didn't, and he was starting to understand what that meant.

She inhaled him, so close to his throat he could feel the feather of her breath. When her hand tightened on his thigh, his cock responded, despite his best attempt to make it behave. She looked at it and then back at him, through that provocative veil.

"Progeny is so saturated with erotic possibilities, people get aroused just pulling into the parking lot. I want you to stay endlessly, achingly aroused, Rev, so everyone will see it. So I can see it, and think of you inside me again, that thick and hard cock of yours. I'm wet enough now to take it right here."

She had that simmering Mistress power ramped up like an engine with the gas pedal mashed to the floor. The silent roar of it took his breath. Her hand moved to his, and he gripped, trying not to crush her slim fingers.

"I want to hold you so tight, and yet so gentle at once," he said. "Don't know how to bring the two things together."

"We'll figure it out," she told him. "I want to make you lose control and yet protect all the things I find amazing and precious about you, Rev. So you're not alone in that."

She started the car and pulled away, but whenever they stopped at a traffic light, her hand returned to his thigh. Proprietary, in a way he had no argument with.

When they reached the club, Rev saw the parking lot was almost full. Some people were making their way toward the entrance from the lot, while others pulled up front to give their vehicle to a valet service.

That was what she chose, smiling at the man in black slacks and matching polo shirt who bent to her window. He had a braided tail of black hair and brown eyes set deep in a hard-boned face. Tattoos were on both arms. Rev saw fierce angels and a grim reaper. Plus a tree with an infant curled up in a nest. An open space next to it appeared to be waiting for a birth date.

"Miss Vera, you giving us the care of your baby tonight?"

"I'd trust no one else with him, Zodiac. But he's no baby. He's a fire-breathing dragon with a double row of teeth who requires respectful behavior."

Zodiac chuckled. "Yes ma'am. Just like his driver. A lady, in the most savage and genteel ways a man dreams about."

"Nice," she said. "When will you have your next poem ready for all of us to hear?"

"By next month, or my Mistress will be disappointed. And I try never to disappoint her."

Zodiac offered her a hand out of the vehicle. That was fine, but Rev exited the passenger side, so that when Zodiac took her place in the seat, Rev was there to give Veracity his arm. Zodiac gave him an approving nod and the wink of a man who understood Rev's desire to take care of his Mistress. Rev found the camaraderie surprising—and reassuring.

The black heels Vera wore had a slash of green sparkles across the toe. The seams of her stockings were different tonight, a chain of dark green roses against the black mesh.

Beside the double doors at the entrance, a neon sign with brilliant orange script and clean white light proclaimed they had arrived at Club Progeny.

"There's an original club, founded by the owners, called Surreal, in Baton Rouge," Vera told him. "So when they started this one, they decided on Progeny."

He noticed the brick path up to the door included a few bricks with words on them. He paused to take a second look at one of them.

"The person first, not the role first." --Tim Emerson

"That one is my favorite," Veracity said. Which also reassured him.

She'd already registered him as a guest online, so they bypassed check-in and stopped at a coat room. Beside it stood an open wooden chest like on a pirate ship, black wood bound by silver straps. It was full of glowing bracelets.

"We introduced this system to reduce awkward situations and misunderstandings," she told him. "One of our unbreakable rules is 'respect the bracelet.' The person who doesn't gets suspended for a month for the first offense. If there's a second, their membership is revoked."

"They take that pretty seriously."

"In a power exchange relationship, there's nothing more serious than respecting someone's choice. Letting a small infraction go leads to bigger infractions."

She pointed to the different colors. "Dom, sub, switch. If you're not sure, you don't wear one of those. But everyone has the second bracelet, because it communicates your status. The green one tells others you want to play, and you're not attached. You're seeking a partner or partners for the evening. Yellow means you're not attached, but you don't want to play tonight. You just want to watch. Someone can approach you to have a chat, in case you're interested in playing in the future. It's a good, no-pressure way to ask questions and set groundwork for later, if the relationship goes that way.

"Red is for a member or guest who doesn't want to be approached for any reason. They just want to watch and be in their own head. Purple means unavailable, because you already belong to someone."

She spoke about each bracelet matter-of-factly, not telegraphing her preferences. "So what makes you feel most comfortable?"

He glanced around him, and she laid a hand on his arm. "Rev, remember what I said. If you decide you don't like it here, we can leave at any time."

"It's not that. It so different, and yet it feels..."

"Like you're not entirely a fish out of water? Just a fish who's not been in this kind of water before?"

He knew this was her world, so it shouldn't surprise him, how well she was reading him. Having lived in New Orleans most of his life, walking along Canal Street or watching the Mardi Gras parade, meant that blatant sexuality wasn't a shock to him. Bare flesh, leather, silver, body paint, he took that in stride. But the intent here spoke directly to him, making him ache.

Not ten feet away, a man in a suit walked with a naked woman wearing a delicate pink collar and leash. He had his hand protectively on her lower back, keeping her close to his side as he escorted her.

There were versions of that where the woman was in control. He stole glances at them, feeling guilty for wanting to do so, but Veracity noticed.

"Rev, right now, you have my permission to look at anything you wish. You can see in action those things we discussed in my living room. Anyone on the public floor is okay with attention. Part of the fun is looking." She flashed him a smile.

"Yes, Mistress. Thank you."

He was expressing true gratitude. Like that box of bracelets, here was the treasure chest of things he'd recognized in himself but hadn't had the chance to experience. He'd dreamed about them, endlessly. Now, everywhere he looked, those dreams had come to life.

Well, mostly. He blanched at a man wearing a cage around his cock, and clamps on his nipples. His back was curved forward, his chin down, his body betraying his discomfort.

His Mistress had noticed. The slim woman with dyed blue hair, woven with silver strands like thin tinsel, placed the crop she was holding under his jaw. She had him straighten, lifting his chin and posture, tall and proud for her. She assessed his effort to do her bidding, murmuring something to him. Though she returned to her conversation with another couple, Rev sensed the greater part of her attention remained on the male suffering for her.

"She knows what his limits are, and he has a safe word." Veracity confirmed it. She was close to his side, her hand on the side of his neck as he bent his ear to her, her breath on his cheek. "She'll monitor his skin tone around the nipple clamps, notice if he's perspiring or shaking. Based on her experience with him, she'll know when he's had enough. If he doesn't safe word as he should, she'll act on his behalf."

She drew his gaze toward a man who wore dark slacks and T-shirt with the club name embroidered on the pocket. The lanyard around his neck glowed red, highlighting DM in white letters. "That's one of the dungeon monitors I told you about. Each one patrols a section of the club."

"Do she get in trouble if she does something wrong?"

"Not if she's being diligent. Ideally, DMs are there to ensure a Master or Mistress doesn't miss something important, because safe play is the goal for all. People are complex in their needs, and this is a very sensory rich environment. Even the most experienced Dominant can miss things. It doesn't hurt to have extra eyes on your sub."

She put her hand back on the wooden chest. "What bracelet best fits you tonight?"

"I feel like I need your permission to wear it."

"Choose it, and I'll let you know."

He reached for the purple bracelet that said he was unavailable, already taken, and offered it to her.

Her eyes gained several degrees in heat. She clipped it around his wrist, along with a submissive bracelet. When her hand remained resting over them, he lifted his other one, putting it on her wrist. He didn't say anything, stroking it with his thumb, but it was a request all the same.

"Did you want me to wear a purple bracelet, too?"

"That's not my call."

"Isn't it? Even for tonight?"

"For tonight...I'd appreciate that, Mistress."

Actually for way more than tonight, but such possessive feelings were new to him, and he wasn't sure if they were a good thing, or appropriate. But when she picked up one of the purple bracelets and offered it to him so he could put it on her wrist, he felt better about it.

"Leave this and your jacket with the coat check." She unpinned her hat with the veil and handed it to him. "It's warm inside the play areas, and I enjoy looking at you without it."

He'd seen plenty of shirtless men already. He wasn't sure how he'd feel about being one of them, here in front of everyone. Had she not asked him to take off the shirt because she could tell that about him?

He chided himself for the thought. Veracity Morgan wasn't a woman who hesitated to ask for what she wanted. She'd told him when she did order him to do something, she expected him to tell her if it made him uncomfortable in the wrong ways. If she could trust him for that, she'd be open about her own desires.

When he shed the coat, the way her gaze lingered on the pull of the shirt over his shoulders and chest told him she did appreciate that view. She unbuttoned her green jacket and pivoted, presenting her back to him. As he helped her remove it, the flared sleeves cleared her gloves and the bracelet she wore.

The lace thing she had on under it was a close fitting, sleeveless garment that showed her satin bra beneath. As she pivoted back to him, her breasts were held up in the bra, her cleavage a temptingly deep valley.

She'd given him permission to look at anything, but he was smart enough to know that didn't include ogling his Mistress to excess. He raised his gaze to her face with effort.

"I like a hungry man, Rev," she murmured. "Give them our coats and let's explore."

The coat check submissive was dressed like a fairy. Glitter on her face, hair pulled up in five or six purple streaked tails. She had on a harness to hold her wings, but that was all she wore, except various splotches of body paint. As he thanked her courteously for the stubs she handed him, her eyes twinkled.

"Have fun, newbie," she whispered, with an amiable playfulness that surprised a smile out of him.

Vera set an arm-in-arm strolling pace for them as they moved deeper into the club. A DJ was throwing out good tunes for the dance floor, edgy, bass thumping choices that fit the environment. He was set up on a stage behind the dance floor, and Rev wondered if they ever had bands. His imagination could conjure plenty of other things for that stage, spurred by what he saw around him.

Public play areas were sectioned off with panels on three sides, creating a defined area while still allowing passers-by to look. An upper-level VIP lounge provided a premium view of those play spaces, as well as the dance floor.

Ros Thomas, Veracity's boss, sat up there. A man stood to her left, leaning against the booth. While his body seemed relaxed, there was a military or law enforcement watchfulness to him. His hand rested on the section of the booth next to her. As Rev watched, Ros reached for it to caress his fingers. She was talking to Cyn.

"That's Lawrence," Veracity told him.

She'd touched on Ros being in a relationship with Lawrence, but she'd also mentioned how some Mistresses had more than one sub. "Is he one of her...regulars?"

"He's her only." Vera's gaze lifted to meet his. "Claimed for life. Not married yet, but when Ros decides she's ready for that, it will only confirm what they already are."

A commotion, loud enough to rise above the music, had Rev turn-ing. He couldn't process what he saw charge through a bead screen archway fast enough to figure out if it was a threat or not, but he did put himself between them and Veracity. Then stared as humans, mostly male and dressed like dogs, raced past them.

Many had on full head masks with long snouts and pointed ears. Others just had floppy cloth ears and painted black noses. Some wore clothing in doglike colors; brown, black, spotted. Faux fur paws covered some hands. Others simply wore jeans and no shirts with their dog parts.

The lead "dog," a shirtless male in a full head mask, bumped into a Dom wielding a cane, a burly man with salt and pepper colored hair and beard. He wore black jeans, jack boots and a black T-shirt. When he gave the "dog" a healthy smack with the cane and scolded him, the leader and the rest of the pack cowered apologetically. Then he rubbed his head against the older male's shoulder and upper arm.

The Master hooked his fingers into the dog's collar, around the neck of the mask, and gave him a light shake. Then he shoved him away with a stern but indulgent look. The pack dashed off joyously, disappearing into another part of the club.

"Puppy play," Veracity said. "There are different versions of it. Pony play, kitten play."

As she explained more about it, Rev thought of the playground near his place. When he drank his Saturday morning coffee there, he'd seen the children act like barnyard animals, or dogs or cats. He guessed people never outgrew the desire for make-believe, but this was also very adult play. The lead dog had tight leather on his lower body, and he'd rubbed it against the Dom's leg with a devotion that suggested the bearded male was his own Master. Or someone he'd played with before.

The Domme with the sub in nipple clamps returned to Rev's mind. The man had been in obvious pain, but even inside that cage, he'd been as erect as the space would allow. And he'd looked at his Mistress like he feverishly wanted to please her.

Sacrifice, service, proof of what he'd endure for her. The element of faith in it was hard to deny. Faith in the strength of what was between them. Perhaps not love, but a form of devotion that gave them both something. Even if only while they were here. Like church on Sunday, giving people something to carry through the rest of their week to help them live their lives.

He thought of the apostle Peter, who, when he was crucified by the Romans, had asked to be crucified upside down. He hadn't felt worthy of being crucified in the manner his Lord and Master had been. A sign of devotion and love. Of sacrifice.

Plenty of Bible stories like that. He thought of Mary of Bethany, anointing Jesus's feet in oil, drying them with her hair. Carrying that scent with her...

"There's nothing I won't do for you, Rev," Teena Joy had told him. *"My love for you is a reflection of my love for the Lord, because you are a gift from Him."*

"Still with me?" Veracity touched his arm.

"Yeah. Just...my mind going in lots of directions."

She studied him. "You feel up to looking some more, or do you need a break?"

"I'd like to keep looking, if that okay with you."

"Yes. We'll go to a quieter spot for a moment, though." He could feel her attention as she gripped his hand, her shoulder brushing his arm. She led him past the dance floor, through another beaded curtain, into a new direction for his mind.

A familiar one. When he was little, he'd gone to the circus with Teena Joy and watched the aerial silk performances. As he got older, he wondered how many people had been entranced for the reasons he'd been, watching the silk tighten around the performer's body, restricting her, holding her, even as she danced with it. As he stared up at her, he could feel the bindings as if they were around his own legs and arms.

A spotter below manipulated the cloth to help her, but in his mind, that man's role was something different. When she'd spun down to land in his arms, Rev had taken all those interpretations home with him, added into a container of desires he'd been too young to explain. Or pursue.

Tonight he was doing just that, and now he was seeing a very different kind of aerial performance.

The silk had been replaced by chains.

A male turned and twisted in them, the metal clinking as he moved. He stopped in a pose that looked like a flying bird, a double length of the chain threaded between his legs, pressed against his testicles, more noticeable because of the flesh-colored hose he wore. Then he turned and the chain was at his waist and ankles. He arched backward in their hold, his arms stretched out and eyes closed as if he were in a trance.

A dark-haired male who stood inside the ring approached and cupped the performer's head. He kissed him thoroughly, tongue teasing his lips. In his crescent position, the erection became far more noticeable.

The Master stepped back and spoke in what sounded like Italian. It apparently meant "keep going," because the man was turning and twisting again. He threaded his legs through the loops so his limbs were spread wide. The Dom slapped his testicles and cock with an open hand. The male jerked, his face suffused with ecstasy and pain both. The Dom put his mouth on the man's inner thigh and bit him, twisting the flesh in the grip of his teeth. The male's thrown wide hands clenched.

Before stepping back, the Dom pushed him like a swing, getting him started again. The man danced in the chains, legs bending, threading in and out, arms outstretched, torso twisting and untwisting like a washcloth in Rev's hands, but all of it so graceful, the rippling tension of his muscles holding the eyes of everyone watching.

The Dom had moved back to the low wall circling the performer, which put him next to Vera.

"Lovely," she murmured. "You're a lucky man, Giorgio."

"I am that, Mistress." He didn't take his eyes off his sub, "He loves to play in the chains for me. Too much. They leave far more bruises than silks, but he likes the sensations. And proving to me the pain doesn't interfere with serving his Master. But there are limits to what I wish him to endure." He offered her a small smile. "Though that will be our little secret, no?"

"Won't hear it from me." She gripped Rev's arm, indicating she wished them to move onward. Giorgio's gaze passed over Rev, an appraisal, but he gave him a courteous nod. Appreciation of Rev's looks, with an acknowledgement that he belonged to Veracity.

She'd told him in this world, the boundaries were clearly marked for a reason. While it brought relief, it brought something else. As he recognized her pride of ownership, he felt the thrill, the deep satisfaction, of knowing he was seen as owned. By her.

At their next stop, three women stood around a male sub lying on his back. One was straddling his head, her high heels on either side of his neck. The Dominant's transparent plastic skirt had gold fringe and was painted with swirls of gold that somewhat concealed her sex and the seam of her buttocks. But since she straddled the male submissive's head, he was gazing at what was under the skirt.

She appeared to be enjoying her drink and discussion with her friends, but the male sub was showing his appreciation and devotion to her by kissing her shoes and ankles, tongue teasing, teeth nipping. As he did, he gazed longingly at what he could look at but not reach. His body was lashed to a flat board with rough one-inch twine.

He wore jeans, but with a start, Rev realized the leash the Domme had wrapped over her fingers disappeared under his waistband, and she kept idly tugging on it. His engorged cock strained against the jeans. When the Domme pulled on the tether, his facial muscles would tighten from the discomfort. Since the leash had metal spikes along the strap, Rev made the disturbing guess those same spikes might be around the man's cock, only pointed in, instead of out.

"The pain is confusing to you, isn't it?" Veracity noted.

"My mind say it's wrong. But other parts don't say that at all."

He hadn't meant anything smart or crude by it, but she understood. "You remember what you told me? How we're all just villages? This is a village. And yes, it breaks down too, if you're not communicating clearly, and connecting, looking one another in the eye to say what's in your heart. You'll see that going on in different ways here. Looking for it, recognizing it, removing all the barriers obscuring it from your vision, is part of the journey. And the pleasure."

She placed her hand on his chest, her palm transmitting heat through his shirt. "Do you feel up to an experiment? I'm feeling a strong desire to get my hands on more of you." Her gaze dipped. "You seem interested in that, too."

He was so hard it hurt. No sense denying it. And the words that came out of his mouth seemed to come from the same place, no thought or conscious understanding to them. "Could you do it...the way you want to do it?"

She arched a brow. "Explain."

"I want you to do it how you like, when the one you doing it with isn't so new. Not so...careful."

He might be crazy saying that in a place like this. But being sensible didn't seem to fit here. And she'd already proven she would protect him from himself. He hadn't understood just how important that would be.

"Yes, I can do that." The radiant flash through her silver eyes spiked his adrenaline. "Give me a word you'll use if it gets to be too much. Not 'stop,' because when we're aroused, we often say that when we mean just the opposite."

He gave her a half-smile. "Code 15."

"Appropriate, since it means possible intervention needed." She crooked her finger at him. "Follow me."

When he did, he saw a shift in her manner. Almost indifferent to whether he was following her or not. No, not indifferent. Expecting he was, so there was no need to look behind her to see if he was keeping up. He watched the flashing, colored lights of the club form lightning bolts across the waves of her hair when her body moved.

His gaze moved to her God-blessed ass under the tight skirt. She couldn't be wearing anything under it except the rose-lined hosiery that made her lovely legs gleam as she clicked along in her heels. When she glanced left, she gave him the curve of her cheek, the pursed shape of her moist, full lips. The sweep of dark lashes.

He would have followed her endlessly for that simple, precious view, and because she wanted *him* to be the one following her.

They returned to the public play spaces near the VIP lounge. She chose an unoccupied one, where the main feature was a section of iron rail fencing with spike tops, like he'd see around one of the fancy houses in the Garden District. Mounted on the wall behind it was a framed photograph, blown up to mural size. A man and a woman were bent over, each clasping one of their own ankles, free arms crossed to clasp the ankle of the other. Standing between them, his back to the photographer, was a Dom, one large hand resting on the lower back of each. On the point of the man's raised buttock was a full wine glass. On the woman's, an ash tray for the Dom's cigarette, which he was currently drawing upon.

Though his shadowed features were in profile, they were familiar. "It's Bastion," Rev murmured.

"Yes. We have an accomplished erotic photographer who visits New Orleans adult clubs a couple times a year. Those interested can sign up to be subjects for his work. They can arrange for a private purchase, or get a free copy and give their permission for him to use the photos for his own showings and sales.

"He and Bastion came up with the pose together, but it was also part of the session Bastion did with these two subs. It's become one of the photographer's best sellers." A smile touched her voice. "It was also the only time Bastion was allowed to smoke within Progeny's walls."

Vera removed the emerald ring and bracelet, and slipped them into Rev's pocket, caressing his thigh before she took off her black gloves. She wore fingerless silver mesh ones beneath. Her nails were painted silver with a metallic black on the tips. "Take off your shirt and hand it to me," she said.

He was aware of people wandering the area, their eyes passing over him, so when she issued the command, he put his head down to follow her command. Her fingers whispered over his neck and shoulder as he shrugged out of the shirt and air touched his skin. His body was tense as a tied rope.

"Any need for Code 15?"

"No ma'am. Just...getting used to things."

"All right." A pause as she waited him out, to be sure, then she nodded at the fence. "Face this and grip these bars." When she indicated the ones she wanted, his arms were stretched out to either side. Not to their full length, but close, his elbows slightly bent.

"Keep your head up. Spread your legs, shoulder width apart." When the pants tightened over his buttocks, she slid her hand over one to squeeze with firm appreciation.

He could hear the noise of other people and feel the air of their passing. Their comments floated in the air around him. By facing the fence, though, it narrowed his focus to her, and made him less self-conscious.

Against one of the panels in the sectioned off area was a cabinet. When she opened the door, she revealed some of the things she'd discussed with him. A crop, flogger, and cane. After she put his shirt on a hook next to the cabinet, her discarded gloves on top of it, she tucked the handle of the flogger into the waistband of her snug skirt, the tassels dangling along her hip. She picked up the crop and cane in the same hand.

Then she stepped behind him where he couldn't see her. Her hand applied firm pressure to his lower back, until he was right up against the fence, his toes between the rails, chest to them, hips, thighs. Two of the bars pressed against his pelvis on either side of his straining cock.

The position wasn't comfortable, but his body adjusted and didn't object. She had his full attention, particularly when she put her toe on one of the fence's horizontal pieces, a foot off the ground, and tugged her skirt higher on her thigh. She unclipped her garter strap from her hose and the lace belt over her panties, a garment sheer enough to show him tempting shadows of what lay beneath.

She wrapped the strap around his wrist, tying the ends together around the fence rail. Then she went to his other side and did the same provocative process. He could pull free, but his inner and outer reaction said he was going to stay where she wanted him to be.

"You're bound, Rev," she said. "You can't move until I release you. You understand?"

"Yes, Mistress." It was easy to be formal now. Her voice told him what to do. So did what was inside him.

She stroked his back and shoulders, and he realized she was doing more than enjoying the feel of him. She was testing his muscles, registering where there was more or less tension. Then she stepped back and the tails of the flogger landed against him.

He jumped, but it didn't hurt. He just reacted to the new sensation, the way the straps hit and then slid down over his skin. She did it a few times, increasing her pace, letting him get the sense of it. Then she did it harder, changing her pattern and the way she hit, so there was more sensation to it, more impact and sting, though it still wasn't painful, not exactly.

It awakened his skin. As it became more uncomfortable, he discovered what she'd meant, about how pain could be welcome. Each impact seemed to send a direct strike to his cock and balls, in just the right way.

He got a little lost in it, such that when she touched his back, caressing his reddened skin, his nerves jumped, but only to reach for her. His back arched so his shoulders pushed against her touch.

"Lay your head back, Rev."

When he obeyed, she leaned against him, her breasts and hip bone against his side. She traced his forehead, his cheeks, his mouth, the parted lips, with her glossy nails and elegant fingers. He captured them in his mouth, and she let him tease them with his tongue as she took her other hand down his back to his ass and kneaded. He quivered.

"Put your forehead back against the bars and show me how you'd move inside of me, if I give you that privilege."

That was a bigger step than just being half naked in front of people, but he looked at that photograph in front of him. The messages in it, and her touch, her presence, were the extent of his world. His hips thrust forward and retreated, pushing his ass against her palm. He thought of how she'd gripped him when they'd lain together in front of her fireplace.

Her thumb stroked the crease between his buttocks, making him shove himself harder between the bars. If his slacks hadn't been in the way, his cock would have jutted out between them, straight and hard. One of the things he'd seen in the play area was a man bound against fencing like this, and his Domme was slapping his cock on the other side of it. He'd looked as if he wanted to die—from bliss.

Veracity stepped back, leaving him with an anticipation like thunder brought.

Hsst. The lightning came. The cane whistled as it cut through the air. The far sharper pain made him flinch and bite down on an oath. And yet, his already aroused nerve endings didn't reject it. She waited a moment to be sure, then did it again. And again. Each time, he registered the pain, flinched, thought it was too much, then something else kicked in and said it wasn't.

His fingers flexed, curled, clenched. When she switched back to the flogger, he jerked at the change in sensation. It hurt less and yet his skin was even more sensitive to it. Then he bucked as a swat from the crop got into the mix, hitting his shoulders, his back, his ass.

His breath was coming deep and hard. As he tried to do it like she'd taught him, and imagine her face, all the expressions that might be on it, he imagined her approval, her arousal, her look as her orgasm had taken her. By giving her this, his reaction to all of it, he was the boat she was riding toward that. Or maybe he was the whole damn ocean, willing to take her as far as she wanted to go.

She put herself against him, her hips curved behind his ass and thighs. Her clothes slipped against his skin, her scent in his nose. She slid her touch down his chest to his stomach. Slipping the fastener of the slacks, she pushed the zipper down before the heel of her hand rubbed over him through the underwear. He stifled a groan. Her knee pressed into the back of his leg.

"I'm taking your pants and boxers down, Rev."

She waited. She was giving him a chance to use that safeword. Code 15. He didn't say it, but when the tip of the cane touched his bare back, a short sting of reproof, he realized she required an answer, for or against.

"Yes, Mistress."

He stared straight ahead and imagined Bastion drawing deep on the cigarette, bracing his hand on the two people submitting to his desires while he thought of what he'd do with the control they'd given him.

The air was cool against Rev's ass, testicles and cock as Veracity pushed his clothes out of her way. When she stepped back and the cane hit his bare ass, he swore he heard her purr at his sucked in breath, his groan. She liked that reaction. He was being hurt...and it was arousing him. Because he liked the pain, or he liked showing her how much he enjoyed giving her what she liked?

Did he have to decipher it? It simply was. Like when he sang, and he knew the Power that had given him that voice liked hearing him lift it to the Heavens, stretch himself to the limits.

Blasphemy? Or just evidence of how much the joys of earth hinted at what awaited them all in Heaven, if they could ever get there.

He lost count of the cane strikes, his body moving with it, the pain lashing fire across his flesh. Then she was pressed to him again, her pelvis pushed to his buttocks, her hand taking control of his cock to rub and stroke.

"Mistress." He choked out the word, a warning.

She gripped his base and dug her nails into it, a bite that could have competed with a crab's pincers. An entirely not-good pain, but it served its purpose. He was able to choke back the climax that had tried to boil forth.

"Take a breath, Rev. Easy and slow. The night is young."

"Apologies, Mistress."

"Rev, if you do something wrong, I'll tell you. I will require an apology, and a punishment to ensure the sincerity of that apology. Otherwise, you don't apologize to me, because you don't know you've done something wrong until I tell you that you have. You understand?"

She eased her hold, stroking him up and down. It was torment, because that climax had been contained, but was an animal still more than ready to break free. The strain of keeping it locked in showed in his voice.

"I don't want to give you more to do. I'm...supposed to serve you."

"You're not abdicating responsibility for your behavior. While this ground may feel familiar, the terrain, the exact address, my desires, aren't. So you follow my lead."

"Yes, Mistress."

"Good. I'll reinforce the point. Sometimes a pre-punishment is a good idea."

And reinforce it she did. With ten more strikes of that cane, followed by the swish of the flogger. His ass and back, his upper thighs, went from surface fire to deep, stinging burn. When he was twitching under the blows, she stopped. As she adjusted his underwear and slacks back over his ass, zipped and fastened the pants, the cloth rubbed the abraded skin. Sitting down was going to reinforce that punishment.

"The club has vampire claw cushions," she said. "We put one on a chair when we want our sub to sit beside us, but not get too comfortable. They have to sit still, too. Sit up straight, not distract their Dom with evidence of discomfort. Having a sub do that while I enjoy a cocktail with friends, knowing he's aroused and suffering at the same time...that has an appeal. Release the bars and turn toward me."

When he did, she was holding his shirt. She stepped close enough to rub his erection with a thigh. As she put a hand on his face, he wanted to kiss her wrist. He asked if he could.

She said yes, and he did, but his knees trembled, which he hadn't expected. He wouldn't grab onto her, but she held him, easing him to his knees, a much better place. He'd retained her wrist, and had his mouth against it. Her other hand went to his head. "You're okay," she murmured. "You're doing fine, Rev."

"What's the matter with me?"

"Not a thing." The emotion in her voice, the curl of her hand, told him it was truth. "You took far more than I expected. You may be more of a masochist than I realized."

"Is that bad?"

"No," she said softly. "I've suddenly found a reason to become more of a sadist."

CHAPTER TEN

"*A*re you watching this?" Cyn murmured. She knew the question was merely a request for input, because Ros had followed Vera and Rev's progress through the club as closely as she had. Vera was usually a private session kind of Mistress, but she'd chosen to do a low-key scene with him in a spot with a clear view to their booth. "He's completely new to it, physically. But she's right. Mentally, he's been there a while."

"Most members here know that feeling," Ros responded. "I haven't seen her get attached this quickly. Ever."

"The fit's there. Hard to miss."

Ros glanced at Lawrence, leaning against the side of the booth. Her beloved submissive would see Vera and Rev's chemistry from a different angle. Because Rev *was* new to this, it could cause unexpected responses, so Lawrence would pay particular attention to how Rev was doing.

Vera's simple test of his responses had dazed him, a light-handed subspace, the knee-weakening kind. He didn't seem embarrassed by it. Vera was right; there was evidence of alpha *and* beta markers in him.

"Might be time to do a deeper dive on this one, boss," Cyn said.

"Vera is our HR rep. You think she hasn't already?"

Cyn shook her head. "If it was about one of us, she'd dive in like a CIA analyst. If it's for her, she's going to do the 'respect his privacy' blah blah bullshit."

She looked at Lawrence. "It's not an obvious fit to me. Blue collar, low skilled job, not well-educated. Vera's not the slumming-for-a-nice-piece-of-ass type."

At Ros's expression, Cyn lifted a shoulder. "You keep me around to say the non-PC shit out loud. It's in my job description."

"Just don't say it around her. Or him."

"I know how to have tact. Or rather, I've seen it done. I can probably fake it."

"Unlike an orgasm," Lawrence said.

Cyn bared her teeth at him. "Faking tact is about being polite. Faking an orgasm is a lie to the universe that could shatter its foundation. More importantly, it's a waste of my fucking time."

Lawrence blinked. "Well, thank God you added that. The universe thing was so poetic I thought Skye had possessed you."

"Can I beat him?" Cyn asked Ros.

"Do your best the next time you're sparring with him at Roughnecks," Ros said absently, referring to the boxing gym they used for workouts.

Picking up on her change in mood, Cyn nudged her. Lawrence shifted closer, offering reassurance from both sides. "She's the most level-headed of all of us, Ros," Cyn said. "All that spiritual juju."

"I know. I just feel worried. I don't know why, but my intuition is usually on the mark."

"I expect it's coming from his family. That cousin of his is a calculating dick. The aunt gives me the creeps."

"From how Skye described them, she's the zealot," Lawrence agreed. "Skye says her certainty she's right, that she's acting in his best interest, sends any conflicting information right to the mental spam folder, so it doesn't interfere with her world view."

Ros brushed her glossy nails over his clipped beard and met his gold-flecked green eyes. In certain lights, they held a trace of blue. "I can hear Skye saying it. Probably in her Mark Gatiss's Mycroft voice. What did she find? I'm sure she dug into them."

Lawrence's lips quirked. "Didn't find anything other than some questionable uses of the collection plate funds."

Ros studied him. "But you're still on the same page with Cyn about them. Particularly the aunt."

"People don't need a criminal background to unleash hell on you. I remember two guys we lost because their team thought a woman was in trouble. When they're close enough, she detonates the suicide vest under her burka. To increase the trust factor, she had her six-year-old daughter with her. The survivors remembered the look of certainty on her face, damn near bliss. So, yeah."

He cleared the shadows out of his gaze with effort and attempted a smile. "That kind of crazy aside, best not to overlook how dangerous a woman can be. Ever."

Or how appealing a dangerous man could be, especially one who delivered a statement like that, with his lips curved in that kind of smile. His tanned skin showed the genes of his Mexican father, while the handsome weathering of his face proved how much time Lawrence had spent exposed to extreme elements.

Ros let him see the heat her thoughts gave her, because she knew it would also help him balance the dark memories he'd just stirred.

She turned her attention back to Vera and Rev. No one was immune from the vulnerabilities their past gave them. Ros knew the wounds Vera carried in her heart. No matter her worries about the unlikeliness of the pairing, Ros felt a healing vibe from Rev, particularly in what he wanted to offer Vera.

She hoped his family wouldn't cause Vera any problems she couldn't handle, but *her* family would have her back if they did. Ros would make sure of it.

Vera continued Rev's tour through the club, letting him see everything. Her short "experiment" had both narrowed and expanded his senses. Anything happening between a Domme and sub caught his attention, his body getting the direct impact of what his mind was processing, while he lost his sense of anything beyond this moment and the next. And the next.

Because of the arousal, the adrenaline, the nerves that made his skin feel like he was out in a summer rain, he knew he was at a gear that might be tuned a little too high. She knew it, too, her hand always upon him. Whenever he got too lost in a spiraling fog of sensual need, her voice would cut through it and bring him back to her.

But eventually the fog got too thick. He misstepped and bumped against her. When she turned toward him, her hand on his shoulder and waist, he curled his arms around her, buried his face in her neck and shoulder. He wanted to bite, to kiss and lick her with the same intensity he'd seen in that male lying on his back, looking up at the sweet, wet and musky gateway to relief for his cock.

It was the wrong thought. His body acted without his brain, swinging them around and putting her against the wall. The sconce mounted there cast red light on everything within its range. A framed photograph next to it showed a man bound on an X-shaped cross, his arms up and out. He was thin, his skin stretched taut over ribs and hip bones. A woman knelt at his feet, her head bowed, her hand on his ankle, her cheek to his knee.

Another woman, in heeled boots and nothing else, was beating him with a flogger. The photo was black and white, except for an artful touch of color, revealing the reddened marks on his chest, and the Domme's dark red hair. Or maybe it was the effect of the light.

His hands flexed on Veracity. Rev almost had her feet off the floor as he pushed his body against her, his cock against her stomach. He recalled himself enough to freeze there, but though he could flex his hands on her waist, he couldn't make himself let go, back off, apologize. His neck was rigid, his head canted low as he tried to figure out what was happening, what had hold of him.

"I do, Rev," she said, telling him he'd muttered it. "It's all right. You're all right."

He tuned back in enough to see she had no fear of him. That was good. He wasn't afraid of himself, because he was familiar with being out of control. The current that would grab hold of him and take him where it willed was a river he'd known from the time he was little.

But he wasn't little, and this wasn't the same. Not exactly. He was caught in a roaring rush of a man's feelings. He wanted something from her so much he wasn't sure he knew how to stop himself from taking it.

He told her that, his voice odd and rough. She dipped her chin, lifted a hand to someone outside his view, but when he would have looked that way, she put a firm hand to his face, keeping his eyes on hers.

"That's easy, Rev," she said. "I tell you when you can take. Right?"

He thought it through. He had no sense of time. He often didn't, not when this feeling came upon him, because it wasn't relevant, but at her words, he was able to find his center. He focused on her breath, her scent, the feel of her clothes against his. She'd lifted one foot and had it wrapped around the back of his calf, her spiked heel sliding against his slacks. It brought their bodies into a tight fit.

He'd heard a lot of crude language tonight, but spoken in tones of reverence, full of raw feeling. *I want to eat your pussy. Please let me suck your cock, Master. Please. Fuck me, Mistress. Please. Let me serve your cunt. I want you to show me your gorgeous tits. Play with your nipples.*

Please your Master.

Please your Mistress.

Please.

He groaned and pushed harder against her. The shot of sensation through the root of his cock, into his testicles, was something he hadn't earned. But how could he pull back? Her hand had moved to his ass and was stroking the curve, nails digging in to encourage the movement. He got one hand up and put it by her neck, his thumb against her pulse, fingers clamped over her shoulder.

"Mistress..."

"Kneel to me, Rev."

It was difficult, but she'd given him an order, and when he latched onto that, it pulled the rest of him into line. He went back to one knee, leaning against her thigh, his breath hot through her skirt. He was steadier there, could almost reach himself. Almost.

He thought of the Lord, walking on the water while his disciples floundered in a turbulent sea. He forced up his chin and looked at his Mistress. She was serene, stern, and held knowledge in her eyes. As she'd said, she knew the ways of this world. She was his shepherd here.

"It's time to listen to some music." She put a hand on his shoulder and stroked. "They're doing karaoke on the top floor, and they have a dessert bar. Do you want some pie?"

Her steady warmth filled him. Cocooned him, took the worries and chaos from his heart. He put his head against her knee, and she caressed his back. She'd told him he didn't need to apologize until she told him he'd done wrong, but a man needed to be a man. He rose and touched her face. "Did I hurt you?"

"No. You are very, very strong, Rev, but I've never known a man with such a gentle touch. You could hold a charging bull at bay without giving him so much as a bruise."

Her brow creased at his startled expression. "Did I say something wrong?"

"No. Just..." He wasn't trying to conceal it; he just didn't want what her words had stirred in his memory to distract from his moment. Then Rev saw Lawrence, Ros's man. He was nearby, leaning against a high top. Nursing a canned soda and watching his surroundings.

"They thought you were in trouble." Shame swept him, but Veracity shook her head, not allowing it.

"They were ready if I signaled that I was. We look after one another here. The DM was here first, but Lawrence came right on his heels. I let them know I was fine. Because I am. We are. Aren't we?"

She smiled up at him, a simple, beautiful thing. She had no doubts. This was her place of faith, he realized. She knew her path here.

She wasn't rattled, but from the heat in her body, the soft look of her mouth and light in her silver eyes, touched with red, she also wasn't as calm as she might appear.

"This is different for you, too, isn't it?" he asked.

She required honesty from him. He wanted that to be a two-way street. He also wanted her trust. The pain of memory he saw said she understood what he was asking.

"Yes," she said. "I don't know what to make of it. So I think music and pie will give us a breather."

"Do they have peach pie? Don't have to be fresh. I like it out of a can, too."

Her lips curved. He saw relief, and gratitude, that he hadn't pressed for more.

"We'll find out."

When they moved toward the stairs, Lawrence had disappeared, reassured by some signal of Vera's, or maybe he'd just recognized his presence was no longer needed.

Rev would talk to the man, though, to assure him of his intentions. This was Veracity's family, and Lawrence was a direct line to Ros, the head of that family.

When they reached the top floor, he saw the karaoke room had a name, offered on a neon sign over the entrance to it. "The Breathing Room." Appropriate.

As promised, there was a non-alcoholic bar that offered desserts, as well as the quick comfort foods most bars had. The stage and karaoke machine were in use, a hefty man with golden beard and blond hair doing a decent version of the Shirelles "Will You Love Me Tomorrow?"

He had backup singers, a middle-aged Asian lady with a bob cut, wearing thigh high boots and a shimmering red dress. The other woman was so pale Rev wondered when she'd last seen sunlight. She wore a schoolgirl uniform with a very short plaid skirt. She had long blonde hair, fluffed out like a lion's mane.

While this wasn't a play area like the floors below, the protocols were still in place. Some subs knelt at the sides of their Master or Mistress, while others stood attendance behind or next to them. But there were also people acting the way he'd expect any friends hanging out together to do.

A lean black man with gold dreadlocks rose from the table he was sharing with another man. As he headed their way, Rev saw tribal tats circling his biceps. He wore belted jeans, boots and nothing else. His torso was like a wiry cable, though he had muscled arms and well-developed shoulders.

He'd been headed toward the bar, but when he saw Vera, he detoured in her direction. Rev got the assessing look he was starting to expect, but it had a different tone from how Giorgio and other Doms had looked at him. This was more man to man, a look between equals. Two male submissives.

"We have a booth over there, Mistress, me and Trey, if you'd like to share it with us."

"Sounds good, Sy. Who's in the running for bragging rights tonight?"

Sy grinned. He had a wide, expressive mouth, the bones of his face cut sharp, his brows dark and thick, one pierced with a gold ring. "Tonight's mostly been a competition for the 'I Need To Keep My Day Job,' award, but these three aren't too bad. You missed an epic Bee Gees mashup with Master L and Frank, and their current pet. They're in town from Baton Rouge on some business and decided to traumatize us with their vocal stylings. Everyone's having a hell of a lot of fun. Converting the top floor to talent show-offs and snacks was a good idea. Mick deserves kudos on that idea. And the dessert chef they hired... wow."

"Well, Cyn got pissed one night when her sweet tooth acted up and all they had were bowls of peppermints."

Sy did a mock shudder. "And as we all know, when Cyn gets cranky, somebody might end up dead. You need anything from the bar?"

"Bring me a sampler tray, and a couple bottles of cold water. If they have peach pie, a slice of that. Put it on my tab." She looked at Rev. "You want coffee with your pie?"

"Yes ma'am, that'd be fine. But I should pay."

Sy lifted a hand. "Let it be my treat, man. I owe the TRA wonder women."

When Sy moved away, Veracity headed for the booth he'd noted, handling the explanation along the way. "Sy and Trey are musicians. They do other jobs to support the habit, but TRA helped them broadcast their talents a little more strategically this year. It's upped their studio and band fill-in jobs. As well as their own group's gigs."

"What do they play?"

"They can do anything, but they like their blues, rock and jazz mix ups. Some funk."

From Sy's arm definition, Rev guessed the man was a drummer, and Trey did guitar or keyboard. As Vera introduced them, Rev noted Trey wore a T-shirt from one of the Frenchmen Street clubs over his jeans. He also had arm tattoos and blue eyes gazing soulfully from beneath shaggy brown hair. Rev expected Trey had no trouble catching female attention.

The man had risen from his chair and nodded deferentially to Veracity as they approached. Rev wondered if both men had done sessions with Vera here. Like what she'd just done with him, only less short, because they were obviously experienced submissives.

Rev wasn't sure how he felt about that. Veracity slid into the booth, making room for Rev on the outside. Trey was on her other side, but with more space between him and Vera, a reassuring signal. When Sy returned, he sat next to Trey. He put the sample dessert platter and water in front of Vera, and coffee and peach pie at Rev's elbow.

"Have what you need?" Vera asked. From the quirk of her lips, he could tell she understood it was a loaded question, but Rev gave her a warm look back and nodded.

"Yes ma'am. This looks real good."

When conversation started up between the three, the topics mostly revolved around the musical performances, and what was happening on the floors below. Rev wasn't excluded, but the men didn't speak to him. Not until Vera straight out said, "You have my permission to talk to Rev directly."

Another way the boundaries set here, the structure, took pressure and worries off of someone new like him, letting him concentrate on what his Mistress wanted.

He did notice that Sy and Trey gave him the same once-over that Lawrence had. They didn't abdicate looking out for a woman just because she was a Dominant. He liked that, even as he still felt less pleasant twinges thinking of more intimate experiences they might have had with Veracity.

It wasn't knowing she'd been with them. It was not knowing if, in this world, it was entirely possible she would be with them again, even while Rev was seeing her. He didn't like that idea at all. Not just because of his feelings for her, but because of what that would say about how she viewed what their relationship was, where it was going.

Leave it, Rev. Let it lie. You letting what you want interfere with what the Lord is giving you in this moment.

A beautiful woman at his side, wanting to be with him, wanting to share things with him.

The Shirelle singers finished to enthusiastic applause. The next person wasn't a singer, but a young woman who visibly shook as she moved onto the stage. Several people called out encouragement to her.

"You're fine, Lottie. You're good, girl."

She didn't seem to hear them. She swallowed and stared at the paper in her hand as if it was the only thing keeping her upright and on the stage.

Sensing her distress, Rev set down his fork, but Vera's hand was on his thigh. "It's okay," she murmured. "Her Domme's got her."

"Lottie."

Proving it, a Mistress two tables away from them spoke. She had spiky black hair and wore snug jeans on her long legs, a tucked-in T-shirt molding firm curves. She leaned forward, bracing booted feet on the floor. "What are you reading?"

"It's from a letter Na...Nathaniel Hawthorne wrote to his wife Sophie. It made me think of you, Mistress. This one section of it."

"Then read it to me. But put the paper away and look at me. I'm sure you know it by heart."

The girl managed it, though not quickly. She creased the paper several times with her nails after she folded it. She wasn't disobeying. She was actively struggling not to bolt.

"Come on, Lottie," Sy murmured, his eyes full of compassion. "You can do it. Just follow Britt's lead."

Rev assumed Britt was her Mistress. Lottie tucked the paper in the back pocket of her jeans. She wore a light blue shirt with a fluttery neckline and small pearl buttons. A gold cross nestled in the valley between her collar bones.

She stuttered, the words spoken in a near whisper. No one called to her to speak up. Britt had the obvious lead.

"Again, Lottie. You're doing well. Try to say it loud enough that everyone can hear."

This time, as she held her Mistress's gaze, she managed it. "'I never, until now, had a friend who could give me repose...all ha—have disturbed me and, whether for pleasure or pain, it was still...disturbance. But p—peace overflows from your heart into mine. Then I feel that there is a Now, and that Now must be always calm and happy, and that sorrow and evil are but ph—phantoms that seem to flit across it.'"

"Very good." Britt's tone stayed firm, but pride filled it. "All right, once more."

This time, Lottie's back straightened. Her expression was less panicked, her voice stronger. She'd responded to her Mistress's approval.

When she was done, Britt sat back. "Very good. Come sit with me."

It was the cue for applause, which the audience generously provided. "Good job, Lottie," Sy called out, raising his hands above his head to clap for her.

Lottie managed a terrified smile, and then headed for her Mistress, keeping to a measured pace with effort. When she knelt,

Britt pulled her hair fondly, wrapping the tail around her fist to tilt her sub's head back and nip at her throat.

"That was a major step," Trey said. "She's gotten up there twice before and scrambled back off without saying a word. We'll make sure to go by the table and give her some strokes."

"You just want to see her blush." Sy nudged him. "Which happens every time you look at her, you fucking flirt."

"Britt told me to do it," Trey complained. "When she starts flirting back, we'll know she's making progress."

"I confirmed it," Vera told Sy. "He's not making that up."

Rev waited until Veracity chose a morsel of white cake from her sampler before he tried his pie. It was good. Mostly.

"Did your aunt used to make that?" his Mistress asked, her eyes upon him.

"Yeah. She liked to have me sing while she made it. Said it made the pie better."

No one in the world would ever make a peach pie that matched Teena Joy's. The memory added to the taste, but it also made his heart hurt. He'd celebrated her arrival in the arms of the Lord, because she'd want that, but the grief could still circle back. Veracity's hand covered his as she leaned closer.

"A lot of people think this is only about sex." She gestured to a Dom and sub near them. The sub wore a pair of jean shorts and a gold collar on her throat. Her breasts were exposed and nipples pierced, a chain between them strung with a gold infinity charm. "It can be. Nothing wrong with that, but it can also open up things that mean a great deal to us, make us vulnerable. And that makes us think of those we miss, who we've lost. You loved her."

"I did. I do."

Trey and Sy were involved in conversation, Trey sketching out music notes on a napkin. If it was deliberate, giving them privacy, Rev appreciated it.

"Mavis said she passed about a year ago."

"Thirteen months and eight days."

Veracity's eyes held his. "That's a major upheaval in your life. Mavis said you lived with her."

"Yeah. I kept saying I should move out, but she'd say I wasn't one of them kids who don't earn his own way. She said the house was too big for her to rattle alone in it, so I said I'd stay, as long as I paid my share."

A faint smile touched his lips. "She say, 'we'll be roommates, then, you and me,' and shook my hand like we was just meeting for the first time. She was always teasing like that." The humor curled tight around the next thought, sunk into it and disappeared. "Then she got sick, and wasn't no question of it anymore. I took care of her, same as she took care of me for so long."

"Did you wish to stay in the house, after she was gone?" Her lashes were dark and thick around her silver eyes.

"Didn't give it much thought. Witford said she wanted the house sold and the proceeds to go to the church, and that was fine by me. The house wasn't the same without her in it, and a good family lives there now. Finding a place closer to the school worked out good."

He had his forearm against the edge of the table, casting a shadow of his hand next to his plate. She drew a line around it with one finger-tip. "That first day, the way you did this to the shadow of my arm, it was like I could feel your touch on my skin."

She put her hand on the shadow, and he couldn't deny the tingle he felt in his palm. She had that way about her, drawing energy and sending it toward him like a blown kiss. Like a flock of blown kisses, landing everywhere on him.

She put her elbow on the table and propped her chin on her hand. "Did you keep anything of hers?"

"Got all the memories she gave me. I have a picture of the two of us from when I was little, soon after my momma died. Yolanda, Witford's wife, she also brought me this ring Teena Joy always wore. She told Witford I was to have it. Just a little gold band, don't even fit my pinkie, but I keep it in a box with a few things. It's all right, Mistress. Giving is how you receive. Possessions don't mean much."

At her surprised expression, he added, "You look like you think I should have been given more. Everything the Lord gives me, every day. That's all I need." He closed his hand over hers. "And tonight I feel squarely on His good side."

He'd won a smile from her, but she had another question for him. "When I said you could stop a bull's charge, that meant something to you."

He should have known she was going to circle back to that. "You have a way of hitting a nail straight on the head without looking where the hammer going, Veracity."

She pursed her full lips. "Does that mean you'll tell me about it?"

"I won't say no to something you want to hear. When I was fifteen, I was on a youth trip to a farm. Some of them boys wandered off. Our assistant pastor noticed and asked me to go fetch them. They was in the bull's pasture, throwing rocks at him, trying to get him to charge."

"Proving why teenagers have to have superhero guardian angels to survive the idiotic things their underdeveloped brains tell them to do," Veracity said dryly. "Though Cyn tells me it's good to hold onto some of that stupidity as an adult, to keep things interesting."

"She full of life, that one."

Vera chuckled. "She's full of something. That's what she'd say to you."

"But you love her like a little sister."

"I do. She drives me crazy, even as I want to hold her and tell her everything will always be okay, because she has us. And now Mick, which I think is why she finally halfway believes we won't all be swallowed up in the ground tomorrow."

"She had it tough before you all."

"She did. Her childhood was a nightmare."

He nodded. "It always the ones like porcupines that need a hug. They gotta draw blood to let you be kind to them."

"I'm going to tell her you said that. Tell me the rest of your story."

"One boy with them was smaller, not so fast. He was smart enough to know it, but they'd made fun of him, called him a chicken, until pride overrode his smarts. He got in the pasture with them. When they aggravated that bull enough he started in their direction, they shoved the boy down and took off. Maybe they didn't mean for the next thing to happen, but when he tried to get up, he twisted his ankle."

Her mouth went to a thin line. "I've never been a fan of the term 'boys will be boys.' There shouldn't be a minimum age requirement for compassion."

"No, but it's what you say, about the brain? Kids sometime don't think about things until they happen. Especially when they in a pack. The brain don't work at all then. Adults harboring a mean spirit because they afraid, or don't like something different from what they know can be the same. When them boys reached the fence, turned and noticed he wasn't with them, the bull was already charging. They froze."

"You didn't," she guessed.

"He was so small. Trying to run, so scared..." Rev lifted a shoulder. "God helped me distract the bull, and we got him outside the fence. The youth pastor gave them all a stern talking-to. Then made them read scripture on the bus for an hour, while the others got to help the farmer milk the cows and feed the chickens. Turned out okay, thank the Lord."

He turned his attention back to their surroundings, to what Trey and Sy were doing, to the flow of conversations around them, to Lottie, now sitting between Britt's spread knees, her cheek on her Mistress's inner thigh.

That wasn't the whole story. The lifted hairs on Vera's neck, her heart punching a harder beat against her ribs, told her so. "You stopped him, didn't you? The bull."

His gaze moved back to the table, rested there a moment, then he lifted it to her face. "Not me. I just said 'God help me save this boy. Don't let those boys live a life knowing they got him killed, bearing that burden. And don't do that to his momma.'"

"So what happened?" She wouldn't order it, because a command felt wrong for this. But she hoped he would tell her.

His brown eyes moved over her eyes and lips. "I ran at the bull and dodged to his right, catching one of his horns. We kind of turned in a circle, and I was able to bring him down to one knee and hold him. I didn't want to hurt him. I sang to him. I don't remember what."

A half smile touched his lips. "But it settled him down a little. I still had a pocketful of grain from where they'd let us feed the goats, and I gave that to him. Once Sammy got to the fence and the others pulled him over it—he was shaking so bad, they had to help him—I let the bull go and walked out of there, calm like the farmer would, so he wouldn't want to chase me. He was calm enough then that he let me."

He touched her hair, feathering a lock through his rough fingers. Silas and Trey had stopped talking, and though she didn't look their way, Vera was sure they were tracking the unprecedented sight of Mistress Vera hanging onto a man's words like a besotted schoolgirl.

Knowing that didn't stop her from doing it.

"You know the thing about that day I like to remember the most? Sammy was so scared he'd wet himself. One of the boys was wearing gym shorts under his jeans because he plays sports after school, and he gave him the shorts. They could have made fun of him, but seemed all of them let God open their eyes to how wrong they'd acted. They put their arms around him, and when it come time for them to sit on the bus reading the Bible, Sammy chose to sit with them. He say he got inside the fence and threw a rock or two, too, so he needed to read the same lessons."

"Sounds like a good kid."

"They all good kids. Just sometimes get off the path, like we all do."

Vera gripped his hand. Rev's eyes fell to that contact. "When I touch you and you talk about the strength and gentleness in my touch," he said suddenly, "that strength is God's, but it part of me, too. So I like that you feel it that way."

Vera explored his palm, stroking his wrist as she considered his large hand, all it was capable of doing. As she did, his head tilted over hers, so she lifted hers to brush her nose along his jaw and cheek.

When she turned so she was hip to hip, shoulder to shoulder with him again, she dropped her touch to his thigh. Her tender caress became something else as she slid a proprietary hand up from there to fondle his balls and semi-erect cock through his slacks, and stroke the muscles of his abdomen above their waistband.

That gingerbread color darkened like brown sugar as she leaned against him and spoke in his ear. "Spread your knees wider for me, Rev. When we're in a place like this, your cock should always be accessible to my touch."

As he stole a glance at the other two men, she dug her nails into his testicle. Just enough bite to yank his attention back where it belonged. "A Mistress exercising ownership is normal here. Sy and Trey won't stare while we're at a table together like this. It's rude and disrespectful to the Dominant. It's only allowed if I give them the privilege of watching."

"Why would they want to do that?"

"They're like you, Rev. As they watch, they imagine their own desires, what shape they take under a Mistress's hand. But I won't do that tonight. Not until I know more about what you really need from my control."

However, she would stroke and fondle to her heart's content. His cock stiffened to full mast, filling up her grip the way a bat would if she slipped her hand up its broadening length.

She knew he'd be thinking of all the things she'd told him, about focusing his energy on her demands, about finding the soul in the gaze. Offering the soul and body together was a mind-altering combination. As she met his gaze, that energy linked with her own.

She wanted to take him to a private room and straddle him, rock back and forth in that seesaw motion that would increase the sensations between their bodies, the depth of their joining, the feel of him inside of her. She wanted his seed and her own response to make that movement all the more pleasurable, the climax even more intense. She would lean back on her elbows and have him suckle her breasts while she cupped his head, rubbed herself on him, felt his cock grow harder and heavier.

For tonight, that would stay the stuff of fantasy. Because though he was responding to her, they'd come up here because of the sensory overload. He was powerfully aroused, but his shoulders were tense, his eyes squinting a little as he processed her touch, what it meant, with all the noise and humanity around them.

She didn't deny something strong was going on between them, but that was all the more reason to slow it down. He needed a slower pace, and maybe she did, too. She was the Domme, in control and in charge of his wellbeing, for this. She'd told him as much, and she would live up to it, taking care of him in the ways she knew. The Mistress in her knew the restless, unresolved feelings he might be feeling could shoot him into sub drop. He needed grounding.

"Sy, Trey." Vera caught their attention. "Would you provide some instrumental backup to Rev while he sings?"

Sy gave her a surprised look, followed by speculation, the experienced musician surfacing. "Sure he wouldn't prefer to choose something on the karaoke machine? Singing with a live band is a different animal."

"He prefers live music. He sings for his church. He'll keep pace." She disengaged her hand from Rev's and tapped the top of it, bringing him out of his head. "Will you sing for me, Rev?"

A look of surprise, followed by relief, for the familiar. It told her she'd made the right call. "I'll do anything you like, Mistress."

"Good. Go to it. They're going to handle the music." She tipped her head toward Sy and Trey.

Rev rose, moving toward the stage as if drawn there by a magnet. Something in him recognized the need for grounding, but it was a comfort zone he hadn't requested; he'd waited until she'd offered it to him.

Sy raised a brow. "He any good, Mistress? I'm not questioning the request. Just want to do what we can to make him look good."

She bounced her eyebrows at him. "That's not going to be a problem."

"C'mon, Sy," Trey said. "She's got a surprise for us."

"Okay, but if he asks us to play Air Supply, I'm out."

"Don't worry, honey." Trey patted his head and fended off the expected punch. "We all know your hard limits."

Trey shot Vera his trademark panty-wetting smile as Sy snorted. The two men went off to join Rev.

Rev was already looking more in his element. Vera caught snippets between the three men about keys, pacing, tone. Things musicians talked about. She watched their doubting expressions become more relaxed, but they shifted back to surprise when Rev shut off his microphone. She suspected Rev had noted the room was half the size of the church. She could tell Trey and Sy thought they'd have to adjust their own sound so as not to drown him out.

Boys, you have no idea, she thought.

She noticed Ros, Skye and Cyn coming in. Lawrence and Tiger, Skye's man, were with them. They grabbed a nearby table, Ros nodding to Vera.

Rev picked up the tambourine and started working it to a beat. As he did, he hummed a few bars of the song he wanted. Trey and Sy picked up on it, then they were ready. Vera felt her heart accelerate as they launched into Jackie Wilson's "Higher and Higher."

The music had the power to make toes tap, turn heads from the bar, and get people to their feet to dance. But then Rev started singing.

"Your love...lifted me higher...than I've ever been lifted before..."

Sy visibly started and exchanged a look with Trey, who gave him a mouthed *what the fuck*. When the men grinned in her direction, Sy shook a finger at her.

"I'll be at your side forever more..."

Vera had her hands in a knot under the table, her body canted forward as she met Ros's blue gaze. Cyn looked thrown, and Skye surprised, in a delighted way. Tiger and Lawrence exchanged a look like Trey and Sy's, the one people had when they discovered a "normal" person could sing like a Motown great.

But Rev had more than that. She'd wondered if it could only be felt in a church space, but as what she'd experienced that day began to build in his voice, it spread out and gripped the room. This wasn't a worship audience, but it made no difference to him. As the power in his voice expanded, the energy behind it made itself known. It brought people to their feet, swaying or dancing, singing the words with him. As he put one hand in the air, they followed suit, celebrating the joy Rev was putting in the music.

"Higher than I've ever been lifted before..."

When the song started to reach its conclusion, Rev, double tapping the tambourine, leaned in and said something to Sy.

Sy's response was loud enough that Vera caught it. "Yeah, man. Get it. We're with you."

"Bold choice," Trey added. "Let's rock it."

The music bounced out of the ending of Jackie Wilson's classic, and Sy used the metal brush on the drums to preface Kiki Dee's "I've Got the Music in Me."

"Ain't got no troubles in my life..."

Trey did the flourish, his hips moving to the beat as he worked the keyboard, and Sy switched out to the sticks again.

Rev didn't overpower a song to impress. He sang it the way it was supposed to be sung, with the right emotions. Joy, reflection, hope, they were all there, along with that other thing. Something like when she channeled Mistress energy and connected with a sub. In that moment, they were in touch with something bigger, even as it didn't change his earthly needs. And her own.

She was glad her friends were here to see it, feel it, because even those words didn't capture it adequately. Sy's amazed look made her laugh out loud, her heart full. And close her eyes to feel it inside her, all the way to the soul.

When she opened them, Cyn was standing beside her. The woman's gaze was fastened on Rev with curiosity, but also a wariness that was second nature to her. Power like this could crack open the toughest person.

But Vera had no fear of Rev. Hurt might come from missteps as he found his way. Once he found it, she might have to accept the likelihood she would be his "gateway" Domme. A first Domme was rarely the last one, especially for a sub who'd held the need in him all his life.

She didn't care for the thought, but that was expected at this stage, too. She wouldn't let him go until it was time, but when it was time, she'd know, because the idea would hurt less then than it did now, in the powerful flush of their beginning. She'd gone through that cycle with Whistler, then Trey, but both men could still play with her easily, club friends with benefits.

She let all that go, because it was interfering with this, witnessing how Rev was captivating and energizing everyone. Moments like this were meant to be celebrated, not drained by future worries.

Rev circled back to an earlier lyric to bring it to a close, and put his own spin on it. Instead of saying he would be keeping his feet firmly on the ground, he locked his eyes upon her and sang it a different way.

"Keeping my *knees* firmly on the ground."

He dropped to them then, for her.

Appreciation for the showmanship made the ceiling vibrate with cheers and whoops. He wasn't aware of that, his eyes on her, registering her flush of pleasure and her response, strong enough to compete with what he'd put into the song.

He bowed his head to her, breathless, his shoulders lifting and falling.

There was singing for celebration, for mourning, for finding your way. For reassuring oneself, when you felt lost or unbalanced.

She'd brought him into an environment where he could experience all of that. That short session they'd done, followed by this, had turned his singing into an emotional catharsis that tears, edginess or sleep provided other subs.

Trey and Sy kept jamming out, transitioning the audience toward the normal dancing and bopping to the music. Grounding them as well.

Realizing Rev was waiting for an acknowledgement, she rose. As she left the booth, she touched Cyn's arm, another reassurance.

When Vera came to him, she put her hand on Rev's shoulder. He pressed his forehead to her leg, his hand resting on her foot. Then he kissed her knee, his mouth moist through the mesh of her stocking.

Sy and Trey's gazes were on him, and her. They all knew about turning points, a full-fledged, honest, uncalculated surrender to a Mistress. A letting go of any defenses. Many subs, caught in the maelstrom, might do it long before they knew the Dom well enough, but with the right Dom, one experienced and looking out for their interests, it was okay.

Because as much as the Domme herself, they were embracing that lack of control they needed, an integral part of themselves. The Domme was just the conduit, the one who took them on the journey and introduced them to the world they wanted and needed, that they couldn't be whole and complete without.

She'd had the honor of being that conduit before. Despite her thoughts of only a moment ago, she realized she wanted this to be way more than that. And it wasn't just because of that nagging emptiness, the pain of watching the other women in her circle find it.

She'd always wanted a relationship where she and her sub were bonded so closely there was no doubt it was divinely inspired. Fate, destiny. Whatever it wanted to be called.

Her heart and soul said it was right here, kneeling at her feet. Later she might rein herself back from that thought, but right now, she had no problem letting that belief enclose both of them.

Dropping to her heels, she wrapped her arm around his back, curving herself over him and murmuring the words she wanted to say. And that he needed to hear.

"You're mine, Rev."

CHAPTER ELEVEN

*R*ev leaned against the wall across from the club's restrooms and changing areas. While benches were spaced along the corridor, he'd preferred to stand, with his arms crossed, head down.

He was dealing with a lot inside. She'd told him that was normal, but she'd also kept close watch on him, mentally and physically. He needed to find his footing and reassure her that he was all right. But first he had to make sure that was true.

He thought it was. He was just caught up in a state of curiosity and wonder. His main challenge was managing a raging need...for something. For her, for certain. To have her, be with her, hold her, feel her bare flesh against his, be inside her, moving strong like an ocean current that would take them places far beyond what he'd even thought was possible in his earthly existence.

He wanted to kneel to her. He wanted to care for her. Help her take off her clothes for bed, kneel by her shower while she bathed, and be there with a towel to press against her skin. He wanted to see that look in her eyes she'd had when she'd gripped him at the table, right there in front of everyone.

It had made him even harder, and she'd understood that, too. He wouldn't have thought that about himself, that he could let a woman do such a thing in front of other people, but it was as she said. Here, it was allowed. She'd used his own words to help him understand this place. This village found such things acceptable. And it opened up a whole new world of things for him to want from his Mistress.

Others passed him, coming and going from the restrooms. He'd almost gotten used to being evaluated in the way expected here. He nodded courteously to each, because even if their faces showed a brief flash of disappointment, they all accepted what his bracelets meant.

Villages tended to accept best what they shared in common, and this environment was no different.

Tisha and Witford had called it a *deviant lifestyle*.

He still hadn't put that one to bed inside him, the vile things they'd said to Veracity. There were things a man couldn't share with his family, that arguably were not their business, but still...their judgment had come from an ugly place, and that ugliness could grow into a monster in his heart, because he didn't know how to fix it.

Because it wasn't his job to fix it. Not until the Lord showed him how. But sometimes believing that didn't make the heart as easy as one could hope. Especially when someone he loved had created the wound and the infection that lingered in it.

"Doing okay?"

He glanced up to see Lawrence coming toward him. The Hispanic male wasn't tall, but he was built solid, his body compact and arms muscular. Veracity had said he was a former SEAL.

"Yeah. I'm all right. You all sure are good about keeping an eye on each other."

"It's the job. And one worth doing." Lawrence didn't smile, but his expression was friendly. "I won't assume I know everything that's going through your head, but just remember, there's being a beginner and being an idiot. Best way to think about it is, 'Is this something I can get better at? Do I want to get better at it?' If the answer is yes, you're in beginner territory."

"What's idiot territory?"

Lawrence pursed his lips. "'I wasn't able to be and do everything she wanted here, so that means I'm wrong for her, or I'll never be good enough for her.' Most of us have been there. Especially if the woman in question matters, and unless we have more cockiness than good sense. These women are good at cutting cockiness down to size, quite literally, if it calls for it."

"I seen that, no question." Rev managed a smile.

"This group of Mistresses, they know their own strengths and weaknesses, and if the weaknesses bother them, they fix them. They don't ask for validation. And they pay attention."

Lawrence leaned against the wall next to him, hooking a finger in his jeans pocket. "They want to notice everything about you, want to know how they can bring things out in you that they'll enjoy the hell out of, but there's a generosity to it. They want you to find your feet in your submission to them, a strength and steadiness that can carry you in the world. Sometimes, when you've dealt with a lot of shit in your life, or your other relationships, you think that kind of level ground is a damn unicorn you're never going to find."

Rev studied the man. "You had a woman like that."

Lawrence nodded, his gaze straight ahead. "It was tough. Her alcoholism only made it worse, and I let myself become part of the whole tangled mess, which, worst of all, didn't help her. Rosalinda helped me figure it out."

His jaw flexed. "A big step in finding that level ground is realizing what happens here is a two-way street. The Mistresses come for what they need, for healing and steadying, as much as the subs do. It works, man. It just works, in ways hard to explain."

He tilted his head toward Rev. "And there's no need to feel uncertain or worried about any of it. In a world where that's all we do sometimes, this is an oasis. If you're lucky, you find the Mistress who'll want to keep you as much as you want to keep her, and you'll have that oasis out in the world, not just here."

Lawrence didn't look like the type of man who indulged in poetic musings, but Rev thought the former SEAL wouldn't see what he'd just said that way. He'd just stated the truth he had inside him.

"Thanks," Rev said. "That helps."

Lawrence nodded. "If you want, I can give you my digits, so if something comes up on the sub side of thing you'd like to talk about with another male sub, one that's part of their circle, you can."

"I don't carry a phone, but if you okay telling me where to find you, a place where it not a problem looking you up, that'd be good."

"Sure thing." Lawrence reached into his back pocket to pull out his wallet and remove a card from it. "I work at this youth rec center, as a coach and anything else they need. You can find me there most days. Leave me a message if I'm not there, and let me know how I can find you."

Rev told Lawrence about the school and the church. "Those are the places I'm at most times."

"Got it."

"How am I doing with Ros and the rest?"

"Not what you need to be concerned about." Lawrence's green and gold eyes met his. "If you take care of her, that part takes care of itself. Understand?"

"I do. I wouldn't hurt her for anything in the world."

"Good."

Rev pressed his lips together. "I don't want to pry into things she hasn't decided are my business, but her family...her born family...they hurt her bad, didn't they?"

"Enough that she rarely talks about them to anyone." Lawrence's expression tightened. He paused, maybe thinking through what he could say while respecting Vera's privacy. Rev stayed silent, wanting whatever Lawrence could offer.

"The first couple of years Rosalinda knew her, Vera left on vacations at Christmas and Easter. The assumption was she went to see family, but she was doing destination holiday vacations on her own. If that helped her, Rosalinda would have left her to it. Maybe even made up an excuse to join her, because though she loves her, Rosalinda's mom drives her crazy."

Lawrence's lips tipped up. "But when Vera came back to work, she always seemed down in the dumps, which isn't her usual gear. So after Rosalinda learned the truth, she told Vera her ass was expected at their holiday celebrations—hers, Skye's or Cyn's. Abby doesn't have any other family, either, so coming to those events with her helped Vera feel more okay about it. And when everyone got paired up, the options only expanded." Lawrence half smiled. "My mother and sisters had us all down at their place last Thanksgiving. That was an experience."

Lawrence's gaze moved back toward the restrooms. "For more, you'll have to ask Vera. But tread with care. It's a wound that still bleeds."

Veracity had emerged. She'd retrieved that little pillbox hat with a net over her eyes from the coat check before she went to freshen up.

As she adjusted it, Rev noticed she'd left the black gloves off, so he could still see the mesh gloves that left the black tipped nails unencumbered. He remembered the bite of them on his skin, the promise of pain. More, if he wanted it. If she decided he wanted it.

"See you later, man." As Lawrence moved away from Rev, he stopped to speak to Vera. She smiled and nudged him with her hip, an intimate familiarity, before he moved on.

It got Rev to thinking. When he and Vera came together in the middle of the hallway, her gaze was coursing over him with appreciation. He'd donned the shirt after the flogging, but she'd had him leave it open, the tie folded in his pocket.

"You look like you want to ask me something, Rev."

"Is Lawrence one of the subs you been with here? Before Ros and he got together? If it's okay to ask that, Mistress."

He added the courtesy, but the words held an edge he needed to get rid of fast. He had no hold on her. No hold on anyone. What God gave, God could take away.

The thought conjured Teena Joy and his mother, but he wouldn't let this be about that. This was about the things he needed to learn about this world, to decide if he could handle them.

"No." The touch of kindness in her tone told him she understood what he was feeling. "Lawrence was hired to provide protection when Ros was under threat from a local gang. He wasn't part of this world," she gestured around her at the club, "though he was in the lifestyle. We could tell when Ros decided he was hers, even before she acknowledged it herself, so he was off limits. Except under her supervision."

"You've...shared him?" His brows rose.

"Once. It was an acceptance ritual. When each of them chose the man she wanted to keep forever, we celebrated and confirmed it among our circle. It differed from man to man, and Lawrence's ritual was the most hands-on."

She said it so matter-of-factly, but it sent his mind spinning again. Dismay, arousal, uncertainty, need. Each time he thought he had a handle on it, the emotions kept surging up, like when rough weather was stirring up the Mississippi, so cat's paws slapped the bulkheads and sent explosions of foam and river water up onto the land. That ambush meeting in her office, the reaction of his family he still wasn't sure how to handle, was part of the boiling mixture. It made all of it even more of a struggle to get hold of.

As long as he was sure of the ground under his feet, he could handle a storm. What was making him feel unstable wasn't something he was sure he should tell her. But she didn't leave him any choice.

She laid a hand on his arm. "Tell me."

He tipped his head, cracking his neck, and closed his eyes, thinking it through before he spoke. "When I was little, and first understood what death was, I was afraid. Then Teena Joy say to me, 'Imagine you standing in front of the door to a new place, and there's a welcome sign and pots of flowers around it, like our porch. Now imagine you wearing your favorite outfit, the one you most like to wear, that's the most comfortable. So comfortable you've worn it out.'"

That's your body, honey. It's taken such good care of you, and it's ready to lie down and let you go. You step out of it and through that door, and God's there. There's nothing to be afraid of, letting go when love is there to catch you. And if you believe it is, it is.

"What you did with me the other night...it gave me that feeling. That if I let go, you're there. Tonight I don't know if that feeling was right. Or if it's like football. You feel good about learning how to catch the ball and run with it, but that don't mean the NFL is looking for you."

So much was pushing and pulling inside him. The singing had helped, but the aftermath, and even the conversation with Lawrence, reassuring as it was, tangled up his mind and gut again. He was like one of the kids, messed up over a crush, all wild and excited one moment, and afraid and tense the next. He wasn't sure he liked the feeling.

"You have a lot to think about." She laced her fingers with his. "How does this feel?"

"Good. But I'm doubting it means the same thing to both of us."

"Is that necessary?" Her gaze remained steady, expression neutral.

That didn't help, but he thought of her guidance earlier. "I don't know. You said that's an okay thing to say."

"Always, as long as it's honest."

"I not sure if that's what I'm being. I not sure of anything in my head."

"What do you usually do when you're confused or uncertain?"

"I pray," he said simply. "I ask God to show me the right way. Then I let it go until that happens. But I feel...I don't want to mess things up with you. I've never wanted like this. Wanted a woman like this."

Her eyes softened and she stroked his jaw. "Do you want to learn to drive?"

He blinked. "What?"

"You said you don't drive. Would you like to learn? We could get together sometime soon, and I can give you some driving lessons. Then you can teach me something I don't know how to do." Her eyes laughed up at him. "Maybe how to sing. We'll learn from one another."

He'd been worried he'd hurt or offended her with his uncertainty. He hadn't. And with the simple offer, she'd told him her knowledge wasn't a way to hold power over him, but a gift she was offering, while asking for the same from him. She was teaching him, and willing to be taught. He gripped her hands. "Okay."

When she took his arm, he looked into her large, silver eyes that offered so many things to him. "I'm here for you, Mistress," he said. "Whatever you need."

A quiver ran through her, a line to a deeper place that seemed to twine itself around his fingers as she slid her hand up to overlap his wrist and knuckles. "Thank you, Rev." A pause, then again. "Thank you."

Her eyes glistened, as if what he'd said had inspired tears. His brow furrowed, and he opened his mouth to ask what was going on.

"Mistress Vera, hold up."

Trey and Sy were coming down the hall toward them, so the moment to ask about that reaction was gone. Rev would roll with it, but he wouldn't forget.

"Mistress." Sy nodded to her respectfully. "We wanted to ask Rev something, if we're not interrupting."

"You are, but go ahead and ask." Her tone was reproving, but her smile was indulgent.

"We'll make it quick." He turned to Rev. "Our lead singer took off with his current girlfriend to California, and we don't know when he'll be back, so we've been looking for fill-ins for the bookings we had before he got lovesick. Me and Trey and the rest of his roommates who make up the band can do backup vocals, but we're musicians. None of us have the punch to be lead. Would you be interested? We have a gig coming up at The Blue Lizard."

Rev blinked. "I sing hymns and songs like I did tonight, ones that we borrow because they fit with worship. I not sure I can sing the way you need."

"Singing is singing," Sy said with a touch of impatience. "What I heard tonight, you can do it."

"Chill, man." Trey elbowed him, then directed his next words to Rev. "We can get together to go over sets between now and then at a time that works for all of us. See if you're comfortable with it. If not, nothing lost, and we can have a good jam session. Sy just freaks out over this stuff."

"Because I like to be paid and not get yelled at by pissed-off club managers who think we didn't deliver what we promised." Sy glanced at Rev. "Seriously, I have no worries. If you do as well as I think you will, Chris can stay in Cali with that fucking groupie until they fall into the ocean."

"Sy," Trey said.

Sy shot Vera an apologetic look but added, "He left us hanging. That shit about musicians being unreliable and flaking out because it's part of their 'art' doesn't wash with me. Bite off your ear and mail it to your girlfriend if that's your kink, but slap on a band-aid and show the hell up when a commitment's been made."

"Some say his friend Paul cut it off when they got into a sword fight," Rev said. "Van Gogh didn't want his friend to get into trouble, so he said he did it himself."

He offered a faint smile for their bemused expressions. "Savita, a student at my school, she did a report on him and told me that."

"Rev works at a middle school," Vera told them.

"Oh. All the better," Sy pressed on. "So you don't have to work on weekends."

Trey punched his shoulder. "One track mind. What do you say, Rev? Are you interested? I'm serious about that jam session. You're not locked into anything."

"Okay," Rev said. "I'll do it."

When he agreed, he had that thoughtful, internal look. As Vera let the men work out the details of when and where they'd be getting together, she noticed Ros at the end of the hall, waiting to talk to her.

Vera put a hand on Rev's arm. "I'll be back in a moment. Don't go away."

"You're my ride," he said, making her smile.

Vera pinched Sy's tribal tattoo covered biceps, hard enough to leave a mark. Which grabbed his attention, for multiple reasons. She pointed a chiding finger at him.

"Keep being this wound up, and I'll turn you over to Cyn. Mick is okay with her doing sessions in his absence, as long as no sex is involved. She'll torment you with orgasm denial. She can make two hours feel like ten days."

"Yeah, that'll help calm me down," he noted dryly, but he dipped his head, a formal apology. "Got it, Mistress. Chris just pissed me off. I need to let it go. Lead singers can be diva dicks. No offense," he added to Rev.

"I never thought of myself as a lead singer," he said. "But I expect if I acted like that, God would cut me down to size. Hopefully using her." He nodded toward Vera.

The two men chuckled in appreciation—and understanding. "Amen to that," Sy said.

Vera shook her head at them and moved to join Ros. As she did, another Domme passed her, Lace M. Tight. Laci had her single tail out and was practicing some flourishes as she moved. It swept around her like a serpent, wrapped her hips and thighs loosely before falling away and coiling at her feet like a semi-tame pet.

"Do you sleep with that thing?" Vera asked

Laci winked at her. "Only the cane comes to bed with me. If a man going down on me isn't doing it right, a couple pops gets his tongue working properly." She glanced toward Rev. "He doesn't look like he needs that kind of help."

"Not so far. But rewards for expertise can look a lot like punishment sometimes."

Laci chuckled and continued on her way, letting Vera do the same.

"I wanted to touch base before you head out," Ros said when Vera reached her. "Everything good?'

"He's spun up, but his head space is getting back where it needs to be. I'll keep in contact with him over the next couple of days just to be sure of it."

Ros lifted a hand to study her manicure. She liked wearing her nails longer, just as Vera did, even though Skye rolled her eyes at the extra key strikes or wonky touch screens that happened because of the dual contact between fingertip and fingernail.

"You make things harder on yourselves than needed," she'd told them, using her digital disapproving teacher voice. But she hadn't argued with Ros's response.

"Trim my nails so I can do texts and email? Or keep them long so that when I have Lawrence tied to my bed, I can leave deeper marks on his gorgeous back, ass and thighs. Let me think about that for half a second..."

Ros examining her nails now was calculated, her way of saying she was waiting for Vera to answer the question she'd actually asked. Sometimes having Dommes for friends could be a pain in the ass.

"He's digging into some old wounds, I won't deny it. It's not intentional," she said, when Ros's mouth tightened. "He's just pure raw submissive. This is all new to him, but he's been immersed in the need so long it pulls him in over his head without much effort. It's a pleasure to watch."

"But it requires you to be more on your toes than you have to be with the experienced ones."

"Yes. He's worth the effort, though." Vera looked over her shoulder. The moment she did, Rev's gaze moved to her to see what she needed. She gave him an "I'm fine" nod.

"Clearly." Ros's cerulean eyes sparked. "We're headed out. Morning meeting tomorrow with K&A's marketing people. If you want to spend more time here tonight, you can come in late."

"No. This is his first time in a club. Best to call it an early night, and you'll need Skye and Cyn with you, so I'll hold the fort at the office."

"You might change your mind about that, even if the decision isn't made here." Ros gave her a significant look, prompting Vera to turn around.

The other men had departed. Rev was back to waiting for Vera.

On his knees.

He'd knelt in the center of the open area. Hands on his thighs, head bowed.

"You know where we are if you need anything," Ros said.

Her words followed Vera, because her desires already had her in motion, headed back toward him.

When she reached Rev, he lifted his head. His look took her breath. "What are you doing?" she asked.

"Waiting for you. Working on what's in my head. Here, in this place, if someone kneeling like this, for a Master or Mistress, no one say anything to him. They cut around him, give him peace and quiet. I needed that."

"You were impersonating a sub to be left alone." She felt gentle amusement. "Except you're not impersonating. You're being yourself. Let me drop you off at home, Rev."

"I'll take the bus. There's a stop close. I like riding at night. Staying on it a couple rounds give me time to clear my head."

"Are you telling me that's what you want to do?"

"Yeah. But I'm also asking if it okay with you, Mistress."

She studied his eyes, his manner, how he held himself. Letting a sub be on his own when his head wasn't entirely right was a judgment call, deciding if he needed the space, and had the steadiness to be okay. In this case, that care also warred with a personal desire. She didn't want to let him go.

It could skew the judgment of a Domme, feeling this much. "One condition. There's a drugstore nearby. I want to buy you a cell phone. You'll text me periodically tonight and tomorrow. I want to make sure you're all right."

"It not the first time in my life my head been messed up, Mistress." He pointed upward, the corner of his mouth tilting. "I got a direct line to Someone to help me get it straight. Don't need no minutes or call plan. But if you want that, I don't want you worrying. I'll pay for it, though.

"And I like the idea of learning to drive," he added. "If we took a trip somewhere, I could help. I want you to know I can do that, serve you how you need me to."

His earnestness affected her, but she covered it with an arch look. "Zodiac has driven for a race team. There's no vehicle he doesn't know how to handle. That's how he earned the right to drive my car from the front door to valet parking. You'll be learning on a car I borrow. And before you start talking about camels, my Aston Martin will be cremated with me, just like Tiger's motorcycles. I'll use a straw to suck the ashes through that needle's eye."

She liked seeing him laugh. They collected their jackets and left the club, walking companionably to the drugstore. After getting the phone, he intended to walk her back to the club, but the bus stop was along the way, and by the time they'd reached it, she'd changed her mind.

"I'm going to ride with you. When you decide to get off at home, I'll take it back here."

"I won't let you ride the bus alone this time of night."

She enjoyed the tingle his intriguing alpha protector side sent through her. "You said you like to ride it a couple times around to get your thoughts together. So we'll do that, and I'll get off here on one of the passes."

"What about your car?"

"Club's open another five hours. Zodiac will have it ready when I get back." She nodded toward the road. "Here comes a bus now. Should we grab it?"

~

This time of night, the bus was mostly for working folks getting on or off shift, or running after-work errands. Both of them were over-dressed for riding, but they knew under the suit, Rev was one of them.

His Mistress was a different matter, and got a second look from everyone. He'd guided her toward a middle seat rather than further toward the back, where trouble sometimes slouched. He also gave her the inside seat. He didn't want to be presumptuous, but he slid an arm across the back, making it clear the role he'd take for her if anyone let the devil guide them.

She sat with elegance, crossing her ankles and adjusting so she was partly turned toward him, leaning against his side. With her hair curling around her face, he wanted to touch. At a slight nod, a flicker of her eyes, she gave him that right. He curled a lock over one finger, brushed his others over her smooth cheek, the firm bone.

She put her hand on his thigh and whispered in his ear. "No talking unless I ask you a question. Or you have something that can't wait."

It didn't take long to realize that order was for him. He didn't have to come up with things to say. He could swim in the high tide waters of everything about tonight, deal with the chop and sudden swells of feeling that lifted him above his comfort zone, but was still a lifting up.

There were a few valleys he couldn't really explain, a raw feeling in his gut. When those happened, her hand, which had found his when he lowered it, would tighten, her fingers stroking his palm. It told him how closely she was tracking his mood shifts.

With a little sigh, she put her head down on his shoulder, a surprising move. Resting his jaw against her hair, he closed his eyes. Letting out his own sigh, he settled into an easier place. Hands linked with his Mistress, together and traveling through the New Orleans night.

"Thank you, Rev," she said at length. "For everything you gave me tonight. You were honest and generous with your feelings. You were everything I need you to be."

Need. It was an unexpected choice of words. Want and desire, those things she'd been very clear about. The word need reminded him of his desire to stand in her darker, deeper places. Be there for her.

Maybe it was more of a need than a desire, too.

That day at the mailbox, she'd talked about how people didn't need to get all wrapped up in finding someone, that that would take care of itself. That they needed to focus on how others needed them.

But it was hard not to get wrapped up in it, especially when right now he was contemplating this miracle, not only of finding her, but hearing that she might need him too. If it was leaning that way, for them to need each other, he couldn't ask for more.

She tensed, and he opened his eyes. She was staring through the window at a run-down shoebox of a house. A crooked For Sale sign was in the front yard.

"Mistress?"

A single word question, which he assumed didn't break the rules. "Thomas Rose Associates supports a domestic abuse shelter," she said. "Laurel Grove. Ros and Abby founded it, in honor of a friend they lost to an abusive husband."

"I'm sorry. Was her name Laurel? If it's okay to ask."

"Yes."

He squeezed her hand and bowed his head. He said a short prayer for Laurel on her current journey, and for the healing and redemption of the broken spirit who'd taken her life. Then he lifted his head. "Why does the house make you sad?"

She'd been watching him, and took an extra beat answering. "A family lived there. We were trying to convince the woman to come to us, and bring her two boys. We didn't convince her in time. Her drug dealing boyfriend killed her and shot her oldest boy when he tried to stop him. The youngest is with a good foster family, but he has a lot of problems. Probably because the night before it happened, a buddy of the boyfriend's shot him up with heroin as a joke. That was what made the mother unleash on him. He got pissed off and…"

She stopped, probably because the hardness in his expression, the regret and anger, told her he'd recognized the story. "The older boy went to our school," he explained. "I remember him. The kids made a memorial wreath and took it to his funeral. I glad his younger brother is with people who want to help him. Even if they can't…it better than being with those who don't care. Nothing harder to see than that. Lot of the teachers, they know those kinds of kids.

"We all try to show them they do have people that care," he added, "if they just can turn to us when they need to. Some of them kids, they got so much on 'em."

"Yeah." She sat back against the curve of his arm. As she did, he started to hum, something soothing and soft. She put her head on his shoulder again. "You make it really difficult to let you go, Rev. To behave as I should."

"How should you behave?"

"As you get introduced to all this, I have to be careful. I can't get lost in my own head and needs."

He touched her cheek, so she would look up at him. "I a student on what you showed me tonight," he told her. "But that's where it stops, Veracity. I not going to school. I'm spending time with you, as interested in you as any of the rest of it. It's about you and me."

"I'm not meaning it in an offensive way."

"I just want you to understand my feeling on it. I'm not a child, and you holding back on me, because you think you have to protect me like one…that won't work."

"It's not like that." Her tone cooled. "I told you exploring this can break open things you don't expect. Me looking out for you on that is no different from you riding the bus back to the club with me. To make sure I'm all right."

He gazed at her a long moment. When he spoke, he didn't address the last comment, because he knew that wasn't the important one. "Teachers protect their students, holding back on them, because they know, at the end of the day, the week, the year... they have to let them go."

He could tell he'd found the nail and hit it square. When she responded, it sounded like she didn't much care for the words herself. "Rev, it's very likely after you explore this, you'll want different things. To expand your reach, to grow in this lifestyle. That may require moving on to different Dommes. It's the difference between a childhood crush and your first real relationship.

"I'm not saying that's what this is. But while we're on the topic of teachers, why don't you take Mavis up on her offer to get you into some adult classes? I know you don't believe God doesn't want you to get an education."

~

Rev's expression went to stone, the one Vera had seen in the office with Witford. She was off her game if she'd made such an idiotic mistake. Normally she was the one Ros called into a meeting to be diplomatic, to smooth things out. She'd gotten defensive. Rev wasn't the only one who'd needed space.

"I done told you why, and it was honest. And it hasn't changed." He leaned in, their eyes close. "When you been hurt bad, you avoid being cut again. Just natural, going that way, and I hate that you been hurt like that. But courage don't exist without fear, do it? I think you're a courageous woman, Veracity Morgan. I sure hope you can spare some of it toward me, because I ain't no crush. You teaching me things, but I also know things."

He pulled the cord, and she saw they were back at the club. He rose and offered her a hand. Silently, she gave it to him, and he took her down the bus steps. The stop was a rock's throw from the club's well-lit parking lot, and there was security circling, so he kept his hand on the door and foot on the step, letting the driver know he wasn't leaving.

Rev leaned forward and brushed his mouth over hers. His big hand gripped the lapel of her jacket, and then he got back on the bus.

As the doors closed and the bus rolled away, he'd found their seat again, and was watching her through the glass. She didn't raise a hand and neither did he.

She'd pissed him off, and he'd pissed her off. But was he wrong, in what he'd said about her? She had to consider it, even as she needed to make it clear she damn well would look out for his headspace and physical well-being when he was under her command.

She wondered what she would text him when she checked on him later tonight.

It took a couple hours to work it out, and even then she found herself hesitating. But in the end, she sent it.

I want you, Rev. In ways that aren't smooth and familiar to me, so I took a wrong turn tonight. I'm sorry. If the road gets bumpy...well, I want to say I'll make sure you're wearing a seatbelt and get us through. Not because I think you're a child who can't protect himself. But because I want you to take that ride with me and make it a journey worth sharing. Respond to me tonight, so I'll know you're all right.

The answer, when it came, made her smile and feel the sting of tears.

I wanted to take a drive with you the first time I saw you, Mistress. You check on my seat belt and I'll check on yours. Think we both gonna need it.

CHAPTER TWELVE

"*L*et's start with this passage," Witford said, marking the page. "Then I can expound on it some and you come in at this point, do a song with the choir that ties it back into the last part of the scripture. Beverly has some ideas for that."

Rev, who'd stopped his task to come stand by the pulpit with him, gave the page a close scrutiny, lips moving as he digested the important parts of what was there. "You could do that verse from Matthew we talked about. It would drive the point home even better."

"Yeah, you're right." Witford made the notation. "Might have to shorten the music program, though. Don't want the women in the congregation taking me to task for overcooking the Sunday pot roasts. You cut it close the other day, with Mrs. Jones and her cancer."

"God might have thought that more important than your invitation to those dinners." Rev gave him an amused look. "You miss a few, you might lose a couple pounds."

Witford snorted, but ran a hand over his abdomen to confirm it was trim. "Don't be teasing me, boy. A man of God should look like he takes care of the temple."

"Long as he ain't so busy maintaining it, he forget what it for. What it serves."

"Now you're sounding like Teena Joy." Witford pointed to the nave. "What do you call dusting the pews?"

Rev glanced down at the can of wood polish and rag he was carrying. "I like to think about the people who sit here, absorb the feelings they left behind, what they came in with, what they left with."

"I'm surprised you have the time. You've been busy."

Rev's attempt at their normal banter vanished. "Don't go down that road again, Witford. I still not right with what you did."

Witford marked the page and closed the Bible. "Then let's talk it out, man to man. It doesn't bother you that she doesn't share our faith?" He gestured at the silver cross on Rev's neck. "The one Teena Joy taught you?"

"Veracity don't share my religion. That a whole different thing. It not our way, but it a different way. Like two paths that lead to the same waterfall. She tell me, in her faith, they say 'And it harms none, do as you will.' In ours, we say 'Do unto others as you would have them do unto you.' Both of them mean to love one another."

Witford frowned. "A lot of our parishioners wouldn't see it that way. But putting that aside, she's taking your focus away from here. That affects your faith. It affects your care for your family. Tisha thinks you're making a mistake, and it's upsetting her. This woman turned her back on her family because of her beliefs. And family is the heart of faith."

Witford had done some deep digging on his Mistress, maybe getting some of the answers that Rev himself wanted more details about. But he wanted those to come from Veracity, when she was ready to reveal them. Witford's disrespect of her privacy didn't please Rev. "Her family turned their back on her because of their beliefs, not hers. You good with words, Witford, but I know music. There are no wrong chords when I'm with her."

Witford's jaw tightened. "A man can be led from below the waist, Rev. Even one as tapped into the Lord as you are. Satan's always watching. The way she likes to enjoy men..."

Rev's expression stopped Witford. Rev waited a beat to reinforce it before speaking. "I holding my temper because you're having the conversation you should have done with me first, but we're not talking about that. Understand?"

"No. I don't. The way she enjoys men is unnatural, and she's enjoyed a lot of them. If you go down that road—"

"I have gone down that road with her, Witford." Rev met Witford's startled look. Had he let his temper say something he shouldn't have said? If so, he would draw that line here and now, but he'd make his feelings on it clear. "There's nothing unnatural about it. Just the opposite. But discussing that is done. I mean it in a way I hope you're hearing. It between her and me. When she comes here, I expect you to treat her the way you would anyone else. If you can't be warm to her, you'll be courteous."

"Or what, Rev? You threatening to leave us?"

Astonishment filled Rev. "What put that fool thought in your head?"

"You're part of the backbone of this church, Rev, and I'm seeing the possibility of a cancer. Do you respect me? Value my opinion?"

"Course I do."

"Then hear me. She may be a fine person, no matter if I don't agree with her beliefs or what she does in her bedroom. But those things make her wrong for you. She is too much part of the world outside, Rev."

"That not for you to judge, Witford."

"I'm a preacher. A spiritual leader for our community." Witford drew himself up. "I pray just as much as you do, and you have a blind spot. I feel it the way Tisha does. What this woman is will change you, break you down."

"Our Lord breaks us down to build us back up new, square in His ways and light. It make sense that there are people in our life He uses to do that."

"Do you really think a pagan into BDSM is God's instrument? Do you hear how that sounds?" Witford stabbed the pulpit with a finger. "There's a special power to you, in your voice, in your heart, strong and pure. You're smart enough to know it, no matter how humble you are about it. And it is susceptible to corruption.

"You said you've gone down roads with this woman, with the way she wants things." At Rev's warning look, he held up a hand. "I'm not getting into that. But I know enough about it to ask you this question. Surrender is important to you. How easy would it be to confuse submission to God with—"

"Witford."

When he used that tone at Veracity's offices, it had startled her people. But it came to him the way the music did, when needed. The one-word warning settled uneasily between him and his cousin, a blanket on a slumbering beast with plenty of teeth. Rev thought of Veracity, standing over him, ordering him to put his mouth upon her, and how those moments made him feel.

He wasn't confused. Not about that.

"All right." Witford pressed his lips together. "But let me say this and I'll be done. Sex feels like something divine, sacred, and it is, in the natural expression of it between man and wife. But its power to make us feel closer to God can be used by the Adversary, a mask of his intent. Just think about it, Rev. You're worrying me, hurting Tisha, spending more time away from the church. No, you're not neglecting your duties, but you used to spend most of your free time here. Now you're not. So what do you think that means? Where do you think it leads?"

As Rev stayed silent, his cousin's words pelting him like stones, Witford lifted his Bible and stepped back from the pulpit. "Bid this woman good-bye, and put her behind you. Will you promise to think about it?"

Rev met his gaze. "I promise to pray about this."

"That's all I ask." Witford clasped Rev's shoulder. The fingers digging into his shoulder communicated his feelings on the subject. "I'm your cousin. I want you to be happy, and I want what's best for you." His mouth tightened. "It hurts me to say it, because I know you care about her, but I can promise you, she's not it. Whatever you need, it's here, in these walls, with your family and this congregation."

When Rev had left Veracity after their bus ride, things hadn't been right between them, but she'd given him the space he needed. Witford had just dumped garbage into it.

Last night, Rev had gotten off the bus at the school and gone to the shed. He liked the way the moonlight reflected on the trees, and seeing the animals that ventured out of the woods behind the fence after dark. He'd sat on the bench and traced those four words, smooth and silky as Veracity's skin, because he'd touched them as often as he wanted to touch her.

Since he didn't make a promise lightly, now he went out to the garden and sat. He didn't feel like praying. That sent up alarm flags, so he tried to set aside his gut level rejection of Witford's words and think about the path he'd insisted upon for Rev's benefit. Walking away from Veracity Morgan and what she offered him.

Rev had only been in love twice in his life. Both times had been short. Once when he was twelve, and once when he was twenty, with the young woman he'd told Veracity about. She'd been accepted to a college a couple states over, so they'd only had the summer after she graduated high school to be together. Teena Joy hadn't interfered, but in hindsight Rev knew his aunt had known it would only last for those two months. Michelle wasn't interested in a long-distance relationship, especially when she got around college friends and a life so much different from the one Rev led...and so much different from Rev.

It had hurt, a lot. Teena Joy had told him that love could be that way. "But God knows what he's doing, Rev. She wasn't the right person for forever. She just helped you learn more about love so when that right person comes along, you'll be ready for her."

"How will I know?"

"She'll be right with God, too, and you'll feel that. And when you look in her eyes, and she looks in yours, you'll see one another, and nothing will tell you different, no matter how anyone tries. Just like your love for God."

Rev let out a tired breath. Yeah, there it was. The truth he needed. Let go of control, and it came. Always. He'd learned to do that early in his life. Be willing to be guided by the right things, but not to be misled.

Rev handled those attempts to mislead him by planting his feet like a mule and letting the other person tire themselves out, pulling on the bridle until they realized he wasn't going to be moved by them. Only by the will of God.

Witford had got ahold of that bridle, all right. Maybe even convinced Rev to take a couple steps in his direction, but Teena Joy's words brought Rev back to himself.

Would she have liked Veracity? Or would she have had the same worries Witford had? He thought both might be true, and spending time with Veracity would have helped end those worries.

He returned to the church and went to Witford's office. His cousin sat at his big desk, staring at his computer. The bookshelf behind him was full, holding the sixty-six books of the Bible broken down as individual volumes, as well as books written to help preachers reach the congregation and counsel their parishioners, addressing the challenges in their lives with the Word.

A printout of his current in-process sermon was by his elbow, marked in red. A half empty cup of coffee and an energy bar were next to it. Witford worked long hours, as most preachers did, though lately more than a few of those hours seemed to be with their bigger donors on golf courses or going to fancy parties.

His cousin and aunt both said it was to keep the donations coming for their community programs and the needs of congregation members when they hit hard times. Okay, but sometimes he wondered if Witford remembered that was why he was supposed to be doing it, rather than liking the way it felt to be seen with powerful people. Or if Tisha bought fancier clothes and jewelry for reasons other than what she told Rev.

"Blending in with the bigger donors, being seen as one of them because of the way I dress and the jewelry I wear, is a way to make them feel more comfortable about their donations."

That was something he prayed about, too. Rev leaned in the doorway, waiting until Witford looked up. "I'm singing Friday night."

"What?" Witford glanced at his calendar. "We don't have anything on the schedule."

"It not for the church. It's a club on Frenchmen Street. Two fellows in a band need a singer for the night. Gonna be some good music, Witford, and I know you and your wife like dancing. Maybe we can even get Tisha to come, stay up past her bedtime."

Witford didn't smile. He tapped a pencil against his papers. "Did you hear a word I said?"

"I did." Rev kept his voice steady. "I glad you care about me, Witford. I love my family, I love this church, I love God. But I also am falling in love with a woman who I know, in my heart, is part of God's plan for me. I considered your words, now I need you to do the same you asked of me. Trust what I feel."

Witford's expression stayed flat. "I don't know if I can do that, Rev. But you're going to do what you're going to do, and we'll do what we'll do."

Rev stared at him. "How about we pray together a few minutes, Witford? Just go out to the garden and pray."

"I've got a sermon to finish so I can do my job on Sunday. So maybe later. If that's all..." Witford put his head back down, and started scribbling in the margins.

It made Rev uneasy, to leave it like this. But maybe he needed to give Witford time to mull on it. "All right, then. I'll see you Sunday."

"Yeah. See you then."

Witford's tone said he wasn't sure they *would* see one another, that Rev's loyalty and commitment were in doubt. His cousin was good at turning a congregation toward the mood he wanted them to have, to get them to question themselves, their faith, and work harder at it. Usually Rev thought that was an admirable talent. His cousin's focus might seem, in his opinion, too much on the collection plate, but the church had bills to pay, and Witford and Tisha needed a living to support themselves. Running the church was their full-time job. As it had once been his.

Troubled, Rev left him. He put the cleaning supplies back in their cabinet and bid Mrs. Byrd a good day before heading out to catch the bus.

~

Witford watched him through the window, a hundred thoughts weaving through his mind, like a needle stabbing through stiff cloth. He had to fix this. He wasn't sure how, but while his concerns were practical as well as spiritual, his mother's feelings on it had been accelerating like a rocket, ever since the meeting in Vera Morgan's office.

She'd weep one moment and rant the next, telling him to take a more aggressive stance with Rev. Tisha was a devout woman with an intense dedication to her family and the congregation. She saw most things through that lens. Her way was the right way. Witford and Rev had even joked about it before, cousin to cousin, but always with affection.

This was different. The years had increased the responsibilities on Witford's shoulders, and deepened Tisha's certainty about the path the church had to follow, as well as Rev's role in it.

You're a good preacher, Witford, but Rev is the personal touch with the congregation. You're our mind, but he's our heart. If we lose him... And beyond that, I promised Teena Joy, and we're failing her. You hear me? We're failing her.

She'd locked herself in her bedroom that night, saying she had a sick headache. Ever since, her behavior toward Witford had been sullen. She expected him to fix this.

Losing her sister had been hard, and she seemed panicked at the idea that she was going to mess up the care and protection she'd promised toward the nephew Teena Joy had raised as her own son.

He shouldn't have told her what he'd learned about Veracity Morgan and the women at TRA, sexual Dominants active in the BDSM scene in New Orleans. Though he tried to talk her out of it, Tisha had called up computer images of men on their knees, led around by leashes. Women beating them with floggers.

One of the pictures had been particularly horrifying, a man on a cross like the Lord's, head bleeding from a thorny crown and barbed wire wrapped around his arms and thighs. Two women were on their knees before him, with their mouths on his genitals.

Witford knew such things were out there, and that they didn't necessarily show their best face on the Internet, no more than porn showed the best side of sex with a woman you loved, like he loved Yolanda, his own wife. He cared for her by making sure she had the things she wanted to have. But the images had shocked Tisha, and led to more hysterical insistence that they had to do something. They had to save Rev from this woman.

Witford knew Rev had a good and steady mind. He supported the things that were Witford's business without interfering in them, even if of late he'd been making some observations that nettled Witford some. It wasn't Rev's way to shove his opinions down someone's throat, though.

But hearing his cousin was going to play music in a blues club on Frenchmen Street was a shock. Maybe Tisha wasn't overreacting as much as he'd thought.

Rev was responsible for at least fifty percent of what went into their coffers, and that was good. But Rev didn't have to worry about paying the bills or handling the books. He didn't have to painstakingly outline a sermon every week. He didn't have to meet regularly with those big league donors and stroke their egos, though Witford admitted that wasn't so bad, especially when it meant he could take his wife to fancy dinners at their country clubs, or go out to parties on their yachts. That made Yolanda happy.

Oh no. Rev just stood up in church and the words and the songs came through him like a river, and the congregation got in the boat and rode that river with joy in their hearts.

That was all right, Witford reminded himself. When his mother said Rev was the heart of the church, that was all right, too. It was Witford's burden to carry, to be the practical one who handled the practical matters. A heart couldn't operate without a mind to run the rest of the body. He was the mind, and Tisha was the soul.

Up until now, that arrangement had worked. Rev had played his part, thanks to Witford keeping him untroubled by the things that could dilute the purity of that faith, of his song. But the world was coming to him anyway, and it would impact all of them if Witford didn't do something.

Witford frowned. Vera Morgan was a wealthy woman. He'd have to think of other options to discourage her interest. Unpleasant ones, but necessary.

She wasn't as invested as Rev, she couldn't be.

Yeah, Rev was mesmerizing, that voice of his, and his faith could be compelling to women, for the short run. Like Michelle, before she'd gone off to college. There'd been plenty of other women in the congregation who'd had a crush on Rev, created by that sense that he stood strong in the light of the Lord. To church women, it was as distracting as if he were a cop or fireman.

Teena Joy and then Tisha had quashed the most ill-advised of the crushes. The others burned out quickly. Over time, the woman couldn't see him as an intellectual equal, or the God thing made them feel inferior to him. They went elsewhere to fall in love and seek a family.

It wasn't the same with Vera Morgan, what was between her and Rev. Witford had felt it and so had Tisha, which was why they'd visited her to deliver the shot across the bow. But the woman wasn't listening, and Rev was getting in deeper.

Tisha had handled the ill-advised ones with frank woman-to-woman conversation. That wasn't going to work with Vera. He really shouldn't have told his mother the things that sent her to those images. She had no interest in even faking a female rapport with Vera.

Thinking about Rev and Vera like that... Witford shook his head with a quick snap, dispelling *those* images from his mind. He rubbed a hand over his face.

"Lord Almighty." Witford turned and looked at the cross on the wall. When he'd taken over the office after Teena Joy's death, it had been mounted across from her desk. After he rearranged the furniture, it was in his peripheral vision. He didn't like having it directly behind him, but it didn't feel any better where it was. Whatever energy hovered upon it sometimes felt like it was crawling up his neck.

"Yeah, we could pray together, Rev," he muttered. "But there comes a time the Lord wants us to get off our knees and act."

If he was going to pray for anything, it was that Vera Morgan would lose interest and move on before she forced Witford's hand, to preserve Rev, the church, and his mother's peace of mind.

CHAPTER THIRTEEN

The music club was a typical one for New Orleans. Too small for how many patrons it attracted, with a bar that took up a third of the space. The walls, mostly made up of old brick and wood trim, were covered with signed photos of those who'd performed there. The vibrations caused by the patrons and bands meant a lot of pictures were crooked.

Because Rev had asked Sy to make sure it was held for her, Vera had a front row two-person table, set off to the right, the wall at her back. Rev would be able to see her there while performing. When he left her for the stage, she would hold the seat for Mavis, who was on her way to join them. Since she'd said she'd never heard Rev sing except in her hallways, Vera wanted her to have the chance to do so. It also meant Rev would have two fans in the audience.

Like Sy, she wasn't worried that he wouldn't please the audience, but she thought her usually unflappable male needed the reminder.

"This way different from a church." He'd said that five times now. Sy had shook his hand when they arrived, clapped him on the back in welcome, and said to come up and join them when he was ready.

She covered his hand. "Are you okay? It's not like you to be nervous about singing. It's no different here than anywhere else, right? Who you're singing for, and why?"

A rueful look crossed his face. "No. It not that. I had some words with Witford. Told him he and his wife could come. He said no. They angry with me. Him and Tisha."

Knowing it wouldn't help, Vera pushed down her own anger. "Because you're doing something they don't agree with or understand."

"Yeah." He pressed his lips together.

"And they see me as the reason for it."

"Because you are." Before the defensive reaction he'd sparked could think of jumping to a flame, he put his hand on hers and doused it. "They just don't realize that's a good thing. They'll figure it out, Mistress. I know their hearts. Just the time getting through to that part of them is hard. The wait, you know. I like it much better when I waiting on a decision from you than when it's one from them."

"Hey, Rev." Sy waved to him. "Let's get this ball rolling."

She squeezed Rev's hand, letting him know she was fine with him answering Sy's call. "Try to let it go if you can. Just enjoy singing."

"Yeah." He curled both hands underneath hers, as if his palms were the nest for a baby bird. He gazed down at her fingers as if they were as precious as that tiny life. The man had such a way about him, and when his eyes lifted, serious and troubled, she had to touch, cup his jaw, stroke his cheek with her fingertips.

"It like getting stabbed by a knife and told it not life threatening," he said. "You got it all bandaged up, but it still hurts, and it's gonna, until you get some time and healing on it. I prayed about it, so I gonna let it go for now. See if I can sing for these people the way I should, with God inside me."

He lifted his gaze. "You look like someone I want to sing for all my life, Mistress. Thank you for being here. And when she get here, tell Miss Mavis I hope she'll enjoy the show and not hold it against me if it not her type of music."

"I don't think that will be a problem. I think she's coming so she can ogle you in a very un-principal-like fashion."

That startled a chuckle out of him, and he tugged her hair before he went up to the stage.

She did some ogling herself, enjoying the shift of his backside in his black jeans. He'd worn that and a snug black T-shirt that said 5 & 2 on it in teal. He'd told her it referred to the five loaves and two fish brought to Jesus's sermon, when he turned them into a feast for hundreds. "You bring the five and two to whatever's needed in your life," he told her, "and God handles the rest. That what 5&2 mean."

"Made it." Mavis plopped down into the chair Rev had vacated, making Vera start. "Didn't mean to interrupt your meditations on the cosmos. Or a fine-looking man's butt. Did I mention I'm changing the custodial staff's dress code to jeans instead of coveralls?"

"Did I mention I might break your fingers?"

Mavis chuckled. "I see we've become possessive of that fine-looking butt."

"Just protecting you from a workplace harassment suit."

"I'm nowhere near work here, thank God. I need a night around legal adults. But my fingers are safe. If I did it, Beau would break out his tight disco era bell bottoms and give me trauma. Are any of your other ladies coming?"

"Yes, but Ros said they'll squeeze in wherever they can find a place when they get here. I was able to hang onto your chair mainly because Rev was parked in it until a few minutes ago. Want a drink?"

"Please. Start with two, because the first one's going down fast. But don't let me have more than that. I have a full weekend. The adult literacy program for our kids' parents is kicking off its new rotation bright and early tomorrow, and I always show up to meet the attendees the first day, to help them feel less self-conscious about it."

Vera signaled the waitress, and they placed an order, which gave her time to consider what she was about to ask. From Rev's reaction on the bus, it was tricky terrain, but she was wired toward giving a person all available tools to succeed. Especially a person she couldn't stop thinking about. Or looking at. He was working around the other men on the small stage, getting set up, smiling at their banter.

"When you talked to Rev about improving his reading and writing skills," she asked, "did he say anything else, other than what you already told me?"

"I was worried he'd be offended, but he wasn't. He just thanked me and said he was good for now.' Mavis grimaced. "'Don't worry about me none, Miss Mavis. My English ain't pretty as your'n these kids, but no one has trouble understanding what I say.'"

She lifted a shoulder. "He's right. Honestly, as an educator, I know it sounds crazy, but I don't worry too much about him."

"Yeah." It was a message Vera kept hearing. "Does that connect to whatever it was you were reluctant to share with me, when I called you about him?"

The waitress brought the drinks. Vera offered her card for the tablet the waitress carried. "Just keep the tab open," she told her.

After the woman headed off, Mavis shot her a narrow glance. "My husband used to say you and I were friends because I needed someone in my life with my own annoying ability not to forget anything, or let it go until I had the heart of a matter."

"Strong women need other strong women." Vera clinked her glass against Mavis's. "Your hesitancy seems...personal. If you don't feel comfortable, don't share. But if you do, I'd really like to know."

A shadow crossed Mavis's gaze. "It might change how you see me. You'll decide I need psychiatric help."

Vera was startled to see the woman meant it. "I already know you need that. You work with teenagers." She kept her tone light, but added, "I respect and admire you deeply, Mavis. Whatever you tell me, I'll give weight because of that. Even if you tell me monkeys flew out of Rev's very fine butt."

"There's an image." Mavis took a swallow of her whiskey sour. "Okay. I'll tell you this up front. I don't know how to explain what I saw, or if it was right or wrong, or whatever it was. It just..."

She shook her head. "Hell. I'll just get it out. About a year ago, a man tried to grab one of our girls."

"Off the school grounds?" Alarm spiked inside Vera.

"From behind that tree where you saw Janis. She'd snuck her phone out of her locker and was texting her boyfriend, who's at another school. When she was at the chain link fence, some guy strides out of the woods, grabs her shirt and hauls her over it. He had it well planned."

If Mavis had been a wolf, her ears would have been pinned back and her fangs bared. "He stuffed a sponge into her mouth—it was soaked with a drug that disoriented her. His van, with a fake utility company magnet sign on it, was on the other side of the woods, parked at the dead end in a neighborhood."

Though Vera knew the story had to have a good ending, she was leaning forward tensely.

"Two people saw it," Mavis continued. "One was a teacher, who immediately yelled out to catch everyone's attention. I was at the basketball court, discussing school dance plans with the class president."

She took a breath. "The other was Rev. He was fixing an anchor on one of the soccer nets. When she shouted, he was already halfway across the field. He ran faster than I'd ever seen anyone run, and vaulted the fence one-handed. When he plunged into the woods, I ran after him while the teacher called the police. Thank God I was wearing athletic shoes that day."

"But I expect you didn't vault the fence." Though her tone was teasing, Vera's grip on her friend's hand wasn't.

"No. When I caught up, Rev had already laid hold of the dirtbag. Lynn rolled free and I grabbed her. She was hysterical, so I stayed with her, ready to protect her if the guy got away from Rev. I found out pretty fast I didn't have to worry about it."

Mavis took another healthy swallow of the drink, her gaze moving to Rev. His head was tilted as he listened to Trey's keyboard adjustments.

"I knew Rev was strong, but when he yanked the man away from her, his feet left the ground, and he slammed against a tree. He tried to scramble away, but Rev had him by the collar and jerked him up to his knees."

Mavis finished the first drink and gripped the second. She didn't lift it, though. She was staring at the floor. For this part, she seemed like she was deliberately not looking at Rev.

"Mavis." Her hand was stiff under Vera's touch.

"I'm all right." But it was still several moments before Mavis spoke again. "Rev got right down in his face, put two fingers against his forehead, and started whispering."

Her gaze lifted, haunted. Even in the humid close quarters of the club, Vera felt a chill. "The wind started whipping through the trees, and hand-to-God, it got dark in that little grove of trees. It was lunchtime, Vera, and no light was around us. It was just gone. I could see Rev and the man. But that was all I could see. And I shouldn't have been able to hear him, but I did. I heard every word.

"'Get out of him. Get out. In the name of God, you are not welcome here. Get out.' Things like that. The man started convulsing."

The club and musicians blurred for Vera like an unfocused lens.

Only Rev was sharply outlined. He'd taken Trey's place at the keyboard, fingers moving over it capably, as if he were showing them something about what they were planning to play.

"Rev squatted next to him." Mavis's voice was unsteady. "He was praying. Not the way you think of it, this subtle, soothing thing people do in church. It *was* quiet, his lips were moving, no sound coming out, but what he was doing, what he was wielding, it was as strong as if he were holding a sword on some kind of ancient battlefield.

"He put his hand out toward me, one finger lifted in the most commanding way I'd ever seen in my life. We held stock still, Lynn and me. The man started...growling. Then he shot up from the ground and Rev knocked him back down, did the two-finger thing against his head again."

Mavis never looked uncertain, but her expression was one of confusion and wonder. "The look on his face...I'd never seen anything like it. If you told me the archangel Michael looked like my assistant janitor, I'd tell you I totally believe it and he keeps his sword in the closet with his brooms and mops."

Vera pushed past the stunned reaction that had taken away her words. "What happened after that?"

"The cycle happened twice more. The third time was different. Something came out of the man. The wind howled like a hundred wolves, and it got so cold I saw the frost on my breath. It was *May*, Vera. May in New Orleans. Then it was gone. The cold, the wind. The darkness was still there, but it was...empty. And okay. Whatever was in that man was gone, like a suit of clothes collapsing without the person in them, only in this case it was the man, folded to the ground as if he were a suit of clothes."

Mavis gazed at the liquid shimmering in her glass. When Sy did a short drum sequence, coordinating with what Rev was doing on the keyboard, she didn't notice.

"It was so quiet. Then a bird chirped one note. Then another. The world started up again, the light, the birds, the kids in the playing fields, all of it.

"Rev helped the man sit up against the tree. He'd started to cry. Rev, this muscle in his jaw jumped as if the part of him who'd knocked the girl out of his grasp still wanted to pummel him. I sure as hell wouldn't have stopped him. But instead…" Unexpectedly Mavis's eyes glistened. Her throat was thick. "He put his arms around this wretched excuse for a human being. He laid his head on Rev's chest and wept."

Mavis lifted her brown eyes to Vera's face. "The high school did a production of Camelot a few years ago. Are you familiar with it?"

"I've seen it at some point. At least the movie."

"Live production is way better, especially with a high school cast. They put a lot into it." Mavis cleared her throat and straightened. She was pulling herself back together.

"You know the part where Lancelot brings Sir Lionel back to life, and it's implied he could do it because of the purity of his heart, his devotion to God? And he didn't doubt he could do it, because it wasn't his power. He was a conduit."

A bittersweet emotion gripped her face. "'I can cross the busiest of streets, if I'm holding my Father's hand.' Rev sang that in the halls one day. He likes putting words to that music in his head."

"Yes."

Mavis sipped the second drink. "It's more than the crazy factor that kept me from telling you. It scared the ever-living shit out of me, Vera. What he pulled out of that man was cold and dark. I know men can be evil all on their own, and they say pedophiles and molesters have something wrong in the makeup of their brains, but this… Lynn doesn't remember much about what happened after I grabbed her and held her against me, and I'm so very glad for that."

"So what happened to the man?"

Mavis's expression became thoughtful. "When the police arrived, he seemed tired. Numb. He told us he was sorry, and that was it. No bullshit protests about him being innocent or having someone call a lawyer for him.

"When I asked Rev about it, he said, 'He let the bad in. He's gotta answer for that. He's got to close up that hole, make sure nothing can get back in. To do that, he gotta do penance for the wrong that evil used his body for.'"

"Did he ever talk to you about what he did? Rev, that is?"

"I had a lot of questions. Still do. But he shut me down. Firm and gentle, like a brick wall with a mattress in front of it. Have you experienced that side of him?"

"I have."

"Catches the attention, doesn't it?" Mavis eyes glinted in a way more like her normal self. Then she sobered. "Though we try to recognize it in ourselves, the formally educated tend to hold a superiority bias toward those with less of that. Book smarts may give me access to the wisdom people have put down on a page, but that doesn't make me wise. Not heart and soul deep. Only applying those words to experience and empathy does that. He's my daily reminder of it. Not just from that extreme example, but from a lot of other things.

"He told me, 'Whatever you saw that day, Miss Mavis, was the Lord. Not me. Might as well thank my mop for cleaning the floor.'"

She downed the second drink. "Hell with it. I'm getting a third before you call me nuts."

"You told me not to let you. And you don't need it." What Vera was feeling charged her next words with sincerity. "You're the most practical person I know. That's what makes me believe every word. I just don't know how to process it."

The musicians started their opening riff with a flourish that made Vera jump. The club, already almost full when the story had started, had reached standing room only in the back. The scents and sounds hit her like a slap in the face.

With a grim and understanding smile, Mavis nodded. "That makes two of us, honey."

Vera remembered the bull, how Rev had hesitated to tell her the details. Now her imagination filled in the blanks, Rev coming up against a thousand pounds of aggravated animal, pushing his shoulder against the bull's, his grip sure on the horn, turning him in a different direction, executing a spiral to the ground as he held him. His straining muscles would have been taut, but he would have also believed they were fueled by a power beyond his own strength.

Did she believe that? She believed the Divine could do anything that was for the highest good. But like any practitioner of any religion, saying you believed it and actually believing it when it happened in your daily life... The Pharisees hadn't believed Jesus was capable of miracles, either.

She ordered Mavis a virgin drink with a skewer of fruit. When it was brought, Mavis sucked the flavor off the cherry and gave Vera a nod of thanks for watching after her. When Vera brushed a smudge of chalk off her blazer, Mavis rolled her eyes and shed the coat, putting it on the back of the chair. "I got out of there late. Otherwise I would have changed so I looked like a hot woman hanging out in a club, rather than a stodgy principal."

"You couldn't look stodgy if you tried. But here..."

Vera leaned forward and removed the combs holding Mavis's hair in a tidy twist. She fluffed it out, then unclipped a couple bracelets off her own wrist and put them on Mavis's. She flicked open an additional button on Mavis's blouse, showing a hint of white lace. "There you go, Principal Mavis. Now you letting the sexy out to play."

Mavis laughed, driving back the darker aspects of her story. The drinks had helped, Vera knew. "If only my husband was still here to witness it."

"You know Landon wasn't much for crowds, but he would have been happy for you to bring that energy home to him." Vera pointed to the stage. "There's some inspiring eye candy up there—not Rev." Her severe look at Mavis had the principal chuckling again. "And they're about to do a lot of muscle rippling and hip and booty shaking."

"Sounds like a fine time to share some details with me about your sessions with Sy and Trey." Mavis winked. "A story for a story. It's only fair. I won't ask you for the ones about Rev. At least not tonight. Ho."

"Don't make me stab you with that fruit skewer."

Trey had sat back down at the keyboard. Whatever he said to Rev had him clapping the blond man on the tattooed shoulder before he nodded to Sy on the drums and stepped up to the microphone.

The lights flickered, signaling the time for the live performance, and the club quieted down a few decibels. Then it went even more quiet as Rev opened his mouth and did what Vera had heard him do at the church.

Instead of a song with recognizable words, he uttered a single note, that connected to another, then another. Notes with a strong hint of R&B.

Sy joined in with a quiet beat on the drums. Trey and the other two members of the band did the same with their instruments, adding to the harmony, letting it build in strength at the same pace as Rev's voice. The audience responded, calling out encouragement.

Rev's eyes were closed, his hand around the base of the mic that once again wasn't switched on. His voice reached every corner and likely spilled out into the street.

A short burst of laughter came from the crowd as Trey leaned over and used a spoon to tap out a tune on three full beer mugs he'd lined up on a table beside the keyboard. The chiming notes worked with the beat. Rev swayed with it, shifting from foot to foot. As he followed the rhythm with the power and versatility of his voice, applause smattered through the audience. More calls of encouragement.

The band was staying with him, doing pure blues improv, picking up his direction, following and expanding it, bouncing off one another with skill and what she thought was a big extra dose of inspiration.

When he hit a final weeping note, she felt like the rest of the room did, as if they were connected to that stage by vibrating threads, threads they wanted to reach for and touch, ask for more of the same current to come into them. Rev had his hand outstretched as if reaching for it himself.

Then he opened his eyes and smiled at the crowd. With a spinning flourish, he produced a harmonica from his back pocket and launched into the opening of "And When I Die" by Blood, Sweat and Tears.

The crowd's response swelled, cheers and shouts of "Go on, now" and "Yeah man." When he hit the first chorus, which picked up like a train gaining steam, the crowd jumped on, ready to ride.

He put the harmonica away but kept one hand out, then up. His body never stopped moving. The crowd picked up on the clapping parts, following along with him.

All I ask of living is to have no chains on me...

He winked at Vera as he said it. A secret message, that maybe those chains wouldn't be so bad, not if she was the one putting them on him. Which gave her some very interesting pictures in her head.

Here come the devil...

Witford should have come. He'd have to be possessed by demons himself to miss how effortlessly Rev erased the gap between faith and sensuality, pulling from the joy music gave generously to both. When she found herself up on her feet with everyone else, she danced and celebrated that feeling, letting it into her.

They kept that momentum going with two more upbeat choices. Then they turned to Teddy Swims' "Losing Control." Rev drove the song's passionate need into every swaying body, filling every corner of the club, all of them gripped by it.

His gaze came back to her, again and again. Her skin held the heat of the club and the heat from within her, a double blaze. Her blouse clung to her, her nape damp. When she shivered, it was as if she could feel his breath there, bringing her coolness. A lower temperature could be as erotic as a high one, when applied the right way, at the right moment.

His voice reached far inside her, setting her off like a tuning fork. Vibration everywhere, low in her stomach, rippling across her thighs, and between them. She wanted his mouth there, wanted to guide his fingers into that wet heat under her silken panties so he could feel her response.

She was turning into a damn groupie, but she was okay with that. Because that wasn't why he looked at her, why it felt like he was singing to her alone.

You make a mess of me...

He made those words a compliment, a desire. *Make a mess of me. Please, Mistress.*

It was another song that included a line about being on his knees to the one he wanted. She wondered if it had been his idea to include it, or if it had already been in the lineup. Either way, how he sang it said it spoke to him, the way it was doing to her now.

Their full set was a mix of rock and blues. The instruments had their own voices, taken in unexpected directions, but pulling the willing audience right along with them. The mass of humanity had become one body, caught in the music, the moment, the haze of sharing that pleasure, so intense it was almost intimate.

Some people thought blues was repetitious, but good blues was an emotion put to song. Letting go of the need for a pattern, letting go of everything, meant it took the listener where it wanted to go.

Same as a session between Domme and sub. Done right, there was a moment where they both let go, and the control belonged to something else. She wasn't oblivious to how that overlapped with Rev's other Master, and His hold on him. Or her belief in the bond between the Lord and Lady.

Watching him get just as lost, as he took them all on that journey, made her want him more.

They wound up with a guitar solo from one of Sy and Trey's band members. As he finished them off, there was thunderous applause and yells for more. Rev had stepped back, taking a breath. His T-shirt clung to his upper body, the club heat having its effect on him as well, but his eyes, alive with that golden fire, told her it had another source. If the club hadn't been shadowed and he wasn't wearing his shirt out over his jeans, it would have been evident. But she knew. She didn't need to see the proof.

She did, however, desire to feel it.

Sy spoke into his mic at the drums. "Fifteen-minute break, y'all. Enjoy the house music, and if you feel we deserve a tip, jar's on the stage. Help us pay our rent this month. Oh, and buy a bunch of drinks so management will invite us back."

He grinned at the cheering crowd. As the band exited the stage, BB King and Bobby Blue Band's jamming version of "Let The Good Times Roll" poured out of the speakers.

Sy sauntered to their table, moving his hips to the music, his fingers snapping as he did an ebullient turn and gave Vera a playful wink. He also offered Mavis an appreciative appraisal, startling her and amusing Vera.

Sy leaned down to speak into Vera's ear. When he did, he closed his hand on hers and squeezed it. "Storeroom down the hall on the left. No one'll bother you. I'll keep her company while you're gone."

He looked at Mavis as he straightened. "Can I get you a drink? It's on me."

"Something non-alcoholic," Vera told him as she gripped the key he'd given her.

Submissives often knew their Dommes as well as Dommes knew their submissives. It was a gift when it was true, and Sy had always been a gift.

"I don't know. I may need the hard stuff to handle that," Mavis teased her, watching Sy head to the bar.

"Trust me. He's better experienced with your head fully clear, so you remember every delicious moment. He's plenty hard enough, I promise."

"Holy God."

The need to claim the man she wanted meant Vera's body was a wire, strung between two equally demanding needs. Still, Vera managed to casually rise, as if she were headed for the restroom. "I'll be back. Have fun."

When she moved toward that hallway, she didn't look Rev's way. She didn't need to. As she arrived at the storeroom door and put the key in the lock, his hand closed over hers. They turned it together. She stepped inside the space, and he closed the door behind them.

The room was dry and clean. Storage cabinets lined one wall, open shelves on the other two for stocked items.

She wasn't the type of woman who attacked a man in a closet at a club. Except tonight she was.

"Lock the door," she said. Then crooked a finger at him.

Rev came to her, his eyes lit with the adrenaline of the performance. She inhaled the sweat that made his skin gleam, and gave his shirt that loving hold on his upper body.

He stared at her, hands curling. "Tell me how to take care of you, Mistress."

She backed up to a shelf and inched up the hem of her skirt, showing him the garters, then her panties, a silky green mesh with flowers embroidered over it.

Now they were onto John Lee Hooker's "The Blues Boogie," the music tumbling over and over itself. The harmonica, guitar and piano were on a ride that was increasing its pace.

Lord, Lord...I'm the boogie man... Come on baby...

She inhaled the scents buried in the walls. Wood, smoke, alcohol, sweat. Life and all its basic needs.

"Slide that crate over here." She pointed to it. When he complied, she put her heel on it, spread her thighs and leaned back against the shelf, gripping the frame on either side of her. "Your mouth on my cunt, Rev. Then your cock, when I say."

"Thank you, Jesus." He went to his knees and put his lips against silk. Despite his fervency, he took his time, nice and slow, breathing on her, tasting her with reverent lips.

He did so well, she had him keep going as the one song finished and another started, the totally fuck-me-slow pace of "Tennessee Whiskey." If Sy had requested it, she was going to make sure he had an unforgettable session with one of the best available Mistresses at Progeny.

She tipped her head back as Rev's mouth sent indescribable spirals of pleasure up through her, strong enough she climbed him, her legs wrapping around his shoulders, hand on his head, nails curved in. He held her hips so firmly they were one being, moving together, pushing, pulling, dancing, lifting and falling. Those strong hands flexed, conveying how deep his own need was to be here with her, giving her this, taking what she was offering.

He pushed his tongue against the mesh, then played around the edges, finding his way beneath it to thrust in, suck on her, take in her taste like he never wanted any other kind of sustenance. His shoulders shifted under the clamp of her legs.

"Oh, Goddess...Rev..."

She worked herself on his mouth, arching back, gripping the shelf, his hands flexing to help her just as she needed him to do. The climax was shooting up, putting sparks in her mind, before her eyes.

They didn't have much time left, but she wanted to draw it out as much as she could. She gripped his neck, the bite of her nails making him lift his head, his mouth wet from her, his eyes holding that flame still.

She pulled open her blouse one-handed, showing him the arch of her rib cage, the rise of her breasts above satin scented with her perfumed heat. "Work your way up."

He did, also taking his time despite the limits of it. Once she allowed him inside her, it would take seconds to get where she intended to have them go. He licked and sucked on the tops of her quivering breasts, cupping them, lifting and bringing them together to thrust his tongue between them. She pressed her thigh against his firm ass, and let her breath wash over his forehead as he suckled a nipple, greedy and easy at once.

Because he had such a secure hold on her, she molded both hands over his head, holding him to her breasts. Both legs were locked around his waist and hips, pressing his cock against her. She rubbed herself there.

"Now, Rev. Inside me, now."

She moved her grip to his biceps, raking the flesh. She wanted him to come back to the stage with her marks on him. She captured his mouth with her own, demanding everything with tongue and teeth. His one arm held her as he lifted her up and braced her hips against a shelf.

"Be inside me, Rev," she demanded again. "Right now."

She didn't help him. She was too busy with his mouth, and she didn't want to give anything else her focus. She didn't have to. That was why she had a man to serve her.

He opened his jeans. He came up against her, so close and urgent, her breasts resting against his chest as he thrust in, pushing her against the shelf. Bottles fortunately secure inside boxes clinked at the force. She gripped his neck, bringing her forehead to his. Felt that energy between them, wrapping them up. "Oh..."

The orgasm was intense, and he covered her mouth with his so she cried out inside it, though there was little chance a sexual release could be heard where the music was so loud people had to shout to have a conversation. Or put her mouth against his ear, as she did now.

"Come inside me. Let me feel you."

His hand hit the edge of the shelf, gripping as he pumped his buttocks under her calves. Driving into her, stroking her. She glimpsed his face, the rigid muscle, the ferocious intent in his eyes as he obeyed her.

But she also saw more than that. In this moment when most men and women lost themselves to their primal nature, she saw he would never forget to give her pleasure, to tend to her needs in the pursuit of his own. He was fully with her, her response to him something he held in both hands and cherished. Caring for her and grateful for the privilege. When she recognized it, felt it, *knew* it, he moved past three decades of defenses and walls and right into her soul. Asked for her heart and she gave it to him.

Oh, Goddess.

His cock was iron heat and slippery friction, a stretching fullness that would stay with her, make her sex tender and sore in the right ways. When she showered tonight, she'd smell him on her body, and he'd smell her on his.

Take that, Witford and Tisha. He's mine now.

It wasn't a magnanimous thought, but right now she wanted to embrace a more savage side. Like the Goddess Kali. Vera locked her arms around him as they rode one another to the finish. When they came to a reluctant halt, both of them were breathing hard, hearts beating against one another.

The more playful piano tones of "Cold Hearted Woman" had

started up. Smiling, she dropped her head back against a shelf edge, eying him to see when he registered the words. When he did, he smiled, too. He framed her face with one big hand, the other helping her slide back down to her feet. He knelt, and her breath caught as he cleaned her with his mouth, tongue and lips stroking her in ways she would remember as vividly as the rest. Then he adjusted her panties and skirt before he rose. He'd fastened his jeans.

"I like knowing you're on me, Mistress."

"I like it, too." She wondered if her eyes were glowing at him like his were at her. She shot a sidelong glance at her phone, which peeked out of her small purse, on the shelf where she'd tossed it. "You have four minutes before your break is over."

He braced a hand by her head. "I'd like to spend three of them kissing you. May I?"

She called up the clock feature and set it for three minutes. Rev lifted a suggestive brow. "Afraid you going to lose track of time, Mistress?"

"If you do it right, yes. And 'afraid' isn't the right word. I'm damn well anticipating it."

That slow smile again, and he leaned in. He explored her with his mouth, his hands on her light and kneading, sliding over flesh and curves and clothing, learning her. She'd slipped her hands behind her, pressing her buttocks against the overlapped knuckles. She wanted to see what he would do, with no further guidance. He kissed her the way she'd always wanted to be kissed, but had rarely ever experienced. He cherished her, hungered for her, took from her and gave back.

It was everything she wanted, but in ways too deep to describe— or even know how to demand. Otherwise she would have given that order to her subs a long time ago. But it wouldn't have worked, because it needed to be the right sub hearing it. The right man. The one who knew how to give that to his Mistress. To her in particular.

"Married to the Blues" had started playing. It was impossible to ignore the pain it unfurled, the female singer's heartfelt cry of loneliness, about lovers lost. Reality and the past always had to have their say, didn't they?

She took her arms from behind her and slid them around him, holding him tightly. She wasn't a needy or clingy person. This wasn't that. It was just holding on in the dark to something she wasn't guaranteed to have forever. So it was best to hold it close while she could.

His hand moved to her neck, his other arm tight around her body. He spoke against her hair.

"I'm here, Mistress. I not going anywhere."

People said all sorts of dramatic things during sex, and especially during power exchange sessions. The better the session, the more likely it was to happen. It was taken and let go, the way it should be, a happening in the moment.

The ache in her throat was because she really wanted the Universe to back him up, the only one who could guarantee such a promise.

"I'd like to come home with you tonight, Mistress. Fix you breakfast in the morning."

"That doesn't sound like a request," she managed.

"It is. It's a request for your trust. In a bit of a forceful way." His voice softened. "Please say yes."

She pressed her forehead to his shoulder, and his hands moved over her back, his mouth against her hair. "Trust me, Veracity. I ain't him. I not anyone that ever hurt you, and I never want to be."

The phone alarm went off. Just as she'd thought, they'd needed the reminder. She lifted her head and looked up at him as he stroked a lock of hair away from her cheek. She let her desire to believe him push back that ache. "All right. You can come home with me tonight. But only if you go out there and make them stop playing that damn song."

"You got it. I break that record in half, just for you."

When he returned to the stage, she went to the bar to get herself a drink. Sy and Mavis seemed to be hitting it off and she didn't want to interrupt them before Sy needed to get back to his drums.

Mavis wasn't a Domme, but she was looking for a flirtation and a fun night out. Sy enjoyed dalliances outside the club, and he'd have a care for her.

Vera located Ros at a high top with Skye and Cyn. Tiger was with them tonight. Lawrence had a night game with one of the rec center sports teams, and Mick needed to work. This was too much noise and stimulation for Abby, but Neil wasn't down range right now, so they'd be at his place in the bayou.

"He's incredibly talented," Ros noted, as Vera put her ear close enough to hear her. "We could help him do something with that, just like we did for Sy and Trey."

TRA's services were in demand and expensive, but they had represented and launched more than one local artist for a scaled down fee.

"No argument. I don't know if he wants that, though."

Ros understood. She brushed a light finger over Vera's cheek. "A little irritation there. Maybe beard stubble."

"I can promise it wasn't the slightest bit irritating."

Ros chuckled and they settled in to enjoy the next set.

She and Rev strolled down Frenchmen Street. They'd taken a trolley to the club from her place, and would do the same to get back to it. Eventually. For now, though, they got on the sidewalk that followed the river, and found a bench alongside it. Rev put an arm around her, buffering the chill off of the water.

"Is that the first time you've performed in front of an audience, outside of a church setting?" she asked.

"Yeah." He shrugged. "But sometimes someone in the church will say I should try my luck at one of those big national talent shows."

"What did you think?"

"It easy to think someone's good when you listening to them at church, and those people want you to be good. More is expected from people wanting to do it for money."

Rev frowned. "But it more than that. I watched an episode from one of those shows. There was these three boys who loved to sing, really feeling it. They did real good, and this big music producer signed them. I watched a video they did after that, and they was all plastic, and sounded just like everyone else. That was a few years back, and they no longer singing. But that first video been downloaded a million times, so I guess they'll always have that."

"That happens way too often. Good marketing shows why something is worth paying attention to and spending money on. It's not about turning it into something like everything else. Ros is adamant about that."

"That follows truth. That's good." He studied her. "Do you think I should go down that road?"

"That's up to you. I may command you to do many things, things that bring us both pleasure, but I wouldn't want you to be different from what you are."

And Rev had no ambitions for fame. From working for TRA, she knew a product's quality alone wouldn't sell it. Marketing was key, but so were the drive and desires of the performer.

Their hands were linked on his knee. "I've been told all my life this gift I have was meant to serve God." he said. "That can look a lot of different ways, and plenty of people have given me their opinions on it. Because of what Witford and Tisha did, I know you have your doubts about whether I've been free to choose."

"Yes," she admitted. "On the path I walk in my faith, I believe how each of us serve is a personal discussion, between you and whatever name you give the Divine in your life. No one else should claim superior knowledge of that discussion. But the more I know you, Rev...the more I think it would be difficult for anyone to get you to do something you think is the wrong path."

He looked out at the river, and she followed his attention there. The occasional white cap gleamed, and the water was dotted with running lights from small fishing craft. The city on the opposite shore provided a backdrop of more lights. "I walking the path I was meant to walk," he said. "When Teena Joy was worried or in pain, or if it helped someone, for me to be what they want me to be, I did it. It was all right, because I got to sing, and be what I am. But if it went against what the Lord wants of me, then I let them know that."

"So all of it has been a conscious, *willing* choice."

"Yes. That the truth, so rest easy on it, once and for all." He met her gaze. "You decide in life what matters, where you have to take a stand, and when you don't. I don't have to prove to people they ain't going to boss me around when I know they can't. I don't have to prove myself to anyone but God." He tilted his head. "And now maybe you."

"Really? How do I fit into that?"

"The yearning to be with you, serve you like I'm doing... Even if you helping me know what that looks like, what to call it, that need's always been there, waiting and wanting to be filled. Having a Mistress...that was the missing piece for me."

His eyes showed the light of pleasure, highlighted by a few shadows. "One of our parishioners, Mr. Ellis, he a widower and so lonely, even though he loves God. He told me, 'My wife, she was the one who could speak to my truth, speak *my* truth, give it a name in a way I couldn't, but knew when I heard it from her. Rev, boy, it'll be such a relief to be with her again.'"

His eyes were thoughtful. "I thought I didn't need no earthly person to speak my truth. God knows it. I just wanted to help people find comfort and strength, help them. But now I understand."

His gaze turned back to her, held her like her hand on his knee. "Long as you know my truth, too, you and God, one on earth, one in Heaven, that's enough knowing for me."

The man was so good at making her tongue-tied, she thought she should punish him for it. But he'd also made her curious, gesturing around him when he spoke of Heaven. "You don't think Heaven is straight above?"

"I think it's inside and outside, above and below, in every direction." He paused. "I want to say something else, but it might push into a room where I not been invited."

"Stand at the threshold and say what you want to say. I'll close the door if it's warranted."

"You like to take care of your...submissives. You're a service-oriented Domme. Sy say that, and that you like to take care of us, but you also like to hold onto the control, which is what puts you on the Domme side."

"That's his opinion, is it?"

Because he was a smart man, Rev noted the sugary edge to her tone. "I not trying to get him in trouble. I'm trying to understand all this better."

"I want you to do that. I'm very okay with you talking to a sub like Sy or Trey," she assured him. "But if you talk to a different sub, always let me know who they are. There are no wrong feelings, but there can be wrong information. And sometimes wrong motives."

"Like sex ed in the classroom, versus what kids tell one another. Like they can get pregnant from a toilet seat."

"Just so." He'd raised another question for her. "Who taught you about sex?"

"I learned the way most boys do. Curiosity and noticing things. Teena Joye answered most my questions. She practical, and didn't want me getting no girl in trouble, or getting a disease. She taught me to respect a woman. I already had that built into me, but she helped me sharpen the tool."

The gleam in his eye amused her. "What did you want to say to me, Rev?"

He lifted their joined hands, rubbing his thumb over her knuckles, warming them. "When I talking to Sy about you, the things he told me... I think you like taking care of a sub, and you'll let him take care of you. Mostly physical things, some not-so-physical things. But deep inside, those needs, you hold those out of reach. Or hide them."

Sy knew her better than she'd expected. "How do you know there's anything there at all?" she hedged.

"I feel it," he said. "So I want to know what I have to do to take care of your deepest needs."

"Be willing to invest the time and care," she said after a long moment. "And make me believe that's what you truly want. To let you take care of me like that, I have to believe in you. Find the will to trust you, more than I've trusted any submissive before. Well, sorry...I trusted my ex-husband that much. My trust was misplaced."

"I'm sorry," he said simply. Sincerely. It touched her heart, and something even deeper.

She cleared her throat. "There's no instruction list for that. All you have to do is be yourself, Rev. Be honest with me. Generous and loving, which you've done so far. Time takes care of the rest, if it's meant to be."

His lips twisted in amused frustration. "I guess I never had something that made it this hard to wait. Now I know why that need for patience all the time be talked about in faith. The more you want it to happen, the worse the wait."

"What would you like to do for me, Rev, that you're having to wait upon?"

It was a question she shouldn't have asked if she wanted to protect herself, but if she was demanding he step outside of his comfort zone, then at a certain point, if she wanted to give him a fair shot at what he wanted, she had to do it, too.

"Be the man you can turn to, Mistress." His brown eyes held hers. "For anything. When you happy or celebrating, I want to share that with you. When you weak, when you need to cry, I want to be the man you know can make it even better, or fix it. Or listen to you while you figure out how to fix it, if that what you prefer. I just want you to know there's one person who thinks you the gift he's been waiting for in his life. And who'll do everything he can to be the same kind of gift for you."

He rose and offered a hand. "Let me get you home. It getting cold out here, and you getting chilly."

CHAPTER FOURTEEN

*H*e stayed with her overnight. In the morning, he scrambled eggs for an omelet, while she pulled two of Cyn's cinnamon rolls out of the freezer to thaw.

He'd offered to visit one of the excellent bakeries nearby, but she shook her head. "Trust me. Cyn's cinnamon rolls are every bit as good. She's a terrible cook, but she is an extraordinary baker. We have a mutual friend, Ben O'Callahan, who's fantastic at both. He could make manna for angels. They trade baking recipes, as well as ideas for giving pain to their devoted subs. Both of them are sadists."

"His submissive...is a woman?" Rev frowned. "He hurts her like Cyn does with Mick?"

"Yes. Ben gives Marcie what she wants, and vice versa," Vera explained. "The need for pain can run deep in some people. And it's hard to understand, but Ben would annihilate anyone who tried to harm Marcie. Though he'd have to get to them before she did. She's a formidable fighter. Trains in MMA. She and Cyn spar regularly."

He shook his head. "Not sure I understand that."

"When you meet them at the club, you'll understand better. There's no missing their devotion to one another. Marcie would fire her 9-millimeter up the ass of anyone who tried to hurt Ben, or anyone she considers her family."

She sat at the table, watching him cook. "Do you have some time to spend with me today, Rev?"

"Yes ma'am, I do. All day if you want." He shot her a smile over his shoulder. "I sure want to."

When she woke this morning and let her fingertips glide along his thigh and up his bare back, an idea had taken hold. She was pleased to hear she'd have time to pursue it.

"Good. After breakfast and a shower, I have something I want us to do together."

He put her plate down and sat down next to her, making the chair creak as he settled. "Got everything you need, Mistress?"

"Looking like it."

He smiled, then bowed his head. His prayer was silent, nothing he imposed on her, but she closed her hand over his and joined him. Saying a prayer of thanks for what was given, whether food or an intriguing man to share it with, wasn't a denominational thing. At least it shouldn't be, to her way of thinking.

When he opened his eyes, she was studying his hand.

"You smiling, Mistress."

"I was remembering coming home from third grade and talking about skin color with my mother. I told her I didn't understand white or black or brown, because everyone is all different colors. Only my hair was black."

She turned his hand over to look at his palm, a lighter color than what was over his knuckles. Then she touched his mouth, that tempting pink seam when his bronze lips were pressed together, like now.

She kept that smile as they curved under her touch. "I pointed out that my friend Elliott's hair was also black, but he was white. Only not really white, more golden brown, the color of the toast she made my father, because Elliot was in the sun a lot. The only truly white thing on him were his legs because he always wore long pants, except when we went to the neighborhood pool."

"I bet your momma was trying not to laugh through all of that."

"I was too young to understand the term 'suppressed mirth,' but it definitely fit." Since she'd also learned the value of not 'suppressing' good memories of her family, she was glad she'd shared that one with Rev.

As always, he waited until she ate her first bite before he picked up his fork and dug in. "May I ask you some things about what you believe, Veracity?"

The question made her wary, but his sincere desire to know wasn't something she'd reasonably refuse. And truth? She was starting to think she'd tell the man anything.

"Of course."

"Do you believe in Heaven?"

"I believe in reincarnation. With each life, we learn and grow. If we did something harmful in a previous one, we have to pursue redemption. Not so much as a punishment, but as a spiral toward an ultimate state of enlightenment, and a better Universe."

She gestured with her fork. "Say I was an abusive husband. In a subsequent life I might be the abused wife, to understand what it felt like to be on the receiving end. Or if something unjust happened to me in a previous life, that might be the cause that's important to me in this one."

"So you just go from one life to the next?"

"After death, I believe there's a place for the soul to rest, recharge, and decide what it wants to do next. Connect with those souls we care about. That's where Heaven comes in.

"During our lives here, I think we also cross paths with certain souls in different guises. Like that husband might be the wife in the next life, but likewise, she might be him, to help her soul understand what made him treat her that way. And they heal, and grow, and move on to the next level."

He grunted. "It sound like kids in a schoolyard, trying to figure out how to play with one another the right way."

"Yes. On a far more serious and intense level." She chewed her eggs. "Mavis told me about the man you chased off from the school."

He'd been about to start on the cinnamon roll, but he stopped. He stayed still, his arm on the table, his gaze steady on her.

"I won't ask you if you don't want to talk about it."

"I'll answer any question you want to ask of me, Mistress. But most questions about things like that want to turn it into something else, so it can make sense to the person asking. I not saying that's what you doing. I just telling you why I don't like talking about it. It like looking at someone else's painting, picking up your own brush and making it something different, then calling it their painting still."

She studied him. "People are bad about not listening, even when they ask for a story or an opinion. We translate what we hear through the filter of our own story, our beliefs, our judgments. But when I'm in session with a submissive, I have to really listen to what he's saying to me. With his mouth, with his body.

"I'm not saying I'm immune to the trap of filtering, but I'll treat what you say like that, I promise. And I know you're not lying to me, but there's more to why you don't want to talk about it. Can you tell me about that?"

He cracked his neck and looked out the window. A mix of reactions crossed his expression, then he shook his head. "No," he said softly.

But it wasn't "no" to her. He'd denied himself something, maybe the right not to tell her.

He turned to look at her again. "When I chased him, I could feel what his intent was. What he would have done if he could have gotten that child away from us. I knew he was sick, but any person that hold hate or harm in his heart is sick. Just different levels of disease, and his was so bad, it had invited evil in to take that sick and make it worse. But I didn't see all that, feel all of that, not at first. I was angry, Mistress. Full of rage."

In his hard face, she saw what she suspected Mavis had. "I was strong enough to hurt him. To kill him. And I wanted to. That rage grabbed me strong, because I love those kids. They my kids, just the way they are to Miss Mavis and the teachers, and their parents. Then, when I got up on him, I knew that feeling wasn't right. It didn't walk with God."

He took a steadying breath. "So I opened myself up to Him, asked for help. 'Lord, what do I do?' And that's when I saw that evil perched on his soul, a darkness on top of his sickness, that had made him go from just being sick to doing something to hurt a child. And I knew what I needed to do. I opened myself up to it, and it was cast out, through me. Lord did it all. I was just the instrument He used."

She touched his hand. "How did you feel afterward? Were you all right?"

He looked at her fingers on top of his. "I was tired. Felt like I could barely move. After the police come and got him, and Miss Mavis leave me be, I sat down against that tree. Guess she thought I went back to work or headed home, because it was last period. I fell asleep, and when I woke, it was the next morning. Ten minutes before time to be at work." He chuckled without humor. "The Lord made sure I didn't oversleep."

He paused. "I did wake up once. Probably about three a.m. There it squatted, a few feet away. That darkness. I said the Lord's Prayer, and it hissed at me, like a mad cat. Then it was gone. I might have dreamed that, but I don't think I did."

His expression cleared, and he looked at her. "I didn't expect you to ask how I felt. I guess I should have. You already done told me. You want to look after me when I need it."

"You did that for me, too, the day Witford and Tisha were in my office. Before anything else, you asked me if I was okay. If I'd been with you then, in the woods, I would have sat with you out there." Their hands were still linked, and they gazed at that connection, feeling it.

"Witford and Tisha think you wrong for me. They say you not Christian. They think you changing me, rather than knowing what I know. You were what I hoped to find."

Tears touched her eyes and she squeezed his hand. When he touched her face, concerned, she shook her head. "You say things that just..."

That quiet all my worries. Heal what needs to be healed. And it's happening so fast, it's scaring the shit out of me.

She didn't say that. Instead she worked around it. "The people we love can know a lot about us, but the deepest wishes of our hearts, I think only we and maybe the person who's the answer to those wishes can see that part clearly."

Vera saw that fit for every woman in the group, with the man each had found for herself. Even Abby and Neil. When he came into her life, because of him being a Dom and her illness, it had been hard to see how it would work. But it had, because they were that person for one another.

"Enough of that." She gestured to the plate. "Eat your cinnamon roll. I have plans for you."

His eyes warmed and he picked up the fork. As he took a bite, she smiled at his expression. "So was I right?"

"If the devil all about temptation, Cyn got this recipe from him."

She grinned. "There are days I think Cyn *is* the devil. Her name does rhyme with 'sin' and her full name is Cyn*bad*."

He chuckled. "You told my aunt there no Satan on your path. But do you believe in evil?"

"Yes. Just as the good that people do permeates all of us and guides us on the Lord and Lady's path, so too there can be evil, created by the darkness in us all, if we let it get the upper hand, through fear or ego. Kind of how you described it, in that man who tried to take Lynn. I tend to believe the literal translation of Satan," she added. "Adversary. That adversary can take a variety of forms."

"Witford call him that, too." He pursed his lips. "Everything you talk about? Don't change my view, but don't disagree with it much, either. There's room for both. You was talking about your momma earlier. Do you have pictures of your family?"

A wall closed around her heart, protecting it from what the question dredged up.

"I do," she said. And left it at that.

"One day," he said, "I'd like to see them. Helps me to have a picture in my mind when I'm praying, and I want to pray that God will heal that rift, take the hurt and confusion away so your love for one another can help you be a family again."

"Okay." She still felt rigid. Brittle.

"May I do something, Mistress?"

"Depends on what it is."

"Saying it might take away from it. Best to show you. Can you trust me, even though I pushed against something that hurt? Maybe because I pushed against something that hurt."

She nodded. Probably because her wariness was as solid as the table in front of them, he kept his next movements slow and easy.

He took her hand, pushed back from the table and tugged her up and onto his lap. Vera sank into his resilient strength, a bulwark against the turmoil of her feelings. As he cradled her, Rev put his mouth against her throat to kiss her. He held her secure, a hand over her hip, the other arm around her shoulder and back.

She drew in a deep breath, pulling it through her, hollowing out her stomach, then let it out, and descended deeper into that embrace, her arms around him, too. A hug, when done right, offered the right messages, that reassured and strengthened the one who needed it most. This was all that and more. It made her want him even more. She craved his submission to her will. Needed it.

"Thank you, Rev," she whispered. "Thank you for coming into my life with such generosity and honesty."

His arms held her even closer. Then he drew back. "You said something about a shower. You want company?"

"Go to my guest bathroom and get started." Because that idea she had? She wanted to do it even more now, and she intended to set it up before she joined him. "I'll be there shortly."

~

When she arrived, she found him stripped and kneeling, waiting on her by the stall. He started the water and, after she slipped off her robe, he helped her inside. Then he submitted to whatever she desired. Which included soaping and exploring his flesh under the running water with mouth and fingertips, and pressing her body against his. Then she let him bathe her, giving him thorough instruction, though she denied them the pleasure of shower sex, or finding a climax. For what she had planned, she wanted that momentum to keep building.

After they got out, he picked up the towel. Though he was still dripping on the bathmat, he dried her with studious attention, sweeping strokes of the terry cloth over her face and neck, upper body, arms and legs. He knelt to do her feet, one then the other, as she held onto his shoulder.

"I dreamed of doing this, too." His voice was a rumbling echo against the tile.

She maybe hadn't thought of this specifically, but it was going into the growing treasure pile of things she was discovering she did want. Could want. That was the way a gift like this worked. The possibilities just kept expanding.

When he rose, she tapped him on his wide chest, rubbing her thigh teasingly against his wet one, grazing his stiff cock. "Dry yourself, Rev. I'm going to go get changed. I want you to go to the living room like this. Start the gas logs. You can take five minutes to look at what I've laid out there. After that, I expect you to kneel facing the chair to the right of the fire. Three feet between you and it. Your knees should be shoulder width apart, ass on your heels, fingers laced behind your head. And I want your eyes closed. Wait until I come and bid you do something else. Do you understand?"

At the club, she'd seen his gaze linger on submissives in that posture. That same interest kindled now, his cock twitching as he digested the potential in her commands.

"Yes ma'am."

She went to her bedroom. Though anticipation had a good hold on her, she took care with her appearance. She wanted to take his breath away.

When she came down the stairs at last, she paused at the entrance to the living room. She'd left the curtains drawn last night, so the morning sunlight was blocked, but she savored what the gas log flame did for the pose she'd dictated. Fingers laced behind his head, the tapering from shoulders and wide back to waist, firm buttocks pressed against his heels. It was worth a long, thorough look.

The story she'd told Rev about skin colors came back to her now, the truth of it in all the gleaming hues of his muscled flesh. She also thought of the religious parts of their discussion, and Rev's opinion, that her views didn't change his, but there was room for both.

There was room for so much, if the heart only opened to it. She wanted to be open to everything this could give her.

She came to stand before him. His eyes were closed, as she'd commanded, but his nostrils flared, the ripple through his muscles telling her he was aware of her presence.

"Open your eyes and look at me, Rev."

His attention climbed her in that intent way that made her feel as if his touch was following the same path. Her lingerie was a peach-colored replica of a 1930s Cadolle. The one-piece garment had a thin lace bra, her nipples pressing against the semi-transparent cloth. The fabric below her breasts to the swell of the hips looked like a boned corset, though the stretch material had no back lacings. A short lace skirt fell from its edge to mid-thigh and barely covered her ass. Under it, she wore nothing.

The outfit was comfortable and meant to tempt, with what her movements would reveal or hide. What it covered would be offered at her pace, while he could only gaze hungrily at it. If she allowed that.

She'd unrolled a mat in front of the fire, and put out a picnic basket containing a coil of rope, a long curling feather, and a set of chimes. She was certain the time she'd given Rev to look at those items and consider their uses had kept his erection flushed and stiff.

Vera sat down in the chair next to the fireplace, a fussy thing with button held cushions. She perched on the edge, her back straight.

As she'd told Rev, in Tantric practice, riding the wave of arousal, experiencing it indefinitely, expanded the body's ability to experience sexual pleasure. Satisfaction was a never-ending current, not a destination.

Rev had said he could give her the whole day.

An eye bolt was embedded in the ceiling, several feet back from the front of the fireplace. She kept a rope of braided black nylon threaded through it. The two tasseled ends looped over hooks on either side of the fireplace, so the rope framed the carved mantel in a three-dimensional way.

"Rev, unhook the rope ends, and bring them to me."

Watching the flow of his muscles, the flexing of his ass, thighs and shoulders, the movement of his erect cock, added to the strength of that current. She wanted to stroke and cup his testicles, taste his cock, bite that strong body.

As she tapped her nails against the chair arms, she counseled patience to her bucking libido.

She'd put in the rope setup for a planned session with Whistler, when he cleaned her house. It had been a memorable scene, so she'd kept it in place, though she'd only made use of it that once. She hung ornaments from the silken ropes at Christmas. A true home "pervertible" had more than one use.

At one of their monthly dinners Vera had hosted, she remembered Skye letting her fingers trail along the ropes before giving Vera a playful look and hopping onto the couch, her feet tucked up under her as they settled in to enjoy dessert and after dinner conversation. Her friend had probably been imagining doing something similar at Tiger's place. He had a fireplace, too.

When Rev brought her the rope ends, she glanced at her feet and he dropped to one knee. "Cross your wrists and present them to me."

Using one end, she bound his wrists with three wraps around both then two loops in between to hold them secure. It wouldn't tighten and cut off circulation, but she'd keep an eye on it. "Can you back up on your knees, Rev?"

"Never tried that, but I'll do it for you, Mistress."

"Move until you're under the ceiling bolt, then stand up and lift your hands over your head."

As he did, she drew in the slack, until it pulled taut, his arms lifted above him. She kept him flat on his feet, though, and tied off the rope on the hook by the fireplace before turning to look at him.

Cock thick and hard, chest expanding with the rise and fall of his quickened breath. He was responding the way a submissive did who wanted the restraint and all it could mean. The pulse point between her legs was hammering.

Vera returned to her chair, moving the footstool so she could brace one foot upon it, which tilted her hips upward. He could confirm it was just her under the skirt. As she dropped the straps off her shoulders, she pushed the bodice down enough to reveal the dark circle of the areolae, though the lace still hung temptingly on the aroused peaks.

"What you doing, Mistress?" Rev asked hoarsely.

"I'm going to touch myself until I climax. You're going to listen. Close your eyes."

When he stared at her in disbelief, she showed him a wicked smile. "Mistresses love that look, Rev. Like you've had something taken away that you wanted more than you could ever have imagined."

"That a good description. I want to watch you."

"Prove to me that obeying me is more important to you than anything else, and you may get that privilege. Do I need to blindfold you?"

"No ma'am." With obvious reluctance, he closed his eyes. His muscles twitched, making the rope sway, the black braid shimmering in the flame's light.

Humming her approval, she began to stroke herself. With the shifts of her body, the little moans, tiny pleas caught in her throat, she made sure he could vividly imagine what he couldn't see. His body was a column, hands clenched, mouth thin, and he kept licking his lips. Precum glistened at the slit of his cock, and his thighs flexed. Toes curled into the rug.

"Oh..." The climax rolled over her, a lovely thing. Not the intense, rip-out-the-soul experience she planned to give them both, but a wonderful appetizer to steady her.

When she could catch her breath, she spoke. "You can open your eyes, Rev."

She reclined in an erotic sprawl, her fingertips still resting on her wet pussy, back arched against the chair, thighs spread. As he gazed at her, he whispered something that she didn't catch, but the tone held reverence liberally tested by sexual frustration. The male fire in his eyes said he was poised to leap as soon as she allowed it. He was already fighting the urge to do that without permission, the animal wanting to take over.

She adjusted the straps, putting the bodice back in place as she rose, smoothing her hands over her breasts and hips. Retrieving the chimes from the basket, she came to him with those and the stool. "I'm going to lean against you to do this, Rev. Don't do anything I haven't said you can. You simply stand there."

"I feel like I got to put my mouth on you."

"I expect you to find a way to control that, Rev." She gave him a cool stare. "Whose will do you obey? Yours or mine?"

"It a battle, between this beast inside me that want to take you down under me, and what'll please you."

"I don't want you to hide your desires. I like seeing the struggle. But I'm teaching you to obey my will over your own desires. Show me how well you can learn."

As she stepped onto the footstool, she pushed her breasts right up against his face, her hips against his abdomen. The devout Rev muttered a creative curse against her flesh, his breath hot through the cloth, but he held fast. Above where his hands were bound, she hooked the chimes to the rope, then stepped down.

"I'm going to put my mouth on you now, Rev. And when I tap you three times, you'll come. I want to taste you, swallow you into me."

As he shifted, the chimes spoke. Her gaze lifted to them, then dropped to his face. "You must remain still. If I hear the chimes, I stop, and I'll resume when I feel you're under better control."

"Even when...you ask me to spill?"

"You must do your very best to come without making them ring. I don't expect you to succeed, but I expect to see the effort to do so. That will determine whether I stop and let you spurt into the air, instead of holding you in my mouth and sucking you to completion."

His eyes held a feverish look, so she laid her hand on his chest and met his gaze. "Testing you, watching you do your best to please me, gives me so much pleasure, Rev. I savor every moment of this. The more you suffer for me, the more I want to give you."

Her indirect reminder of what he said he wanted to do more than anything else—serve her—seemed to settle the maelstrom in his head, even if he remained caught in his struggle to deny his body what it demanded he take.

"Thank you, Mistress. That all I need to hear to keep doing it."

"Good."

She put her mouth on his chest and began to work her way down, enjoying the journey. Tasting and biting, nipples, abdomen, hip bones, upper thighs, then around his cock. He shuddered, but except for a couple tiny *tings*, the chimes were staying remarkably still.

The strained muscles, the chaos in his eyes and vibrating energy around him, told her he was putting everything into serving her as she'd demanded.

She drew that hot wave tighter around them, letting him have the benefit of it, in the way she slid her fingertips over him, and in how her mouth tasted, her teeth nipped, her lips sucked. She dedicated her full attention to his cock, exploring it, sucking on the head and laving the shaft with her tongue. Taking the whole thing in and working it in her mouth, she went as far to the root as she could get. As she slid back up to the head, she relished his taste.

The next time she went down on him, she cupped his testicles, rolled them in her palm, pressed in between them and reached between his spread legs to stroke his perineum.

His breath was harsh but shallow, making it sound like a growl caught in his throat. His body was sculpted iron as he fought to stay still, to keep the chimes from singing. The effort built the response, making sure it didn't rise too fast, drawing it out.

She'd love a bronze statue of him, just like this, to put in her back-yard. She had artist contacts. She might commission one.

So even when he's out of your life, you'll have the memory...

She shut that voice up, not wanting to taint this moment with insecurities.

She tapped his thigh those three times, and gripped his buttocks, taking him in as his release jetted into her mouth, bathing her tongue and throat with his seed. She dug her nails into his ass and sucked harder as the strangled groan became a cry. She scored him with her teeth, earning a jerk and a ring of those chimes, like a call to worship. She heard him give himself a chastising oath, even in the throes of his orgasm. Her lips would have smiled if they weren't stretched by his still spurting cock.

Oh, Rev, you are a Mistress's treasure.

She kept on him even after he was done, until he was jerking a little, his cock hypersensitive. He was still trying not to move. This was also a teaching moment, him learning that her playing her mouth over him, squeezing and stroking, was something she would do as long as she wished, because what she held was hers, to do with as she desired.

When he understood the lesson, she was rocked by a powerful wave of gratitude from him, for her demands, for giving him the opportunity to strive to please her. To honor her demands and desires over his own. His Mistress wanted him enough to take and take. And take some more. And that was what he'd said he wanted, most of all.

At long last, she rose. Her knees were shaking, butterflies in her stomach and chest. She leaned against him to grip his neck and kiss his mouth, letting him taste himself on her lips.

"Spending a day with you might kill me, Mistress," he noted in a rasping whisper.

"Would it be worth it?"

"My aunt didn't raise no fool. You got me tied up, so only one answer to that question." Then he sobered and pressed his forehead against hers. "Yes. God in Heaven, yes. You so beautiful, Veracity. So strong and beautiful. I grateful for you, too."

So strong and raw, the words came straight from the heart. From his soul, directly to hers. Time for part two.

She moved away to unhook the rope end. "You can lower your arms," she told him, but even as she spoke, she was already back at his side. When his arms came down, they fell around her. Then his knees gave out. He tried to do his part, so they didn't end up in a tumble of limbs, but she glanced significantly at the band of his bound arms as they arrived on the mat on their knees. "I think you did that on purpose."

"Long as you don't ask me direct, I don't have to lie," he told her, that light in his eyes again.

She laid her head on his chest and listened to his heart for a few beats before she eased back and had him lift his arms so she could remove the rope from his wrists. "Stretch out on the mat on your back. Put your arms out to either side of you."

"May I look at you, Mistress, or you going to have me close my eyes again?"

"You can look at me, for now. But I'm pleased you asked."

When she knelt next to him, his gaze coursed over the high hem of the skirt. He extended a fingertip and touched one knee just below the lace, glancing at her before it landed on that spot, to see if it was okay. "I can smell you," he said. "Your desire. Mixed with that perfume you wear. I'll dream of that, too, now."

"Do you know what henna is, Rev?"

"Some of the girls have henna tattoos. They want the real thing, but that's what their parents will allow."

"I'd like to do a henna design on you. It'll last about three weeks, though if you need to remove it sooner, it can be scrubbed off."

"Where you going to mark me?"

She liked that he used those words and let her fingers map her response, aware of how he trembled beneath her touch. "Around your cock, up to the base of your throat. Your forearms, around your wrists. If it feels right, after I do that, I'll do your back, base of spine to your nape."

"That seems real specific."

"It is. There's a spiritual association with the designs, and the process itself. In Tantra, erotic energy is known as *kundalini*. It moves through the body, stimulating the *sushumna*, which are the central energy channels. The chakras form that column."

She traced a path from the left testicle up the right side of his spine, following its track from the front of his torso, and came to the matching side of his nose. "This is the solar energy channel, representing masculine power, the Lord, or God." She did a mirror process. When she stopped beside his nose on the left side, her smallest finger was on his lips. "That's the lunar channel, for the Lady, or the Goddess."

Using the concave space provided by his lower back, she slipped her hand beneath him, pressing against the base of his spine, the upper rise of his buttocks. "The *sushumna* starts here, with this chakra. Sometimes the energy paths are depicted as a serpent, because with its sensual movements, it can bring to mind the awakening of erotic energy, its sacred power. What I'm about to do is map those chakras, and call the unique power and focus each can bring."

His gaze had flickered at the mention of the snake. "Does the serpent symbolism make you uncomfortable?" she asked.

"No. Moses healed the Israelites with a carved serpent on a stick. It a symbol, just like what you described. A voodoo priestess lady near the St. Louis cemetery say snakes are sacred in lots of paths."

"That sounds like Faustine."

"You know her." He didn't seem surprised, but neither was she. Coincidences, common friends and crossed paths had always shown up in her relationships with someone destined to be an important part of her life.

"I do. Are you friends?"

"Yeah. I like to walk that neighborhood near the cemetery, and she has a bench out front next to a Catholic cross. She got it from a church that burned down. It seven feet tall."

"No HOA to impose restrictions on giant lawn ornamentation."

"If there was, she just turn them into toads and make them hop away. That what she tell the neighbor kids, to play with them." His lips gave an appealing little quirk, his eyes darkening as she smoothed her palm over his chest and abdomen, the upper length of his thigh, as she listened to him.

"Go on," she urged, her voice throaty.

He cleared his and obeyed. "People leave shells and pebbles on it. When I stopped to do that myself, she come out. We sat and talked. Since then, I go by there now and again. I helped her with her plumbing one weekend. She has a couple snakes that hang about her place, and one holed up in her gutter drain. I helped her get him out."

"An appropriate dilemma for a voodoo priestess." She wondered if there'd ever been a time she'd been coming to visit Faustine when Rev might have just left her company. The good vibes Vera took in at Faustine's place would have had an extra boost that day. His energy might have lingered, as if to say to the matching unconscious part of her: *"Soon."*

She retrieved a razor and aloe-infused shaving cream from her basket. "I'm going to shave the areas where I'll be putting the design, if that's all right with you."

When he nodded, she shot him a feline smile and bent over his cock. "Don't move."

"Yes'm. Don't need to tell me twice."

She began to remove the hair around the base of his cock. She also planned to clear a path from abdomen to chest. After she was done with the design, she would rub coconut oil over the affected areas and tell him to keep doing so, to hold the design and soothe the skin.

"What do you wear when you go to bed, Rev?"

"Usually shorts and a T-shirt."

"While this design lasts, you won't sleep in anything. You'll touch each symbol on your front every night before you go to sleep, and remember what I tell you about them now. You'll think about what I want from you, and how you want to serve me. As you do those things, you'll do the breathing exercise I showed you, pulling sexual energy in and arousing yourself, but not to climax.

"I'm not tormenting you," she added with a smile. "In Tantra, these exercises teach us how to hold ourselves on a plateau where we take our arousal to a deeper, more spiritual level. When we do at last release, it's a sacred, intense act that increases our connection to one another and to the Universe, God, Lord and Lady; however we feel the Divine within us."

She blew a shaved hair out of her path, and he shuddered. "If you could touch me now, Rev, how would you do so?"

"I'd start with your hair." His gaze latched onto it. "I'm watching it fall forward, so soft around your face, and I want to curl it over my fingers, stroke it. Then your mouth."

His voice deepened. "When I was away from you, I held your face in my mind, like you told me about. I could feel it against me, your lips, the way they wet, just the right amount, and how they press and give against my skin. Then your throat."

His attention dropped there. "I never looked at a woman above the shoulders so much in my life, and wanted to stay there. It not because the rest isn't worth looking at, but everything you are and want from me shows itself plain there. In your eyes, the shape of your mouth, the looks you give me..."

She'd paused as he spoke, her hand on his abdomen, her thumb just above his cock. Her touch straddled two energy centers. The base spine position under her thumb offered grounding, while creative energy rested beneath her fingers.

Skye did graphic design work for their clients, and she'd talked about how she felt it "in her gut," when a design direction was right. It made sense that creative energy was there, and sexual energy could connect both points. Vera closed her eyes, letting his words sink into her, pull the two of them closer together, increasing her focus.

"Good," she murmured. "That's good."

She didn't have to tell him to be quiet after that. The moment wrapped them up, what she was doing, why she was doing it, and how they wanted to experience it. As a result, when she finished shaving him and set aside the cream and razor, she was in the right headspace to start on the design.

The blue-tinged henna came from a shop in New Orleans that specialized in different mixtures. This one had a fragrance, and the powder contained sparkling crystal grindings that lent additional properties to the application.

Henna designs could be complex, but she was competent enough with simple ones. She liked doing the lines and dots, the teardrops. Rev's gaze held her like clasped hands as she worked on the underside of his outstretched forearms. Lines were drawn by holding the paste tube just above the skin and letting them lay themselves down, rather than by direct contact with the skin. Flooding filled in the space between those lines the same way. The teardrops were dots applied with a slight drag.

"This stays on four hours before I wipe it off. If I kept it on six hours, it would darken even more, but it will still get dark enough over the next few days."

She was ready for a break before she did the rest. Setting the henna supplies aside, she stood, gazing down at the work she'd done so far, the man lying at her feet, arms straight out to either side, legs straight and together, his cock rising from his pelvis.

"Don't move," she reminded him. Then she stepped over him,

straddling his hips, and lowered herself so her still damp cunt pressed his cock against his belly.

His lips pressed together, his eyes locking upon her in a way that told her how much he wanted to lock himself around her. Inside her.

She wanted that, too, and she showed him, circling his cock with one hand to guide the ridged head into her cunt. As she slid down onto him, biting her lip, his attention latched onto her mouth. She saw the truth of what he'd said, how much he liked looking at her face and all it told him. Gave him. The strength of his regard made her shiver.

"Oh...yes," she purred, rising and falling upon him in slow, easy glides. She squeezed down, sucking in an erratic breath at the resulting ripple through her sex and lower belly, her own chakra areas.

"Those energy channels I was talking about? Solar and lunar? As I rise, I draw through the solar, and release through the lunar, but I imagine them going into you and doing the same. Can you do that, too? A circle of fire, of energy, of fuel..."

She could tell when he figured it out, because the small movements of his body, to accommodate her pleasure and yet respect the need to keep the paste undisturbed, gained a noticeable synchronicity, and that energy strengthened. The ripple became a wave, for both of them, strong and carrying them higher.

"Goddess..." she breathed. His eyes moved to her breasts, the quivering of the curves above the lace, nipples hard against it. Flames from that Kundalini fire shot from the base of her spine, spiraling around her, spearing through each chakra, flooding them, taking her over.

The lace of the skirt let him see tempting hints of her cunt, stretched by his cock. She caressed the sensitive skin where she'd removed the hair, and came down on him, a full, hilt deep contact. Determined to let that power fuel what she was doing, she found that plateau at the edge of release and stopped herself there, channeling it, cycling it through. He was still breathing the way she'd shown him, so she knew they were holding onto one another there. The sensual need evened out, spreading over that surface, surrounding and securing both of them. No climax. Just blissfully balanced on its threshold.

She stopped. They were both shuddering. Leaning down, she put her lips against his, sharing that irregular breath with him. She stroked his hair, ear and throat as she tasted, licked, bit, and drank in a long, deep kiss.

She laid her hand on his chest and lifted her head only enough to put a small amount of distance between their mouths. His presence, power and life, all up against hers. His musky male scent, his flesh and muscle, heat and need.

"Keep breathing with me, Rev. Imagine your breath, your life energy, coming up through those centers, to your crown chakra and above it, to the energy of the Universe, and let that energy fill you as you exhale."

When she straightened, he was with her. Gazing at her with a double helix of calm focus and sexual furor which reflected her own state.

She drew herself off of him, holding him with her muscles until the very last scintillating friction of his head against her slick tissues. When she went back to her knees next to him, his lips were parted, still damp from her mouth, his gaze clinging to her.

It took a few more breaths before she was steady enough to resume the design, especially since her next canvas was around his tempting cock, bathed in her own aroused scent.

She did a teardrop and arch design over the base, against the newly shaved skin. She put a mandala around his navel. Then she laid her hand over his heart and sternum.

"Every one of these has multiple meanings. This one, the heart chakra, is associated with the desire to serve, and compassion. It's your center, Rev. I'm doing a mandala here, too."

"What the mandala mean?"

She loved the sound of his voice when he was in a deep sea of arousal. It was a song meant just for her.

"The short response is the Universe." She put several rings around it, adding flowers on either side, with the close humps around the central petals. At the base of his throat, she did another arch, with the tear drops raining above it.

She sat back.

"You gonna keep going, Mistress?" Rev's light brown eyes were filled with her. He was still on that plateau with her, a mix of heavy arousal and stillness. "It feel like you want to."

"I do, but no, I'm done with the front. I'm resisting the urge to do too much." She knew her look held some of the ferocity she was feeling. "Dommes tend to have a strong urge to mark their territory."

She set aside her tools, rose, and returned to her chair. While he watched her, held down by the restraint of the wet fragrant paste, she propped her foot once again on the stool. His cock became stiffer at the view. Its involuntary movements might affect the design, but that didn't bother her. Each time she looked upon it before it faded, she'd know how and why it had been altered.

"What are you thinking, Rev?"

"I've never felt owned by no one except God."

"Does this conflict with that?"

"No. It feels...balanced. A line between Heaven and Earth, kind of like how you done drawn it on me." He glanced down, his chest muscles shifting slightly.

"Do you have any difficulties standing for long periods, Rev?" He bore some of the scars she'd expect for an active man. Nothing that suggested severe injury, but because his job was physically demanding, there could be repetitive motion damage.

"No, Mistress. I'm on my feet most the time."

"Moving on your feet and standing still for a long period can be different. Tell me if anything starts to hurt. If you injure yourself, you can't serve me, can you? Not as well."

"No, Mistress."

"Good. Stand carefully, and move back under the hook."

When he did, she brought the rope ends back. She had him lift his arms straight out to his sides and then wrapped the rope over each hand to help him hold the arms up. "Don't straighten your knees too much. It can cut off your blood flow and make you pass out."

She had to resist the urge to brush her thighs against his cock. She might decide to close the gap between their bodies and really ruin the set of the henna.

Fortunately, she had a new canvas to distract her. His back. She retrieved her paste and moved behind him, gaze sweeping the drum tight buttocks and broad shoulders, and what was in between. The next mandala went on the base of his spine. From there she created a serpent trail of dots and circles, winding her way up that path. At the center of his back, where the heart chakra was, the mandala she created radiated outward like a sun.

The work drew her in, everything quiet again except the rush of the gas logs, and the clicks and shifts of her house. Rev kept his head up, his body straight. Even without his eyes upon her, his attention circled her as if they were dancing with clasped hands.

Applying henna was a very intimate process. If he'd been holding and kissing her, she would have felt as connected to him as she did right now. She considered the last design, for the base of his neck. The chakra for intuition, communication and expression was there.

She did two vertical lines, flooding them with the henna, then did the same horizontally. A cross. She wrote *John 13:34* in cursive beside it on one side, a flower chain on the other that went around to touch his collar bone. As she did it, the quote went through her mind.

A new command I give to you, that you love one another.

She put her hand over the unmarked part of his shoulder, and thought about the command to love. Jesus was the ultimate Dom, knowing all, protecting those under his care.

Imagining Cyn's reaction to that thought, she suppressed a snort. Rev's fingers twitched. "All right, Mistress?"

"Yes. I was thinking about Cyn. She's not the biggest fan of Christianity."

His shoulder tightened. "She don't want me with you?"

Vera stroked that muscle. "She's concerned about you being with me. But it has to do with her, not you. As I mentioned, she had a very hard start in life, and saw a lot of bad things. She's a fighter, so in her mind, if there's Someone there, It's guilty of unforgivable neglect. If there isn't, then we're all just foolish for believing."

She paused. "But being with Mick, I think she's learning how unfathomable and limitless love can be. Which means she's starting to open the door to faith, more than she has in the past."

"Sometimes a person needs more than themselves to find it, to start that conversation inside." Rev's head dipped, as if thinking. "Some people, that door don't open because of everything they piled up against it. They have to dig it out. She got the mad in her, but she got the good, too. You can feel it. With a will like hers, after all she been through, and now with a man who love her, the good will win out."

"I agree. It takes most people a while to figure that out about her." She wiped her hands on a cloth. "I'm done. Stay in that position for now, but you don't have to worry about small shifts to keep comfortable."

Vera put away the supplies and cleaned up. When she returned to her chair, this time, she stood before it, her back to him. She slid one strap off her shoulder, then the other, then sinuously pushed the garment down until it fell to the ground around her bare feet.

When she glanced over her shoulder, she saw a strong man drinking in what she was offering, his hands held by her ropes, his body decorated by her henna. It was a view she would capture and call back again and again.

He was doing the breathing exercise to help him control his reactions. When she let him release this time, it should feel like nothing he'd ever experienced. A Tantric-driven orgasm was impossible to describe. It could go on and on, the ultimate Dom and sub space. Their bodies twined around one another, the aftermath forming a vessel of connection that would carry them on a river of bliss until it bumped against the shore of reality.

They came back to it in a better state, because the Universe had confirmed it was there, and far bigger than anything anyone knew, a comfort.

He took an unsteady breath. "I feel...incredible."

"You look incredible." She let him see how much she meant it. "When I wipe off the paste, I plan on enjoying you in every way I'm imagining, Rev. And in every way you're imagining." She showed him a dangerous smile. "So for the next four hours, I'm going to keep your mind on that."

She withdrew a thick book from the magazine holder next to her chair. It had gold edged pages and a blue cover, the title of the book stamped on it in the same gold. "I picked up this Bible this week. Tell me your favorite passages, and I'll read them to you."

After a long, stunned moment, a chuckle rumbled from his chest. "Mistress, I may be rethinking what evil truly is."

CHAPTER FIFTEEN

"*A*ll morning, you've been humming, singing or smiling like you don't have good sense," Beau noted. "It must have been a good weekend."

"It must have been," Rev answered.

"Well," Beau said with exaggerated somberness, "I expect it has to do with the Lord seeing fit to let you wake up on the right side of the dirt."

"That's entirely it, Beau. You called it."

His boss snorted. "I know the look of a man who spent his weekend in the arms of a fine woman." He gestured to Rev's forearms, revealed from the rolled-up sleeves of his coveralls. "Was that Miss Vera Morgan's work?"

Rev grinned and kept cleaning the glass of the foyer trophy cases. He'd finished the sports ones and had moved on to the nerd boxes, as some of the kids called them, because they held the awards for the math, science, chess and debate teams.

The vinegar scent of the cleaner brought to mind painting Easter eggs with Teena Joy while she read the resurrection story to him.

"She and the women at her company help out a lot in the community. But people are more than one thing, and sometimes those other things aren't as good."

Rev stopped at the unexpected comment and looked over his shoulder. "What nonsense you talking, old man?"

Beau lifted a shoulder. His humor had been banked, his gaze careful but concerned. "I want all good things for you, Rev. But she's different from you. Not better or worse, I'm not saying that. But awfully different. When you're interested in a woman, your heart gets involved quick. Are you sure she's not just... Well, women like the way you look. You know that."

Vera's face, her touch, her words, were in Rev's head. But at times she'd made it sound like she didn't expect this to last. He thought of the club, the BDSM world unfamiliar to him. How she'd emphasized that the "scenes" there mostly didn't translate to relationships outside the walls. He thought of how easy it was for her to introduce him to men she'd had scenes with like she'd done with Rev.

With all that, and Beau voicing words uncomfortably close to Witford's, two people he valued, the seeds of doubt could be planted. But only if he gave them the right kind of ground inside himself to do so.

She'd taken him to her home, something she'd made clear she didn't regularly do. Plus they were talking about and doing plenty of things outside of the club things. So as important as that part of her life obviously was to her, and how much he yearned to do those things with her, it wasn't all of what had brought them together.

"I'm not saying you're not worthy of a woman like that, Rev." Beau was gazing hard at his introspective face. "Not even close. You deserve a loving woman. Never mind me. I should have stuck one of my big feet into my mouth."

"No." Rev gestured with the cleaner. "You my friend. You say what's on your mind. I appreciate it, Beau. I really do. It's okay. I done here. I'm going to go fix that bent locker handle on Hall C."

He paused, though, looking at the "nerd" awards. "You know, when people hear someone talk smart, they figure they worked hard to get smart. That someone who don't talk smart wasn't smart enough to do good in school, or was too lazy. They don't dig into who a person is. She's not like that, Beau."

Beau met his gaze and nodded. "I'm glad to hear it. If she sees you the way we see you, then she's pretty *and* smart. In the right ways. And I hope the best for both of you."

"Me too. God gives us plenty of gifts, but most of them come with a time limit. It's why we gotta value them. Can you take the cleaning stuff back to the storeroom? All I need is the toolbox."

"Sure." Watching him go, Beau really wished he hadn't said a thing. Witford had stopped by on Rev's day off and expressed some worries. He'd noted how much he wanted the best for his cousin and appreciated Beau looking after him, since Rev respected his counsel.

Normally Beau would have dismissed Witford's concerns, because Rev was a grown man, and Beau had seen plenty of evidence of Rev's common sense. But falling in love with a woman could mess with any man's compass, and he was pretty sure that was what Rev was doing. It didn't hurt for Beau to throw it out there.

Though it somehow felt it had.

Rev would have reassured him if he could, but he did have some chewing to do on it. Noting the time though, he quickened his step. He wanted to get the locker repaired before the next bell. It was a narrow hall, and he'd be an obstruction as the students flooded the space, headed for lunch in their usual exuberant fashion.

Watching the kids be kids always lifted his day. Even as he used the bell changes to take a closer look at those he knew had more trouble being happy. He liked to get a sense of how their day was going and give their next period teacher a heads up if they needed a boost in attention.

He tried to keep an eye on all of them, even the ones who seemed to do fine, because a bad day was a bad day, and every person had them. But some days he missed the warning signs.

This was going to be one of those days.

He'd turned up Hall C when he heard the first shot.

"So should we skip this bullshit, and I'll clean out my desk?"

Vera looked up to see Watt Bellini filling her doorway with wide shoulders, a belligerent attitude and weary frustration. He wore pressed slacks and a plum-colored dress shirt that complimented his thick dark hair, keen brown eyes and a jaw that tended toward a five o'clock shadow, no matter how clean shaven he started his day. He had a strong but amiable personality and, according to Cyn, was a consistently excellent account manager.

"I see you have an idea of why I requested the meeting." With a cool look, Vera gestured to her guest chair. "Close the door and sit down. And please keep the profanity where it belongs. Not here."

Watt's jaw tightened, but he complied. He sat in the guest chair with a straight back and braced legs. "Sorry. I'll turn in my notice and work my two weeks from home to transition my replacement. I guess I can forget a referral, but that'll give me time to get some ducks in a row."

His fingers tightened on the arm, the ruby in his University of Georgia class ring catching the sunlight from her window. "I screwed myself on this one. I should have come to you up front, but I figured you wouldn't believe me, and I let her get out ahead of it. So the bi— she wins."

Vera sat back, crossing her legs. "Watt, no decisions have been made. You're here so I *can* hear your side of the story."

She'd effectively thrust a stick into the spokes of the bicycle he'd been pedaling so hard. "What?"

She tapped the arm of her chair. "There are many abominable instances of women being sexually harassed. But every situation has to be thoroughly investigated, without bias, because a man is just as vulnerable to being harassed, *or* falsely accused. Power can be political or emotional, not just in accordance with company hierarchy. Abuse of the power is the driving factor, not gender."

She put that frost in her tone again. "Whoever is at fault, whether you or Henrietta, will be shown the door. Any employer seeking a reference from us will not get it, and they will be told that history. But first we will determine who deserves that treatment and who doesn't."

Vera nodded to Watt. "I'm listening. Take a few moments to lose the attitude and change gears. When you're ready, don't embellish, and be honest, even if it doesn't reflect well on you. I'm seeking the truth, and I'm very good at recognizing lies."

"Okay." Watt pressed his lips together. Took a deep breath. "Henrietta and I had a reciprocal interest a few months ago. We went out for a couple of dates. Ended up in bed together. Three times."

He cleared his throat, shifted. Vera said nothing.

"Then my mom got sick, and Henrietta felt neglected. She didn't get how important my family was to me. I told her I needed to focus on that, to help my dad. She didn't take it well at first, but then she started to approach me at work..."

He looked out the window at the live oaks framed there. "I hate this," he said through gritted teeth. "It's no one's business and she made it into...this."

"I know this is embarrassing and difficult, Watt," Vera said quietly. "It's why these details go no further than this room, unless it becomes necessary."

"I guess I have to trust you on that one. You haven't ever given me a reason not to." He laced his hands between his spread knees. "She'd rub against me when I was getting coffee. Try to talk me into hooking up after work. Jesus..." He shook his head. "I don't think I meant all that much to her. She just doesn't like to be the one told *no*. That kind of attitude makes her an aggressive account manager, good at securing the deal."

It was an accurate assessment, since that quality had gotten her hired. The company was full of strong women, including those who ran it. Ros didn't like to lose. Neither did Cyn. But they both knew where the line was in a situation like what he was describing.

Watt sent Vera a tired look. "My mom is doing really harsh chemo. Dad doesn't drive. I've been trying to keep all the balls in the air. When I come into work and pour that first cup of coffee... I know it sounds idiotic, but that's become an important five minutes to me, Vera. It's like my reset button. Up until the day that landed us here, I'd been brushing her off, handling her. But that morning, I didn't react well. I told her I couldn't be her little fuck-toy right now and piss off. I tried to apologize later."

He shook his head. "I know that was bad behavior on my part. But for her to take that and claim I was sexually harassing her... I didn't think I'd hurt her that badly. I didn't mean to do that. Maybe I should have asked for a leave of absence, but work helps to keep me sane."

Vera had told Watt she was good at detecting lies, and she was. The key was setting aside bias and listening. Then asking the right questions and assessing reactions.

When she'd interviewed Henrietta, the woman had spoken of Watt cornering her in the supply closet, stopping her at her car after work. He'd pushed against her in the open car door, grabbed her hand

and put it on his crotch. He'd told her, "We've hooked up before. Fucking is no big deal. Let's keep scratching one another's itch."

"I told him no, that I wasn't interested," Henrietta had told her. Her body language projected the expected combination of embarrassment and anger. "I told him I didn't want to do the casual thing anymore. He won't take no for an answer, and he waits for when I'm by myself to...ambush me. My nerves...it's making it terrible to come to work."

Her hands had been shaking as she wrung them in her lap. "Maybe I should just give my notice. I don't want to cause any problems, and maybe this is my fault, because I went to bed with him to begin with..."

Which was where Vera's flags had gone up, because Watt was correct. Henrietta was aggressive in her job. Forthright in meetings. She neither possessed nor showed any empathy for the insecurities that dragged many women into a victim mentality, or the guilt trap when it came to sexual harassment or abuse. She also had excellent skills with clients, and knew how to work a room. Not insincerely, not exactly, but she knew the right buttons to push, how to read someone. How to get the result she wanted.

Except in this case.

"Watt, what's your mother's chemo schedule?"

"Six more weeks, twice a week."

Vera tapped the note into her computer. "All right. For those six weeks, we'll put you on a flex schedule, so you can work remotely as much as you need. If you have a face-to-face client meeting which conflicts with your mother's needs, let Cyn know. She'll get it covered."

"You'll tell her?"

"She already knows." Cyn missed nothing about her people, and had been digging into all this a day ahead of when Henrietta brought her complaint to Vera.

Watt was correct. Him not coming to Vera right away meant Henrietta had had time to cover her tracks. Watt had assumed in a female-led company where the staff was eighty percent women, and he was one of only three male account managers, he wouldn't have an ally or sympathetic ear. Vera was about to fix that impression.

"But...I...you're not letting me go?"

"No. Henrietta's employment will be terminated this afternoon, which is why I want you to leave this office and go straight home. Focus on your mother. When you next come into this office, your five minutes with your coffee will be undisturbed." Vera's lips twitched. "Unless Cyn needs something from you right away, and pounces on you as soon as you hit the parking lot."

"Yeah, she can be like that." His lips twitched, but he ran a hand over his face, his eyes suddenly suspiciously wet. "Jesus. Sorry...just... sorry."

Vera nudged her tissue box to the edge of her desk, letting him grab one to swipe at his eyes.

"Watt...she's your mother. You're under a lot of stress. You have a demanding job and now a difficult family situation. Henrietta exacerbated it to the breaking point, and we all have one. That's why we watch out for one another."

"Yeah." He pulled himself together and gave her a wry look. "When I took this job, a buddy told me I'd never advance my career, 'working in a hen house.' His words, not mine. But TRA has made such a name for itself in marketing, I figured hell, even if I can only work there a few years and then have to go elsewhere to make a vertical move, it'll look good on my resume. But then Cyn promoted me to account team manager, and I'm doing work I love. The idea of leaving here because of something like this, it felt like the straw that broke the camel's back. Henrietta..."

An unhappy look crossed his face. "I didn't want to hurt her, Vera. I mean, we had some good times. I just didn't expect her to turn on me like this. I know I was an idiot for hooking up with someone at work, but we head up different teams, and I thought we understood each other."

"Your judgment might have taken a hit, but you tried to resolve it the right way. You explained your situation to her, and she kept pushing. You apologized for snapping at her, and she chose revenge instead of accepting the apology. You bear no blame for her behavior, which was reprehensible."

"She's not..." He sighed. "I want to make excuses for her now that I know I'm not going to be canned as an accused sexual harasser. I don't like thinking I got her fired."

"You didn't. She did." Vera locked gazes with him, so he understood how much she meant it. "Keep that in mind. As I'm sure you're aware, this situation shouldn't be shared with other staff members. You can communicate further concerns with me or Cyn."

"Yes ma'am." He rose, and gave her a grateful nod. "Thank you, Vera."

"You're welcome."

After he left, Vera took a breath. *Well, shit.* This was going to derail today's schedule. She'd need to meet with Cyn, and let Cyn vent her desire to kick Henrietta's yoga-toned ass all the way out to the parking lot. Then they'd review the proper exit interview process, which would include how to handle Henrietta if she threatened to bring a lawsuit against TRA for her firing. Vera thought it very likely the woman would react that way.

Companies often headed off such a situation with severance pay and a written agreement that the reasons for her firing would never be disclosed to another employer, but Ros didn't play that way. Which meant the CEO might need to attend that exit interview.

Ros didn't respond well to blackmail. As unpleasant as it would be, Vera had no doubt about the meeting's outcome. No matter how aggressive and tough Henrietta was, she was no match for Ros. She'd make it clear to Henrietta if she went that way, she'd be incurring a lot of legal fees...and TRA had deeper pockets.

Vera pushed back from her desk. Before she got started on all that, she'd give herself five minutes to dwell on something far better.

It had been an amazing weekend. She'd accompanied Rev to church on Sunday, ignoring and mostly shutting out the effect of Tisha and Witford's baleful looks. Instead, she immersed herself in the joy of Rev's singing. When they shared a pew together afterward, she basked in the warmth of his hand around hers, the press of his shoulder and thigh against hers.

She'd liked the hint of the forearm henna beneath the cuff of his dress shirt. The cross showed on his nape, and though it had drawn some curious looks, it wasn't inappropriate to the environment. They wouldn't expect he had the other designs, including one around his cock. But she knew, and the knowledge was like having sugar on her tongue.

This time, when the service concluded, Rev introduced her to some of his favorite congregation members. Including Mrs. Everett

Meriweather. The flirty ninety-year-old widow had a ready smile for Vera and took her hand. She wore black heels and a trim sapphire-blue church suit with a magnolia bloom in the lapel next to her rope of pearls.

"Rev needs a good strong woman in his life." She spoke bluntly, the privilege of a confident woman her age. "One who takes care of him the way he takes care of all of us. I like the look of you. Almost as smartly dressed as me."

"Thank you. I'm doing my best. On the taking care of him." Vera swept an appreciative gaze over her ensemble. "I obviously have work to do on the clothes."

"Sincere flattery and a sense of humor." Mrs. Meriweather captured Rev's hand, creating a circle between the three of them. "Good for you, boy."

Those kinds of welcome dissipated the tension Witford and Tisha's attitude caused her. She did see a couple looks at the same disapproving level as theirs, most noticeably from two ushers who'd taken up the collection from the front half of the church. When Rev introduced her to Simon and Tyson, they were stiff in their responses, unwilling to be drawn in. They'd excused themselves to flank Witford and Tisha, a chilly backdrop to the wall of Rev's family.

It brought back some incredibly unpleasant memories, no matter how much she tried to squash them.

Rev had drawn her closer, his arm around her waist. "Don't worry none about them," he said. "They'll come around. Let me introduce you to the choir ladies and Beverly, who leads them."

"Palma Webb on line two for you, Vera."

When Bastion's voice came through the phone intercom, his message yanked Vera back to reality like a bucket of cold water in the middle of an orgasm.

Fucking hell.

The Henrietta situation, the problems with Rev's family, were minor issues compared to her reaction when Bastion said her sister's name. The spike through her chest could have done an ice pick proud.

"Vera? You there?"

"Yes."

"She says it's personal and you'd take the call. Rather imperiously, and not in the good way," he added. "More bratty and petulant. Can I teach her a lesson by taking a message? Threaten to spank her if she doesn't learn better manners? Don't lecture me. It's only a workplace faux pas if I threaten a staff member with that."

Bastion's irreverent manner helped get her back on track. Even if her hold on that track was taking all ten of her tensely curled toes. "Stop getting your advice about professional office behavior from Cyn. I'll take the call. Do you have any Rolaids in your desk?"

"Honey, you know I do. I buy them in bulk."

"Good. I'll come get a couple after I finish the call."

Lord help me.

Hearing a gunshot at a place one should never be heard took a precious second to process. By the time Rev turned the corner of Hall C, three more had rung out, competing with the screaming that had erupted with the first.

Kids were bursting out of Mrs. Cuddy's class, wild-eyed and frantic, rabbits trying to escape a wolf. Most went toward the exit door at the end of the hall, rather than coming his way. The ones that didn't, he waved them past him as he moved forward, sticking close to the wall. Watching for the wolf.

Teachers who heard the shots would follow the drills they'd practiced. Lock their doors, tell the students to get down on the floor so a shooter couldn't get a good target through the upper panel of glass, and report status to the main office through the intercom system.

With a stutter of his heart, he saw one child lying motionless in the hall. Another staggered out of Mrs. Cuddy's room and collapsed, blood soaking the front of the nice striped shirt his momma had probably bought him. The wolf emerged right behind him.

It was Craig, a slight, pale boy with thick blond hair. He was one of the students who held himself apart, a hooded ghost in the hallways. He'd transferred in a couple months ago, his dad having won custody of him in a nasty divorce. Mrs. Cuddy had made the most progress with him. She handled the yearbook and had gotten him involved, helping to collect some pictures for it.

He wore baggy jeans and his usual dark hoodie. It had a skull-faced reaper printed on the back, one bony hand reaching out as the other clasped his scythe.

Rev had a chilling view of that empty eyed specter, because Craig was ignoring the kids he'd shot and was turned toward the children fleeing toward the exit door. He raised his gun, taking aim on Mary Wharton's back.

"Craig, *stop.*"

Craig spun around. Since he had his finger on the trigger, it went off, hitting the lockers to Rev's left with a loud clang. A sizzling burn across his arm suggested a ricochet had hit him, but Rev barely noticed. He was focused on Craig's lifeless eyes, hopeless and tired and confused and far away from the reach of anything or anyone.

No. No one was beyond Love. God would give Rev what he needed to reach him. He gripped that calm certainty with all he had and stood still and tall, while Craig pointed the gun at him and gave him that empty stare. Rev couldn't tell what was going on his mind, but it hadn't yet told him to pull the trigger again.

Lord, save those two children, and whoever else is hurt. If this be the day the Lord calls me home, thank you for Veracity. Keep her and love her, the way I wish I could have stayed around and done. Amen.

~

"You abandoned us, Veracity."

Vera had her heels planted as if she expected a gale wind to gust through her office. "I go by Vera. I'm not a child anymore."

Hearing her full name on Rev's lips made it special, and didn't remind her of her childhood at all. So only he had her permission to use it. Or someone who used it out of love, which meant her sister didn't qualify. "If you've called me for money, do you think guilt is the way to go?"

"Do you expect me to grovel? Would that make you feel more high and mighty than you already do?"

"I expect you to be courteous. Respectful, the way I'm trying to be to you."

"You lost my respect a long time ago."

Anger took over, and so many awful feelings Vera knew a full bottle of Rolaids wouldn't handle it. "Mama told me not to come back. That's not abandoning you."

"She had no choice. You insisted on living wrong, and you wouldn't agree to counseling—so yes, you turned your back on us. A path away from God was more important to you than your family."

If she'd had any doubts over why she had such a negative reaction to Tisha and Witford, the passive aggressive undercurrents—plus the not-so-passive ones—made it as clear as one of Rev's vinegar-cleaned windows.

Step back, she told herself. *This is barren ground, the earth too worn out for anything to grow in it again.* Holding Rev in her mind, thinking of his patience, his honest way with his feelings, helped balance the way-too-familiar ache spreading through her, like a garden overrun with weeds. A garden she'd thought she'd kept well-tended enough to keep out those weeds, but weeds could and would shoot back up overnight.

She would treat this like a meeting with a difficult employee. She would focus on what she could resolve instead of what she couldn't. "Tell me what's going on, Palma, and why you need the money."

"Me telling you that your family needs it should be enough. You don't need a reason."

"Since it's my money you're asking for, yes, I do. I may also have other resources that can help."

"Fine. Daddy had a heart attack about ten months ago. He hasn't been able to work, and Mama is running out of ways to make ends meet. She got herself a job, but it doesn't pay much. Me and the others have kicked in to help with the mortgage, but we got our own kids and bills, and we're running short. Bethany said there's no reason we should strap ourselves when you have money."

"How will our parents feel about you coming to me?"

"We'll make it seem like we came up with more. They've had a hard enough time letting us help. When I started paying their power bill, they threw a tantrum. Bethany pointed out all the years they took care of us, so it's not charity to accept our help when it's freely given. They've been better about us helping since then, but you know they won't accept anything from outside the family. Best we not tell them. And—"

You know they won't accept anything from outside the family.

Did her sister know how that one sentence, so carelessly uttered, cut Vera to the quick? Would she care if she knew? "How much do you need?" she interrupted Palma.

Palma's tone went flat. "Twenty thousand would get us through the year. We're filing for disability programs and early Social Security, but it's a quagmire, and they're throwing up roadblocks."

"Fine. Here's my cell." After giving Palma that info, Vera continued. "Text me your bank information. I'll transfer the money. Send me what you and Bethany have done on the government programs so far. I have contacts that can remove some red tape."

"So just like that? That's how easy it is for you? While we're scraping by, you have the kind of money to—"

"Palma, if you don't want my help, that's up to you. If you ever want to have a conversation that isn't about accusing me of not being part of a family that doesn't want who I am, call me. Otherwise, use your text finger for future communication. Got it?"

The sharp tone was what she used on employees trying to bullshit her, or submissives needing a stronger hand. It worked for this, too. Sullen silence filled the phone.

"If you'd been here, he wouldn't have had the heart attack," Palma said abruptly. Then she hung up.

A minute later, the bank information arrived on her phone. Vera choked on a bitter laugh. Tossing it on her desk, she went to her windows, folding her arms against herself.

She didn't have to recall her father's granite expression as her mother told her to pack her things and get out. It was like a picture on her wall, waiting for her to turn in that direction to see it. He'd had her mother execute the sentence, but he was the head of the family. The decision came from the top down. After her mother had said it, he'd turned away from Vera. Except for the iron set of his shoulders, she would have felt like it meant no more to him than switching off a TV program he was done with.

When she'd gone to the room she shared with Bethany, Bethany pleaded with her to stay, to just work it out. *Act like what they want you to be. Be whatever you want to be when they're not around.*

"I'm not a liar like you," she'd told Bethany, speaking out of hurt, her throat flooded with tears. "They should be able to love who I am."

Because they didn't. They hadn't said, "We love you, but you can't stay under our roof if you don't believe as we do." It was just, "If you don't believe as we do, then you can't be part of this family." Full stop.

She would have given so much to have them add in that "We love you." It would have helped, to have something that suggested time would bring them back to one another. Like Rev had told her he'd pray it would.

But she knew now it was better that they hadn't. No false hope. And she routinely reminded herself that, before those events, she hadn't lacked for love or care. Cyn had understandable, horrific reasons for her cynicism toward religion. Vera had been raised in a loving family, with plenty of opportunities. She couldn't deny that. Maybe that was why she'd never held a grudge against Christianity when that love had been withdrawn. She knew plenty of Christians who never would have turned their backs on their child for choosing a different path.

Wicca had its own adherents who were intolerant and disrespectful of paths not their own. That was a human trait, not a spiritual one.

The raw pain in her gut was bad enough, but it was the anxiety she really hated. Transferring the money, dealing with the bureaucracy surrounding disability care, were challenges she could handle. The anxiety wasn't from that. It was the old feeling of the bottom falling out of her world, the safety net gone.

She wanted to reach out to Rev, but he was at work. She'd do what she'd done before she'd met him. Pull herself together and use the strategies she'd taught herself, to rebuild the walls Palma's cutting cruelty had just damaged. One of which was thinking about the people who cared for her, who were the foundation of her world.

Which now included Rev. She believed that.

"Vera?"

Bastion was in her doorway. His expression darkened at what he saw in her face, but she shook her head. "Just don't. Not right now."

Some people needed to fall apart in the company of others. She wasn't one of them, and he knew it, so he put the bottle of Rolaids on her desk. "I'm sorry. I assume that was a family member? Snotty voice aside, she sounded like you."

"Yes." Emotion made her voice throaty. "I have a one o'clock, to go over a contract with Earl Livingston."

"Should I push it to another day, or give you an hour?"

"Two o'clock is fine if that works for him. If not, reschedule to his convenience. Thanks, Bastion."

"All right." He gave her a hard but understanding look. "Buzz if you need anything else."

He closed her door without having to be asked. She sank into her guest chair, and put her face in her hands. Eventually, she would try steady, meditative breaths, good thoughts, prayer. Call Rev up in her mind, in full, wonderful detail. But right now, the tears pushed forward, and she wouldn't deny them.

A cathartic cry, for what couldn't be helped or fixed, would give her the strength to get back up. After that, she'd fix her face, and handle the bank transfer.

"Vera." Cyn came in without waiting for a response to her urgent knock. Seeing Vera's tear-streaked cheeks, she stopped short. "You've already heard?"

"Heard what?"

Bringing her phone over to Vera, she pressed the replay button on a news video.

"...shooting at Roberts Middle School happened at 9:40am. We're getting reports that at least one teacher has been killed. Several students and a custodial worker have also been shot. Police are holding the names of the victims until the families can be notified. The shooter was a 14-year-old male—"

Vera bolted from her chair, grabbing her cell phone off her desk. She tried the burner she'd given Rev, but it wasn't on. Mavis's went straight to voicemail, no surprise. She didn't have Beau's number, something she'd correct later, but there was no use trying the school number. A million parents would be trying to get through.

Skye showed up at the door, using her recording software with flying fingers. "He's at UMC."

Later Vera would realize she'd never thought "custodial worker" meant anyone but Rev. Not that Beau was any less brave, but as she'd already learned, Rev had a way of being at the right place at the right time to prevent a tragedy from becoming worse than it already was. If he was close enough to try and protect the students, he would have stepped between the shooter and his targets, no matter that he was unarmed.

Bastion was back, the keys to Cyn's truck in his hand. "Ros and Abby are still at their meeting in Baton Rouge, but I'll let them know."

"Wait until we know his status," Cyn said. "There's nothing they can do until we know more. Skye will handle things here."

Vera had presided over her share of memorial services. When it was someone's time, it was time. But right now her spiritual acceptance of death as a part of life had zero room inside her. Rage and fear had sharpened into a weapon she fired at the Universe. *Don't you* dare *take him from me.*

Cyn had pulled Vera's purse from her drawer and handed it to her. When Vera reached the door, Bastion and Skye stepped aside to let her pass, though Skye gave her a brief embrace and a steady look. Bastion used the cover to snag Cyn's elbow. "She got spun up from a call from her family a few minutes before you came in," he said, low. "As insane as this sounds, she might need your help keeping it together."

"I've been known to keep my temper," Cyn said, her brown eyes like stone. "Except when someone needs their ass kicked. I'll have her back, either way."

"I know it."

Cyn wasn't much on PDAs, but Bastion squeezed her arm, his worried gaze following Vera. "Keep me posted. Anything she needs."

"Yeah. And you already know—"

"If Ros and Abby need to be called, they will be. Go, Cyn. She could run track in those heels right now."

"Karman Leone," Vera said at the ER desk. "He goes by Rev."

The admin typed in the name and reviewed the screen while Vera did her best not to yank it around and read it herself. "He's out of surgery and in recovery," she told them. "You can go up to the waiting room."

As soon as the woman told her where it was located, Vera was headed for the elevator. Cyn's long legs helped her keep pace. "They don't have him in the ICU," her friend pointed out. "That's a good sign."

Yes, it was. *He's alive*. But it didn't reassure her enough. She needed to see him.

Cyn stood close enough to her in the elevator that their shoulders brushed. Their relationship could be contentious, because even as close as they were, Cyn saw Vera as an authority figure, and her dysfunctional subconscious was predisposed to needle her, even without provocation. But right now, Cyn projected nothing but unconditional support, which included the willingness to go full-on pit bull. Whatever Vera needed was what she'd provide.

Vera expected nothing less from her, but she stomped the surge of emotion it caused, trying to break through her wall of control. She didn't know what was ahead of them, but she would figure out what Rev needed before she'd indulge her own reactions. That was what Cyn and the others were used to from her, because that was the way Vera was. It wasn't an act.

She thought of him in her home, stretched out under her touch, his eyes upon her as she painted his skin. They'd have seen the henna when they worked upon him. Did they know it had been put upon him by someone who wanted him marked as her possession, with her protection?

With her love. New though it was, she couldn't deny its existence when it was pounding in time with her heart.

When they reached the waiting room, she saw Witford and Tisha sitting in two of the chairs. His cousin's lips tightened, and Tisha's expression went stony. Witford rose and turned to the hospital volunteer sitting at the desk.

"This woman isn't welcome," Witford said. "She can't see my cousin."

"That's not your call." Cyn's posture was a sword halfway out of a scabbard.

"We're his family," Tisha said. "She's not."

A dangerous reaction gripped Vera, but before she could unleash it, she saw Mavis coming down the hallway. Which meant Rev was okay enough to receive visitors, though probably only one or two at a time, explaining why Tisha and Witford were out here.

"Thank goodness." Mavis clasped Vera in a light embrace and whispered in her ear. "He's all right. Take a breath."

As Vera did, gripping Mavis's forearms, the woman drew back and looked toward Witford. "I'm so glad you called her like he asked you to do." She glanced back at Vera. "The nurse said he's been asking for you since he woke from surgery."

The volunteer at the desk, a retiree in a pink smock, looked like she routinely handled families in crisis. Or in this case, conflict. She'd been following the conversation, as her words now proved. "Sir," she said briskly to Witford, "your cousin is awake and stable. He can choose who he wants to see. That said," she looked toward Vera, "I should verify with the nurse he's asked to see you. Name?"

"Veracity Morgan," Vera said stiffly.

Witford curled a lip. Tisha's gaze held hate and revulsion. Neither was bothering with a façade for their true feelings.

As Mavis drew Vera a few steps away for a private conversation, Cyn slid into the line of sight between her and Rev's family. Whatever Witford saw in her expression had him returning to his chair beside Tisha, though with plenty of attitude. If there'd been a target painted on her, Vera couldn't have felt the thrown knife of his gaze more keenly.

It told her how rattled they were, but it didn't throttle back her urge to react in kind. She had enough anger to pull it out and use it on the bastard herself.

The nurse said he's been asking for you since he woke from surgery.

"What happened?" Vera asked Mavis.

"A troubled boy, Craig, brought a gun into the school. He shot four students and Janice Cuddy." Mavis suddenly looked so overcome that it was Vera's turn to put a steadying hand on her shoulder. Mavis gripped it tight.

"They're all mine, Vera. Rev is, too. They're my responsibility."

"And you take care of them," Vera said. "You can't be in every child's mind, anticipating every problem they're facing or how they'll react to it."

"I know. I know. God, Vera." Her face crumpled. "Janice is dead. Two of the students are in critical condition."

Oh, Goddess. "I'm so sorry, Mavis."

Vera leaned in and pressed her forehead to her friend's. "You breathe with me. We'll handle all of it, but let's take a moment."

Mavis's head moved in a slight nod. When she lifted it, they were both in a better place. Vera had better control of the urgent need to bolt down the hall and find Rev, refusing to let anyone stand in her way.

"I talked to one of the two students who was less injured," Mavis said. "She was shot in the leg but will be fine, thank God. She was lying just inside the classroom door, and saw what happened after he shot Janice."

Mavis's lips twisted. "She admitted she recorded it on her phone, which she'd had hiding in her bag, the little miscreant. I gave it to the police."

"Tell me you transferred that file to your phone before you handed it over."

"I did. But you don't need to see that, Vera. Watching it once was more than I ever wanted to see."

She wasn't eager to see it either, but she needed to do so.

Recognizing it, Mavis cued up the file and transferred her earpiece to Vera's ear so she could hear the audio without anyone else doing so. Then the principal stepped away, proving she'd meant it. She never wanted to watch it again.

Vera turned toward the window to conceal her own reactions as she watched the nightmare unfold.

When the girl had started recording, Craig was still in the classroom, so Vera saw a few seconds of static images, a portion of her leg and the door jamb. Then Craig stepped over her. Though the phone shook with the girl's trembling, he ignored her. Vera saw his sneakers, the frayed cuffs of his jeans. The erratically moving camera lens shifted up, capturing his back, the tilt of his head and movement of the gun in his hand. He was wearing a hoodie with a stark white grim reaper on the back.

Jagged steel jammed into her chest when Vera saw Rev. He shepherded children past him, sounds of pounding footsteps and screaming bouncing off the hall lockers, drowning out everything else. Until Craig turned toward the exit and raised the gun. Rev called out Craig's name, in that resonant, seize everyone's attention way.

When Craig spun toward him and the gun went off, Vera's heart leaped into her throat, almost choking her.

Though blood appeared on his upper arm, Rev didn't flinch. He started to move forward. Calmly, as if none of this was happening.

"Craig, you all done now. You need to just lay it all down, boy."

"Go away. Just leave me alone. I want everyone to leave me alone."

He fired and Vera jerked as if the bullet had hit her. A gasp caught in her throat, a tiny protesting moan, as Rev stumbled a little. Blood welled up on his neck.

"Oh Goddess..." She was in a chair, which was good, because her knees had given out. Mavis was next to her, Cyn on her other side, a firm hand on her shoulder. Her friend was keeping a watchful eye on Witford and Tisha, while also watching the video over Vera's shoulder. She'd probably made sure Vera ended up in the chair instead of on her ass on cold hospital tile.

Rev straightened and walked up to Craig as if the boy had shot a water gun at him. He murmured something that was lost, but his body language said it was a reassurance. When he took the gun from Craig's hand, it went off again. Rev jerked once more, but he wrapped his other arm around Craig and brought him to his chest. "You okay. You did a bad thing, but we gonna help you find your soul again."

Mavis stared out the window into the parking lot, but she had her arms wrapped across her. Her fingers were a metronome, ticking off moments against her rib cage.

Craig fought him some, but when he gave up, he collapsed against Rev. During that time, Rev had put the gun on the ground and kicked it away. Beau arrived then, picking it up. The screen wobbled and fell against the girl's leg, offering a view of the classroom. Vera saw the teacher, her head down on her desk as if she'd decided to take a nap. She was grateful that was all she could see. Vera expected the girl had passed out, another small mercy.

She handed the phone back to Mavis. The pressure of Cyn's hand on her shoulder increased. Vera was sure her friend could feel the volcanic eruption building within her. If that volunteer didn't get a favorable response from the nurse, she wasn't waiting. She'd break Witford's legs to get to Rev.

"What happened after that?" Her lips felt numb.

"When the police arrived," Mavis said, "Rev was coming out of the school, holding Craig against him. He told them Craig was the shooter. He was so calm they thought the blood wasn't his. But the boy had blood on his face. That was the first indication they had that Rev had been hit. The second was when he collapsed while telling the police where the other kids were, and about Janice."

"Where was he shot?" Vera's voice sounded hollow in her head. Palma's call had caused an ache in her gut. This was drilling a hole to her spine.

"Upper abdomen, but close to the outside. Missed anything important. The other bullet grazed his neck. Craig was drunk. He'd gotten into his father's liquor cabinet. He walked up to Janice's desk and shot her. She tried the most to help him. It never makes sense."

Mavis's voice shook again. Vera and she sat holding hands, until she could continue. "Then he turned around and started firing. If he'd been sober, he might have had better aim. Though if he'd been sober, he might not have done this at all. When he came into the hallway, he'd just loaded the gun with a new magazine. He could have used ten more bullets if Rev hadn't stopped him."

"Yes? I'm calling about Karman Leone. There's a woman here he's asking for, and I'm just confirming."

Vera's head snapped around as the volunteer finally connected with the nurse. By the time she'd thanked her and hung up, Vera was standing over her.

"You can go on back," she told her.

"You need company?" Cyn asked Vera.

"Only one at a time," the volunteer said, though the last word hitched when Cyn gave her a baleful stare. Vera put a hand on her friend's arm.

"I'm all right. Promise. Um..." She rubbed her forehead. "We need to fire Henrietta before the end of the day and get an exit interview if we can. Watt's working from home for the next few weeks because of his mom's chemo."

"Story was what I thought, right? She got her panties in a bunch over the rejection and decided to be a conniving bitch. It backfired on her," Cyn said shortly.

"Yes."

"I'll take care of it with Skye. She has access to all your forms and HR procedures. Focus on this." Cyn met her gaze. "Go let him know his Mistress is here for him."

Vera nodded and hugged Mavis once more. "I'm here if you need me," she told the principal. "We all are."

"Same goes," Mavis said, despite her own hollow-eyed state. "He's tough, Vera. He'll be all right."

She ignored Witford and Tisha and headed down the hallway. When she reached recovery, she was directed toward a curtained area.

Vera stopped, feeling lightheaded. If she passed out and they had to tend to her before she could see Rev...well, that was unacceptable.

Steadying herself, she looked through a crack in the curtain and saw him. His eyes were open, and he was looking for her. As soon as he found her, his hand was out, reaching. He sat up, his feet swinging to the floor. The crazy man was getting up.

She needed to stop him from doing that, but she also wanted to be in his arms before another breath was drawn, but she couldn't seem to increase her pace. She was swimming through quicksand, like one of those dreams where she couldn't get to someone in trouble, no matter how hard she tried, or how much she called out.

She wasn't that kind of person. She kept it together in the worst circumstances. Especially when someone needed her.

He'd pulled off the things they'd stuck to him and was moving toward her, his gait stiff but steady, his back straight. The machines monitoring him were beeping angrily, but he was indifferent to them. Then he had his arms around her.

She pressed her face against his throat, that wonderful pulse beating against her. He was holding her up, she'd realize later, holding her with those strong hands as she held onto him. The fabric of the hospital gown was an annoying barrier, but she could feel his body, vibrant and *alive*.

The roaring in her head faded as she put her hand on his chest and found his heartbeat, the energy coursing through that chakra an unstoppable current. He stroked her back.

"I'm all right, Veracity. God and I, we get along good, but if he has plans for me, I done told him I need some time with you, that you need me, too. We need that time."

When she finally eased back, her hand ended up resting on the bandaged part of him beneath the gown. Just above his waist, close to the outside, as Mavis said. They'd put a bandage on his neck, too. She noticed a cut on his arm that they'd dressed with a topical ointment.

"Let's get you back to your bed before the nurses throw me out."

"They not going to do that."

But a moment later, a nurse pulled back the curtain. The blond fortyish woman had a hawk's hooked nose, broad hips and an insistent look on her face. "I'm going to lie down now," Rev told her, heading off her protest, "but this woman, she gonna stay with me."

"Is she family?"

"Yes," he said.

Veracity saw he wasn't making up something to keep her there. It was how he felt. What that made her feel weakened her knees again. "You moving me into a room anyway. She can go with me there."

"But our policy—"

"The choice is she stay with me, or I sign one of them forms and leave," he said steadily. "I not trying to be hard to get along with, Nurse Amy. But this is the way it's gonna be. She won't get in the way. She's efficient and smart, like you."

Nurse Amy fisted her hands on her hips. "You think a handsome man giving me compliments will make me overlook proper care for one of my patients?"

"No ma'am, not at all. I'm telling you she's the best thing for me right now."

Nurse Amy fastened a pale blue gaze on Vera. "If you being here means I don't have to tie him to that bed, you can stay."

When another nurse called to Amy, asking for help, Vera muttered, "I can take care of that part myself, I promise."

Rev's chest hitched with a half-chuckle. But she noticed he flinched at whatever that chuckle made his body do, and when they moved toward the bed, he did have to lean on her some. She was fully on board with Nurse Amy on getting his ass back into the bed.

The nurse returned seconds later to replace the monitoring lines. "They'll move you to a room in about a half hour," she said. "Try not to cause me any more trouble. I've got plenty of patients worse off than you."

"Yes'm. I got everything I need now."

Once he was assured Vera was going to stay, a weariness had grabbed hold of Rev that made him seem to sink even further into the bed. His eyes closed, though his hand remained wrapped around hers. Filled with worry, reminding herself that he was fine, Vera held onto it.

She sent a text to Cyn and Mavis, giving them their status, then she held that large hand with both of hers, occasionally brushing her lips over his chapped knuckles as he dozed. When his chest hitched, either from pain or something else, she moved her palm to his heart.

His eyes opened, confirming pain. Terrible, overwhelming, and not physical. It reminded her of his expression in the garden, before he knew she was there. His plaintive cry to the heavens. "I know," she whispered.

"Mrs. Cuddy was a good woman. She had two kids, one in college, one about to graduate high school. Her husband and her been planning what to do with retirement, though she say she worried about kids not having enough teachers with good sense to teach them. I saw her. Folded over her desk like she was taking a nap, only in her own blood."

The phone screen went through Vera's head. She put her hand on his face, knowing her own reflected his anguish.

"And those two kids in bad shape... One got shot in the stomach. They say he'll be having a lot of problems, and infection... God might take him anyway."

He shook his head. "All that, but the worst of them all is Craig, because his soul is so sick. If he ever heal enough to know what he done, he'll wish he was dead. I could feel him thinking about it, some part of him knowing. Thinking it would be better if he just go ahead and turn that gun on himself. God help me, I'm not sure if he not right, the hard road ahead of him."

He lifted pain-filled eyes to her. "But then I think of what you said about reincarnation. He'd have to face the same things all over again that he didn't figure out in this life. Wouldn't he?"

"Yes. Suicide just puts it off."

"That's a hard thing."

"Yes." Their hands were in a knot on his chest, and she wanted to give him something for the pain he was feeling. He already knew so many of the things that could bring comfort in times like these, but the reinforcement from somewhere other than his own suffering heart might help.

"What would you tell Craig, if he realizes what he did?"

Rev's eyes shadowed. "God's love don't falter," he said slowly. "Even when we do the worst things possible. He'll require justice, redemption and penance, but He never stops loving."

"The ultimate tough love parent."

"Yeah. Don't give no quarter, but don't leave you, neither." Rev didn't quite manage the smile. "You was having a bad day. I sorry. I made it worse."

Surprise shot through her. "How in the name of all that's holy can you know that?"

He treated her to his appealing lopsided smile. "I can just tell, Mistress. What happened? I don't want to think of the other for a while. I'll be praying on it a lot, but right now, it hurting my chest and making them bullet wounds burn."

She told him about Henrietta and Wade's issue, no names. He watched her as she ran through it. When she was done, he waited a beat. Then spoke. "What else?"

At her look, he added, "That's your job. You know how to handle it. It give you weight on your shoulders, but you strong. You can handle weight. What I feeling from you on that...it like this bullet. Just something that happened on your way to fix a problem. But the other thing you haven't told me about, that's like the way I feel about Craig, Mrs. Cuddy and the kids. Something you don't know no way to fix or make better, that just hurts."

"I don't feel like talking about it right now."

"Okay. I just lie here and think about how bad I feel. No distractions."

She narrowed her gaze. "How about I pinch you really hard somewhere that *will* be distracting? There's a term called topping from the bottom, where a sub tries to get his Mistress to do what he wants."

He sobered. "I not trying to do nothing like that. I teasing you, Mistress."

"I know. My sense of humor has taken a battering today." She sighed. "Fine. My sister called me. My father had a heart attack."

Rev pushed up on his elbows. "You don't need to be here, looking after me. Where they got him at?"

"It was ten months ago. He's okay, but he can't work. Palma called to guilt me into giving them money."

He sat back, gazed at her. Then he opened his arms.

She lay down against him. She did it gingerly and stayed in the chair, only her upper body in his hold, but when he guided her head to his chest, and tightened his embrace, she could feel his desire to hold her close. Take her weight.

She laid her hand on that bandaged spot on his side. She thought about what would have happened if that bullet or the other had been closer to places that would have taken him from her.

He'd wait for her to tell him more, and wouldn't push further. By holding her, he was letting her know she wasn't alone with it.

"I'm giving it to them, of course," she said. "They need it. But it dredges it all back up again. My family, my ex-husband, Donovan, they all wanted me to be someone I'm not. For my family, it was being their kind of Christian. For my husband, it was some of that, but we were just the wrong fit, and he wanted to give my soul a lobotomy to fix it.

"Bethany, my other sister, asked me why I couldn't just pretend. Act one way around my parents and then just live my life the way I wanted when I got out on my own. When I met you, saw you in the church that first time, for one terrible minute, I thought about walking out, because I was sure I was setting myself up for it again."

His arms tightened around her. "Glad you didn't."

"Me too. It felt like there were more things connecting us than separating us. That the things we're different about don't have to become a virus that infects the rest. That maybe it can all be part of the whole."

"The whole what?"

She paused. "The whole way we love one another."

"Did you just say you in love with me?"

He said it with humor, but when she looked up, his expression was far more intense. "Yes, I did," she said. "And if you don't feel the same way, I will smother you with a pillow. Even Nurse Amy won't be able to save you."

He stroked her cheek. "It was so easy to fall in love with you, I afraid it was too easy. That it wasn't real. Or I was being like one of the boys at school, all caught up in a pretty face and a nice backside. Or front side."

"Really?"

He swept her with a meaningful look. "Difficult to overlook those things on you, Mistress. You's been blessed by the Lord in many ways. But I know what lust feels like, and I a grown man, knowing the difference. Nothing ever felt so real to me. And falling in love is easy, but loving, staying in love, usually isn't. With you...I feel like every day it will be the easiest thing I do, loving you. So, I don't want you to worry about that."

"I don't plan on being so easy to get along with all the time."

"I didn't say you was easy to get along with. I said you was easy to love." He caught her hand as she threw a mock punch at his shoulder —though a very light and careful one—and held onto it. "Teena Joy used to say I got a stubborn streak when I think things need to go a certain way. So maybe we balance one another."

"Maybe we do."

His certainty filled her with something she had stopped believing in, though she hadn't stopped looking for it. Acknowledging the dichotomy in that, she let him hold her hand in his bigger one, reassure her with that strength and his own certainty.

Which was when she realized why she was still feeling so anxious.

She was going to believe in his love, let herself fall as deep into it, explore every room of it, as she wanted. She was going to be all in.

She didn't doubt his love. Or even her own feelings. No, she thought of him walking up to a boy holding a gun, to an angry bull. Chasing a criminal into the woods.

It wouldn't be his love that was taken from her. It would be him.

But when she found the man she wanted to keep, she'd always promised herself, no matter what baggage she had, she'd give her heart, all of herself, to him. And she'd cherish whatever the Fates had given her, no matter for how long.

Ros and Lawrence, Skye and Tiger, Cyn and Mick; when they'd met, all three men had held dangerous jobs. Neil still did. Active SEALs had a harrowing mortality and debilitating injury rate. A truth that wasn't easy on Abby, especially with her own challenges as a paranoid schizophrenic.

But they'd decided it was worth it. Probably because they felt the way she did now. No matter what Fate had planned, she wanted to lie here and just be with Rev. Hold his hand, talk to him, tease one another.

Tomorrow would take care of itself, and they'd handle it when it got here. For now, he needed her, as much as she needed him. They'd take care of each other.

CHAPTER SIXTEEN

*T*wo weeks later, Rev joined her for a volunteer day at Laurel Grove. During her visits, Vera helped guests with legal advice, aid paperwork, job applications—whatever her skillset could offer them.

They all did their part. Cyn gave self-defense classes, and Skye taught computers. Ros offered general business principles and tips on acing job interviews, while for Abby it was accounting and bookkeeping. Learning employable skills and care for themselves built confidence in people who'd had it stripped from them, or never had it before.

The men helped, too. Tiger worked on vehicles, and fixed up old beaters to expand transportation options. Lawrence coached the kids on sports. When Neil and Mick were in town they came, too, doing maintenance, and interacting with the kids to prove real men weren't cruel and mean.

Though Vera showed Rev the rules for volunteers, she knew he wouldn't need much guidance. His church did charity work for NOLA's homeless shelters and associated agencies. But the main reason he didn't need much direction was simple. He was Rev.

She turned him over to the day manager, and went to the small room set up with folding table and chairs to meet with her scheduled appointments.

As she finished the last one, Skye appeared in the doorway. "Come see this," she signed.

Vera followed her friend through the big rambling house to a communal living space. Rev was sitting on a stool far too small for him, but made it look comfortable, his feet braced and hands resting loosely on his spread and bent knees. A child stood on the outside of either knee, listening attentively to him.

He was telling Bible stories, and integrating some singing into it. Though what he sang were playful rhymes and he kept his volume low, his compelling voice had drawn a crowd. Mothers perched on second-hand sofas or folding chairs, kept stacked in here for group counseling sessions. Many held children in their laps. Others lined the walls to listen.

While many of the kids were young, some were teens, including a boy so skinny a good wind could take him away. Rev's gaze strayed to him several times. He was remembering Craig, she knew. He'd gone to the juvenile detention center to meet with him a couple times, though the boy had been unresponsive to anyone, even his own bewildered and horrified parents.

This scene was poignant and heartwarming, a needed contrast. Skye touched her arm, directing Vera's attention toward what her friend really wanted her to see.

Cyn was leaning against the wall, listening to the stories with as much attention as anyone else. Mick stood next to her, his hand braced above her head. Like many here, they'd seen the worst side of humanity. Rev's words offered a balm, maybe in a way they hadn't expected. He had that effect.

Since Cyn was as situationally aware as a feral cat, she noticed Vera's arrival. Saying something to Mick, she tugged on the front of his shirt, an affectionate gesture, before sliding over to Vera and Skye.

"At first, I watched him because I didn't want him bible thumping," she admitted quietly, "But he's not like that."

"No, he's not. I wouldn't bring him if he was. I wouldn't be with him if he was. I'm also bringing him to dinner tonight," Vera added.

"We'd be pissed if you didn't." Skye responded, signing.

"The Bible also say there a time to dance." Rev said, concluding his story. He swept his gaze around the room. "I think now is that time."

"'Says,'" one of the girls declared. "The Bible also *says, there's* a time to dance."

"Is that how it go? Well, that works, too." Rev smiled at her. "It important to go to school and learn how to speak proper. See, you already taught me better. Maybe you be a teacher one day."

She beamed at him. "Then I'll tell all the students what to do."

Vera suppressed a chuckle and exchanged a glance with Cyn and Skye. "Next generation Domme, in the making."

Rev's attention moved to the emaciated teen, dropping to the phone in his hand. "Anything on that have a beat that'll work?"

A tentative smile crossed the boy's face. He called up his music, scrolled through and pressed play. A tinny version of Olly Murs "Dance With Me Tonight" started, with the toe-tapping drumbeat.

There was a set of speakers nearby, and the boy connected his phone to them. As the music filled the room, its cheerful vigor and Rev's smile had even the shyer kids slipping off their mothers' laps to dance with him.

Rev swayed back and forth, clapped and spun. He led them in some nonsensical dance moves, making the children laugh. Then he picked a child to choose the next dance move. Then another.

A woman at the wall was tapping her foot, despite a bruised face and her arm being in a sling. Rev offered her his hand in his gentle way. "Let's show 'em how it's done."

A considering pause, then she put her hand in his. He back strolled them into the circle, snapping his fingers with his free hand, and guiding her in a turn under his arm, being careful of her one in the sling. When she smiled, the bruises on her face didn't disappear, but held less weight. Her six-year-old boy came with her, and Rev incorporated him into the dance they were doing until Rev relinquished her to her son. "You take over now," he told him. "A boy should always be willing to dance with his momma."

"Fucking hell," Cyn murmured. "I'm half in love with him already. No offense," she told Mick.

"None taken. I'm totally smitten myself, and I'm as straight as a Roman pillar." Mick shot Vera an amused look.

After several songs, a staff member announced it was lunch time. When the boy disconnected his phone from the speakers, Rev was talking to him. The boy stiffened as Rev put a hand on his shoulder, but relaxed into the contact as Rev kept talking. He nodded and saun-tered off to lunch.

As Rev moved toward Vera, a little girl with an eye patch and an earnest expression intercepted him. She wore jeans with daisies embroidered on the pockets, matching the daisy fasteners in her dark hair. She reached out and gripped his hand. "Will you come sit at the table with me and my mom?"

"I need to do some more chores. But I appreciate you asking. It always nice to have a pretty little lady wanting to spend time with big old me."

She giggled and left to find her mother. As Rev reached Vera and the others, he spoke low, but with feeling. "They want daddies so bad, it breaks the heart."

"It's a good sign for her, though," Stefanie said. The staff member was leaning against the wall on Vera's other side. "When she first came here, men scared her half to death. All she expected from them was yelling and hitting. She's made great strides. Now we work on the deeper stuff."

At Rev's curious look, Stefanie added, "We build up her self-esteem so she doesn't backtrack in her future relationships, looking to fill that need for a father by trusting anyone who comes along, and ending up down the same path her mother did. But her mom's made good progress in that direction, and she's the most important role model her daughter can have in valuing herself."

"You have a hard job," Rev said. "That's a lot to work through and figure out."

"Volunteers like you remind us that learning to have fun and enjoy life is a big part of that healing process. And helps with the harder challenges. Thank you. Thank you all," she told Vera.

Vera could tell it helped Rev to hear that. Craig would be going through counseling, part of his road to trial and sentencing. Cyn touched her arm. "We're headed out. We'll see you tonight."

Her gaze rested on Rev as she said it. Though she'd seemed to enjoy his singing and Bible stories, Vera could tell Cyn had more on her mind on the subject. She'd likely bring it up at dinner. Vera considered slipping a tranquilizer in her drink. Or taking one herself.

Cyn and Mick moved away, Mick giving Rev a friendly nod.

"Tonight?" Rev asked.

"We have a once-a-month dinner, Ros, Cyn, Skye, Abby and me, and their men. Bastion has a standing invite to it, and he comes every once in a while, but he prefers different haunts. We rotate the location between our houses. Tonight it's at Neil and Abby's place outside the city. It's a bit of a drive, but would you like to go?"

"Would you have invited me if it hadn't come up just now? I know you a very polite Southern woman."

"Not that polite. For your information, I told them I was bringing you a few minutes ago. I was debating whether I wanted to do that, or skip the dinner, take you home and do other things with you."

He raised an intrigued brow and leaned in, hand braced by her head, those gingerbread-colored eyes heated and close. "Maybe we can do both, Mistress. I got a lot of stamina, but if I run out, the Lord will provide."

She laughed. "I'm moving before lightning strikes this doorway."

The evening's mild weather made it a good night to have dinner outdoors, lit torches and the breeze keeping mosquitos and gnats at bay.

Since he and Abby had married, Neil had made some changes to the small house he lived in on the bayou, including a deck built off his boat dock, accommodating a grill area and scattered chairs. He'd also expanded the screened porch for a treated wood table that could seat a dozen people or more.

"I helped," Abby noted.

"You sure did." Neil slid an arm around her. "You were cute as a button, with bouncy ponytail, shorts, sneakers, and sawdust on your nose."

He was able to catch the thrown punch, though only because he had the training to do so. Thanks to Cyn, Abby was no lightweight. None of them were.

"Don't ask me why I'm hesitant to hand her power tools," Neil told a grinning Tiger.

Vera sat next to Ros, enjoying the relaxing pastime of watching her closest friends and their men socialize. Tonight that pastime included Rev, but her attention on him wasn't casual, for several reasons.

She'd meant what she said to him, about being the earthly person he could lean upon. Physically, he'd recovered from the shooting, but he was dealing with the emotional fallout. The hurt he carried over it was deep.

She also watched him because the monthly dinner was a true family gathering. She was surprisingly nervous about it, which had no basis in anything. Everyone here would be kind to him—even Cyn, in her own way—and he was easy with people.

Her nerves were because there was a significance to her inviting him to be here, and they all knew it.

He and Skye were sitting together, and he was trying his sign language on her. Rev took his mistakes with humor, just as he had with the student at the school, and followed Skye's lead when she showed him the right way to say what he was trying to tell her with his hands.

Skye looked pleased. Though she was proficient with her voice recordings, her reaction to sign language fluency—or the attempts to become fluent—was no different from how anyone in a foreign country felt when they crossed paths with someone who could speak their language.

Tiger, standing at the grill with Neil and Lawrence, watched his Mistress. His look held a million things, light and dark, primal and elevated, all under the heading of love. Desire, interest, protection, regard, respect, hunger, possession. Need. Joy and care. Happiness, contentment. It forged the bond anyone with eyes and a heart could feel when they saw it, and it was expressed with the same elements between all the couples.

Tiger had been part of the Club Progeny world when he and Skye had gotten together. Before that, every woman here had enjoyed sessions with him. Lawrence and Mick were committed alpha submissives, so understood that without confusion. Neil was a unique Dom in his understanding of Abby's needs as another Dominant, but likely because of her illness and its management, he'd gotten a quicker than usual crash course in how essential every stabilizing bond in her life was, including those with former submissive partners like Tiger.

When Cyn had found Mick, and Vera had become the only one without a soulmate, seeing those ties had made the dinners less enjoyable to her. Not something she admitted to anyone. The gut-deep "they don't really need me" feeling she despised was a hydra whose heads could never be terminally pinched off.

Tonight, she understood how pathetic that feeling had been. Having a man like this with her, who made her feel the way Rev did, reminded her of the many different ways that love expressed itself, and how strong her ties with the other women were, built on the experiences and times shared.

She hoped, if she did have to give Rev up, that she would remember that, and not let that feeling return.

All that said, having her own man looking her way, often enough to make sure she was doing well or didn't need anything, was a nice new feeling.

Now Rev was half singing, half speaking a hymn to Skye in a low voice, with lots of starts and stops. She was showing him how to sign the lyrics. Vera imagined him doing it at the church, where the sweeping movements of his large hands would add to the beauty of his voice.

"So how many bodies have you dumped here, Neil?"

Cyn and Mick were sitting on the bench at the end of the dock, Cyn's leg casually looped over Mick's thigh, his arm around her back and hand resting on her hip. They were close enough to the grill to listen in on the conversation between Tiger, Neil and Lawrence, but far enough to do their own reconnecting, since Mick had returned a day ago from a special ops consult in Texas. He'd offered his experience to an agency attempting to shut down criminal organizations active at the Mexican border.

However, since they were now bantering with Neil, Vera knew it was a good moment for her to handle something else. She caught Cyn's attention with a raised hand. "Come sit with me a minute and let Mick supervise Neil, make sure your veggie burger isn't touching the dead animals."

"Neil knows better," Cyn said, but agreeably rose, Mick's hand sliding over her hips to help her to her feet and enjoy the contact. She shot him a heated look and half smile from under her tangle of brown curls and came to sit next to Vera. Ros strolled over to the grill to lean against the rail next to Lawrence, hips brushing as she sipped her drink.

Cyn nodded at Rev. "He handled himself well today."

"He's comfortable with people. He works with kids during the day, and is a leader in his church."

"I thought his cousin was the preacher."

"Yes. But Rev...I think he's the talent. The real deal that strengthens the faith of the congregation."

"He's the sales guy."

"No. I wouldn't put it that way. Not the way you're meaning it." Vera nudged her. "What's going on? I thought you had made peace with some of this."

"Yeah, and no. It became less important. I think he's just rubbing me the wrong way."

"Him or his faith?"

"Are the two separate? They don't seem like it."

"When you do it right, they're usually not. I follow the Wiccan faith, and it speaks to me, guides me in my choices. You know that about me, and it doesn't seem to bother you."

Cyn took a swallow of her drink. "I'm just able to accept your version of the spiritual hoodoo because it's more like Halloween than Easter, and I like Halloween."

"That is an insulting oversimplification of two very powerful and complicated spiritual paths."

"I aim to offend. It's my reason for getting up in the morning."

"It used to be." Vera glanced at Mick, who'd picked a soda out of the cooler and taken a seat in a chair near Neil and Tiger. "I think you have other reasons for getting out of bed."

"Uh, no. He's my reason for staying *in* it."

Vera tapped her bottle of water against Cyn's. "What you believe in, deep in your heart, what helps the world make sense to you, that's a big part of your personal fabric, right? Your love for Mick, no matter how you shrug it off, is your spiritual compass."

"Spiritual compass *and* fuck toy. They go hand in hand in my one-woman church."

"Are you planning to expand the congregation?"

"Not if I can help it. It makes arguing about dogma a lot easier." Cyn sobered, her eyes on Rev. "I have my own shit about it, Vera, but be careful. Just because he has his head on straight, doesn't mean his family does, and their dislike for you oozes out of their pores.

Lawrence gets some serious weird vibes off the aunt, and after the hospital, I agree."

"You think an elderly church woman is going to jump me one night while I'm leaving my favorite coffee shop?"

"Someone's beliefs can make them do stupid, violent shit, no matter how harmless they seem." Cyn's troubled dark eyes turned to Vera. "I know you can handle yourself, as long as you don't forget to watch for a threat. But what I worry about more is how they might mess with his head, so he breaks your heart.

"I know I'm impulsive," she added, "but my gut doesn't lie to me. I like him, I do. I just wish he didn't come with all the rest."

Vera couldn't deny Cyn's perspective made her uneasy, but she kept her tone light. "Do we know any man worth the trouble who doesn't come with baggage? And would we like to turn that mirror on ourselves?"

Cyn made a face. "Stop pointing out stuff that makes sense or I'll start calling you Mom again."

"And I'll do what I did last time you tried that. I'll have Skye leak doctored pictures of you at a Taylor Swift concert, wearing a sparkly rainbow unicorn shirt."

Cyn's grin ended the conversation's serious tone. "I love it when your inner sadist comes out to play."

Rev was aware dinner was an audition of sorts. Casual lovers were not brought to this. Only family.

He thought of what Lawrence had told him at Progeny, that his job wasn't to worry about what they all were thinking. It was to care for Veracity, what mattered to her, what she needed. This was an opportunity for a deeper understanding of that.

He was different from the other four men. In one way or another, they had the heightened awareness of their surroundings and keen attention to detail that came from dangerous career paths.

Neil was an active SEAL and Lawrence a former one, and the two men were closely bonded from having served together. Tiger owned a successful local garage and liked to customize motorcycles as a side business. His former life as a member of the Fallen Angels, an outlaw

MC notorious in the New Orleans area, still rested behind his eyes, though, a lightly sleeping lion. Mick was a former cop and undercover agent from the human trafficking world.

Even if Vera hadn't told him, Rev could tell which man and woman were together. Those puzzle pieces hooked directly together, while the rest formed the full picture, a unique family of Dominants and submissives.

Lawrence made sure Ros was never low on her wine or in need of anything. She watched him banter with Neil, a light smile on her lips, a warmth in her eyes that said she had her hand on the thread to whatever was going on in Lawrence's head and heart.

Tiger used sign language with Skye. She almost never used her recorded voices with him. Rev could pick up the tone of their conversation from gestures and facial expressions. When Tiger sat down on the bench by the grill, Skye climbed into his lap, her knees bent, his tattooed arm going around her to hold her secure as she obviously teased him with quickly moving hands and a dancing light in her eyes. Though his own dark blue gaze rested upon her with devotion, a moment later he groaned and dropped his head back at whatever she'd said, making Mick and Cyn laugh.

Cyn's razor-sharp edges didn't come out to cut her man, except maybe in the ways Mick wanted. When Cyn's hand rested on Mick's arm, Rev noted her nails bit into his skin, a promise of the pain she could inflict. When she did that, Mick adjusted his hand on her shoulder, his thumb sliding along the side of her throat to caress her. Their bodies were so close, it was as if they wanted to be one person. Or already felt like they were.

Then there was Neil and Abby. Vera had told him that before Skye and Tiger got together, Tiger had been a regular session partner for Abby. Every woman here had "played" with him, and it showed in Tiger's easy intimacy with them. However, now that he was fully claimed by one Mistress, Rev could also tell—with relief—that bond had priority.

Vera said that when Abby came to the club with Neil, sometimes they would choose a male sub for her to enjoy as a Mistress, but always with Neil present and participating in some way that made it clear who she was going home with.

When Neil had the burgers and shrimp ready, they sat down on the screened porch, gathering around the yellow pine table a friend of Neil's had built for him. There was cucumber and tomato salad, fresh corn on the cob, bread baked by Cyn, and green beans from Vera's canned garden stores.

Rev intended to bow his head for a brief silent prayer, but Vera spoke. "Would anyone mind if I have Rev say a prayer over the food?"

"Since Neil cooked the shrimp, it might be needed," Lawrence said.

"I spit on yours, Munch," Neil told him. "It's all good."

Rev noticed Cyn's expression wasn't encouraging, but not against it. Just neutral, her gaze on Vera.

"I'm fine doing it quiet," Rev told Vera.

"I know. I'd like you to say a prayer for us, Rev. I wouldn't presume to command you on your faith, but I'm asking."

"If you asking, Mistress, it no different than a command to me."

His response brought everyone's attention to him, but he saw no reason to say less than the truth to her. As he bowed his head, Vera's hand curled around his. He'd left his other hand out and Skye took it, her clasp certain. He didn't have to look to see what the others did. He felt it when the circle closed. It infused him with warmth. The tightening of Vera's hand confirmed what he could feel.

"Thank you, Lord, for the food before us and the blessings you give us, but most especially for Love, the greatest blessing of all. You taught me early that Love comes to us the strongest when we surrender to it. I see that in those around this table tonight, and I'm grateful they and You let me be here to witness it."

He paused, Craig's face in his mind, Mrs. Cuddy's, those kids who'd been hurt. He didn't turn the reaction away. Grief like that should be felt and honored. "And I know that whatever happens to us, You there to help get us through. I can feel it, that every person around this table know that Love is there, as close and ready as the hand they clasping. Amen."

"Blessed be," Vera murmured.

The conversation bounced around as they ate, comments about the food and work. Sessions at Progeny were also brought up.

"What did you think of that portable stock you can suspend from ropes or chains?" Cyn asked the other women. "Mistress Lace M. Tight tried it out last weekend."

"I think it would choke someone with a neck as thick as Tiger's." James Earl Jones voiced Skye's opinion through her recorder.

"The pads on the inside can be removed for someone with a bigger neck," Cyn told her.

Seeing Rev's puzzled look, Vera explained. "You remember the big stock you saw at Progeny, anchored to the floor? With holes for a person's neck and wrists?"

"Yeah. I remember."

"This one is more portable. It's a square, formed by two pieces of hinged wood. It's about eighteen inches long. It's fitted around the submissive's neck, holding him in place, whether standing or sitting. The weight of the wood is taken off the collar bones by attaching suspended chains or ropes to the two hooks screwed into the wood."

"It requires careful attention," Ros told him. "If you bliss out your sub and his knees buckle, or he slumps over and that board's in the wrong position, it could press on the throat in a dangerous way. But for early stages in the session, it's nice. Gives the sub a different experience. Whistler got pretty wound up over it with Laci."

"He gets bored quickly," Vera observed. "So that was a good option. It keeps him guessing and on his toes."

"Literally, if she takes up the slack on the chains." Cyn pointed at Ros with cornbread for emphasis.

"Speaking of which, the club has switched out a few of the restraint systems with Tetruss cuffs," Abby noted. "You can keep subs up on their toes with less abrasion to the wrists."

The Dommes moved from that to other equipment at the club that they liked, the pros and cons. The submissives weighed in on them from their perspective.

No matter how matter-of-factly the subject matter was presented, Rev couldn't avoid his body's reaction to it. Vera's hand slid up and down his leg, slow, her head tipping up so she could gaze at his face. She was pleased he was getting worked up.

And he wasn't alone. Ros's hand was also below the table. Rev couldn't see where it was, but the heated way Lawrence was looking at her, the curl of his fingers on the back of her chair, gave him that answer. Skye was leaning against Tiger, his arm hooked over her neck, thumb brushing the upper curve of her breast. The sensual tone in the voices of those talking ran smooth through Rev, like hot syrup off a stack of pancakes.

Then the conversation took a different turn.

Throughout the meal, Cyn's eyes had returned to Rev. On the next lull in the conversation, she changed the topic.

"So Rev... Do you have your people's pat response to why bad things happen to good people? Pedophiles, tsunamis that kill thousands, every kid or puppy out there crying alone in the cold, hungry or hurting. We don't know what the fuck that reason is, but that's okay, just keep tripping along, happy as clams in the sunlight of God's love, and it will all make sense eventually. God's all powerful, God doesn't make mistakes, God's shit don't stink."

"Wow," Tiger observed, stretching out one leg under the table to nudge Cyn's boot. "Way to put a guy on the hot plate."

"Yes, and *don't*." Vera pinned Cyn with a hard look. "I mean it."

"Veracity." Rev put his hand over hers. "I thank you for your care, but I can speak for myself."

His thumb slid over her palm, a secret caress to confirm it. Then he turned his attention to Cyn. "You angry, like a lot of people. Angry for the pain done to you, yes, but especially to those you care about. Ain't nobody understand it, Miss Cyn. Everyone I ever met, including me, struggles with that, no matter what we believe. Only belief that answers it is no belief at all, but that emptiness has a cost too big."

He moved his hand to where the bullet had hit his side. His pain-filled eyes, the harsh ache in his voice, showed Cyn and all of them what Vera had felt churning inside him for days, how he'd struggled with what had happened.

"I don't know why a good teacher had to die, or how a boy get so messed up in his head that he think killing someone is the way to deal with that pain."

Silence gripped the table. Vera knew his words found the vulnerable spots in all of them. For Neil, Lawrence and Mick, it would be the lives they'd seen end—sometimes because they'd had to be the ones to take them. For Ros and Abby, it was Laurel's death from her husband's abuse, as well as the death of Abby's own mother, who took her own life rather than deal another minute with the illness her daughter had inherited.

For Skye, it would be the father she'd lost with her voice, who'd died within arm's reach of her. And for Cyn...she'd been born having to fight, and lost more of those battles than she'd won. It hadn't defeated her, but she carried scars that still festered.

"But when I was growing up," Rev said, "a preacher told me you can lean on your faith to give you the strength to deal with pain, or you can be angry and hate and turn your back on it, to punish it for not riding to the rescue. Now words is words. They don't mean much. But he backed it up with his own experience.

"He say, 'I've done both, and I can tell you, the second one, it don't do you or anyone else around you any good. The first, somehow, it help you get through it and appreciate the blessings in your life, which manage to show themselves, even in the worst times.'"

Rev shook his head. "Hate just don't do anyone any good. If you feel it in your heart, your first job is to find a way to get rid of that poison before it infects everything about you."

As his gaze moved to each of them, Vera could tell that Rev felt those currents of memory and experience, even if he didn't know the details. He hadn't told them he had the answer, or even that God did. His words acknowledged their confusion and pain, and offered all he could. His understanding. And hope.

She was tense, waiting to see what Cyn would do. The intelligent brown eyes had rested on him throughout the explanation, her mouth a thin line. Now it eased a fraction. "Okay. Decent answer. Next question."

"Great Goddess," Vera muttered.

"Tonight's interrogation dinner will include a rack of testicles over a bed of marinated nails." Skye was still using James Earl Jones' voice, only now it sounded like his Darth Vader character, complete with heavy breathing.

Ros leaned over Lawrence to murmur to Vera. "If he can't handle Cyn, you chose the wrong person, and I don't think you did. Look at him. He's fine. He wants to answer her."

Mick was leaning back against one of the porch support posts, his fingers caressing his Mistress's shoulder. He sent Vera a look that included a flicker of amusement, a tug at his firm mouth. It was reinforcement of Ros's reassurance, she was certain.

Cyn ignored the byplay to deliver her question. "Your family doesn't like Vera. Why are you so sure they're wrong, sure enough to be here, instead of kicking her to the curb?" Her attention slid to Ros. "If I'm being an ass, I'll stop. But Vera is important to us. To me."

Cyn met Rev's gaze again. "She's been our spiritual backbone for a long time. She helped me believe there's something out there to have faith in. I don't want anyone messing with hers."

Thinking this had been about exorcising Cyn's own demons or testing Rev's mettle again, Vera was taken off guard. And deeply moved. She found herself at a loss for words, but that was all right, since it was Rev that Cyn was expecting to answer her.

Rev propped his elbows on the table, his fingers laced together as he dipped his head, thinking. No quick response. Cyn waited him out, as did everyone else. They respected taking the time to do things right. To answer from the heart, and Rev would search his to do it.

"Faith is something that's always being messed with. Ain't strong unless it's tested." Vera saw a tightness around his mouth and a different kind of shadows in his eyes. Just like the school shooting, he wasn't hiding how his family's behavior was making him feel. Vera put her hand on his back, feeling his heart beat through his shirt. He gave her a look of gratitude.

"My family don't understand, but I believe they will, in time. They'll learn that they wrong to worry about me and Vera. Because seeking love, when it true and pure, and what it should be, is always God's will. I think sometimes even when it's not what it should be, because you got to learn the way of it, and that means mistakes, failing at it.

"There's a man in our church, Vince. He done had two marriages, and losing both through divorce nearly did him in, because he has a heart made for love. But this last one, she was the right one. And he told me what he learned from the other two helped him find her."

When Vera moved her hand back to his leg, he laced his fingers with hers, looking down as he traced the tip of a manicured nail. Then he raised his gaze back to Cyn. "What I said that first day in your office is still true. No matter what happens, Miss Cyn, I'll care for her heart. I promise you that. I promise all of you that."

Just as he had that day, his gaze moved to Ros, acknowledging her as the head of the family.

"I know Vera can take care of herself, Rev," Ros said. "She's handled some deep hurts in her life. I'll give you an assurance, too, because I know you mean what you say. If you end up being one of those deep hurts, not because you intend her harm, but because it's another step in the journey, like you described, she'll be able to handle it. Because she has us, always."

His mouth tightened, but he nodded. "Thank you, ma'am. I glad to know that."

He glanced at Cyn. "If it all right with you, Miss Cyn, I think it might be time to enjoy this fine meal without more serious talk. Maybe we could talk more later, if you want."

"Amen," Abby said, inspiring laughter around the table. When Rev winked at Vera, she freed her hand from his to squeeze his thigh.

Neil nudged a bowl of sugared pecans closer to his plate. They'd had them out as appetizers before the meal, and transferred the remainder to the table to have with dinner. "Noticed you tucked away a couple handfuls of these," the SEAL said. "I think you just earned some more."

Rev chuckled. "My sweet tooth can get away with me. I like those in particular. They sell heated ones at the candy shop along my bus route."

Cyn gave Vera a "we okay?" look. Cyn's expressed feelings about their friendship and faith made Vera feel like hugging her. Such a gesture would horrify Cyn, which was reason enough to do it. However, since Vera didn't want to move from the warmth of Rev's side, she gave Cyn the "I'm watching you" gesture as her answer. It made Cyn grin, as expected, and restored things to an even keel.

For a few moments at least. Once the dinner was concluded and the dishes were cleared, her contentious younger sister-of-the-heart had another mission. She brought it up as they were lounging in chairs on the deck, letting the meal digest before coffee and dessert.

Neil was cleaning the grill while Lawrence and Abby perched on the rail. Tiger leaned against it, a beer clasped in loose fingers. Mick and Cyn had chosen two side by side chairs, and Ros was in one that gave her a good view of Lawrence. Skye sat on the bench near Tiger, her knees folded up and heels on the edge of the wood as she sipped a soda. Vera and Rev were on the two-person love seat with canvas cushions.

"What kind of fight skills do you have, Rev?" Cyn asked.

"This is her soap box," Vera informed Rev. She rested against his side, her fingers playing with his on her shoulder. "She thinks everyone should be a trained assassin."

"I believe everyone should have the skills to protect themselves and others," Cyn corrected. "And from what I've seen, it seems like he could use some."

She was remembering the video she'd watched over Vera's shoulder. The slight tension in Rev's body told Vera he'd made that connection himself. "I wouldn't have hit Craig," Rev said.

"No? Even to keep him from shooting anyone else? There are tactics you could have used to disarm him."

"Yes, I know. I used them."

Rev and Cyn's gazes locked and held.

"Cyn." Vera spoke, low, drawing the woman's gaze. This was raw wound territory, and Cyn had to know it.

"She trying to protect you. And me. I'll take that as a compliment." Rev attempted a smile, moving them to more amiable ground. "You're right, I haven't had much call to learn how to fight like that. Never needed to know how before, don't exactly know why, because I been places where people are too used to fighting. But don't hurt to be prepared. The kids I played with growing up were afraid Teena Joy, my aunt, would take a strip off them if I came home with a scratch."

"Overprotective females are the worst, aren't they?" Mick commented to Lawrence. He gave a narrow-eyed Cyn an innocent smile as Lawrence grinned at his own Mistress.

"I wouldn't know."

Ros shook her head at them and turned to Rev. "Whether elbowing your way through tourists on Bourbon Street or breaking up a fight with middle school kids, it doesn't hurt to have some moves." She shot a glance at Cyn. "Despite her breathtaking lack of tact and timing, she's a very good self-defense teacher."

Neil gestured at Rev with his beer. "Don't worry. Her trained assassin shit is a more advanced class. That's where she requires a blood oath."

"I think that's a blood donation." Lawrence squinted as if trying to remember.

"I'll be happy to draw some of yours later," Cyn promised him. "Asshole."

"Hey, hey, hey." Tiger wagged a finger at her and Mick. "None of your foreplay shit in front of the rest of us. I've just eaten a heavy meal."

Cyn rose. "Neil has a workout area out front. I'll show you a couple things, Rev. We can spar."

Rev stood, but looked her up and down and shook his head. "No ma'am."

"You pull the 'you're a woman' shit, and we'll go a round right here."

"Cyn." Ros drew her attention. "It's not always about that."

"Not entirely true," Rev said courteously to her boss. "I won't lift a hand against a woman."

"Cyn," Vera snapped and stood up as Cyn took a step toward him. She wouldn't put it past Cyn to throw a punch to make him rethink that position.

In an adroit move, Rev put his hands on Vera's shoulders and moved her in front of him. It brought Cyn up short and made Tiger laugh outright, a sexy, masculine rumble. When Cyn shot him a venomous look, he lifted one hand in an "I'm Switzerland" move.

Rev gauged Tiger's considerable size. "If you wouldn't mind having him show me what you have in mind," he said, "we can do that."

"He would have chosen you, Munch, except sparring with someone your height just doesn't seem fair," Neil said to Lawrence.

"I didn't get this shit when you all needed a guy to get into a tight tunnel," Lawrence noted.

"Yeah, you did. We were just a little nicer about it." Neil formed a narrow space between thumb and forefinger. "Little. Like you."

"Munch?" Rev asked.

"Munchkin," Neil told him, and ducked Lawrence's lunge at him with the grill brush, the men ably demonstrating their skills, even in mock sparring.

"Dinner and a show," Skye signed to Ros. "Can't beat it."

"It's a nickname our team tagged him with early," Neil explained. "They call me Twizzler, because I was a bean pole in BUD/S and they found a picture of me when I was a kid, sunburned to lobster red."

Rev had stayed behind Vera, fingers firm on her shoulders. She leaned back, her hips pressed to him because it felt too good not to do it. If he got an erection from it, the women would notice with as much appreciation as they were giving to Neil and Lawrence's wrestling match. His hands tightened on her, and he shot her a wry look before it switched to grave courtesy.

"You seem to know a lot about fighting, Miss Cyn. I wouldn't mind learning some things, thank you."

"Yeah, yeah. Fine. Stop using Vera as a human shield, you big pussy."

The dinner party relocated to the front, their interested audience securing vantage points on the porch and steps.

"Might be better for me to take the lead on this one anyway," Tiger advised Cyn. "Since he's not planning on formal martial arts classes, what he needs are street fighting skills, defensive moves to defuse a situation fast."

"Nothing defuses a situation like a knockout punch," Cyn responded. "Or a broken knee cap."

"Probably not the best way to break up a fight between students," Rev put in helpfully. "Miss Mavis wouldn't be happy, and the parents might be upset."

"Bunch of bleeding hearts," Cyn grumbled, but she yielded to Tiger's take on things.

As Tiger and Cyn began their instruction, Vera wasn't surprised that Rev picked up on the tactics well enough to suggest he had some natural skill. When Neil stepped in to add his input, Vera saw a flash of memory on Ros's face. Not a good one. Her boss was remembering the close call that had happened here on this porch, when Abby's meds hadn't been working and she'd had a knife.

Ros had told Vera how Neil had disarmed her, without leaving so much as a bruise. Which meant Neil was a good choice to provide Rev useful tips for a do-no-harm-if-possible situation.

Though Rev had made it clear he wouldn't have done it differently, Vera wouldn't mind knowing he could bring additional skills to a situation like that, other than the hope and faith that it wasn't his time to die. God approved of those who helped themselves, right?

Rev had ducked out of a hold with Tiger and Tiger was showing him how to do a leg sweep and bring him down to the ground, their bodies pushed into one another, Tiger's arm extended as he showed Rev the kind of hold he should have on it.

Now that she wasn't as worried about Cyn's motives, Vera could indulge herself. Watching handsome men grapple *was* stimulating. The others were watching attentively. Abby sat in a chair, her knees drawn up, head resting on them. Rcs stroked a hand through her friend's long red hair as she sipped a glass of wine. Cyn perched on the rail, throwing in tips. Skye was just below her on the steps, but she had her tablet out. When Vera leaned over to see what she was creating, a smile crossed her face.

A graphic rendering of Rev and Tiger, gladiators in an arena, while intrigued women in Roman dress watched.

"Gladiator Night," Skye wrote on the screen.

"Make sure that goes into the suggestion box at Progeny," Vera said.

During dessert and coffee, Vera helped Abby finish up the dishes in the kitchen while Cyn and Rev walked to the end of the pier together. Vera expected Rev was giving her the chance to have more of that conversation he'd promised.

Vera had thought about going with him, but he'd squeezed her hand, and brushed his lips over her temple.

"No need to babysit me, Mistress. I be all right with her. I can see her heart, same as you."

She trusted his take on it, but she still kept her eye on them. They sat caddy corner to one another on the dock benches, Rev listening while Cyn spoke. When he responded, she had a thoughtful air, but not a tense or unhappy one.

"She's gone from evaluating him on your behalf, to accepting and wanting to understand him better," Abby said. "It's a good sign."

"I always hope we don't put them through too much to be part of this inner circle, but..."

"But they wouldn't be who we want, if they didn't embrace and meet the challenge."

Abby pressed against Vera's shoulder. The wind through the screened window lifted her hair, blowing it against her delicate cheek.

Abby's unearthly beauty sometimes added to Ros's constant worry about losing her.

She looks like an angel who took a wrong turn and ended up here.

That worry had fortunately lessened, thanks to Neil and Dr. Maureen Whisnant, Abby's wonderful psychiatrist and a fast friend of the TRA group.

"How do you do it, Abby?" Vera said, watching Rev. "Love Neil so much and not lose your mind worrying about him being where so many bad things could happen to him?"

"I've already lost my mind. Got the certificate and everything. So that box has been checked." Abby slipped her arm through Vera's. "Seriously, having practice dealing with unpredictability helps. I have superhero crisis coping skills. And what's the alternative? Not love someone who's offering me every part of himself? He's the person who made me want to keep breathing, living, and dealing with all the bad shit in my head."

She looked at Neil, who was having one of his quiet moments, leaning on the dock rail and gazing out at the water. Feeling her regard, the tall man glanced over his shoulder and gave her a half-smile, his slate-colored eyes fixed upon her.

"Makes my knees weak, every time," she murmured, and shook her head. "When I let go of the fear and guilt about inflicting my crazy on him, I gained a new truth, and that truth was that he wanted to be with me through everything. He feels that desire and need as much as I do. The few minutes of peace and joy I have with him, whenever the world gives me that break, has proven to be enough to make it all worth it. Something I never would have believed before I experienced it."

Her eyes twinkled. "Doesn't hurt that he's terrific eye candy, gives me fabulous orgasms, and is willing to care for me in whatever way I need."

"Yeah, there's that."

Cyn rose. She put a brief hand on Rev's shoulder and said something. From the softening of Cyn's face, Vera thought she'd said something about the school shooting. Whatever it was helped, because it showed in his expression.

Cyn joined Mick, sitting in a deck chair, his feet braced on the unlit fire pit. Lawrence and Ros sat across from him. Cyn took the chair at Mick's side.

Rev got up and moved down the ramp to the floating dock where Neil kept his boat tied. He gazed out at the water, his shoulders set.

Because she'd stood at that spot at other dinners, she knew the flowing current would mute the sounds of land. Facing the water at night, a person could imagine they were alone, except for the whispering cypress trees and pines, and the occasional splash as fish jumped, or frogs or alligators entered or left the water.

Rev would be listening to those sounds echoing through the open space between sky and water, the movement of the water a constant.

He'd be thinking about Mrs. Cuddy, Craig and the kids. Or the people at Laurel Grove he'd seen today. The weary but persistent staff and volunteers, the kids and mothers, the lonely teen with his music player, the little girl wanting a father to share a meal with. So many bruised and battered bodies and souls.

Was she so connected to him after such a short time, that her soul could reach out and feel all that from him? Understand how the most spiritually connected person could feel overwhelmed by all of it, not know what to tell someone seeking counsel on how to make sense of it? How not to abandon caring, giving and offering whatever was needed?

She didn't know what he'd told Cyn, but her expression was more serene than usual. She was listening to a conversation between Ros and Mick, but then they stopped, their attention going toward the floating dock.

Tiger and Neil paused, and Skye turned around, straddling the rail, her sneakers propped on the bottom railing.

Rev was singing. He'd started out low, the melody drifting over the bayou. As his tone gained in volume, she recognized it.

"Jesus Loves Me."

She left the kitchen and crossed the deck, the eyes of the others on her as she followed the narrow dock out to the boat ramp, her footsteps quiet on the boards. When she reached his side, she laid her head on his shoulder. He put his arm around her, smoothing her skirt over her hip.

As his voice rose, she looked at the tops of the trees, where roosting birds would hear the notes. The song spread outward as well, into all the dark, moist corners where life was born, lived and struggled to survive. She thought it would soothe and elevate all who heard it. God, the Lord and Lady, every face of the Divine, had to be smiling.

When he finished, she stayed silent, waiting for the last echoing note to melt into the moving water, blowing wind, the ears of frogs and other nighttime creatures. She wiped away the tears on his cheeks, the heat and dampness of them a sacred anointing she felt deep inside.

"Why that song?" she asked.

"A little girl sung it to me today, to show me she knew a 'Jesus' song. She told me when her daddy pushed her down the steps and she broke her leg, she sung that to her momma in the hospital, so her momma wouldn't cry so much. Said her momma sung it with her and promised she wasn't going to let no one hurt her no more. Now her momma has a job, and they going to a new apartment next week, a real home where there's no yelling or hurting. She says she thinks Jesus made that happen, because of her singing that song."

Vera slid her arms around his broad chest and put her head there as he closed his own arms around her. "The faith of children."

"Yeah. I don't see she wrong, though. I think her momma saw that faith, and realized her daughter needed to have faith that her momma would take care of her, and she found the strength to do just that."

He took a deep breath, easing back enough to give her a half smile, though she saw a lot of things moving behind his eyes. Not all of them were about bad things in the world. "So how many bodies *has* Neil thrown out here for the gators?"

"None. But I routinely sacrifice Christians here to my pagan alligator gods." She touched his curved lips. "Thank you for coming with me tonight."

"I liked being with your family. They like all families. Some easier to get along with than others, but they love one another, and that all that matters."

"Yes." She saw the flash of unhappiness in his eyes and knew its source. "Witford's still giving you crap, isn't he?"

"He say I'm changing, and taking a path that's not God's will. He says I think I need to know all these new things, but those things may not be according to the plan God has for me. He say you not my path, that you're not God's will."

Vera bit back ten things she'd be willing to fire at Witford for that bullshit, but he wasn't here.

"I know he doing it because he's confused and hurt and worried," Rev added. "But it's hard for me not to listen sometimes. Not because I agree," he assured her. "What he thinks on that is wrong. But it make me think of things he's done or said in the past that I let slide, because I know the struggle in his heart."

He sighed and released her to cross his arms and frown out at the water, a man working a problem. "He's battling what's inside him, not me, so I don't feel the need to lift a shield or weapon in defense. Yet lately...I feel under attack. Got something I want, and they telling me it's wrong, people I care about and respect. It don't change the love, but it hits that respect part hard. Makes it hard to be around them. After them showing up at your office, then what happened at the school..."

He gave her a bleak look. "Think I maybe need a break. Get some space from all of it."

The question in his voice, a seeking, told her he was trusting her for guidance, just as she'd asked him to do. She would live up to that faith. "I just happen to have a free weekend, if you'd like me to share that space. And if you don't, if you need time on your own, I'll give that to you, too."

He framed her face in his hands, a sudden fierce movement. "Let me do something for you, Mistress. Let me give you pleasure and joy, find it together. I don't want to be further away from you than a breath. I want to steep myself in you. Spend the weekend serving you. May I do that for you, Mistress? My head gets clear when I do that."

She tried to keep her voice steady. "Yes, you may. And when I let you up for air, I'm going to give you that driving lesson."

He put his forehead on hers, held her. "All right," he said. "Thank you."

She offered him her hand and walked back up the dock with him toward the others. When she was close enough, she called out to Tiger.

"Do you mind if I bring Rev out to your place this weekend to give him some driving lessons?"

"You're going to let him drive the Aston?" Tiger's expression warred between doubt and shock. "I've changed my mind. You crazy kids are moving way too fast. How about you get married instead?"

Vera laughed as Rev's brows rose. "Could we use one of your older shop trucks? That was part two of my request."

"Sure. I'll leave the keys in it, so if you come while I'm at work, you don't have to wait on me."

She smiled up at Rev. "Sounds like a plan."

CHAPTER SEVENTEEN

*N*eil and Abby had offered all of them a place to sleep, but it was a small house, and Vera liked having her own space. Because it was late when they returned and they were both tired, Vera had invited Rev into her bed, him in his cotton boxers and her in a silky nightgown that clung to her curves and was translucent enough to kindle heat in his gaze. But as she rested in his arms, the two of them merely held one another, engaging in quiet pillow talk. Some topics were more serious than others.

"You don't seem to have hang-ups about me being Wiccan," she noted, "even though I'm sure more people in your congregation than Witford or Tisha would find it objectionable."

Her infuser lamp emitted a vanilla scent in the room and cast tiny dots of light along the wall. He gazed at them, one arm behind his head, one around her.

"Teena Joy told me that my heart was pure, and to trust my heart, that God would never lead me astray. He led me to you."

"To convert me?" She'd never gotten that sense, but she would ask, to know what to expect if Witford or Tisha put that kind of pressure on him.

"No." He looked down at her and touched her chin. "To serve you. Love you. Belong to you. Protect you." She closed her eyes as his words sunk into her, took root. "I hear it in my head, another song ready to be sung, only a song with my whole body."

He hummed it, what was in his heart. "Let me serve you. Give me a name to call you..."

"Mistress, Rev," she whispered. "You can always call me Mistress." *You can also call me yours.*

"Do you believe Tisha, that I can corrupt your soul, change it? Make it less godly, more worldly, where you think less about praising the Divine and more about reward on earth, instead of heaven?

He hummed another few notes, then subsided. "If God give us that full table I talked about, a well-lived life is our thanks and praise to Him, too. Earthly joys have their place. Maybe everything life offers, all the choices we make, how we help, love, fail and succeed... how we grow from all that, that's another way we praise him."

He shifted so he leaned over her, his head a silhouette above her. "No, Veracity. I don't think you corrupt my soul. I think you make it stronger. I been in a hard place this week. God and praying have helped, but so has knowing I have you, your care...your..."

She gazed up at him. "You can say it. Because it's true."

"Your love," he said. "Thank you, Mistress."

She slid a finger along his waistband, a mute demand. He removed the cotton boxers, his hands finding her under her silken nightgown, pushing up the fabric as she guided him over her to settle between her legs, press himself between them. He brought his mouth to hers, a long, swimming kiss, full of everything they both needed. When they came together, it was such an easy coupling, an easy rhythm. They fell into that rising and falling breath together with the same effortless coordination, everything anticipated and accepted, offered and given.

She arched her back and he helped her take off the nightgown, so they were skin to skin, moving together as he went deeper, thrusting, her heels coming up to lock over his buttocks, her hands latched on his shoulders.

They rocked together. He'd learned from her, so that rocking went on and on and on until at long last, she whispered "now," and they rode that strong river current to a climax that left them shuddering and boneless in one another's arms, no need to move or doubt the Universe's plan in bringing them together.

~

As they drove to Tiger's the next morning, Rev told Vera he'd agreed to do another gig or two with Sy and Trey.

"Their lead singer called in and said he'll be back soon, but they have a couple commitments they'd like to keep before then."

"Good. Sy says the club owner where you performed the other night is interested in having you come back. Do you think you'd do that, if they play there again?"

"If they need me and I can make it work with my job and the church, sure. I like helping out." He shrugged, his fingers coiled over the Aston Martin's open window frame as he turned his face toward the wind. "But I'm not interested in becoming a rock star."

"Well, that's disappointing. I had a whole fantasy going. You, shirtless, in leather pants, hugging up to a mic. Your muscles gleaming with sweat, hand reaching out to the crowd but your eyes looking for me..."

A slow smile slid across his face. She continued. "I see all those young groupies in the audience, trying to catch your attention by screaming their love for you, wearing their tight shirts and short skirts. Maybe throwing some underwear onto the stage."

He blinked. "Maybe I been working at a school too long. I be thinking, what would their daddies think?"

"I think most fathers abdicate the teen years to the mothers, to save the lives of young men and reduce the chances of early onset gray."

The grin deepened. "You'd be a good mother, Veracity. No nonsense, patient. You want kids?"

She sucked in a breath. Rev immediately reached out to touch her hand. "Mistress?"

"Yes, I'm fine." She didn't say anything for a few miles. He waited her out, but kept his hand near hers, knuckles brushing her wrist where she gripped the gear shift.

"I had a plan. I'd have one and adopt two, when he or she was about three years old. Out of diapers but starting to need siblings."

"How old would the adopted siblings be?" he asked.

"I'd look at six or seven years old for one, nine or ten for the other. But I'd likely just let the adoption counselor tell me who most needed a home and see if my reaction to their story tells me that's who belongs with me. Who my found family is, like Ros and the rest are."

She took a more leveling breath. "How about you? Do you want children?"

"Yes," he said simply. "But if all I'm given are my schoolkids, I'd be all right with that. I've thought about having a kid of my own, though, plenty of times. I like the feel of it. Maybe a son, and we'd both dote on his momma. Drive her a little crazy."

"Probably drive her a lot crazy."

His fingers tightened on hers. "Why did it hurt you, me asking?"

"It didn't hurt, not exactly. Guess I never expected a man to ask me that. Not the way you just did. Most men stay away from the topic until the woman brings it up, even deep into the relationship. You asked like the answer mattered. And you liked my response." She sent him a half smile. "Which thrilled and terrified me at the same time."

"I don't know where the Lord is going to take us, Veracity. But if He take us down that road together, I feel nothing but right about it, no matter how soon it seems."

She thought of the other four members of their group. With the exception of Skye and Tiger, their men had come into their lives and, in a remarkably short time, each woman had known. And the group usually knew before the woman herself had believed in it.

She recalled the glances at dinner, the way each of them had been getting to know Rev. As if they knew they were talking to a man who would become one of them.

Who might be father to the children she'd always wanted.

Her phone buzzed. After glancing at it, Vera dipped her head toward him. "I need to take this one. It will make you smile."

He gave her a curious look as she had her hands-free pick up the call. "Hey, Jasmine. I have you on speaker with a friend of mine, Rev. Are you calling to give me good news?"

"I *so* am," came the effusive reply. "Only you might want to hang up on me. Joss and I finally decided on a date. We want to do it at the next full moon King Tide, at that park we picked out."

Vera calculated the date and blinked. "That's soon."

"We're going to keep it simple, but please tell me you're available. We honestly will change it if you aren't, because you're who we want to handfast us."

"I can do it." Vera suppressed a laugh as a squeal came through the phone.

"I'm so happy."

"I'm happy for you. The first time I introduced you, I knew you two were meant for one another."

"May God bless your union and your love," Rev said.

"Thank you. Wow, you have a great voice." Jasmine's voice dropped to a dramatic whisper. "Vera, are you hanging out with a Christian?"

Rev blinked as Vera laughed. "Yes. I'm living dangerously. Maybe he'll come to the ceremony, and you'll get to meet him."

"I'd love that. Consider yourself invited, Rev. Oh, that's my mom calling. I just left her the message about the date, and she'll be freaking out."

"Okay, go talk to her. We'll touch base next week on what ritual elements you want. Tell Joss congratulations. Blessings on both of you."

When she disconnected the call, Rev put his hand on hers again, and gripped it. "You marry people?"

"Yes. Some Wiccans call it handfasting."

She told him more about Jasmine and Joss. Jasmine was a gardener, and Joss a passionate fresh food cook.

They'd met at a Beltane festival. Joss had been helping with the after-ritual refreshments, and Jasmine came with her friends. Their fingers brushed when he handed over the cup of mead and a napkin full of crescent-shaped almond cookies. He admitted he gave her one extra. That had been the start of it.

"Joss is very shy, and as you could probably tell, Jasmine is like one of her garden flowers. She turns her face up to the sun and soaks it all in. He sat with her after the refreshments were passed out, and they talked about his favorite vegetables and herb seasonings. She arranged for him to visit her garden at the community college. She teaches botany there, and he cooks for a vegan restaurant in NOLA. We can go there sometime, unless you have an objection to a meatless meal."

"I tend to eat what's placed in front of me and be thankful for it." He touched her hand. "Your blood family. I don't want to pry too much, but will you tell me more about why you had to leave them?"

Even with him, it took effort not to withdraw, physically and mentally, from the question. "If you'll tell me why you need to know."

"Witford tried to find out more about it. Said your family shunned you. I don't need you to say another word about it to me," he said, tightening his hand on hers when he saw the anger in her face. "But I not asking because of that. I asking because I want to know how to share that hurt. Help you with it when it comes upon you the way it does."

She'd worked on this wound in her soul, knowing it did no good to deprive it of oxygen. Maybe because of that, and because of Rev himself, she knew she could believe him, and finally talk to him about it.

"Faith should guide your life. I don't believe religion should dictate it. There needs to be room for questions, growth. It's a marriage, where you and your faith bond with a respect for individuality and free will. People can choose different religious paths. My family didn't feel that way about it. It was a painful road, and it ended with them telling me I couldn't be part of the family anymore."

"I hope they weren't that cruel about it."

"No." They were worse. She didn't have to say it, though. She expected it was vibrating off of her.

"You know the saying about not burning your bridges? I realized a bridge only leads to one side or the other. When they burned that bridge, I could see the water again. And I thought, if we all get into the water at some point, maybe somewhere downstream, we reach a together point again. But that's not up to me. It's up to the current, and where it takes us."

She drew a breath. "I constructed a bridge out of twigs, burned it in my cauldron and then scattered the ashes in the Mississippi. Watched it flow away." At his raised brow, she explained. "It's similar magic. A small version to replicate your bigger intent."

She gave a half laugh. "Cyn would say what it boils down to is, 'I kicked that shit to the curb and got on with living my life.' I guess that's true, too."

His gaze was thoughtful. "What are you thinking?" she asked.

"I thinking about Witford and Tisha." He pressed his lips together. "There's something bad wrong between us, Veracity. I gave it to God to fix, because the answer to it isn't before me, but it's getting worse."

"What makes you think that?"

"The silence," he said soberly. "They talking, they mouths moving, saying the things we normally talk about, but there's this big silence

290

behind it. I don't know what to do about it. It like they hiding in a room and not showing me what's going on there. I've never had that happen with us. When you talk about your family, the pain I feel from you, it's what I feeling..." His eyes darkened. "I'm worried."

She turned onto Tiger and Skye's long and winding private driveway, but stopped to let the engine idle, so she could give him her full attention. "I'm so sorry. I wish I could help, especially since I'm the problem."

"No," he told her with gentle authority, reaching out to touch her mouth. "You not. The problem is in our hearts. We haven't figured out how to understand one another on this. It will come."

She slid her arms around his shoulders, held him to her, felt the strength of his hands at her waist as he took the comfort and gave her back some of the same. That closed circle that could reassure, that could provide an emotional fortress when needed against the battering of the world.

When they eased back from one another and she resumed driving, he glanced around him. "Tiger and Skye got some good land out here."

"Yes, about twenty-five acres. Skye's kept her loft in the Industrial District because it's closer to work, so often they'll stay there during the week and come out here on the weekends."

"Abby and Neil do something like that, don't they?"

"Somewhat. Abby stays at her house in the Garden District when he's down range, but when he's home, she usually works from his place. He's made sure she has the wi-fi she needs, which he says is the greatest sacrifice he's made in their relationship. Though she says he's not sorry he can get better reception for his favorite sports channels and history documentaries."

Rev smiled. "Was it hard, making room for the men in your family of women?"

"Not as much as we expected. They expanded that family, and each relationship brought out different traits in each woman. As close as we are as friends, those qualities weren't always accessible or as noticeable before they fell in love. You see it most significantly in Cyn, but really, it's happened for all of them."

"Does it bother you, that they found that first?"

She glanced at him. "I apologize, Mistress," he said, but she shook her head.

"No. You pay attention to how I feel about things. I would have been surprised if you'd missed that."

"It one thing to notice. Another to confront you with it."

She looked at their clasped hands. "It feels less difficult to talk about these days. But yes, it did bother me. I recognized it for what it was, though. I didn't let it make me desperate, or willing to settle. There were plenty of nights I felt the bite of that loneliness, of flying by myself while they glided along next to me in pairs, but we were still in the same flock. How about you? Have you felt lonely, Rev?"

"Yes." He gave her the same honesty, not willing to let her fly alone with her own experience. His brown eyes showed hints of gold as they turned upon her. "Maybe I didn't ask myself the same questions you did, because all my life I been told whatever happened to me, or didn't happen to me, was because that was how God wanted it, and I never was alone as long as I had Him. But I think God know, as much as we need Him, we need a helpmeet, someone who recognize our heart, and let us walk our earthly path together."

They pulled up to Tiger and Skye's compound, which included a long brick house and outbuildings, like the barn garage for his at-home motorcycle and vehicle work. A concrete pad with a pavilion covering it created a generous outdoor space, complete with grill, wet bar and comfortable furniture. The track for vehicle testing was beyond it.

Rev exited the Aston Martin, came around and opened Vera's door for her. He hadn't expanded on what he'd said, made it personal, but she knew that was what they were becoming for one another. Help-meet. She could try to protect herself by denying it, but with him, that insecurity seemed to be disappearing, carried down the river with the ashes of that bridge she'd created.

Tiger had helpfully left the truck they were going to use parked on the track. When they reached it, Rev opening the passenger door for her, she turned, curving her hand around his nape and pressing herself against him. He was ready for her, circling her waist and bringing her closer with one arm. Lifting her foot, she slid it around his calf, her other hand dropping to his ass to knead for the pure pleasure of it. His cock hardened against her, as if merely waiting for her to require that from him.

Ready to serve her, just as he said.

His hand flexed on her waist. "I want to touch you like you touching me," he whispered against her mouth.

"Not right now," she said, sensually cruel. "I like that you told me. But all I want is to enjoy you, kiss you, grip your beautiful ass and know that you're waiting for my command to do more of what I want."

Then she took his mouth again. He wasn't passive, his mouth telling her of his hunger, teasing her lips, her tongue, stroking and pulling stronger desires from her. Wanting her to give him that order, willing to wait, but also wanting to let her know how worthwhile he could make it if she decided she wanted to deliver that command sooner.

He pressed his forehead against hers as she broke the kiss. "Good thing we starting here instead of in traffic," he said.

"Safe driving practices are important," she said solemnly. "That's your first lesson." As she drew away from him and caught his amused but exasperated reaction, she shot him a wicked grin. "Slap my ass the way you're thinking about and you will pay dearly," she informed him.

His laugh warmed areas already heated, but it was the kind of warmth that settled it, a promise that the pleasure would be ready to revisit later, and the way they spent the time in between would be worth the wait.

He had to adjust himself to make the fit of his jeans a little less constricting as he got into the driver's seat, a pleasant thing to watch. She leaned over and stroked him, cupped him as he spread his thighs, anticipating her desires.

"Since you've ridden in plenty of vehicles, I assume you've paid some attention to how it's done," she said. "Why did you never get a license?"

She took more pleasure in his effort to answer her, but he knew what she expected. His voice, though hoarse, was coherent. "Never seemed to have a need. Trolley and bus get me where I want to go."

"So why do you want to learn to drive? Other than to give me some relief on hypothetical road trips?" She sat back against her seat, her shoulder against it, her legs crossed, knee up near the console. She'd worn a flirty blue and green paisley skirt, its wide waist band decorated with dark buttons. Her breasts were hard to ignore, clad in a short-sleeved blue top with a scoop neck. But after his gaze slid from there and down to her legs, the return trip brought him back to her kissed lips and luminous eyes.

"You want to show me, and anything you can teach me, that let me be with you, I like that."

"That's a very good answer. Let's get started." As she went through the basics, she learned how much he'd absorbed from watching others. When she at last told him to start the vehicle, he leaned over, gripped her seat belt and drew it across her body. His fingers brushed her hip as he latched it. The truck was an older one, without the nanny beeping if the seatbelt wasn't on, but that didn't matter to Rev. Keeping her safe did.

With a whimsical smile, she leaned over and did the same to him, sliding her fingers over his chest, tangling briefly with the chain for the silver cross. She lingered at his hip as she clicked the belt in place, and discovered he was carrying chewing gum in his pocket.

"Bubble gum?"

"For the kids," he told her. "And sometimes for Beau. You can have a piece if you want."

She smiled and replaced the package. "Start the truck."

He proceeded carefully, listening to her instruction as he made several circuits of Tiger's test track, showing a decent grasp of driving skills.

"Tiger said you can come out anytime and practice," she told him. "It's an old truck and he leaves the keys under the mat. It's usually parked next to the barn."

"He don't worry someone going to steal it?"

"Not a big issue out here. Plus, even without his outlaw biker history, anyone who sees the man is going to think twice about pissing him off. And then there's Skye. With her tech skills, she could ruin someone's credit, put them on an FBI watch list and worst of all, empty their music playlists and cancel their social media accounts."

He chuckled. "Best not to mess with a Mistress's man."

"You got it. Like Cyn says, 'I'm the only one allowed to beat or psychologically torture you.' Let's do a few more rounds here, then we'll test out some of the back roads around Tiger's property."

Once again, Rev handled himself well for that step, though he pulled off when faster vehicles came up behind him. He didn't get flustered, but he was attentive and cautious in the way new drivers were.

"How does it feel?" she asked when they took a break on a shoulder.

"Good. I like learning things that can help someone else. When I first started working with Beau, I wanted to learn all the stuff he knew, which made him sure they brought me in to take his job. But I just wanted to pull my weight so he could count on me. Once he figured that out, we got on fine. Every budget cycle, if it a tight year, I tell Miss Mavis if they have to cut our staff, then it should be me. I won't let them do that to him, and I always got my job at the church."

His jaw set. "Beau wasn't too sure about you either, said some of the things Witford and Tisha did, only Beau's reasons for telling me were different. He was more worried about how it affect me as a man."

She narrowed her gaze. "What things?"

"I don't want to get old Beau in trouble. He was just worried about me."

"Are you refusing to tell me?"

"No. Just protecting him." He gave her a rueful smile. "What you'd expect. Why some fancy, beautiful woman might be interested in someone like me."

He spoke casually, but she could see Beau had managed to plant a doubt or two, and they'd taken root. Shallow ones though, easy to pluck out if addressed early. As she did now.

"Rev, I respect you as an equal. You submitting to me, me being your Mistress, that's a decision made from both sides. I am attracted to you. No, let me correct that. I am *fiercely* attracted to you, and it's not just your beautiful body, wonderful mouth and that limitless desire to submit you carry. It's the whole man, everything I'm learning about you."

She leaned in to slide her fingers under the collar of his shirt, stroking heated skin. "So, at the risk of offending Beau or anyone else acting out of true concern for you—which I appreciate—if they're suggesting you're some boy toy I'll tire of because of our different economic or educational circumstances, they're feeding you garbage and can fuck the hell off. I'll drive that garbage out of your mind, like Jesus and those money lenders. I have no problem using a whip to do it."

The comparison startled then amused him, but she saw the

doubts he'd harbored give way to belief, allowing him to move from there to need. The need to feel the weight of a control that strong, reinforced with the kind of pain she'd shown him could open him up to dormant feelings only recently come to life. But they'd been there from the first time he'd gotten on his knees before the Virgin Mary.

"I apologize, Mistress. You're right. I letting things come between us that don't belong there."

"Yes. But that's why you told me about them, which is the right thing to do. That's how we take care of them. Together, and by trusting me with what's happening in your head."

She sat back. "Drive us back to Tiger's. We'll go get some lunch."

When he stopped the truck by the barn, he turned off the ignition and slid his hands along the wheel, a marveling look on his expression.

"When he was young, Witford and his friends liked to drive fast, like young people do. Some time I might do the same, just to see what it like to be the driver when doing that." He shot her a glance. "I sound like a kid."

"But you're not. Not at all."

His gaze swept over her. "I thank the Lord for that."

When they were back in her car, she twisted toward him. "I'd like to see the home where you grew up, before your mother died."

He didn't seem bothered by the request. "It ain't much to look at. The neighborhood is pretty run down. I don't have the exact address, but I know the name of the street, if you want to put it in your navigation screen there."

She complied. As she turned onto the highway that would bring them back into NOLA's city limits, Rev had his own question for her. A startling one.

"Do you ever wish you back with your ex-husband?"

"Lord and Lady, no." She jerked the wheel when she looked toward him, and Rev's hand was immediately overlapping hers, helping her to steady it.

His expression eased at her forceful response, though he looked like he regretted asking. It had upset her, but she realized she wanted him to know.

"It's hard, even when it's your choice and even when it's already been over well before you make that decision. But I mourned the loss of the 'wished for marriage' more than the actual one. There are so many could-have-beens and dreams that die with the relationship."

"It is a death," Rev said soberly. "And you had to grieve. You ever see him?"

"No. Donovan moved out of the area a long time ago. He won't be back. I check his social media now and again, but we haven't spoken in years. He got married, had a couple kids, and lives in DC. We were planning to have some, but I made excuses for us to hold off. Something felt wrong, and I'm grateful we never had any. I wish him joy in his current marriage, and hope they're more compatible than we were."

"Did he...submit to you?"

"Some. But he liked submission as play acting, to spice up the relationship. Which was fine, but it runs far deeper for me than he wanted to go."

"That feeling, that wanting to surrender to a Mistress, was always just waiting inside me," he said. "Least it feels that way. Was it the same for you?"

"Strongly enough that it was part of why my family and I had to part ways. My faith is inseparable from what I want in a relationship with a man. While I didn't feel an in-depth discussion of my sex life was necessary, they heard things, and found out what I liked."

"And what's that, Mistress?"

She gave him a sidelong glance, a feline smile. "A strong man, so well set with himself that he can submit beautifully to a dominant female. Or submit in a less than beautiful way. They both have their moments."

They'd reached the part of town he'd given her, so their attention shifted to him directing her through the turns that brought them to the home he'd shared with his mother.

The square cinderblock structure with one solitary front window, covered with bars, looked like a casualty of Hurricane Katrina. Though it was probably too damaged inside to meet code, a realtor somewhere was sitting on the deed, hoping for a future where the area might get gentrified, and the small lot would make him or her money. But for now, it just looked like an abandoned building. With some notable exceptions.

The property had reasonably fresh exterior paint and the thatch of grass in front was mowed. A steel magnolia wreath was on the door, and shells were piled at the doorstep like a cairn.

"I go to the beach each year just before her death," Rev said, looking at it. "Get some shells, add to it. The steel magnolia wreath, that's the kind of flower she was, so it fit. I found it at a junk store, cleaned it up and painted it."

"You keep up the house?"

"The outside, since the door locked, and the realtor don't want anyone but him inside."

Rev's gaze rested on the wreath, his hands spread on his knees like uneasy spiders. "Teena Joy favored my momma. So growing up, sometimes when I'd look at her, it was like I could almost see her. I'd feel this need to reach out and touch Teena Joy's face, as if I'm touching that memory, feeling my momma living there, under the skin."

He glanced at Vera. "Like what I feel when I look at you. I'm seeing something I want so much, I want to reach through, inside you, and touch your soul. Just one touch would be enough, and I'd know it was eternal."

He looked toward the door again. "I don't remember her real good. Teena Joy was my momma in most my memories, but when I'm here, I feel her strongest."

She touched his shoulder. "I'm sorry you lost her so young. And I'm sorry about Teena Joy. Even when it's time for death to come, that doesn't mean we're ready for it."

"No." He turned toward her. "If you decide...if you want to try to reach out to your daddy, because of his health, I can be there for you."

She drew her hand back. "I appreciate that, Rev. I've tried various ways to reconcile with them, but when I burned that symbolic bridge, I was done being rejected. I got the message and moved on, just as Cyn said. You ready for lunch?"

He gazed at her but nodded. She pulled away from the house. "Anywhere in particular you'd like to go?"

"I like breakfast for lunch."

"Me too. Let's go to Mother's. They serve it all day."

"Sounds good."

It wasn't far from his old home. She found a parking spot near Mother's, but when they stopped, she didn't immediately exit the car.

"I've been through countless rounds of guilt and pointless what-ifs,

Rev," she said. "I've accepted that sometimes it takes more than exerting my will to achieve a desired outcome."

When they left her car and began to walk together, he slid his arm around her, his hand overlapping her hip. "You can exert your will where it's welcome. I'm very welcoming of it."

Her tight lips eased into a smile. "Noted."

They headed toward the diner's open door. From the outside, the old brick building didn't look like much, but the cooking smells wafting into the street could get the stomach rumbling.

"When someone not ready to let the Word in, you have to do what the Lord say," Rev said abruptly. "You shake the dust off your feet and move on, but you've given them the message, the offered hand, and that don't go away. They can come get it when and if they ready. Till then you just keep your heart open. I think it maybe like that with your family."

Vera pressed her lips together. "I had to shake the dust from my feet, but it didn't leave my heart. And I still deal with so much anger over it. What do I do with that?"

"Forgive every day. Like Jesus say. Not seven times, but seven times seventy. His way of saying do it as long as it take." He tilted his head to look down at her. "Want to come to service tomorrow? I'll sing a song you like. Just tell me which one and I'll put it in the lineup."

"Highway to Hell, AC/DC?"

He laughed out loud. It turned heads in their direction, because Goddess, laughing was just another form of singing, and his voice had that mesmerizing quality for both. 'Tisha's eyes would pop right out of her head."

"Will the Beatles scandalize her? How about 'Here Comes the Sun?' Do you normally take requests?"

"No, but if it's right, that song will come up." His hand tightened on her. "And I have a feeling it will be just right."

CHAPTER EIGHTEEN

*S*he preferred to sit in the back of his church, not like a student trying to avoid the teacher's notice, but because it offered the best view of him when his singing propelled him into the nave, toward someone who needed extra attention.

She considered whether forgiveness needed to be asked for strategically positioning herself so she claimed the best view of him, but the Lord and Lady would understand.

You created him, after all. Every fine inch.

Today, he was drawn toward a couple struggling over their relationship with an estranged relative. If it had been anyone but Rev, she would say he did it deliberately, to point a finger toward their conversation the day before. But the Powers-That-Be were multi-taskers; they put information out there that addressed more than one person's problems.

"The people we love are the hardest to understand," Rev told the couple. "They can hurt us the deepest. But God love us. That's all of it. Beginning and end. You don't have to figure out more than that. Don't have to control or direct anything.

"When you look at your grandma, you look at her with your heart, not your worries or your head. She a good and loving person. She don't think the way you do. She don't think the way I do. She don't need to. We all get to be petals on a sunflower, all of us grouped around the same sun. No matter what we call it, we connected to that light and to each other, you understand? He know her heart, which means you do, too, deep down.

"What's that song? 'Here comes the sun.'" His gaze shifted to Vera before coming back to them. They were holding his hands, three sets overlapping. Clutching.

"It going to be all right. We let that warmth in, there it is, just waiting for us to let it in. Open that door, all right. It just starts with this. You go find her, you go where she is, sit down and hold her hand. Just be quiet and still, let God see that and let the sun come out in all of you..."

He rose, singing a line or two of the song before coming back to the point. "We all got someone like that. Your neighbor, a friend who's not so close to us anymore, a coworker. Someone is upsetting you, and you haven't told them or talked it out. You go to them and you say, you can help me, brother, sister. I don't know how to feel better about this, but I don't want to have anything in my heart but love for you. It makes me heart sick to know this poison is between us. So help me. Help me understand. Help me get rid of it. Help me let the sun in again. Let *Him* in."

He spread out his arms, gesturing toward the cross. "Here comes the Son."

Calls of praise came from the parishioners. Rev had been singing pieces of the song in between his spoken words, but now he started singing the whole tune. Vera saw lips moving, the congregation singing with him, but it was soft, the murmur of the ocean on a peaceful day. They wanted to hear him. Though it had no problem reaching every person in the congregation, he sang it in a softer tone, as it was meant to be sung, filled with hope and a tender optimism.

Only when the choir joined into the chorus with joyous enthusiasm did the audience volume increase.

It's alright... Here comes the sun...

Witford had said Teena Joy had given Rev a "simple" faith. Vera recognized the word for what it meant. Maybe Witford had once known it as well, instead of how he'd meant it in her office, a hundred indirect cuts disguised as well-meaning concern.

Everything she'd learned about Rev, felt from him, especially since the shooting, said that he searched his own soul with the perseverance that God's adherents had needed to wander the desert. When he saw pain or need, he used his faith to help and protect, and asked nothing but the opportunity to be in the right place to be God's instrument. He didn't let his despair or pain over humanity's failings stop him.

That kind of faith wasn't simple at all.

Though she'd told herself she wasn't going to engage, she also refused to cower. Tisha sat in the front pew, her back to Vera, so the dagger glances were coming from Witford alone. He sat next to the pulpit, waiting for Rev's singing program to finish. He smiled and nodded, adding *amens* and lifting one hand. All the right responses.

But when their gazes met, she saw a mess of bad feelings. She gave him a cordial nod. His gaze moved on like he hadn't seen her.

She could keep the cold war going, or respond a different way. The lesson God was teaching through Rev today was for all of them. This was hurting her man, and Vera knew how much worse it could get. She wasn't having that.

She'd invite Tisha and Witford to dinner at her place, with her and Rev. A home cooked meal, where they'd have the chance to get to know her, and let her do the same. The offer of a clean slate, wiping away preconceived notions that weren't earned or deserved. She needed to give them the same chance she wanted them to give her.

She and Rev dropped her car at her house and picked up a trolley to Jackson Square to grab lunch at the French Market. As they strolled the square, petting the carriage horses and checking out local art vendors, she ran her idea past Rev.

"I think that'd be good. Witford like fried chicken, maybe better than he love Jesus."

"I don't know if I can live up to that, but I do make an excellent fried chicken. Cyn has me buying from a humane supplier through a farmer's market, where the chickens are given a natural outdoor life, until they're killed." She grimaced. "That's as close to vegetarian as I get."

"Still better than not thinking about the animals at all. Everything we put in our mouth goes into us, and if the animal was afraid or mistreated, that goes into us too."

She raised a brow. "You have highly developed empathy. It's something seen more often in people who've...left the environments in which they were raised."

"Like a bunch of traveling. Or going to college. Reading lots of books."

"Yes." She squeezed his arm and he covered it.

"You didn't offend me, Mistress. Wouldn't mind doing some traveling, but everyone I meet is like visiting a new place. Couldn't learn everything about them, even if I had a million years."

They had reached a vendor with hand-drawn cards. Rev pointed out one with an axolotl, a lizard creature with the cute face of a stuffed animal. Probably a disarming way to lure in prey. She should tell Cyn it was her spirit animal, just to hear her scoff at the idea that anyone would call her cute. Only Mick was that brave. Or foolish.

The artist had a blank card with a watercolor sunrise on the front. The script below was *Here comes the sun*...

She bought the card and slipped it into her bag. "I want to take you home, now," she said.

"If we had your car, you could let me drive."

He was teasing her, but she linked her arm through his and gave him a look. "It's time that I drive. Wouldn't you agree?"

His biceps flexed under her touch. "Yes, Mistress."

When they were on her porch, she handed him her key so he could open the door for her. One of her favorite things about a power exchange relationship was how many layers of meaning such seemingly ordinary acts could have.

Her desire to take control had grown on the way home. She'd had him be quiet, put her hand on his leg, told him to hold his knees open. Since they were on the trolley, she hadn't touched him intimately, but having him do that had him fully attentive and deeply aroused by the time they arrived.

It was the state she wanted him in. Nothing to think about, not their families, not the shooting; just what was between them. A haven and resting spot.

Putting her keys on the kitchen counter, she moved into her living room and sat in her straight-backed chair. "Come stand behind me."

When he did, his hands settled on the chair on either side of her shoulders. His thumbs brushed them, an incidental thing. He was waiting for her permission.

"Stroke my hair and shoulders, Rev. My neck. Let me feel your desire through your touch."

His hands moved over her curls, fingers sliding under and over them to find her scalp to stroke her skull, then he moved out and down to her shoulders, kneading, caressing.

In anticipation of their lunch plans, she'd brought a change of clothes to the church, and so had he. She wore a purple knit shirt over a pair of snug jeans. More than once, she'd felt the heat of his gaze on her ass when she strolled ahead of him among the street vendors. When she sent him a reproving look, his lifted shoulder said, "How can I help myself?" his expression guilelessly charming.

His thumbs moved beneath the neckline of her shirt and bra straps. When he traced her collarbone, sensation radiated toward her breasts. He moved to the round part of her shoulders, down her upper arms, then back up. When he found his way back under her hair, he massaged her neck, clasping her there with a brief tantalizing pressure, giving her the strength of his grip.

She tilted her head back against his abdomen as his fingers slid down the front of her throat, stopping at a spot at her sternum that obeyed her dictate, but also sent more of those sensations outward and lower. Then back up, following ground he'd already covered, but changing pace and pressure so she knew he wasn't just doing it to kill time until she'd let him get to more interesting places. He was treasuring each touch, treating it as new, something wondrous.

Just as he'd described how he viewed every person he met. A new place to discover.

Hell, he was good at this.

When she felt like she could melt against him, if the chair wasn't in between their bodies, she had him come stand before her.

"What's going on in your mind, Rev?" She crossed her legs, folding her hands over one knee. "And why are you standing over your Mistress?"

The flare of heat in his gaze showed the energy shift between them to full-on Domme and sub. He dropped to one knee, denim stretching over ass and thighs. His linen shirt had wooden buttons, two open at his throat. The fabric was thin enough the hue of his bronze skin was hinted at beneath it.

"I thinking about a Sunday school lesson. The structure of a prayer."

She arched a brow, waiting.

"First you honor God. You seek His will. Ask for what you need, and trust He'll respond. Not the way you want or you think He should, but how He know you *need*. You forgive, to help open your heart. And then you finish by honoring Him again."

"Why are you thinking of that?"

"God say no false idols. But God is Love, and so if you honor Love in your life the same way, it doesn't feel blasphemous. There God's Will, and yours, Mistress. I'm good serving both, especially since I'm pretty sure He sent you to me. Or me to you. So..."

He bent forward and put his lips on the top of her foot. "I honor you, Mistress. I want to serve your will, and I trust you to hear my heart, understand my words, my reactions to you, and know what I need. And I hope to show my honor for you, with whatever you command of me, here and now."

Enlightened. That was what the man was. Pure and enlightened, while also a hundred percent primal, erotic pleasure, in a six-foot frame.

"I like the way your mind works, Rev. Sit up and move back for me. I want to sit in front of you."

When he complied, they sat cross-legged, their knees touching. She put a hand over his heart. "Lay one hand on your knee, palm up."

When he did, she put hers in it, and had him place his free hand over her heart. "A closed circle, our two bodies," she said. "What I'm imagining is you, sitting in the center of my heart, breathing with me. Even when we're apart, this connection," her fingers tightened on his, "is there. We can reach out to one another through it. No matter how far apart, we'll feel that energy. It will only become deeper as we serve it. Trust in it." A smile touched her lips. "Honor it."

She stayed that way, and he held her gaze, no self-consciousness, that power growing as if it had merely waited for the two of them to reach for it. If she closed her eyes, it was a flickering, multi-colored flame against her lids, reflecting what was surging through her body, through those energy channels and points of contact between them.

Confirming that bond and connection was real, strong, and only going to get stronger, as long as they were open to fueling it. It made her tremble.

At length, she drew back and stood. When she swayed, he stood up on his knees, his arms sliding around her hips to hold her securely. She caressed his jaw with quivering fingertips. "Take me to bed, Rev, and serve me there."

"May I ask a favor, Mistress?"

"You may. I won't promise to grant it. What you need, I will always give you. What you want is a gift for me to grant, at my own pace."

His smile didn't dilute the intensity in his gaze. "I want to carry you there."

"Why?" She shoved aside that idiot and typical female reaction, gauging her weight and if he was overestimating his own strength, which might have been sufficient if only she hadn't had that extra cookie from the metal lunch box full of them Cyn had brought to the office. A vintage Wonder Woman lunch box. Mick had bought it for her.

"You know that poem, about the Footprints?" Rev said. "You a strong, strong woman, Veracity. I want to carry you so that you know I can. You care for me, but a submissive takes care of his Mistress when she need it, because that's part of how he serves her. How this one wants to serve her. Serve you."

Her trembling increased. She'd held the reins on so many submissives, enjoyed the give and take of those sessions, some more intense than others. But none of them had claimed her whole heart, and she hadn't been that for them, either.

This was...different. So different. Rev had involved her heart from their first meet. From the first time she saw that quote on the wall of the maintenance shed. And with the exercise she'd just had them do, she'd linked their hearts even more.

She was the Mistress, she was in charge, and he was submitting to her. And yet somehow the two of them were caught up in something so powerful, those roles had nuances to them she'd never thought they could have.

She'd been foolish to think it would be otherwise. Didn't she have four in-her-face-every-day examples that proved how limitless and undefined those connections could be?

"Carry me to my room, Rev," she said.

When he rose, she slid an arm around his neck, molding her hand over his broad shoulder. He bent and put his hand beneath her knees, the other behind her back, and lifted her. The gratitude in his expression, tinged with an intriguing possessive satisfaction, made joy skate through her, doing a few twirls and flips along the way.

He took her to her bedroom. As he moved toward her bed, the narrowness of the room, its length, gave her the sense of a journey that ended in just the right place.

"Put me on the edge, Rev."

As he did, she had him remain standing so she could press her lips to his abdomen, stroke her hands along his sides, over his hips and upper thighs. She stood, putting the rest of her against him as she unfastened his jeans, and indicated with the pressure of her hands that she wanted them off. All of it, except his cross.

When he complied, she trailed her fingertips over his neck, gripping the cross briefly to feel the engraved words about faith against her skin. Then she moved down his abdomen, tracing a circle around his cock, suitably stiff and straight. The henna designs had faded away, but she would plan to do them again. "Undress me, Rev."

He gripped the hem of her shirt, easing it over her head, careful not to snag her hair. The bra unfastened in the back, so he leaned up against her, his breath at her temple as he did that, her hands on his bent arms. His hand slid over her cat and pentacle tattoo, the most sensitive place on her back.

He removed the jeans next, his thumbs pushed into the sides to ease them off her hips. They were snug enough the panties had to come with them. She sat down to let him finish it, him going to his knees to slip them off her legs with her shoes. He straightened, leaning in between her spread knees to remove her earrings, her pentacle, and her Maat and Isis pendant, cradling them in his large palm. As he twisted around and rested them on the nearby dresser, he corralled the earrings in loops of the chain.

"Give me your belt," she ordered.

He bent to pull them out of his jeans while she let her hand wander down his side, along his bare hip, the flexing muscle of his ass.

She looped the belt around his wrists and backed up onto the bed on her knees, tugging him up onto it with her.

She liked the effect, him looking like a prowling cat, shoulders and head lowered, his gaze intent upon her. She laid down, parting her legs so his knees were braced between them. As she brought him down over her, she had him put his bound wrists above her head, forearms framing her face.

The heat of his skin was welcome against her. She lifted her legs and clasped them over his bare backside. With the pressure of those legs, she eased him into her slick tissues, tightening her core to lift and pull him in, take him deeper, hold him there.

The light filtering through the tall window turned his face into a sculpture, the striking cheekbones and firmly held jaw. She traced the tender pink seam between his brown lips. "In Tantra, the goddess Kali is the passionate teacher, the female showing the male what she desires, letting him be a witness of what female sexuality is, how it intertwines with his. 'A naked goddess, with disheveled hair; symbolizing freedom...' That's from the *Chakrasamvara Tantra*."

His eyes moved to her hair fluffed around her face. When his attention came back to her eyes, she parted her lips, drawing his eyes there as well.

"Start moving inside me, Rev. Move slow, just as slowly in as out, and keep doing it that way, no matter how much your body says to do more. No matter what I do to you. When you're close to climax, stop. Remember your breathing. Impress me with how long you can keep that energy channeled, cycling, building, but not releasing."

He obeyed, muscles corded in his biceps and under her heels. She trailed her fingertips over his shoulders, scraped him with her nails. Reached up and put her mouth against his throat, bit him, licked him. Rocked her hips up and took him deeper.

His growl, his erratic breath, was music she used to choreograph the way she touched him, stroked, gripped him with her inner muscles to increase the friction from his thick cock. Goddess, he felt so good. That energy was there between them, that link, and she focused on it. This too was a closed circle of energy, their bodies joined.

She reached above her, so his gaze was on her lifted breasts, so close to the heat of his puffing breath, the stretch of his lips that showed his teeth. She gripped the belt, his bound hands, and wrapped her own hands in the free part of the strap, her knuckles brushing the smooth wood of her headboard. The hold gave her more leverage, but it was also an intriguing message. Choosing to be bound to him.

"Mistress…" he said, after a gratifyingly long time. He was learning how to internalize that arousal, drive it deeper into his core, into the root, and hold it there. His gaze was glazed, his mouth tight. She licked his lips, his teeth, nipped his jaw, and a muttered oath escaped him.

"Be still, Rev."

He did, body shuddering. "Stay still inside me and worship my breasts with your eyes, then your mouth."

When he stared at them, covering every inch, the swollen curves, the tight nipples, the damp crevice between them, the bliss was indescribable. After the right amount of time, he dipped his head and began to breathe on her, then brush his lips there, a touch of tongue. When he finally dipped his head and latched onto a nipple, he drew it in deep. The hard swell of response through her cunt seized her whole body.

Keeping herself in check, cycling those same orgasmic currents, she began to work herself up and down his shaft. He fought to hold his lower body still and obey her.

"Submit to my will," she reminded him in a breathless voice. "And tell me what you need. What do you need, Rev?"

"Whatever you know I need, Mistress…God, great Lord in Heaven…I love your breasts…"

Fervent admiration. He lavished praise upon them with his mouth and teeth, his lips, the brush of his rough jaw.

She wanted this to go on forever, the two of them here, nothing in the outside world to take them away from it. A spike of fear came with the thought, a reaction she wasn't expecting.

She let go of the belt to clasp his head as it moved over her breasts, her thumb against the pulse crashing in his throat. "Rev," she whispered. "Karman Leone. Inside me, in every way. Mine."

His bound hands shifted, moving under her head. He held her, his elbows pressed outside her shoulders, his body suddenly having more weight, as if reminding her of what he'd said about carrying her. About being there for her.

He had felt the anxiety, and he was answering it.

There was no absolute protection from everything in the world.

But the desire to protect, the measure of it, strengthened the bond two people could have, especially when that desire was accepted and reciprocated, welcomed not as an obligation, but an honor and privilege they would work to earn. She wanted to take care of and protect him as well, with everything she had.

"Now, Rev," she said softly, and the two of them moved together, bringing their bodies to that pinnacle, where they rocked and shuddered together, his jaw to her cheek, his body driving strong into her. She cried out against him, flesh and bone, the rush of blood and life between them.

When it ebbed away, he was damp with perspiration, his expression locked upon her. One of his bound hands had a noticeable grip on the back of her neck. "You're not intending to let your Mistress go."

"It crossed my mind."

Another little shiver went through her at the look in his eyes. "You don't look like that bother you much," he said.

"No. It doesn't. Not when I feel it from you. It matches what I feel, too."

She slid her hand down his back. "But I admit I'm having some trouble breathing."

With a grin, he lifted off of her. She turned inside the circle of his arms, adjusting them so she had his bound hands cradled against her breasts, the end of the belt clasped in her hands. His body spooned behind hers, so their chakras aligned, just as she'd described that to him. Contentment gripped her.

"I'm going to sleep for a little while. You should do the same. If you need to get up, let me know and I'll unbind you. But don't do it yourself. I like knowing you'll wait for me."

"Yes, Mistress." His mouth was against her hair, his heat behind her, his strength around her.

She liked that, too.

"When I sleep, I invite you into my dreams, Rev. I want you there, and I want that unconscious part of us we access in sleep to tell us what our path together should be."

So nothing in the waking world will screw with it. She didn't say that aloud, but she held onto him tighter.

"See you there, Mistress."

She woke just past two in the morning. She slipped the belt free of his wrists and rubbed the reddened skin. She hadn't had it tight enough to affect his circulation, so she'd slept easy on that, but when he'd pulled against the hold, stroking inside her, she'd known the skin would be affected. Another mark to replace her henna designs. For now.

She slipped from the bed, murmuring a reassurance to him before she went into the bathroom. After she emerged, she leaned in the doorway, watching him sleep. Thinking of a lot of things. Things he'd said, things she felt with him.

Following the currents of those feelings down to the kitchen, she saw the card she'd bought on the counter. *Here comes the sun.* Here comes light, illumination. Warmth.

She made herself a cup of tea. When she turned, he was there, standing tall and dark in the entry way. He'd put on his jeans. She'd have to talk to him about getting dressed before his Mistress told him it was okay, but she didn't mind this look, the top button open, his hip bones and sculpted upper torso visible.

He came to her, and she slid her hand over his side, into the back of the jeans to caress his buttocks. He hadn't put on any underwear, which mollified her some.

She brushed a kiss against his lips. "Rev, bring me that pen over there."

When he did, she opened the card. Her kitchen nightlight offered enough illumination to see the blank white interior. Her feelings were a tumultuous sea, but she put the pen to the page and wrote in flowing cursive.

I love you and pray for all of you, for our family, every day. Reach out to me anytime, or come visit me in NOLA. Veracity.

She put the pen down carefully, slid the card into its envelope and wrote her parents' names and address on it.

Rev had his hand on her lower back. When she was done, she looked up at him, her heart in her eyes. Aching, broken, but functioning, fully capable of love. Without a word needed, he picked her up and carried her back to bed.

CHAPTER NINETEEN

*A*s Vera got out of the Aston Martin, she paused to gaze up at the night sky, kneading her aching neck as she did so. It was her turn to be on call for Laurel Grove, and late this afternoon, after a full day of work, they'd reached out for help with a new arrival.

Atalaya Summers had taken her husband's beatings for the last time. Because today he'd gone after their eight-year- old son when the boy tried to protect her. She'd scalded her spouse with a pot of coffee and knocked him unconscious with a fury-fueled swing of her cast iron skillet. Since she'd never been anything but a cowering shadow around him, he hadn't seen it coming. Fortunately, because the man was built like a mountain.

Atalaya grabbed whatever she could and ran. When she and her son had gone into a convenience store bathroom so she could clean up, it had been stocked with cards and stickers for domestic abuse and human trafficking hotlines. Which had connected her to the right people to bring her to Laurel Grove.

Vera had been contacted so she could be present when the police were called, so Atalaya could explain what happened with a legal advocate present. Her son's split lip and fractured wrist, plus her bruises from her last beating, faded but still visible, had worked in her favor. As had the fact she'd called an ambulance for the concussed piece of shit when she and her son reached the convenience store.

Sorry, Vera apologized to the Universe. *I mean the misguided soul that needs spiritual healing—along with some prison time to help reinforce the lesson.*

The police had to take the mother into custody. Dequan, her son, hadn't understood. He'd clung to Atalaya, shouting at everyone, trying to keep them from taking her. He thought he'd never see her again. Vera had sworn to him she was going with his mother. She would get a judge on the phone, despite the late hour, and see if he would agree to let Atalaya be released into Laurel Grove's custody immediately after processing.

One of the officers had stuck with Vera, telling the judge the mother wasn't a flight risk, and verifying she was unquestionably the victim of a serious domestic abuse situation. She was back with Dequan within a couple hours.

So it had been a worthwhile day, though a long one. And not just for her. Rev had had a church commitment tonight, leading a prayer circle at the homeless shelter. He'd warned her it usually led to one-on-ones with some of the guests and a possible overnight to give further succor to lost and hurting souls. He was going to have breakfast with her, though. Since she'd given him a key, the thought of him coming to wake her was appealing.

She closed the door of her detached garage, putting the Aston Martin to bed for the night, and headed for her back porch. She was going to have a hot bath and a glass of wine. Terron, her neighbor, was still up, his upstairs light on. An economics professor, he was often up late with his lesson plans, grading assignments and helping students who contacted him through the college's messaging system.

The scrape of a shoe on her porch, a movement in the shadows, had her grabbing for her pepper spray. She opened her mouth to scream her loudest, but the figure lunged, arm sweeping forward. Pain exploded through her skull, spinning her around and dropping her against her metal chairs. She grabbed them as she went down, hoping they'd make enough racket to draw Terron's attention.

Except he wore earphones that blasted seventies rock music at him while he was working.

Her attacker landed on her. Despite her spinning head, she fought, kicking and punching, wiggling and trying to force a scream out of her frozen throat. A grunt said she'd succeeded in hurting him. She'd also thrown the asshole off of her. Her mosaic table fell to the boards as he sent it toppling. He cursed and she was hit again, dazing her further.

In the next horrifying moment, her mouth was muffled, a cloth jammed into it, a bag over her head shutting out light. The panic was almost worse than the pain in her skull.

"Had to wait longer for you than I thought," a male voice grumbled. "Should have known. A witch prefers the devil's hours."

Her shriek against the cloth was strangled, jaw and limbs going rigid as agonizing electricity rocketed through them. She scrambled to hold onto consciousness, knowing her life depended on it, but with the Taser and the head blow, the battle was lost.

Everything went dark.

At eight in the morning, Rev paused in front of Vera's house, thinking of her curvy body nested in her bed, the chestnut-colored skin of her arm and shoulder visible, her lush curves barely clad in something silky. Yesterday, when she'd told him to wake her for breakfast, her tone suggested they might not make it out, so he'd brought some. Two pastries and coffees from the café down the street she liked. If she wanted something more substantial, he'd go get it, but she wasn't normally a heavy breakfast person.

As he went around the house and climbed the steps to the kitchen entrance she'd told him to use, he noticed the chairs she kept flush against the siding had been adjusted, facing one another. The mosaic table between them had cracks, a couple tiles missing.

Maybe she'd had company last night and someone had knocked it over. He rapped his knuckles on the back door. If she was already up, he didn't want to be presumptuous, just walking in on her. That key was a gift he wouldn't disrespect.

Yesterday, he'd taken out his ring of keys and held that one in his hand, as if it held the warmth of her body. Beau had caught him at it. When Rev admitted Vera had given him her key, Beau had told him he was acting like a girl who'd gotten engaged, staring at the sparkly diamond on her finger. But his friend had squeezed his shoulder, the ribbing meant to be good-natured.

As Rev listened for the sound of her stirring behind the door, he noticed a color that didn't fit with the colors of her azaleas. He moved to the railing and peered down.

His mind froze.

It was her purse, the red one with little pearls and gold on it. She wore her black skirt and red blouse with it, and a gold chain belt.

In the next instant, the coffee and pastries were left behind and he was in the house. Turning the key in the lock wasted precious seconds. He almost forced the door open on its frame before the deadbolt drew back.

He called her name as he strode through the rooms and to her bedroom. Her bed was still made. No coffee cup in the sink, no TV remote tossed on the couch before she'd gone to bed. She was neat, but she wasn't obsessive about it. She liked a house that looked like someone lived there.

He returned to the porch to retrieve the purse, then thought better of it. Fingerprints. The police would want to see where everything was. But then he saw a scrap of white stuck between two of her potted plants. When he crouched down to look closer at it, his heart thudded in his ears.

New Orleans had its share of crime. But he didn't know of many criminals who carried wallet cards with the service and event schedule at Rev's church. The special, more detailed kind printed for volunteers, including the ushers.

No. No. *No.*

It just wasn't possible.

But in Rev's gut, he knew it was.

When he dialed the church office, Mrs. Byrd answered.

"This is Rev, Mrs. Byrd."

"Why Rev, using a cell phone. Miracles are happening every day. I—"

"Where's Witford?"

His terse tone had her pausing. "He picked up a message left on the machine by Tyson. Said he had the package Witford told him to get, and he'd brought it to the old mill. When I asked Witford about it, he said it was supplies they want to store there, for the upcoming revival. Witford took Simon with him to help sort them out."

Simon and Tyson were the two ushers who'd shared Witford and

315

Tisha's distrust of Veracity. Rev had talked to them about it, but they'd brushed off his concerns. Much as Witford had, when he'd shut down further conversation with Rev about her.

Simon and Tyson were part of an ex-con rehab program the church sponsored. They weren't the only ones in the church who were, and the program did good for men and women with records. However, Simon and Tyson often acted like Witford's personal bodyguards. Witford didn't discourage that impression, and Rev had wondered what his cousin had them do to reinforce the notion. Or what his cousin did for them.

Had Rev's willingness to let certain things "resolve themselves," put Veracity in harm's way? Just imagining that Witford might...

"Oh, and Tisha went with Witford."

His heart slammed against his ribs. Tisha wouldn't be part of something like what he was thinking. But hearing she was with them wasn't making him feel any better.

"How long ago did they leave?" he asked, cutting off whatever Mrs. Byrd was saying.

The startled tone in Mrs. Byrd's voice suggested the dread and anger he was trying to suppress had come through. "About an hour ago. Is everything okay?"

"I don't know. I'll call you back."

Rev looked at his burner phone. He needed to call 911. He needed to send the police out to the old mill. But he didn't know what was going on, what Witford was doing. He could be wrong. All he knew was that Veracity was in trouble, and everything in him told him she was at the mill.

His cousin and his Mistress.

His aunt.

Please God, help guide me. Whatever I do next, let it be the right thing to help her.

He dropped to his knees on the kitchen floor, his hands clasped to his chest. He opened up everything. His heart, soul and mind, those chakras that Vera talked about. Call the police or go to the mill. Or both. Or call her friends.

When he lifted his head, he'd made his decision. He just hoped it was God's, too. And that he wasn't too late to stand between his family and whatever evil might be guiding them.

Vera woke in darkness, in a place that smelled of dirt and old wood. Her wrists had been bound with a zip tie behind her. Her ankles were bound too. Not being able to move was a terrible, helpless feeling. The hood over her head and the cloth in her mouth was the worst, causing a mind-numbing panic that made her feel like she was suffocating.

But she wasn't. She'd been unconscious for a while. *Breathe.* She needed to breathe. She was able to spit out the cloth gag, but they had something tied around her neck to hold the hood in place, so the balled-up rag dropped and stayed, a damp weight against her chin and neck.

She'd done breathing exercises to handle emotional stress, but that was hell and gone from terror like this. Still, she knew she needed to think clearly, so she made herself do it until she could access some cogent thoughts.

Was this an opportunistic rapist? A husband or boyfriend, wanting vengeance or access to a resident of Laurel Grove? TRA had gotten a lot of press these past couple years. Maybe this was an attempt to extort money from Ros and Abby.

That last one made sense, but it didn't fit the brutal way she'd been treated. Whoever had taken her didn't really care what condition she was in, only that she was still alive.

Focus on your surroundings.

She was alone. Her movements as she regained consciousness hadn't resulted in anyone speaking or moving toward her, and she didn't hear anyone breathing. She thought the hood was a pillowcase. It had a laundry detergent smell, making the situation even more surreal.

She felt like she was in a small space, like a shed.

She also had a phone.

Cyn had given her the garter phone holder as a joke, a poke at how Vera liked to wear her "turn of the nineteenth century" fashions. Such fashions weren't big on pockets, and a phone could ruin the lines of the form fitting garments.

Cyn had rolled her eyes. The initial discussion had been about Vera carrying a gun, but that wasn't Vera's thing. So Cyn had gifted her the phone holder. She'd told Vera to carry the phone in it, particularly when dealing with Laurel Grove issues or traveling New Orleans streets at night. *If someone throws your purse away from you, thinking that's where you're carrying it, they've left you a weapon.*

Damn if the woman hadn't been right.

She writhed and twisted, pulling at the hem of her skirt until she could pluck out the phone. It dropped from her trembling fingers, stiff from the cutting hold of the zip tie. She bit back a curse but reclaimed the device, working it around in her hands until she had it in a position where she could operate it.

As she touched the screen, she heard the tone that told her the battery was low. Her stomach tightened into a hard knot. So it would die soon. She'd had a half charge before she was knocked out, so she'd been out for a few hours. She didn't know what kind of cell signal she had here.

The earliest someone would be looking for her would be in the morning, when Rev was coming for breakfast. She didn't know if it was still night.

A phone with raised buttons would have been *so* fucking helpful right now. She reminded herself that she activated the voice control on her phone all the time without looking. Muscle memory.

It took some fumbling, but she found it, hearing the tiny beep as the microphone engaged. She left the phone on the ground, and turned so she was over it. Her head swam from the movement, wanting to pull her under again. If she fought it, stress would make it happen. *Keep breathing, keep calm.*

"Dial Ros," she rasped.

911 might make more sense, and it would be her next call if she had time, but Ros would cut through any delays, any red tape as the police got to the bottom of things. Ros had access to Navy SEALs and Matt Kensington and members of the police force, like Leland Keller. No matter that he was a sergeant in Baton Rouge; he was a resource that would launch into action without delay if Ros told him it was needed. A dead cell phone could still tell them her last known location. If there was cell service out here.

Ros's voicemail picked up right away, which made her want to wail her frustration. Ros never turned off her phone, but even through the hood, Vera could hear the static. The signal was very weak. She'd been lucky to get the voicemail.

"Help...help me..."

Her voice was raspy and barely audible, her mouth and throat dry. She probably shouldn't raise her voice. Someone might be standing outside the shed.

Shit.

Someone was coming, shoes crunching over gravel. She turned off the volume button on the side of the phone and scooched back, pushing the device into a dusty corner where she encountered a web and its occupant, skittering over her hands. Funny how what would make her shriek and recoil made zero impression on her when her life was at stake. She rolled back into the spot where they'd left her, just in time to hear a door being rolled back. A meager light filtered through the pillowcase.

"You're sure she didn't have a phone," a gruff male voice said.

"I tossed her purse in the bushes. Her outfit doesn't have any pockets. And she's been out of it most the night."

"How about her bra? Some women carry them there."

"No, I didn't..." An awkward pause. "You check her, Simon. I don't want to do that."

"Christ, Tyson."

Tyson and Simon. The ushers at Rev's church. *What the hell?* Her mind spun. Witford and Tisha hated her, yes, but this...it wasn't possible.

Except it was. Cyn had warned her, as had Lawrence. They had a sixth sense for wrong intentions, and a person's capability of acting upon them. Wearing nice clothes and attending church didn't change that.

Oh Goddess.

Rough hands pushed her to her back. Vera tried not to react as her breasts were groped and she was patted down. The touch was functional, nothing sexual about it, but the impersonal nature chilled her. To Simon, she was an object.

"Nothing," Tyson said. "See? Satisfied?"

"Almost." Metal scraped, a sound like a bucket handle being lifted. A breath later, ice cold water struck her face and chest. Vera yelped and tried to roll away as more followed it.

"Stop," she shrieked. "Stop it, damn you."

"I'm not the one damned here, bitch. Get her up."

As she was pulled to her feet, the hood was left in place, to keep her manageable she assumed, since they weren't making any effort to conceal their identities. She knew what that normally meant in kidnapping situations.

But she was still alive, which meant they wanted something.

Take advantage of any opportunity to get away. Ask questions, get information. Don't act like a victim.

She was never again going to lose patience with Cyn for badgering her with self-defense directives.

"Why are you doing this?" she demanded.

The tie around the hood was loosened, but any hope that her vision was about to be restored was dashed as a big male hand caught the balled-up gag before it could fall free. He jammed it back into her mouth.

She tried to use her teeth on those fingers, but he was too brutal and efficient. And when her hood was jerked back down, she was backhanded. He hit her in the same place, which made the pain already throbbing there triple through her cheek and nose, her eye socket. She would have fallen if he didn't have a hard grip on her arm.

"Shut up."

They'd taken off her shoes. She was being half-dragged in stockinged feet across gravel that tore the fabric and stabbed tender flesh. They didn't slow down for her. That further detachment made the dread inside her morph into uncontrollable terror. This was the way people treated animals being herded up a chute for slaughter. Villagers in the path of an oncoming army. Prisoners in concentration camps.

Witches being burned at the stake.

I'm not the one that's damned.

To do whatever unspeakable thing they planned to do, they had to disengage like this. The gag prevented her from saying anything to prove she was a fellow living soul.

She heard falling water...a waterfall? Or a big fountain. An earthy water smell penetrated the hood.

"It's time for you to stay away from Rev."

Witford. His voice was little different from how it had sounded in her office. Sure, arrogant, patronizing. But there was strain, too. He didn't necessarily want to be doing this, but Vera didn't take any comfort from that. She recognized the tone of someone who felt *she* was to blame for *making* him have to terrorize her.

She'd managed to spit out the gag again. She spoke as forcefully as she could through the hood. "You think me being dead and out of the picture will keep Rev loyal to you?"

"Killing you isn't our intent. We're here to make the point you refused to hear in your office." Witford paused. "When we drop you off, there won't be any way for you to prove we did you any harm, I can promise you that. It will be your word against ours. I'm well known in the community, a pastor. You're a witch, a pagan sexual deviant, pursuing one of our beloved but confused church members, a simple man with a learning disability."

Now she understood the purpose of the hood. She couldn't claim she'd seen their faces.

"You think Rev won't believe me?"

"You won't tell Rev about this. We can make things much worse for you, a woman living alone. As we're about to show you. Have you heard of the drowning test for witches? Throw a witch in the water. If she sinks, she's not a witch. If she floats, she is one."

Which proved how illogical fear could be, especially when provoked by those with a self-serving reason to incite it.

Reaching for that cold analysis helped her cling to self-control. And the hope that he was trying to scare her with words. Not actually carry out what he'd just described.

The day-to-day survival of many Laurel Grove residents had often depended on them behaving exactly as their abusers expected. Until an opportunity like what Atalaya had experienced last night opened a door toward freedom.

"I am not the enemy here," she said.

"You are the enemy. You are the Adversary, sent to draw Rev away from the Lord's path."

Tisha's voice, the confirmation of her presence, didn't shock Vera. Lawrence and Cyn had predicted that as well. Hell, it was possible this whole thing was being driven by Tisha's fear for Rev, and the pressure she'd put on Witford to fix it.

Witford made a noise of protest, as if he'd counseled her to stay silent, but Vera heard the rustle of her clothing. As Tisha came closer, she smelled the faint scent of her perfume. The woman's voice was tortured but defiant. "We have to protect him."

"He's protected by the Lord," Vera said. "You think you do a better job than Him?"

Before anyone could stop her, apparently, Tisha yanked off the hood and slapped Vera. Her rings cut Vera's mouth.

As Vera focused blearily on Tisha's hard, glittering eyes and tight mouth, the woman spat at her. "You dance and fornicate with Satan. He shows you how to twist words and plant doubt in God-fearing hearts."

"I already told you, there is no devil in my faith," Vera snapped back. "Only human evil, which is more than capable of insanity like this."

"Hold her," Tisha instructed Simon and Tyson. When they seized her arms, Tisha tore open Vera's blouse, ripped off her pentacle and tossed it away. Then she started to prod Vera with sharp fingers.

Vera struggled, but Simon seized her hair, pulling her head back. Witford's gaze flickered in mild alarm, but when he saw Vera's eyes on him, the look disappeared, his face dispassionate. Tyson held her in a tight grip, but he didn't look comfortable with what Tisha was doing. He tried to look anywhere else but at Vera's breasts, exposed when Tisha yanked down the bra cups. Simon stared at them as if he'd like to cut them off.

It's not you they're doing it to. It's a mannequin, and you're watching from somewhere above them.

Witford was the con man, a preacher who liked money and what it could buy. Tisha was the zealot, driven by ideology and the certainty she was right, that she had God on her side. Simon was a thug, on board with anything that allowed him to do violence. Tyson was more in Witford's camp, but short of murdering her outright, Vera expected they would all stick with the basic plan, to scare the shit out of her so she'd leave Rev be, for the greater good. To serve God's will.

Ros, check your voice mail. Check it. Now she was wishing she'd dialed 911, though her logic had been sound. She had no idea where she was, or if the signal would have been able to target her whereabouts to find her...in time. It was the wrong thought, because it dropped the bottom out of her stomach and set loose a starburst of fear.

"There." With a sharp fingernail, Tisha stabbed a spot under Vera's arm, beside the curve of her breast. "A witch's mark. Told you it was there."

"It's a birthmark, you horrid, sick woman."

Tisha slapped her again, then leaned in. Her breath on Vera's face was minty. Get dressed, brush your teeth and hair, go torment the woman you'd kidnapped. Just like the laundered pillowcase, it made the moment even more bizarre. Tisha's makeup was impeccable, her clothes as stylish as ever.

"Witford doesn't understand. He wants to scare you. I know better. I know you won't be scared for long. Unless you believe we'll do everything we promise. I swore to my sister I'd keep Rev safe for the Lord. He's a gentle soul who doesn't understand the likes of you."

"He's not that gentle." Vera refused to look away from Tisha's flat eyes. "He won't forgive you for harming me."

Her lips tightened. "He'll never know. Unless you want more of this, you'll tell him you don't want to see him anymore, because you're tired of him. Because you're done playing your sick games with him. He'll return to us, where he belongs."

Tisha drew Vera's gaze toward the deep, fast running creek, and the mill wheel attached to a larger building, the original mill, she assumed. "The wheel still works," Tisha told her. "We run water through the chute to make it turn for the children, for youth events. It sticks sometimes, but Rev is so handy. He always gets it started up again." Her eyes held Vera's. "But he's not here right now, is he?"

She turned to Witford. "Tie her to the wheel."

"What?" In that moment, she saw that Witford hadn't been prepared to take this beyond the threat. Whereas Tisha had planned for it.

"She has to know we won't stand for her evil. That we'll stand up to it, that if she persists in trying to corrupt Rev, we won't back down."

"Mother..."

"Witford, I'm not evil." Vera spoke over them both. "You know that. I love Rev. I'm in love with your cousin and he is in love with me. Evil doesn't love."

Simon grabbed her by the throat and tightened his grip, cutting off her air and making her choke. When her eyes rolled toward him, he gave her a humorless smile. "Keep mouthing off, witch."

"Simon, ease up," Witford ordered. Simon did, but not before Vera was seeing spots.

Simon didn't want to torture her. Or maybe he did, but he wanted a different end result than Witford.

He wanted her dead.

And she knew Tisha did, too.

Tisha was clutching Witford's shirt. She gave him a sharp shake. "Look at her. She knows what to say to get in a man's head. Do you want to lose everything we've gained because we don't obey the Lord's Will in this?"

Witford stared down at her.

"We just need to convince her we mean what we say," Tisha coaxed him, her voice softening, even though Vera was sure the glittering hate in her eyes didn't. "That we'll stand against any evil that tries to poison our church. We need to send the serpent crawling back under its rock."

Witford's mouth set in a thin line, and he raised his eyes to Vera. The corruption in his soul meant that what he had the power to do to her, with her so helpless and at his mercy, was starting to grip him. Giving him the twisted shot of adrenaline that corruption craved.

"No." She tried to counter that feeling by making the word strong and defiant. But a wavering note had crept into it, coming from that place inside that knew when it was up against forces so unimaginably terrible.

If you can't find hope, use hate.

Holy Mother, another Cyn-icism, as Skye liked to call those pearls of wisdom.

"You're a coward," Vera snarled at him. "And you know this is wrong. Rev knows your soul is in trouble, Witford. Don't prove him right."

Simon hit her in the mouth this time, breaking one of her teeth and sending her to her knees. He gave her a kick that sent her rolling. "Don't talk to the preacher like that, witch. You pray for your soul. That's all you got left."

Then he jerked her up by the elbow, so violently she was afraid he'd dislocated her shoulder. "Tyson," he snapped. "Get in here and help me."

Did Witford miss that they hadn't asked him for permission, that Simon had decided to run with Tisha's desires instead?

As they took her toward that wheel, Vera struggled and screamed, but every defensive move she had was thwarted. Her wrists were bound to one of the wheel slats with rope, Tyson holding her waist as Simon did that. Then they shoved her into the water, her weight pulling against her shoulders. Cold and slimy, dark. Tyson adjusted the manual crank, turning the wheel backwards to lift her out.

As Simon leaned out to bind her ankles to a lower slat, she kicked him in the face. With an oath, he punched her in the stomach. Her breath wheezed out of her. He tied the ankles so tight she'd lose her feet if they were left that way.

Her body was curved over the wheel, the rough edges digging into her shoulders, back and hips.

They had a rack at Club Progeny, with padding and protective measures. Being put on it was exciting and pleasurable for the submissive, with only the amount of fear and pain they wanted from it.

This was not that.

Triumph and darkness gripped Tisha's round face. If Vera died, Rev's aunt would convince herself it was God's will. In a saner moment she wouldn't be able to face the reality of what she'd done. Or why.

If hope fails, hate can't be the answer. Not for the last moments of my life.

She hadn't expected her mind to go there, but Vera had spent almost as much time in her adult life as Rev providing spiritual guidance, which meant she'd had to search her soul endlessly for answers to the worst that life could hand out. Like this.

"You're lost." Vera's voice shook from the cold, the fear. "Whatever this is, it has nothing to do with the God that Rev knows. The God that I know." Her gaze moved to Witford. "Don't do this. Don't stain your soul with this."

"Take her under." Tisha crossed her arms over her chest, that defensive move she'd shown in Vera's office. "We'll do this until I believe you when you say you'll stay far away from Rev. Now and forever. Or you die here."

Tyson shot an alarmed look at Simon. Simon sent him a *shut the fuck up* look. Witford stared at his mother, but she was only looking at Vera.

"Rev will look for me. My family."

"You have no family. They knew what you were and put you behind them. I'll make sure Rev thinks that you left."

Simon pulled the lever. With a grinding sound, the wheel began to move, taking Vera down into the water again.

Vera screamed for her life, hoping anyone was close enough to hear. But as the water rose up and the panic closed in, she took a deep breath and began to pray.

Every second was like an hour when a person had no control over what was being done to them. The water was freezing, and the underwater foliage crawled across her body, making her think of the snakes that populated creek waters.

Please...please...

She'd almost blacked out by the time they brought her up, but her lungs knew what to do. As she wheezed and coughed, sucking in oxygen, she tried to appeal to the one person whose amoral practicality could override Tisha's mania.

"Witford, please..."

"Not there yet," Tisha snapped. "Take her down again."

Vera had no breath to scream, only to wail, a plaintive sound, asking for mercy. She reached for her faith, for prayer, for help, but the terror was so large, carving a wound inside her. It wanted her to bleed out and let go, give in to the desolation of abandonment.

Her parents were in her mind, her sisters, but she pushed them away and reached for Rev. Ros, Skye, Cyn and Abby. For Bastion. For all the good souls she'd met, some she'd helped, and many who'd helped her. Mavis, Stefanie. Atalaya.

It might be her time to go. It might be. She didn't want it to be. But it might be. She just hoped she could find Rev in the next life. He was hers. She was his. They would find one another.

She'd told him they had a connection, that they could reach for that connection. She reached for it, called to him. She knew she'd been doing it subconsciously since she woke up in the shed, an SOS call like her dying phone, hoping the beacon would reach him.

But sometimes things born in faith were wishful thinking, if Fate had a different plan. She just didn't want to believe that right now. She didn't want to go. Didn't want to leave Rev, or her life. But she supposed no one really did, did they?

When they brought her up the third time, she knew she wouldn't survive the next dunk. Even above the waterline, she barely had the strength to pull air into her lungs.

"Tisha, she's had enough."

"Look at her eyes, Witford. Still defiant. She doesn't have the repentance of a reformed soul."

Witford stepped closer to the wheel. "Woman, repent," he told her. "Tell me that you'll leave Rev be and this can be over. I will end it."

His eyes held hers. He wanted her to do it. Knew his ass was on the line here. But his image swam away, their surroundings dissolving. She wasn't alone anymore. She was floating with a flock of connected souls, all those who'd ever been tormented like this, for not believing as the tormentor did. Not being what they wanted them to be. It happened over and over and over again.

"Please..."

"Do it," Tisha said, and though Witford's hand lifted as if he were going to protest, Simon sent her back under. Her last view was of Witford's conflicted, grim expression, his gaze following her down.

This time when the water closed over her head, she thought of her tears, becoming part of the water. Terror and pain slipped away from her, even the cold, which was such a relief. She reached for Rev, for that bond, one last time.

Her body was jerked. The wheel had started, then stopped. Then it did it again. It had gotten stuck, she realized distantly. Just like Tisha had said. But Rev wasn't here to fix it.

So even if they didn't mean to kill her, it was going to happen, even so.

The jolt of the wheel had jumpstarted her survival instincts, though. She tried to strain against her bonds, but she was too weak. She was fading, disappearing into the darkness of the water.

Pain shot through her wrist, as if a knife blade had struck it. Her arm floated free of the rope. Her brain couldn't drive its motion, reconnect her to it, so she just regarded the unguided muscles with vague curiosity. Another pain, and her other wrist was free. Then her ankles. A strong arm was around her, pulling her away from the wheel. Tyson, or Simon? Or had Witford decided to get in the water and do his own dirty work?

She was drifting away, leaving it all behind. They were too late. Would Rev think of it as God's will?

She didn't want to leave him. She didn't want to be without him. But some things you didn't get a choice about.

Then she felt him. That energy connection they'd created on her living room floor, it was there, winding its way around her arm, her hand, holding her with his gentle, implacable strength. Her beloved man.

I here, Mistress. Please come to me. I would come to you, because that's what I supposed to do, not supposed to make you come to me, but this one time, you come to me. Don't deny me.

She frowned. Things hurt. The coil tightened around her arm, and expanded to envelope her upper body, her throat, her legs. Not a terrifying binding like Simon had put on her. This was a cocoon, enveloping her, with something pulling her back toward Rev. But she was so tired, and pain was waiting in that direction.

I here, too, Mistress. Please. Don't you leave me. Don't you do it. I need you.

She erupted into consciousness, cocoon replaced with cold, pain and fear. Her chest heaved, fighting that drowning feeling. Goddess, it was as horrible as she expected. Hands turned her as she vomited water, her body shaken by the expulsion like an already broken doll. She was on wet boards. A nail head dug into her arm.

But amid all those discomforts, she realized one of her hands was being held tight, and out of all the other pains, large and small, that grip didn't hurt at all. And it was familiar in a way that helped drive the fear back like a door opening and showing her the way home.

When she cracked her eyes open, despite her waterlogged lashes, Rev was bent over her, one of her hands in his, his other hand on her chest. He had his head down and was praying over her with fierce concentration. Lawrence sat back on his heels, his wet T-shirt plastered over his heaving chest. He'd been doing CPR on her, she realized.

His stunned expression, locked on Rev, suggested maybe he'd had to quit doing it, knowing she was gone. Because she had been. Until she'd thrown up the water.

"Thank you, God," Rev was saying. "Thank you."

She was hurt, she was cold, she felt miserable and traumatized to the depths of her soul, but she was alive.

She was alive.

CHAPTER TWENTY

$\mathcal{W}$itford, Tisha and the others had bolted when they'd come on the scene. Rev and Lawrence had gone into the water to cut Veracity free, and Tiger helped pull her out. While Lawrence started CPR, Ros called an ambulance.

Now Veracity was breathing, and she'd gifted them with that brief precious moment when her eyes opened and took them all in, before she passed out again.

Ros gripped Lawrence's shoulder, and knelt in the muck next to her friend. She lifted Veracity up against her and stroked her hair while her eyes closed, her face wracked with sorrow, anger and relief.

Rev bent his head over Vera's hand and pressed his face there. He couldn't let her go, couldn't relinquish her. That lifeline between them still hummed, and he had to hold it tight, be sure of it. *Thank you, Lord. Thank you.* Everything else was tearing him up inside, but he would take that, take any level of suffering, for the gift of her survival.

His family hadn't killed her. Five words that shocked him to the foundations of everything he'd thought he'd known about them, about what they called love for him.

"The police need to know where to find them," Ros said.

It took a few moments to realize she was talking to him. Rev lifted his gaze to meet hers. When he didn't immediately provide her an answer, those blue irises went arctic cold, the eyes of a vengeful goddess. "You have a problem with that?"

What he saw in Lawrence and Tiger's hard faces told him they might overrule him. He understood, but he knew what he had to do. "I'll go get them to turn themselves in."

"And if they won't?"

"They will." He looked down at Veracity. One side of her face was badly swollen. Thinking of who might have done it, and who was responsible for all of it, turned the rage in his heart into a frightening force.

It must have shown, because Lawrence touched his arm, drawing his attention. "It might be better for the police to go get them," he said.

"Yes. But my aunt...I need to do it. If it isn't done in the next hour, then call the police."

When he looked back down, Veracity's eyes were open again. Mere slits, but she was gazing at him. Shock and trauma meant she probably wasn't entirely aware of what was happening, but he gave her the main thing she needed to hear.

"You're safe," he said. "You're with your family."

Vera's gaze moved to Ros. Her boss had her halfway over her lap. Vaguely, Vera wondered what shoes she'd worn for the rescue. Lawrence was kneeling by her shoulder, and Tiger stood tall and strong over them. Rev had said she was safe, but their faces held a tension that suggested something was unresolved.

Rev's expression had that dangerous look he could get, but he was suffering beneath it. She understood why, but she couldn't reach for what she needed to help him. But he wasn't asking for anything. Instead, when he touched her face, softly, his eyes held onto every part of her. He told her again that she was safe and okay.

Then he told her other things.

"You taught me to imagine the details of your face, to hold you in that heart chakra. But that don't take no effort or practice at all. You all up in me, in every way."

Something else was going on. She'd heard them talking over her, and the meaning of the words was there, if she could recall them. When she did, she wished she hadn't.

He was leaving her. The anguish in him, the suppressed urgency, was the war between his need to seek her understanding, if not her permission, and realizing she couldn't handle anything else right now. Particularly that.

She might understand at another moment, when she was far enough away from this one. But the knowledge throbbed under her heart, an overwhelming pain. He was going to confront his family. Which meant, in a convoluted way, he was choosing them over her, when she needed him with her, right now.

She knew it wasn't as simple as that, that she wasn't thinking clearly. But damn it, she shouldn't have to. He needed to stay with her. Let the police handle it.

But he wouldn't.

She'd taught herself, over and over again, to stand on the foundation she'd created for herself. It was the place from which she could handle whatever life threw at her.

Somehow, she dragged herself to that center point now. If she could get through the next few seconds, she'd reward herself with unconsciousness again.

"Go do what you have to do, Rev." Her voice was hoarse. From the water, from screaming, from dehydration. "Thank you...for coming to get me."

His confusion at her tone was brief. Painful acceptance replaced it. He relinquished her hand, but he didn't just let it go. He guided it to one of Ros's hands, folding her fingers over Vera's, and holding both for a weighted second. He met her boss's angry eyes. "I'll be back to her, soon as I can be."

When he rose, he gave them a grateful nod. "Thank you," he said.

When he walked away, Vera pressed her head against Ros's chest. She held out for about a minute. Maybe less. Just enough time for her to know he was gone. Then everything started to spill forth. Ros held her as Vera sobbed, her infamous control so beyond her grasp she wasn't sure she'd ever find it again. She shook so hard that Tiger and Lawrence knelt on either side of Ros and wrapped them both up, holding her inside their strength.

She begged for the peaceful grayness to take her, and this time it did. Right as the ambulance lights flashed over them all.

Rev hitched a ride to his church in a pickup full of migrant farm workers. Though they might have known more English than they were letting on, his state of mind didn't need translation. After offering him a bottle of water, they left him with his thoughts, his ass planted on the heated metal of the rusted bed, his feet propped on a coil of rope.

When he'd thanked Lawrence the man had murmured, "We'll take care of her."

The agony that went through Rev like lightning splitting a tree hadn't needed any translation, either. Lawrence's mouth had tightened, his eyes showing he understood what Rev felt.

Taking care of her is supposed to be my job.

But he had another job, too. Leaving Veracity's side when she needed her man, her sub, the person who wanted so much to serve her in all ways, tore him to shreds. But it had to be done.

He found them at the church, as he'd expected. Witford was sitting on the step in front of the pulpit, Tisha in one of the pews. Simon and Tyson were there. The Bible talked about lost sheep, but wolves could be lost, too. Maybe sometimes they were even more lost.

Rev walked down the aisle, holding Witford's gaze. His clothes were still damp from the creek. He hadn't realized one of the workers had wrapped a blanket around him until he got out of the truck. Rev hoped he'd thanked the man for his kindness as he handed it back.

Though he didn't look toward Simon and Tyson, he stayed aware of them. They were looking at Witford for a cue, to tell them what he wanted them to do.

He came to a halt a few paces from Witford, Tisha in the pew to Rev's left. She had her head down, hands clasped, body rocking as she prayed silently.

"When we leave here, we going to the police station," Rev said. "You all are going to tell them what you did, and accept the consequences."

He sensed Tyson and Simon's shift. Witford looked toward them. The knife in Rev's gut twisted, because he knew what that look conveyed.

"Whatever lies you thought up to cover yourselves, they lies." Rev spoke evenly. "God knows when you lying, and that's who you answer to. Right? So you stand away from the lies. If God in you at all, then you should be under a terrible weight of fear and regret. You go to the police, tell them what you did, be honest and let a lawyer get you what fits with that, and you'll stand right with the Lord again."

"Rev—" Witford began.

"You won't speak to me."

He didn't raise his voice, yet the sound echoed through the nave, up to the ceiling, and rattled the windows. Tisha jumped, and all four heads snapped toward the window nearest her. One of the panes had cracked, leaving a jagged line like lightning.

Rev ignored it, keeping his gaze on his cousin. "This between you and God. I'm here to make sure it's done. If you push me for more, I will put your head through the fucking floor."

He registered their shock, but it meant little to him. In his heart, all he saw was Veracity.

It flashed through his head again, that moment when the presence of Witford's Lincoln at the mill had confirmed his cousin was involved. Him, Lawrence and Tiger coming up on the three men gathered around the lever for the wheel, working on it, Witford looking panicked and angry.

They hadn't seen Veracity, but then Rev's attention had gone to Tisha. Standing apart, her eyes fixed on the wheel itself, her face a mask of hatred and fear and triumph, a look he would never get out of his mind.

Rev had followed her gaze to the wheel and seen a nightmare. Vera's bound wrists and curved fingers, the only thing above the water. He'd burst into a run and jumped into the well of water around the wheel. So cold. His Mistress was in that cold, dark water.

He pulled out his pocketknife and sawed through the ropes on her wrists, only to realize that wasn't the only place she was bound. He took a breath and dove down. Lawrence had joined him. When he felt his way to her ankles, her hands were floating limply above him. He felt the brush of her fingertips, only there was no life to them. His heart had hammered like a blacksmith's tool on cold steel. He'd sawed one ankle free, Lawrence the other.

Now, standing in the church that had been a haven for him most of his life, he thought about the damage to her face, the abrasions on her wrists, her torn clothing. Blood from a cut on her lip started bleeding again because her mouth had stretched out, trying to pull in air.

When her eyes had first opened, he'd seen the fear, because after something like that, it would take a moment for her to realize she was safe. It would take far more time for her to *feel* safe again.

They'd done that to her. His family.

Whatever Witford saw in Rev's face was so close to the surface, it had him stepping back a pace.

Wrath. It was the right word.

I did not come to bring peace, but a sword.

It was real fucking tempting.

Instead, he spoke through stiff lips. "I love her, and the Lord gave her to me to love and protect. She was a gift to me. You..." Rev stopped, shook his head.

He pivoted and moved into the pew. He sat down next to Tisha, leaving enough room that he could turn on his hip, put his knee up on the wood. He braced his hand on the back of the pew in front of him and gazed at his aunt. She looked frozen and afraid, her eyes on the cross at the front of the church. Her hands were clasped hard before her.

Her face was closed in on itself. Strong women did that when they were hurting, when they were confused, afraid. Even angry. And when they'd messed up so bad, they'd dropped themselves into a dark hole. Everyone was afraid in an abyss, because they thought no one knew they were there, or didn't care that they were. That they were forgotten, unseen, out of the Lord's favor.

He thought of Veracity blindfolding him, putting him in darkness, but her scent, her touch, her very presence, was so strong. He'd known he wasn't alone, no matter what, as long as she was near.

He had walked away from her, when it was the last thing he wanted to do. The damage from that decision could be irreparable.

No. The connection between them couldn't be broken, even by something like this. He had to have faith in that, and do what needed to be done.

Tisha had broken out of her trance, and turned her head toward him. She had some strategy in mind, he could see it in her face. "Rev... Karman..."

He put his hand over hers. His grip was a little tight, because she winced. He eased it, which took a startling amount of effort. He wanted to squeeze until he ground bone, until she felt what he was feeling, all through his body.

"I can't think of what you done. If I put it in my mind, in front of my eyes, I might burn this place down as an abomination in the sight of God."

Her eyes widened, but he bowed his head. "Pray with me, Tisha. Pray the way you did when you was growing up with Teena Joy. When you couldn't have thought you'd ever do something like this."

"She was taking you away from us, Rev..."

"Hush," he said mildly. "Do as I say. Really open your heart to what you done. Let God show it to you. Put down all the excuses and things you telling yourself to make it okay. All right?"

I'm lost, O Lord. She lost. We all lost... We need our Shepherd.

The words were in his head, then on his lips. He couldn't sing it the way he normally did. His voice was broken and raw, but that was how it needed to be sung.

She'd bowed her head with him, but he felt her rigidity. She couldn't find it right now. But it gave him a moment to take a breath, to find what he needed so he could make sure this went the way it needed to go.

Her free hand reached toward him.

"No." His forbidding tone arrested the gesture. When he lifted his head, she'd closed it into an ineffectual ball that landed on her lap.

"I don't belong to you, Tisha. I your family, but I don't belong to you. My path is my own, and it lies with her. And here. The two things aren't wrong together, or with God. When my Mistress smiles at me, I feel God's smile in that too. Sometimes a Goddess's. So I know Veracity Morgan is part of that path right now, and maybe for forever. I surely hope so."

He reached for her throat, and she shrank back. Her fear hurt him, but he didn't stop. Gently, he removed the gold necklace she wore, with its ruby pendant. Then came the earrings. Three rings, including the big diamond she'd bought last year, when the house Teena Joy had lived in, where Rev had grown up, had been sold.

He'd always known that Teena Joy left him the house. So deep in his grief over her loss, he hadn't cared when they told him that her will said to sell the house and give the proceeds to the church. He was fine with them getting the money. He'd signed whatever documents they wanted.

At the time, he told himself Witford had seen how hard it was for him to be in the house without her, and had given him an out.

He shouldn't have let the lie stand, even if the motive had been pure like that. Which it hadn't been. All this time, he'd seen the warning signs, told himself they'd find their way back to truth, but he should have held them accountable sooner for turning their backs on that truth. If he had, maybe they wouldn't have gone so far down this road.

When Veracity's bruised face came back into his mind, her limp body against his in the water, he twisted around to set Tisha's jewelry down on the pew seat. He took his time with it, arranging the neck-lace around the earrings and rings, until he was calm enough to face her again.

Then he pulled on memories, let them take over his mind, so that when he finally found the strength to give her a faint, sad smile, it startled and cut her at the same time. Tears spilled down her cheeks.

"There she is. The aunt who'd stop when she was cleaning the church with Teena Joy and listen to me sing. She'd sing with me, too, because I wanted her to. We all get lost. Teena Joy told me that, plenty of times. I've found my path, the one that works for me, and it may go different places, but I've chosen it, and I want it, and I feel the Lord's power in that choice. I feel His happiness and smile. I want you to feel His smile again, too. But the only way back to that is through some hard things. Through repentance. You have wronged her, and wronged God."

Her mouth thinned, but his hand was on hers, tight again. 'Never be so sure you're right that you fail to listen, care, connect and under-stand.' Your sister taught me that. Maybe things be interfering with your hearing and seeing. If you accept the consequences for your actions, you the family I know, that I have loved all my life."

He rose, and gazed at her, then at Witford and the other two men. "If you don't, if you run from it, if you lie, I will speak truth, and it will go harder on you, and not just because the law will punish you for deception and violence. Your souls will get even sicker."

Witford stared at the floor, fear and anger coming off of him. His mind wasn't on what he'd done, but what he'd lost. Which meant his thoughts were turning to how he could change that, the devil pulling him his way. Maybe somewhere in there, the Witford that Rev had once known better was digging in his heels, trying not to go down that road, but the energy in the room said the battle was starting to turn in an ugly direction.

Rev could feel it, not just from Witford, but from Simon and Tyson. It was like an uneasy ocean current, the kind that caused seasickness. Back and forth, back and forth. Up, down. Up, down. They were ex-convicts who would face an even stiffer prison sentence for the violence they'd done today, and they were thinking about that.

Rev squared himself in the aisle. Whatever came was meant to come. When Witford lifted his gaze, Rev met it.

"What's it gonna be, Witford? You can kill me to save your mortal life, but it'll cost you your soul."

"Witford," Simon said, a hard note to his voice. Witford tore his gaze from Rev and looked toward him. "You know it's got to be done."

Tisha looked up. "No," she said. "Rev...Rev is right. We're lost. We need to—"

"Shut up," Simon told her. "It's because of you that we did this shit."

Rev looked at Simon's hands. And then he thought of Veracity's face.

Simon read his look and answered it. "You want a piece of me, you sanctimonious asshole? Mouthing off about God while your cousin handles all the work around here?"

Rev stepped toward him. A creak and thud stopped him, the sound of the nave doors opening and falling shut again. When he turned, he saw Lawrence, Mick and Tiger standing in front of them. As their intent gazes evaluated the situation, they spread out, shoulder to shoulder.

"You okay here, Rev?" Lawrence asked. "Thought you might need some backup."

"The cops are on their way." Tiger's cold blue gaze, as predatory looking as his name, landed on Simon and Tyson. "You can try to make a break for it, but we'll just drag you out into the parking lot and beat the shit out of you. Your chances are better with the cops."

Witford had deflated at their appearance, and Tyson did the same.

Simon held out the longest, but when Tiger shifted forward with a "give me an excuse" look, he muttered a curse and sat down on the transept steps.

"Fuck you," he said. But he said it with his head down and shoulders hunched.

Rev drew a deep breath. That desire to take Simon up on his challenge was still there. He wanted to yank him up and make him fight. He wanted blood, tears and fear in threefold measure to what Veracity had endured.

Her faith believed that the harm they did would be visited on them threefold. But like his own faith, it didn't say inflicting that punishment was the right or job of the one who most wanted to do it.

Deliberately, he moved his gaze to the cross and all it represented. He couldn't feel it the way he wished right now, because everything was so locked down. Facing what his cousin and aunt had done, all of it, and what had happened to Veracity, what role Rev had and hadn't played in that...it was all too much.

"Rev?"

He turned toward Tisha. Her voice was low and timid. "What will happen to the church?"

"I don't know." He didn't know anything right now. Except that he didn't want to be here. He wanted to be with Veracity.

He looked toward Lawrence. "After we take care of this, I need a ride to the hospital."

"That's the second reason we came," Lawrence said. "Your Mistress needs you."

~

It took the expected amount of time, which meant far too long. Rev had to go to the police station. The detective handling the case had interviewed Veracity at the hospital. He questioned Rev hard, the words like nails, because Rev was hammering the questions into himself. But he gave the detective whatever he needed, holding nothing back, so he could get to his Mistress.

He'd told Lawrence he'd take a bus to the hospital, because he was sure Ros was in need of her man, too. Instead the former SEAL waited patiently until he was done and drove him. Lawrence said little, but his presence offered an unexpected reassurance to Rev.

When they arrived and went to the floor where Veracity had a room, Cyn intercepted him in the waiting area. Her expression was neutral, her voice coolly cordial. Rev recognized a guard dog when he saw one.

"Ros is with her. They're going to discharge her in the morning. She doesn't want to see you right now."

"All right. I'll be out here if she changes her mind."

Her expression stayed flat. "I don't think she wants you here, period. Not right now."

Rev inclined his head, acknowledging it, but then he turned to Lawrence. "Thanks for bringing me here, and sticking with me at the police."

Then he moved to a chair that faced the hallway that held Veracity's room and sat down. After exchanging a glance with Lawrence, Cyn pivoted and went back down the hall.

Lawrence gave him an approving nod. "Good call."

"I messed up bad, Lawrence."

"They messed up bad. You made it right. That's what matters."

"No. I mean...leaving her so I could handle Witford and Tisha. Because of her family...she not going to understand."

"Yeah, she will." Lawrence gave him a sober look. "Vera might be hurting, and you have to give her the room to feel that, but she'll understand. You had to make sure that they couldn't hurt her again. That's part of taking care of her."

Lawrence came close enough to grip his shoulder. "You're the real deal, man. We all see it. It's why Cyn didn't tear you a new one. She might do it later, though. I'm going to touch base with Rosalinda, then I have to go to the rec center for a little while. I'll be back soon, though."

Left to his own thoughts, Rev stared down the hallway.

His mind wasn't done punishing him. The images cycled through, again and again. Getting to the mill, not believing what he was seeing, not comprehending his family was responsible for hurting her like that. Then getting into the water, nothing else mattering but getting her out.

He gripped the chair arms. Tiger had gotten Simon and Tyson out of Rev's path, advancing upon them with a wall of rage and physical intimidation. They'd bolted for the parking lot. Witford had hurried Tisha to his car while Tiger was occupied with the other two.

Rev thought of the cold dark of the water, his Mistress bound there. It had made his own soul cold and dark.

When she was free and he had her in his arms, his flood of relief vanished when he realized he couldn't feel her breath on his neck. Her heart didn't beat against his, no sign that her soul was within her.

Tiger lifted her out as the other two men hiked themselves out of the water. When Lawrence started CPR, Rev clasped both his hands around one of hers. Her long brown fingers, her palm a sweet light sand color, with a touch of pink. Two of her polished nails were broken.

Lawrence had had Ros wait in the car until they figured out what was going on, but now she was here, too, kneeling next to Lawrence as he administered CPR, her eyes fixed on Vera's face.

Rev had put his other hand on Veracity's chest, below where Lawrence was trying to get her heart to pump. He didn't register when Lawrence realized there was nothing more to be done and Ros choked out a protest, a hard sob. Rev had put it all away, everything gone. It was just him with his head bowed, his heart, mind and soul praying, reaching out to his Mistress, looking for her in the void. He wouldn't let his heart beat again until hers did. That was all there was to it.

He'd thought of the structure of a prayer, just as he'd described it to her.

Ask for what you need, trust that you will receive it. *Please let her life be what is needed. Give her back her life. Don't take her away from us. Not like this. Please God, she serves you as I do. She loves. She is full of love. Please...*

He'd never consciously reached for that energy within him, that well of pure belief and faith. It just came and he followed its lead. But he'd grabbed hold of it, plunged into it, willing to drown in it like Vera had drowned in the water, just to bring her back. *Please...please... Please...*

When she jerked and started to cough, the power was a triumphant jolt of electricity through him. He immediately bent his head lower to praise its Source, even as he couldn't let her go. Didn't ever want to let her go.

Rev came back to the present. His hands were clasped hard in his lap, as if he still held her hand. He'd also somehow fallen asleep. It was a couple hours later, and things were quiet. Outside the windows, it was night, the lights of New Orleans bright. And Rosalinda Thomas sat across from him, watching him.

She'd changed into the most casual thing he'd seen her in, light blue jeans and a tunic top with silver thread at the neckline. Her boots had silver braid sewn around the ankle.

"You should go home," Ros said.

He rubbed a hand over his face and straightened. "She needs to know I won't leave, even if she tell me to. She needs to know I'm not like her family. I'm never going to abandon her just because we not seeing eye to eye on something. I not a Navy SEAL, or a cop, or a big scary fellow like Tiger. But I don't need to be. My strength come from Love, and the love I feel for her... no one is going to make me abandon her. Not even her. Or you."

He said the last with a respectful but firm nod. Her eyes stayed expressionless. "You made her feel abandoned."

It hurt him to the core to hear it. Thinking Veracity had told Ros that, drove him to the edge of his control. He needed to go to her, be with her, and take that pain away. It was the one pain for sure he could ease, because it didn't change the truth. As Lawrence had pointed out.

"No," he said. "Her family done that, so when I had to make the decision I did, it took her back to it. That's all. Which is also why I need to be here, to see her. To remind her that this ain't that."

He gave her a bitter smile. "I not any more likely to be driven away than your own man, or any of the men who belong to you all. She a very strong woman, but even a strong woman has limits. She needs me to help her find her strength. I know it, so I sit here until she ready to call that strength to her."

Ros rose. Her expression changed, suddenly showing so much emotion he had to rise, too. "I'm so sorry, Miss Thomas. For all of it. If I could have been there sooner, if I could have known what they planned, I would have done anything to stop them from hurting her like this. God forgive me, I do mean anything. I'd have sold my soul and gone straight to hell to keep her from it."

His faith had been shaken tonight. Not his faith in God, but his faith in those around him. Life could be unpredictable, but when the earthly ground you were sure of gave way beneath you, it was the toughest loss to take.

Ros stared at him. He'd reached out and gripped her hand, too moved by her distress not to make contact. Her fingers were cold. She stayed at arm's length, but her eyes were damp. "All right," she said. "Room 6A."

Then she cleared her throat. "I'm going home for a little while."

"Will Lawrence be there for you?" He was worried about the things he felt from her.

"He's always there for me."

She moved around him, headed for the elevators. After he watched the doors close on her, he reached for the phone Veracity wanted him to carry and carefully typed in a message.

Your Mistress headed home. She needs you.

Just pulled back into the parking lot. I'm her ride. But thanks for letting me know.

Rev put the phone away and walked down the hall, his shoes squeaking. Through open doorways, he saw patients sleeping or watching TV on low volume. A nurse making her rounds gave him a nod.

As Rev reached 6A, Cyn was coming out. The phone she held suggested Ros had sent her a text, letting her know Rev was on his way. Thinking of what Lawrence had said, he braced himself for the possibility of a more forceful tongue lashing, but once again Cyn merely gave him a short nod. "I'll be in the lobby when you're done," she said.

"I'll be here until they throw me out," he told her. "So if you need to go home and get some sleep, I'll be here when you come back."

"I'll see if *she* throws you out before I make that decision." Cyn glanced over her shoulder, and Rev saw a rare look of tenderness on her resolute face. "I've never seen her this fragile. Go easy. Else I'll break your legs."

"Yes'm."

She surprised him with a light pat on his arm, and left him.

When he stepped in the room and was able to look upon the woman he most wanted to see, Rev felt a wave of relief so strong he gripped the doorway to keep from staggering.

Veracity was asleep, but her expression was troubled, deep lines around her mouth and forehead. Her fists were clenched on the top of the covers. He knelt by the bed.

I dreem of kneeling...for her.

For you.

He murmured that, then put his hand next to her fist, and bowed his head to pray. It took a while, but he used what he knew of prayer and what she'd taught him, about those channels and the energy to fill them. He pulled it through him, offered it to her, his hand shifting to cover hers, to create a channel between them. When her fingers seemed looser, more relaxed, he reached across her body to grip the other hand, to keep that circuit closed.

Eventually, he felt an answering pressure, but he simply kept praying and channeling. Somewhere along the way, their breathing started to synchronize. He thought their hearts did, too. With every in and out, every beat, he gave her his will and love. Anything she needed. And he asked for her forgiveness.

Throughout the night, even when the nurse came in to check on her, he remained in that position, holding a vigil. No words spoken. Just a million thoughts and feelings passing through that connection, but one in particular, the same one he'd prayed for when they brought her out of the water. Only this time he was asking not for her life, but for the return of her trust and faith.

Come back to me.

Vera woke to see two things. One, Ros at the door with a flat of three coffees in hand, and Rev. His head was on the covers next to their clasped hands, his folded-over big body wedged in a small chair.

She wanted to touch his head, give him a Mistress's approval for his care, but she felt numb.

When she slowly extricated herself, he woke. As he straightened and came to himself, his gaze moved to her face, taking in everything at a glance. The automatic smile on his face died.

"Got this from that coffee shop you hit sometimes on the way to work." Ros put the cups down, one near Rev, and leaned in to kiss Vera's forehead. When she drew back, her blue eyes were measuring. From the tightening of her mouth, Vera assumed the bruising was substantial. Everything on that side of her face felt swollen. "How are you doing?" her boss asked.

"Ready to get home." Vera cleared a thick throat and discovered it also hurt like hell to speak.

She remembered the nurse checking her vitals. Rev had accommodated her when the woman needed to take his place at Vera's side. He'd held up the wall until she was done, his eyes always on Vera. She recalled the deep rumble of his voice, responding to the nurse. She'd offered to bring him a cot. He'd declined.

"I good, ma'am. Thank you."

Then he'd sat his big body back in that small chair, leaned over her, taken her hand, and started praying again. Sometimes he'd knelt on the floor. But he'd stayed close, no matter what.

"The nurse said I'd be discharged this morning," she told Ros, trying to ignore the fact that talking made her eyes water. Her face really hurt.

Ros arched a brow. "I'll drive you home once they take care of that."

"That would be good."

When Rev moved to put his hand over hers, Vera lifted it to pluck at the hospital gown, as if she hadn't noticed him reaching for her.

She didn't pretend like that. But she needed the defense mechanism. The spell that the night, the relief at not being dead, had spun, had no hold over her in the daylight. She had no armor. Someone torturing her, trying to kill her, denying her value, meant she was floundering in a cauldron of emotions she didn't want to examine. She was going to break if anyone wanted anything from her.

Especially him.

"Vera," Ros spoke softly. "Look at me, dear one."

It was an effort, but she managed. She knew her gaze was pleading for something, she didn't know what. Fortunately, Ros did. Reminding Vera why, when she needed a leader in her life, it was usually the woman in front of her who provided that.

"You've always been the one who helps us when we're adrift," her friend said, "and we've learned things from you. Enough to say what you need to hear now.

"Whatever you're feeling is okay. You've been through a serious trauma. It's going to take time and counseling to help you deal with it.

But today, we only have one thing to do. Get you home. I'll get you settled, and then I'll work from there, in your home office. I won't bother you, but if you need anything, I'll be there. Tomorrow, if you want me to give you space, I will, but today, it's best if someone is there with you. Not you."

That last part wasn't to her. Rev had begun to speak and, anticipating him, Ros had issued the short statement. Her expression toward him wasn't unkind, but it was uncompromising. Pure Domme, pure CEO, pure Ros.

"Not today, Rev," she repeated quietly. "Last night, how you felt about being here, it was right. But now, this is the right thing."

"I understand." His voice was tight, though, his expression the opposite of the words. He shifted his attention to Vera. "I'll do whatever you need," he said. "I know you not ready to talk about any of it, but I need to say one thing to you. What they...my family, did to you... it was awful. What they did to their souls by doing it... I had to go to them, had to make them see that."

She'd flinched when he said "my family," and he'd seen it. The pain in his gaze pierced her, and she didn't want to feel that. "I do hear you, Rev. But I can't handle hearing it. I'm not all right. Do you understand?"

"I do, Mistress."

"*Don't* call me that." The anger she felt startled her, and she shrank back, from herself as much as from him. "Please...I can't...not right now."

Rev rose and took a step back from the bed, even as Ros drew closer to the other side. He gazed down at the bill cap he was turning in circles, like he'd done outside her office that day. He wasn't ashamed to meet her gaze, she knew. He was obeying her, trying not to put any pressure on her, add to her pain. If he looked at her, with all he was feeling in his eyes, that she heard in his voice, he knew he'd do the opposite of that.

Please go. Just please go.

"I understand. I don't deserve to call you that. I didn't serve you the way I should. And I'm part of the family who did this to you."

He was connected to those who'd done this to her, but that was the only truth he'd spoken. But a mean, petty part of her wouldn't contradict him on the rest. She closed her eyes, hoping when she opened them, he'd be gone. But instead, his arms slid around her. His wonderful, strong arms, that she could barely bear to touch her right now. Even so, he held her close to his chest. "I love you, Veracity. I love you."

She nodded, a quick, reluctant thing. She was fighting not to push him away. It was barely a second before he let her go, stepped back again and turned to Ros.

"Please let me know if she needs anything...I can provide."

She could tell leaving was terrible for him, not knowing if she'd ever want to see him again.

Not knowing the answer to that question herself was one more blow she couldn't handle facing. Not right now.

CHAPTER TWENTY-ONE

*W*hen he walked out of the room, Rev felt like he was walking away from home.

His Mistress was home. Especially right now. She was the only thing that made sense to him.

But that was no good. He had to get his head right, to know how to be there for her, not to lean on her too much when she'd had such grievous hurt done to her.

The day he'd helped out at the shelter, there'd been a volunteer counselor handling a session with one of the guests. Rev had found her daughter sitting somberly on a chair outside the closed door of the little room. She'd been too worried to go play with the other kids, and was holding a container of glitter in both hands. He'd pulled up a chair next to her.

"What's that?" he asked.

"Fairy dust. When you sprinkle it on people, it gives them magic. Sometimes the ability to fly. Want to see?"

"I was hoping you'd offer."

He'd obligingly bent forward so she could sprinkle a pinch on his head. He'd widened his eyes, stood up and stretched out his arms to do a zooming plane maneuver up and down the short hallway. "Why, look at that. It do work. Isn't that something?"

She smiled and cradled the container against her. "You were

praying with Lucas and his mom in the playroom," she said. "Is there magic in that, too?"

"Yeah." Rev took a seat beside her again. "It a lot like fairy dust. It touches those who need it, gives them the ability to lift themselves up."

He glanced toward the door as it opened. The mother's eyes were red, but she looked like the session had helped. Her daughter rose to hug her, and they walked away, hand in hand.

The counselor leaning in the doorway had coffee-colored hair, one blond lock twisted like a ribbon against it. She also had the look of the TRA women to her. That Domme look. Her green gaze slid to his glitter-anointed hair, and a smile curved her mouth.

"Maureen," she said, offering a hand. "Known as Dr. Mo around here. You're Rev, Vera's man."

He rose and shook. "I like the sound of that."

"Good. I think she does as well."

"You help the kids too?"

"Yes, sometimes. My approach with them is more like yours. I sit with them, play with them. Listen and use what they give me to nudge them toward healing and healthy emotional responses. Some sessions I don't make much progress, or I feel like we've taken a step backwards."

She glanced at the mother and daughter, now on a couch in the living room, the little girl in her mother's lap. "Time in a safe mental and physical space contributes most to their healing. Too many questions, too much prodding and poking at the wrong time, can feel like more of the same thing they left behind."

Yeah. So Rev knew he'd messed up, saying anything to Veracity at all about his family and what had happened. Her telling him not to call her Mistress tore out his heart. He'd tried not to show it, but how she turned her face away from him told him he had. She couldn't handle his feelings right now, and she was the most generous person he knew.

It was one thing to see the terrible thing done to her. Another to see how it had dug deep into her, upsetting all she knew about herself, what she believed about the world.

It put a weight and hurt on his heart he didn't know what to do with. He got on a bus, but he didn't get off at his home. He kept riding, staring through the window sightlessly. He couldn't pray, which he knew wasn't the right thing, but it didn't change it. He had things in his mind that rejected everything. What he wanted most, to be with her right now, wasn't right either. She needed him with her, even if she'd pushed him away, but she needed the man who wanted to serve her with his whole heart, not a man toting around a tortured, angry wreck of a soul.

He saw boys playing basketball. It was a bad neighborhood, but the court was part of a church's grounds. The stone structure had been here for over a century, but funds had been found for some long-needed renovations. Nothing fancy, just what was needed to keep it up, and the front stoop was clean, the landscaping tended. Jesus didn't care about stone and a roof. He cared that the door was open and welcoming.

When Teena Joy had first started their church in a big tent on the property where the building now stood, she'd told him that.

He exited the bus and went to the church steps. The outer doors were unlocked, because one of them rested an inch or two in front of the other. It was unusual for a church to be unlocked this early in the morning, well before time for the pastor or church secretary to arrive.

He looked at the door, then at a bench in front of the chain link fence around the basketball court. He could sit over there. Think.

One of the songs he'd practiced with Sy and Trey had been "Some Things I'll Never Know" by Teddy Swims. The far-too-true and sad words were in his head now.

His feet took him up the steps and inside. It was a non-denominational church like his own, with a mix of Christian practices represented. Like a table of candles on one side of the transept, and a wooden cross centered before the chancel. A painted wooden lamb rested beneath it in a manger of straw. Statues of the Virgin Mary, St. Francis and Buddha were placed behind the cross in the chancel.

Near the candle table was a well-tended olive tree, hung with mementoes. A bracelet, a pet collar, a small family photo. A shrine for loved ones. Photos were stuck in potted flowers, grouped around the tree's sizeable wooden planter. He guessed it had been built by a devoted parishioner. Words were carved along the planter's wide top lip. *Psalm 96: All the trees of the wood rejoice before the Lord.*

Going to the cross, he put his hands on the base, his forehead on the polished wood above it. But that didn't give him rest. He wanted to beat his head against it, use the impact to give him answers he didn't know.

He backed away, and sank down in a pew in the middle of the church. As he leaned against the wooden side, he put his head into his hands.

A movement had him lifting it. A woman wearing jeans and a T-shirt had come in from the chancel door. She had close-cropped hair and caramel-colored skin.

She was also blind. She wore dark glasses and used a white cane decorated with colorful stickers to navigate the space before her. The casual way she swept it left to right told him she used it only to be sure nothing unexpected was in her path.

The reason for her familiarity with the surroundings became obvious as she turned his way, making the swirly white letters on her T-shirt easier to read.

I'm the pastor. Really.

(Yes, God does have a sense of humor.)

She wore a military dog tag in a silver frame. The short chain it was on was threaded with jasper beads and a cross, the cross lying against the dog tag.

Her head cocked in his direction. "Hello. Are you all right?"

A kind question. If he was fine, just here to pray, she would leave him be. If he needed something...

He was used to being the one who offered what she was offering. Veracity was the first who'd offered Rev, as a man, things he'd finally allowed himself to need. Or maybe she had pushed through the doors he'd kept closed on that.

He didn't know what to say. He needed to say something, because she couldn't see if he was nodding or shaking his head. But a paralyzing mix of grief, rage and helplessness gripped him, and an overwhelming desire to act how he shouldn't. If he so much as twitched, he feared he'd become an agent of destruction, a tornado he couldn't control.

The woman moved toward him. Though barely past five feet and small-boned, there was a toughness to her that made him think the dog tag could be hers.

She slid into the pew behind him, leaned forward and put her hand on the pew, sliding it toward him until the side of it touched his shoulder. "I'm here," she said quietly.

She said nothing further. Just sat with him, with no expectation, no pressure on him to say or do anything. It helped him let some of that pressure out and keep ahold of himself. It also meant the words that came from him had no prompting other than being what covered all of it.

"I failed her. My Mistress."

A peculiar stillness gripped the woman. He'd likely confused her with the odd word choice. But he couldn't think of how to change that, so he just kept going. "My family...they think I chose her over them. She thinks I chose them over her. I tried to follow my love for all of them, and that sword, both sides, is cutting me to pieces. I don't know how to put myself back together to help either one of them. And there's such anger in my heart for my family, I don't want to help them. I only want to help her."

He trembled with the terrible truth of it, said aloud in God's house. She gripped his shoulder, just a light, brief contact, but it was a powerful connection, like two live wires. The woman understood the path. Like Veracity did, even when hurting and confused.

The wound in him was bleeding, and he would let it keep flowing. He told the pastor everything that had happened tonight. She didn't interrupt once, and her hand tightened during the worst parts. Relaxed when he said how Veracity was okay, and with her chosen family—it hurt to not include himself in it—and that he'd made sure his family had done the right thing.

The kids from the basketball court abruptly burst in, laughing, busting each other's chops over the pickup game. Rev started, and rubbed his face, wiping away the tears he hadn't realized were there. The pastor squeezed his shoulder, a reassurance, and twisted around.

"John Walter, if I hear that basketball bounce on this floor, I'll rearrange your internal organs by putting a combat boot up your backside."

"I know better, Reverend Dana," he promised. "Do you have any of them sausage biscuit roll things in the kitchen?"

"I made up a breakfast batch. Leave me a couple of them, you pack of wolves. There's bottled orange juice, too. Look in the fridge. And be quiet and respectful in this space."

Out of the corner of his eye, Rev saw her dip her head his way. The kids minded her, quieting down and sliding past him with sidelong looks, the one in the lead murmuring, "Sorry, sir."

They disappeared through the door she'd used in the chancel, likely the best way to the church kitchen. They resumed their banter once more, though at a lower volume, their shoes thumping along with them.

When Rev turned on his hip toward her, Reverend Dana had a fond smile on her face. "They're good boys," she said. "Go on, if you have more on your heart."

Rev did, but he spoke it slowly, thinking it through. Letting the rest out had helped him dig deeper. "There are moments that say, take this in your own hands, take up the sword. I think God does use us that way, when you have to protect innocents. I would have fought them to protect her. I would have taken life to do it. The life of my own cousin, raised like a brother with me."

It was another terrible thing to say aloud, but it was the truth. "I'm glad it didn't come to that."

"Me, too," Reverend Dana said. "The lives you take never really leave you, even the ones where you had no choice, not if you want to protect what matters. You relive it, though, thinking, if there'd been more time, more space to make the decision, it could have turned out differently. But with humans, it doesn't always work that way."

"No ma'am. Some things, people I know, I can help put back together, but I can't fix them permanent. They keep figuring out ways to get broke again." Craig passed through his mind, that poor boy's flat dead eyes. The families of his victims would say his soul had fled his body, but the soul didn't have that choice. It was cowered down in him somewhere, miserable and afraid.

Teena Joy didn't let him watch the news much, but he recalled a story of a man who'd killed his wife and kids. Teena Joy had said he had a powerful sickness in him. Rev asked if she thought it was best for them to put him to death. She said God made those decisions, though sometimes He did it through a court and a judge or jury. She'd said, "That man might like donuts, Karman. He might go into a donut shop every day and pick out one, sit at the counter, drink his coffee and enjoy it."

He'd asked her what that had to do with him killing his family.

"Everything and nothing. You just think about that whenever you're dealing with someone, with things they've done. Be just, and don't allow harm, but don't decide you're their judge, either. You offer love and forgiveness, and let God take care of the rest. You be human, and let God be God. Your soul will be lighter because of it. Lighter in weight, and more lit up, with less darkness to hide things from you."

It was far easier to follow that path when the person harmed wasn't someone you couldn't breathe without. He gazed at his hands. He'd held Veracity, willed her soul to stay in her body, even as he could feel it being cut free. It had terrified him. Made him determined to change its mind. Change God's mind. Had that been wrong?

No. Because God would have taken her, if it was meant to be. Rev had no power to stop Him. But it still felt like his effort had torn the fabric of the universe a little. "I afraid there's nothing I can do to fix this," he said.

"It's been my experience," Dana said carefully, "when we think we've failed our Master or Mistress, what we've really failed to do is trust them enough. There are only two things they expect. For us to trust and serve them. Just like with God. They're not God, but the principle is the same, because they're both based in love and devotion."

He stared at her, then his heart eased a little more. God had sent him to someone who understood, who could stand on the ground where he was floundering. "Yes ma'am. Guess that's true enough."

She cocked her head. "There's another poison in your gut."

"If...they'd succeeded. If they'd...killed her." When his voice broke, her surprisingly strong hand gripped his shoulder again. "They were going to make me think she'd just left. If they'd convinced me of that, I would have looked to my family for comfort, never realizing they was the ones who took her from me. Why people like this? How they make that okay in their minds? How they let hate and fear and lies take them over that way?"

"We are flawed creatures," Dana said softly. "But it didn't happen, and maybe that's because this time good triumphed over that kind of evil and darkness. We take our victories where we get them."

Her voice became firmer. "Though she needs some time, when she's ready, your Mistress will need you to trust her enough to show her just how badly this affected you. You have to show your hurts, because to fully heal from them, you have to do it together. Open your souls to one another."

She tapped his hand, resting on the back of the pew. "You start opening that door when you're falling in love, but when things like this happen, you have to open it wide and take each other into the back rooms, into the basement and attic. We talk about how love can handle anything, but it's another matter to have the courage to trust it, and each other, that much. The depths of love are infinite, and it will go anywhere you need it to go."

She paused. "Just like the love you have for your family. They've done something terrible, but you love them because that doesn't go away. And since you say your Mistress has been down a difficult road with her family herself, she can help you with that.

"We need to stand on our own two feet, but we also need to know when we need help. When we need healing and care, too."

She drew his attention to her blind eyes and a cochlear implant behind her ear. "I nearly died from an IED when I was in the Army, but worse than that, I wished I had. It took my Master to bring me back to myself. Both of them. The earthly one and the Heavenly one."

Because of her proximity, he'd noted the name stamped on her dog tag. *Winston, Peter R.* He nodded toward it.

"He the earthly one."

"Yes." She clasped it, her lips curving with a hint of mischief. "Sometimes he tries to convince me he's the Heavenly one as well. Doms can get carried away with the whole know-it-all, protective thing."

Her humor opened his heart to more light. "I didn't expect to find a pastor called to the same thing I am."

"No? Faith is all about the beauty and challenges of submission." She offered her hand to him, palm up. "If you want, we can pray together. For you, your family, and especially for your Mistress. We can give thanks, because she's alive, and you have the chance to show her how much you love her and want to be with her."

"And hope she feel the same way."

"If it's God's will. Or the Lord and Lady's." Dana winked. "I have a friend who worships your Mistress's chosen path."

She touched the dog tag again. "Rev, I don't pretend to know God's plan for you, but I'd be surprised if it didn't include your Mistress wanting you back at her side. Just be patient and allow time for her to heal. To think and pray."

He took her hand. "And most importantly, have faith."

"Amen. And blessed be."

Vera stared out her kitchen window at the birds wrangling for the best position on the tray of her feeder. The whimsical metal piece, designed to look like an antebellum house, was swinging from the jockeying birds. It was twilight, the setting sun glinting dully on the metal.

It had been nearly three weeks. Jasmine and Joss's wedding, their handfasting, was coming up. She thought of Jasmine's phone call, that day in the car with Rev. Her delight when she heard the girl was ready to set a date, that two people who were good for one another were choosing to walk forward together in this life.

Last night, she'd sat in her living room and recalled the henna exercise with Rev, every moment. Marking his flesh, enjoying his body, the way he responded to her. The feel of his eyes upon her, when she let him open them.

She hadn't mailed the card to her family. She'd considered burning it in the cauldron she kept on her home altar. Instead, it rested on that same altar, until she was in the right frame of mind to know what to do.

Her head would be fucked up for a while. No one had ever committed violence against her the way Witford and Tisha had. She'd had several sessions with Maureen to talk it out, and it had helped. So had a wine and chocolate dinner with Ros and the other women. At work, Bastion made sure her tea was always hot, that she had the best of the baked goods, and fielded her calls as if he was a knight protecting the walls of her castle. When she told him she was fine, he pretended he wasn't doing any of that. And kept doing it.

She wanted Rev. Needed him here with her. He'd known that, too, that night in the hospital. She was being stubborn because she could, because her whole world felt upended. Because she was coming into her house through her front door after nightfall, because she didn't feel safe doing it the way she normally did. Because she was doing stupid things, like blaming him for being family to the people showing up in her too-frequent nightmares.

She was hiding from him. That knowledge made her angriest of all.

It wasn't the best mindset for officiating a joyous occasion like a wedding, but she could pull it off, bring the right energy to it, if she meditated on it, if she...

Goddamn it, she couldn't. Her faith in love was shaken, which affected everything else. She should call and ask someone else to do the ceremony.

But Jasmine had asked her to do it.

The radio was playing. Don Henley's "End of the Innocence" which seemed too close to home. She wasn't innocent, but anytime one's world, one's paradigm, was shattered, proving how at the mercy of Fate each of them was...it wasn't an easy thing to accept, because then every bubble one created for oneself felt like an illusion that would disappear, like dreams did shortly after waking in the morning. Nightmares didn't suffer from that problem.

She went to her living room, turned on the fire because she felt cold, and sat down. She cried again, so frustrated and angry, and hurt... and afraid. She wasn't this weak, weepy woman. She *wasn't*.

Surging up, she marched through the kitchen and yanked open her back door, just to prove she could do it after dark. She'd scream her defiance at that darkness, dare it to come up on her porch. She'd kick its ass.

The shout caught in her throat. As she looked at her pots of flowers arranged on the porch stairs, so many bright and beautiful blooms, a different, better idea presented itself. Her backyard fountain gurgled, water splashing around the bronze girl dancing, a smaller version of what she'd bought for the office. When she walked slowly down the steps and looked up through her live oak branches, she could see stars.

Do the things you would tell someone else to do, and believe they will work, the same way you believe it for them. Maureen had suggested that. *And realize it will take more than once for it to do so. It's like mental PT. It's going to be really difficult at first, but it will get better, the more you do it.*

So she sat on the bench by the fountain and centered herself. She called upon the meditations that she'd summoned plenty of times these past weeks. The usual peace and balance they brought her had stayed out of her reach, but each time, they'd been getting closer. Just as Maureen had predicted.

She let go of the desperate need to be back to her normal self and breathed. She didn't push the frustration and uneasiness out the door. She just opened it, let them see the way out as she turned her attention to other, better things. She imagined herself baking something, taking out the ingredients, getting her hands dusted with flour. Preheating the oven, feeling the heat against her legs as she worked at the counter next to it, mixing fragrant dough by hand.

She coaxed her subconscious to turn away from the fear and frustration as if it were a separate being from herself, a hurt child that needed to know it was okay.

The pathway to her favorite quiet place in her head was there. It had gone from opaque in the first week to murky in the second, a path through a haunted forest. Tonight moonlight was shining on it. As she moved along it, slowly, she inhaled the scents around her on the outside, felt the presence of the elements, the wider turnings of the universe.

The path became even clearer.

Several more deep breaths, and then she was ready for the idea that her flowers and peaceful yard had given her. She rose and shed her clothes. On this bench, the oaks screened her, and no one could see her in the darkness.

Terron, bless his kind heart, had a spotlight on the corner of his house, with enough wattage to throw light into her backyard as well as his own. Normally and considerately, he only used it in brief spurts, like when his brother was visiting and his greyhound needed a last trip out before bedtime.

The police presence at her house meant her neighbors knew the basics of what had happened to her. A few days after she was home, Terron had come to her front door and told her anything she needed, he would do, and had offered to keep the spotlight on at nights for her. Or to install a spotlight of her own for her, if she wanted that.

She'd been twitchy and not herself that day, but it had helped, the reminder of the good in others. She'd taken him up on it for the first week and a half, but last week had told him she wanted him to start turning it off again.

She was glad she'd done so, because here she was. She needed to feel the night, the moon, the strength of the Goddess through her. She tipped her head back, her hair brushing her shoulder blades, her hands reaching up.

As she let all that into herself, she knew when she wasn't alone. She wasn't afraid, since she'd invited that energy into her before. She'd reached out on that link that awful night, and he'd felt her. He'd come, the Powers That Be helping him know how to get to her in time.

He'd come now, because it was time. She was ready.

She lowered her chin. Rev knelt a few paces away from her, his head down. Waiting on his Mistress's desires.

"How long have you been here?" she asked.

"I been coming by for a brief spell every night." His voice moved over every inch of her skin, a warm blanket being pulled up over her body on a cold night. It settled into her heart. When his head lifted, his gingerbread-colored eyes, the thick lashes and strong inner light, held her like his arms did. "Just to watch the house a while. Make sure you're okay."

When she reached out, he rose and took her hand. As they touched, her body swayed, and his arm went around her, holding her up as she put her face against his chest.

It didn't matter that she was naked, and he wasn't. He was giving her this, making her feel powerful. Showing her that power was still there. It hadn't been taken away by what had happened.

"Jasmine and Joss's wedding is soon," she said. "I don't know if I can do it."

"Do you want to?"

"Yes."

"Then you will," he said simply. "What can I do to help you, Mistress?"

She touched his face. "I'm sorry, Rev. For your family. I'm sorry I couldn't tell you that sooner."

"That wasn't your job, Mistress," he told her brusquely. An answer not from her sub, but from the man who wouldn't back away from the responsibility of being a man. "They turned themselves in. Lawrence told you that, right?"

"He did. You took care of it, just as you said you would."

If she stayed immersed in that night, her life really would end at that moment, nothing else but that defining her.

The strength of his hands was welcome. She felt safe and protected with him. He'd given her that from the first, a surprising need she hadn't expected to have as strongly as she did. She told him that, and his eyes darkened with pain, but she wouldn't allow his guilt to mock her words.

"I still feel safe and protected, Rev. You came for me. You helped save me. Even if it hadn't turned out that way, it's not a physical safety I'm talking about, but an emotional one. It was how you felt about your family that made me feel abandoned. Not the other. I was wrong about that. I understand why you did what you did." She paused. "I need you, Rev. Come inside."

"Yes...ma'am."

He'd remembered what she said at the hospital. She put her hand on his chest, then her head on top of it. She could hear the beat of his heart through it. "You're mine, Rev," she said softly. "And as long as you want that, you'll call me Mistress. Do you understand?"

"Yes, Mistress." The relief in his voice was a powerful wave surging through her.

"Let's find that ground again. Come inside and watch over me. Keep me safe."

When they reached the door, he stopped and looked down at her. His hands fell to her waist, flexed. "I need you powerfully, Mistress. All of it, in my head, what could have happened, I've about lost my mind over it. Wanted to rage and howl, go find Witford and those others, even my aunt, and do terrible things to them. I knew that was all wrong, but this feeling, to be inside you, take you over, kiss every inch of you, wrap your hair around my hand, all of it...it feels so strong, so different. Something dark to it, but something good, too."

Her hand curled into his biceps, and she used her nails a little harder. "Why do you think I want you to come inside?"

As she drew him over the threshold and shut the door, he was behind her. She sucked in a breath as he pressed her against her laundry room wall, his body fully on hers. He put her palms flat to the wall, his own over her hands, and they stayed that way, her naked, him clothed, both trembling.

Then he dropped to a knee. He bent all the way down, put his mouth on her ankle, and started working his way up her calf. Slow, tasting her everywhere, his hands following, gripping her legs as he moved up and rained kisses over her thighs, her buttocks and lower back. She curled her fingers against the wall and remembered when she'd ordered him to touch her shoulders and stroke her hair. This was a different form of that, a worshipping and a hunger, tied together. She felt it, in a language universal to every living thing.

He rose and slid his arm around her waist, fingers exploring her navel, her hip bone, her mound. He didn't go further than that, until she dropped a hand from the wall, clasped his wrist and guided his hand between her legs. At the near violent response of her sex to his touch, she arched against him, hair brushing his face as he buried it there, finding her neck to taste, bite, suckle.

"Yes, Rev," she said, her voice throaty. "Inside me, now."

He opened his jeans, guiding himself into her from behind. The angle required him to go slow, but he pressed in deep. Taking his hand back to her cunt, he sealed his hand over it, fingers spread over her clitoris, her stretched labia, his cock buried between them.

She shuddered at the sensations, such overwhelming proof of *life*. He nipped her throat again, tasting. She brought his other hand up to her breast so he could stroke, explore the taut nipple, the swollen fullness of the curve.

"Oh. Goddess...Stop, Rev. Stay still inside me."

He stopped stroking, their bodies quivering. It didn't make it all better, but it was the right step. A reminder of how willing he was to be what she needed, how much he wanted that, too. She closed her eyes at everything such intimate stillness could bring.

She knew his soul enough to know how difficult it had been for him to leave her that terrible day. He'd had to obey a different Master, the one that made him Rev. He needed her forgiveness for that, but he needed to forgive himself.

Feeling all of that restored and reminded her of the power she had as a Mistress, to help him. To have the honor and pleasure of giving him that forgiveness.

She pushed against him, a nonverbal cue, and he reluctantly slid from her. When she turned to face him, she linked her arm around his neck, hooking her leg over his hip. He understood. In the next blink he'd lifted her up against the wall, and was back inside her. This time, the angle was the right one for what her eyes told him he could unleash.

"Give me your strength, Rev."

A cry broke from her throat as he thrust into her, his hand slamming against the wall as he braced himself there. The power of it vibrated through the house's frame. His other arm banded around her waist, his hand clamped on her hip as his buttocks flexed under her legs, locked around him.

His body, so strong and solid, his need, was all around her, inside her. She put her face against his jaw, and wrapped her hands over his neck, his vulnerable neck, as he bent his head to her. He brought her to a climax that had a serrated edge, the slicing reminder of the past few days. But their souls were open to one another and joined, able to handle it, soften that edge.

"Yes..." The orgasm rushed in, the dam breaking, and she pushed herself down on him. "Now. Right now."

He released, and kept working himself in her as her cries rose, a catharsis of sobs and tears. Her fear, her anger, the whole big tangle of emotions that she didn't yet know how to fully untangle, but she would. She wouldn't accept defeat, wouldn't let fear and anger rule her.

When they both slowed and she was still crying, he was pressing against her, also still inside. He stroked her hair and held her so tight, letting her know he was there. He would always be there.

He was murmuring that. Telling her how sorry he was, how he'd be where she needed, when she needed him.

Life didn't always allow it, but believing in that person's love, how fervently they wished for that, meant so much. She wanted to believe.

"Rev." She spoke his name softly. When he wiped away her tears with his thumbs, she did the same to him. A strong man's tears. Was there anything more certain to help heal a woman's heart? Those tears said, *I love you, you're not alone with this, I want to fix it.*

"Rev," she repeated his name, because she wanted to do so. She gazed up at him. "Are you hungry? I made soup."

He didn't smile, his eyes holding her as tight as his arms. "Have you eaten tonight?" he asked.

She shook her head. He plucked a towel from the stack on her dryer and pressed it between her legs. Then he dropped to one knee to blot the seed he'd left on her thighs before using the same towel on himself and fastidiously tossing it into the wash.

"I'll make us two bowls," he said. "Any bread to go with it? Maybe one of those muffins?"

"I'm not sure you've earned muffins yet."

It was a weak attempt at humor. The flicker in his eyes acknowledged it, but he gave her a solemn nod. "Maybe some soup crackers. I'll go get your clothes from outside."

He'd noted the cotton robe she kept on a hook by the door, so he helped her into it first, even tying the sash, caressing her hips. She kept the extra robe there, because sometimes she liked to sit on her back porch after she'd changed into her nightgown. The robe helped if there was an evening chill.

She *would* do that again.

"You can keep your jeans on, but leave your shirt off," she said.

More relief, that she wanted to be able to look at him, touch him as she wished. But when he touched her face before he went to retrieve her clothes, she could tell he wasn't expecting her to be the same as always. She appreciated that.

After he returned from the yard and deposited her clothes in the hamper, per her direction, he followed her into the kitchen. Sliding onto a stool, she let him do as he'd said, fix them soup. Serve and wait on her.

"So who's doing the service at your church this Sunday?" she asked. It brought that uneasiness crashing back through her, but she was feeling like she could win the battle with it right now.

He gazed down at the vegetables swimming in a seasoned tomato-y broth. "Me."

"Have you ever done that before?"

"No. It'll be the first time I ever done it by myself. But I helped Witford come up with enough sermons. And it needs to be me. The congregation is confused, and hurting. I hope God will show me what to say, to help."

In the pause that followed, she expected he was thinking of

inviting her, and talking himself out of it so she didn't feel like he was pressuring her. She wasn't sure herself, so she asked a question to fill in the awkward silence.

"Are you taking over the position permanently?"

"I don't know. The church was started by Teena Joy, Tisha, and Tisha's husband, my Uncle Mel, before he passed away. Witford grew up in it, like I did. We never had to choose a preacher."

"So you could just take over doing it permanently. No vetting process."

"Yeah." He found her soup crackers in the pantry and, at her nod, put a handful into her soup before he did the same for his own. "But I think I'll ask the congregation to choose. It's their church, after all. If they want someone else, I'll fill in until they ready to take over."

"Would you want the job?"

He lifted a shoulder. "Sunday sermons are only one small part of being the preacher. I couldn't work at the school anymore, and that's important to me."

"What if you hired a co-preacher, and you shared the responsibilities? A partnership, so you have an equal say in the church's management and direction."

"Maybe." He slid onto the stool next to her, and stirred his spoon in the broth.

"Rev, look at me. What's going on?"

He lifted his head, his expression troubled, at a perilous depth she recognized. She'd seen it in her own mirror, these past few weeks. "It shook me up, my faith in certain things. It isn't the church's fault. Isn't the congregation's fault. But that poison was there, and I having a hard time understanding how it happened, and if I missed something I should have seen."

"It's a wound," she said at length. "Only thing is to let it heal and see what life offers you."

His gaze slid over her in the robe, and the corner of his mouth quirked. "Is life offering me you, Mistress?"

She nudged him. But she got up and went to her bread box. Bringing forth one of Cyn's giant muffins, she cut it in half and put his portion next to his soup. When she slid back onto her stool, she made sure she was close enough their hips and shoulders brushed. Even if it meant she might elbow him while eating her soup.

"I don't have a lot of answers tonight," she said.

"Is it all right that I'm here with you, being with you?"

"Yes," she said simply. "This part is good."

"Then that's enough, and I'm grateful for it." He gripped her hand. "I been feeling like I have a knife in my lungs, because even breathing hurts, and when you touched me here," he put his hand on his chest, "you took it out."

She put her other hand over his. She couldn't say anything, because his words made her own heart hurt. But this time, it was the right kind of pain.

CHAPTER TWENTY-TWO

*R*ev stood at the pulpit, gazing at the polished wood top. Unlike Witford, he had no notes in front of him, no carefully reviewed pages. The congregation waited, and he drew in their energy. Uncertain, unbalanced by what had happened. Much like he'd felt, all the way up to this moment.

He hadn't asked, but Veracity had said she might come. She hadn't, and he understood. But it sure would have been nice to see her in the sea of expectant faces before him.

"Let's pray first thing," he said. "I think it will help."

And it did. He did what he did in the garden behind the church, offering up everything, hiding nothing. Asking for guidance, showing gratitude for his blessings. Hoping he served God's will in all he did.

When he lifted his head, he was calmer. He looked at the people before him, and he smiled. "It all right," he said. "Things happen. We all get lost."

A few murmurs of assent. "I see hope in your faces. Hope that I have some answers. I don't think I do. But that's okay, because God give us the answers we need."

He thought of Tisha and Witford. He felt their absence keenly. "We get lost in fear, in hatred, in anger. We get lost when we put store in the wrong things, and forget the only things that really matter."

He lifted his gaze. "And what are those things? Honoring and caring for others. Forgiving when forgiveness is needed. We hurting because we don't understand what happened to Tisha and Witford, to Simon and Tyson. But we know if they look to God, if they ask God to help them find Him again, He will. God's forgiveness is limitless. No matter how short we fall on it, we have to try to be like that."

He drew a few random lines on the wood before him. "I always had family, but they come and go too often. My momma, Teena Joy. Now Witford and Tisha. They not passed on, but they apart from me right now, and I don't know if they'll find their way back. It hurts, almost as bad as from them dying."

When his attention slid over the elderly members of their church, he saw understanding. They'd lived long enough to know what he was saying. They would help him with the younger members of the congregation, would take his words and use them to help heal others.

"I not sure if I done right, if I missed things I should have seen. If I should have done things I didn't. We can all ask God's help today. Faith isn't always an easy path. But love carries us down the right road. Love for each other, our families, families we born into and those we choose.

"When we hate, we separate ourselves from one another. That's when we get lost most of all, and when we invite evil in. We think it belongs to the person we've separated ourselves from, when really it's infected us, too."

His gaze lifted as the rear door opened. Veracity entered the nave, wearing a form-fitting golden orange suit with black trim. The colors reminded him of a monarch butterfly. Her pillbox hat was black with a little gold net over her eyes. Her black gloves had sparkling orange lace at the wrists.

As she took a seat, the vise around his chest dropped free with a resounding clank.

～

Vera had been drawn as tight as a gallows rope when she drove into the parking lot. She walked up to the doors and stopped, perilously close to bolting back to her car. No usher came out to change her mind. She should take that as a sign and do just that.

But it was Rev's first sermon in front of a congregation. She'd come this far. Gotten dressed up and everything.

She put her hand on the door, opened it, and was standing in the narthex. She clasped her hands together, head down, and listened to his words, coming through the next set of doors. They reached for her, brought her closer to the entry. Maybe his words opened them, or maybe her grasp on the handle did it, but it didn't matter. She was in the nave, and sliding into her preferred back row pew.

He kept talking, but his eyes touched her with a light that told her just how glad he was to see her.

She saw Ray, a couple pews away from her on the other side of the aisle. No phone on his knee, but no collection plate either. His expression was troubled, fixed on Rev. She expected Rev had told them today wasn't going to be about collections, or keeping an eye on the parking lot. It was about being fully present for the service.

"Repentance is important, because to be forgiven by those we love...there's a grace there more priceless than anything made by man. 'I once was lost, but now I'm found.'"

As he sang the "Amazing Grace" line, straight from the pulpit, the effect was immediate, a spring rain on parched earth, the promise of the morning sunrise. Vera could feel the way it sank into all of them, the worst parts of the tension and worry easing, heads lifting, shoulders dropping, gazes exchanged, hands clasped.

He left the pulpit, still singing. He repeated that line in the way a blues song would do it. Strong like a declaration. Then soft and fragile, a man weeping before a cross. Quiet, the sound of a brook, all of them resting on its grassy banks, at peace. With rejoicing, with laughter, strong and lifting up to the heavens.

When he'd started, some of the parishioners had come to their feet. Less than normal, though. That changed as he kept uttering the line, bringing a few more individuals, then clusters of people here and there, and finally whole sections rising. At his gesture, the choir joined in, and the energy surged. Those on the aisles reached out to him as he passed, so he could clasp their hands, a confirmation of solidarity.

"Reach out to one another," he sang. Then he sang it more fiercely, a call to action, a piercing light. Michael's sword, cutting darkness away. "Reach out to your sisters and brothers. We all here for one another. Pray for each other. Pray for Witford, for Tisha, for Simon and Tyson. They strayed into the darkness, and they need us all to raise God's lanterns, to guide them back to the light."

Amens rang out. Calls for Jesus's help, proclamations that Jesus was Lord. As Vera watched it happen, she recalled every joyous energy raising at her own Wiccan and pagan celebrations, offering hope and healing, all from the same source, the same well. Everything connected. Every soul. Every heart.

When Rev reached her in the last row, the congregation had turned, following his progress. Once there, with no self-consciousness, he dropped to one knee and extended his hand, palm up.

"I asked your forgiveness," he said huskily, "but I want so much more than that, Veracity. I need your heart and love, just as much as I need God's love, because they one and the same to me. I need to belong to you in Heaven and on Earth, same as I belong to Him. You my Goddess, He my God. The balance I need. Let me serve you both. Let me love and care for you."

He wasn't raising his voice, and for once, despite the fervor behind it, it didn't resonate. This was just between them and him, only his body language telling them it was a moment of import, the question being asked.

Tears rolled down her face. When he'd come to her the other night, she'd realized that yes, she was hurt, and more than a little afraid of what was going on in her. But she'd also realized she couldn't heal by herself. She needed him to help her. And she still did. She told him all that with her eyes, which was her answer.

Here I am.

His eyes lit up and he pressed a kiss to her fingers, held them to his forehead, that third eye, before he rose, drawing her up with him. He turned to the congregation. "This is the woman I love," he said. "Veracity Morgan. She a caring and loving woman, who stands in God's light."

He began to back down the aisle, and resumed "Amazing Grace," incorporating the words and sentiments thrown to him from his audience, as was his way. Since he didn't let go of her hand, he took her with him. She allowed it, because she didn't want to let go of him, either.

Then they surprised her, people reaching out to grip her free hand as she passed, offering her warm greetings with fervent sincerity. But all of them, herself included, were in the grip of the words God had given Rev, had given to all of them. There was no room for anything here right now but truth and love.

"Peace to you, sister..."

"Welcome..."

"God praise you..."

When she reached Mrs. Meriweather, the woman took her hand and spoke a matriarch's blessing. The words she chose had a significance Vera couldn't deny.

"Welcome to our family."

Many things, large and small, happened for more significant reasons. She'd lost her birth family, but then she'd found Ros, Skye, Cyn and Abby, Bastion, and people like Sy and Trey, Mavis. Now that family was expanding even further.

She'd faced the real possibility of her death. It had opened her not just to this moment, but to healing the wounds of past losses.

She could mail that card. She could truly forgive her parents and siblings, and give them a home in her heart, where they'd always belonged. She could embrace the gifts she'd been given, and where those gifts had brought her.

To the man who held her hand, and her heart, in his gentle, strong hands.

After the service, Rev asked her to stand with him at the door. She saw some uncertain looks at her pentacle, but mostly they looked to Rev, drawing on the reassurance and strength he'd brought back to the pulpit after he'd escorted her to a seat right up front, giving her a wink as if he expected her to admonish him later for putting her in such a conspicuous place.

Yes, there would be repercussions. But for now, she settled in to listen, just like everyone else.

He'd held up several different books. The Bible, the Torah, the Koran. Hindu texts, Buddhist texts. "All these talk about what God is," he said. "They men's way of trying to understand, to make sense, to know how we should follow God. None of these paths are wrong. But here," he touched his heart, "is where God make the most sense, if our heart be right. This is where we can always find and follow Him.

"I don't think it matter to Him what we call Him, or the paths people take to Him, long as one thing the same. The most important thing. If everyone called him Love—not God, not Allah, not Jehovah or Yahweh, not Lord and Lady"—his gaze touched Vera's before rising to his listeners again—"how you think we might treat one another, no matter what path we following?"

So yes, there were some uncertain looks at her choice of jewelry, but he'd made them think. Or, from his perspective, God had given him words to help them that way. Though in her opinion, God had chosen a darn good channel, one not only with great reception for the message, but who believed in it fully.

When the parking lot emptied, Rev turned to face her. "How are you today?"

It wasn't a casual question, so she took her time answering. "I'm feeling not quite so lost at sea. You being with me...it helped. I'm finding my way back to myself."

He gazed at their interlaced hands. "Is it all right if I say something to you, then? About that day. It's okay if it's not. It'll keep."

A faint quiver went through the connection and his mouth tightened. As he lifted a hand to her face, she shook her head, even as she leaned into him.

"No. I can hear it. I want to hear it."

"We do this first. So it might be easier." He drew her into his arms until her head was on his shoulder, face to his neck, and his voice was above her ear, like soothing thunder during an easy rain. "You tell me if it's too much."

Her other hand moved to his biceps, held, as he pressed his forehead to hers. That third eye contact, instinctive between two souls reaching for one another. Trying to reconnect, and realizing that, too, was a fragile thing, something that couldn't be forced.

"Walk with me in the garden," he said.

He understood. She nodded, and they walked hand in hand around the outside of the church, through the cemetery, to the garden archway.

"I stopped at a church that night," he said. "After I left the hospital. Spoke to a Reverend Dana, and she helped take the sword from my heart. She was...like me. In your world. Our world. Submissive."

The way he said it sent a welcome spark of sexual electricity through her. "Yes," Vera said. "She is."

"You know her?"

"The BDSM community isn't large. Dana is married to Peter Winston, operations manager for Kensington & Associates. They're a client, and Matt Kensington and Ros are good friends."

"Is Dana a friend of yours?"

"As a matter of fact. There's a 'Faith is Universal' event each year. Cyn calls it the FU conference." Vera's eye roll made him chuckle. "It started as a small get-together in Audubon Park, a collaboration between a Buddhist monk and a Catholic priest. Dana and I have shared a booth there. And a hot chocolate afterward."

Rev nodded. "I talked to Christophe, one of our Sunday school teachers. He been taking seminary courses online and wants to be an assistant pastor. We gonna split it up, the services and pastor duties, and let other active church members share the responsibility. A church is way more than just one person."

"Sounds like you won't have much time for anything else."

"Everything I plan builds in time for you, Mistress."

The bright sun caught the golden brown in his eyes and lit them up with all the heat and life he carried within. She saw his desire to dive deep into her, and the wish that she herself had. Standing in the garden, with beauty around them and sunlight on their shoulders, she would let the right feelings course through and strengthen them, bring them forward on a path together that would never split apart.

"What you did with Witford and Tisha was the right thing, Rev. It was the thing a strong man, a just man, would do." Because of how fragile the place inside her was that the words touched, she said it slowly, carefully. "But I'm also glad that Lawrence, Mick and Tiger followed you. You're mine now. You'll have a care with yourself, and think about that before you walk into situations with bulls and bad people. Understand?"

His lips twitched. "Yes, Mistress."

"I want to say something to you, too. About that day."

She had him sit on the bench near the stern but kind angel statue, but instead of sitting next to him, she sat down on his lap, sliding her arms around his shoulders. He put his around her hips, his eyes warm and curious.

372

"I remember you there, Rev. In my soul, my heart and head. I know I was leaving my body. You reached out and held on, telling me to come back. I felt it, the Divine power flowing through you, winding around me. I looked into your eyes and saw your soul. Do you remember that?"

"Not entirely." His sheepish look had her raising a curious brow. "What I do remember...it might be the first time I wasn't sure if I let God speak through me, as much as I spoke my own mind, and asked God to please take my wishes into account. I maybe asked Him a little more forcefully than I should have."

She kissed him. A sweet glide into pleasure, the two of them holding onto one another. When she drew back, she gave him her best reproving look.

"Since a Mistress has to hand out the right kind of punishment to help a sub feel better about taking the lead when he shouldn't, maybe God will leave that to me. Given the circumstances and all. Plus, I plan to do terrible, evil things to you for putting me up in the front pew like that without any warning. In those circumstances, a woman likes to make sure the back of her hair looks as good as the front."

"I promise to remember that in the future," he told her solemnly, and patted the back of his short hair. "It important to me, too."

"Wise ass." She stroked her nails along his nape. "Do you want to come to the handfasting? Jasmine did invite you."

"Yes. I'd like to see it done. I been looking through your ministering books, about that, and some other things." His expression became more intent. "Once you ready to go home, I'd like to do something with you I been thinking about. Will you trust me on that, without me telling you much about it ahead of time?"

"Does it involve spiders or reality TV?"

"No ma'am."

"Then yes." Her eyes held his. "I trust you, Rev."

⁓

Once they reached her house and entered her kitchen, he slipped her purse from her shoulder and asked if she would go out into the back-yard and relax on her bench while he prepared. Showing that his request hadn't been a spur of the moment thing, he'd had her stop at his place so he could retrieve a box of things to bring with him. He'd asked her to wait on him in the car, and when he came out, the box was closed.

As she sat on the bench, gazing at the falling water and dancing girl, she felt a mix of things. The emotions of the day, of the past weeks, were powerful. She worried she'd never be the same person again.

"You're not," Maureen had said during their latest session. "Events like this change us. There's no escaping that. But you have to decide what you want to reclaim and what you want to leave by the roadside. What matters is *you* make that choice, not those who did this to you."

She closed her eyes. Inevitably, when she did that, some of the worst moments came back to her, her inability to move, the wheel taking her under, the water stealing her ability to breathe. At first, she'd fought to get away from those images, but with Maureen's help, she was making herself relive them in limited doses. As she did, she told herself it was over. She'd survived. She was on the other side of it.

It didn't stop her from starting off the bench when he touched her, her hands fisted in defense. "Oh, Goddess. Rev, I'm sorry."

His expression held deep pain, shared with her, but he held out a hand. "You owe me no apologies, Mistress. Please, will you come with me?"

She put her trembling hand in his. He held it, just looking at her, then tipped his head back. He'd shed his suit jacket, the sleeves of his dress shirt rolled up to his elbows, the shirt tucked into belted slacks. He'd removed the tie and opened the collar so she could see the smooth skin of his throat, and a hint of the scooped neck of the cotton T-shirt he wore under the shirt.

"Sure is a fine day. I might have done this outside, but it involves some things I'm not sure you'd want your teacher next door to see." He gave her that stirring alpha look of his. "Or that I'd be okay with him seeing."

She summoned a smile. "Maybe we come back afterward. Have a Sunday dinner out here. We'll cook it together."

"Sounds good."

He guided her to the back door, her hand secure in his, and paused there to look at her, then out at the backyard. "You got a nice space here. Good place to sit, good sun. I expect some good and bad things have happened at this very spot, over the million years it been here. Do you think that change the good things about it?"

She looked up at him. "It can. But we shouldn't let it."

His firm lips brushed hers. "Exactly."

Once in the house, he took her to her bedroom, though he paused in the doorway to explain what she was about to see.

"I been reading your books about the Tantra stuff," he said. "I thought maybe this is something that you'd like."

He put both hands on her shoulders, the calm strength that riveted members of his congregation in his touch, vast and immutable as the ocean itself. While it had a similar effect on her, she also knew what it cost him to find it, and offer it to her. She wasn't the only one who'd been scarred by what had happened. Her hands overlapped his, holding onto him, as he was holding onto her.

"If it don't," he added, "you'll tell me and I'll stop. And that will be fine. Mind me?"

"I do." She caressed him. "Have I mentioned I like how you use that phrase?"

Giving her a lopsided smile, he moved so she could see what he'd done.

He'd laid a mat on the floor and placed four bowls of water around it, marking the quarters. White and red flowers floated in them, the colors of Shiva and Shakti. A bouquet of mixed flowers was at the head of the mat.

"May I undress you?"

At her nod, he slid the orange coat from her shoulders. "This a butterfly's colors. When you came into the church, that's what I thought you looked like. A monarch butterfly."

He hung it up in her closet, then returned to slip the buttons of her blouse and unzip her skirt, leaving her in garters and stockings. He knelt to remove those. As he did, his hands slid over her skin with the soothing pleasure of a hot shower after a long, hard winter day. Coupled with the erotic stimulation that his touch could bring to her.

His decision to pause a moment, to look at her in the garters and underwear, his gaze covering every inch of skin, added to both feelings. Though the erotic part took a decisive lead.

He showed his pleasure for handling her body, touching it, appreciating it, and he made sure each article of clothing was hung up or folded the way she liked. Over the short time he'd known her, he'd internalized so much about her preferences, including her care of her clothes.

Each movement, each act, built the power within the space he'd created.

He'd started the gas logs in the bedroom fireplace, so she wasn't cold. When he came back to her, he took her hand and dropped to one knee, looking up at her. Fully clothed, while she was naked, and yet, just like the other night, the gesture, his expression, told her he saw her as in charge, in control. His Mistress.

"I was reading about *nyasa*," he said, pronouncing the word with care. "Honoring the divine and inviting it inside you, so you know what I say is true. I know you a human woman, Veracity. But I also know you a piece of God, what you call the Lord and Lady. I think...I think what happened damaged that connection a bit. Same as it did for me, with the face of God I know. I thought this might help heal that some, for both of us."

He invited her to lie down, in a knee-weakening way. He rose to lift her in his arms, then squatted down, an impressive show of strength, and placed her on the mat in a supine position. He touched her face, then her throat, her chest, her abdomen, her mound.

She trembled. It was a unique feeling, to give her submissive the lead like this, and yet feel how strongly he was *serving* her. Taking care of her.

He drew the bouquet closer and knelt beside her. "I gonna place a flower at each of the chakra points, and each flower honors a Goddess."

"You've been reading my Encyclopedia of Goddesses."

"Yes ma'am. Got some interesting female deities in there."

When he removed his pocketknife from his slacks to cut a lush red azalea bloom out of the bouquet, she wasn't prepared for the sudden memory that wrenched her away, making her lose time. When she came back, he was leaning over her, his hand on her shoulder.

"Veracity."

She shook her head, and a tear rolled down her face. "This is beautiful. I don't want to ruin it."

"You can't ruin anything." He folded the blade back into the knife, put it in her hand and closed her fingers over it. "This helped me free you."

"Yes." She felt the heat of his hand lingering in the metal and held onto that, closing her eyes. It was as he'd said on her porch. Good and bad. This had been a weapon of good. It had helped save her.

She offered it back to him, and he continued, easy and calm. He laid the bloom on her mound, the petals brushing her clitoris. "The Goddess Kali. Folks think she scary, bloodthirsty, and she can be, but you made me think of her a different way, and what I read said she also is passionate. She know creation comes from destruction, from pushing ourselves, facing our fears to free us from them."

He met Vera's gaze. "Things end so other things can begin."

"Yes," she whispered.

He selected an amber colored rose next, laying it on her abdomen. "Freya," he said. "A goddess of fertility, among other things. Her name translates to Mistress. I liked reading about her."

When he put a yellow peony on her sternum, over her heart, her breath hitched in a near sob. "Kuan-Yin," he said. He stroked the side of her breast, her upper arm. "Her name means 'she who hears the weeping world.' She a goddess of compassion and healing, who stayed human instead of becoming pure light. She wanted to stay near humanity and help them." He nodded thoughtfully. "She reminded me of Jesus that way."

He put a white azalea bloom on her throat, the petals a light caress against her pulse. "Hecate. Goddess of witches, a moon goddess, sometimes an earth goddess. Connected to earth and God power, and she understand the balance between the two. She bring that under-standing back to you, to bring you peace and balance."

He stroked her cheek, traced her ear, caressed her hair and took away another tear with his thumb. His face showed anguish, love, care. Resolve and determination.

"All of them are within you. They *are* you. You stand apart from whatever earthly harms are done to you, because whatever happens, you come out on the other side, just as Christ did, showing death, pain and torment had no lasting hold upon Him."

She knew reading wasn't easy for him. She imagined him holding the books in his hands, bent over them, his mind taking those words into him, absorbing them into who he was, to remember what he'd read and repeat it like this, in his own way.

He unscrewed the dropper top of a small brown bottle, tucked next to one of the flower bowls. "I anoint your crown chakra, to reinforce and bring my Mistress that balance."

Rev leaned over her. While he left a drop of lavender on her forehead, she rested her hand on his abdomen and closed her eyes again. Inhaling its calming properties and the almond oil base, she kept his image inside her mind, every detail of him over her like this. His body, his words, what he'd created here, all of it was a forcefield, keeping out anything unwelcome.

When she opened her eyes, he was replacing the top of the bottle. He set it aside and sat back, his hands on his knees as he bowed his head.

"And now I await my Mistress's desires."

She felt the flowers resting upon her, and all they meant. She welcomed the familiar touch of that power into her and didn't shrink from it. It closed around her, helping and healing. Giving her back the power she'd been too fragile to embrace this fully, up until this moment.

She'd come back from church wanting to immerse herself in pleasure with him. This took that need to a far more transcendent level.

She slid her hand over his knee and touched his fingers. "You remember that first fantasy I described, leaving your handprints on a chalkboard as I did what I wanted to you?"

"I remember it." He kept his head down, his fingers tightening on his knees under her touch.

"All the things I've done to you and with you. They go through my mind a hundred times every day. They make me aroused, make me content. Make me miss you, need to be with you." Joy surged through her as the words came to her the way she wanted them to come, unfettered by anything else. "Even as I'm also able to wait, to do what the day demands of me, knowing you're there, at the end of it, but also throughout it, and at the beginning of it."

He swallowed. "It sound a lot like my day, Mistress."

"Take off everything but your cross, then sit back down, legs Indian style."

A little smile crossed his face as he rose. "Teena Joy, when she taught me history, the part about Native Americans, she had me sit that way and we made feathered headdresses out of construction paper. She told me stories about the Choctaw, Natchez and Chitimacha, the tribes around New Orleans."

"I'd like to hear those stories. But right now, I want to see your beautiful body, every inch that belongs to me."

Heat flourished in his eyes, in the energy shimmering over his flesh and the muscle beneath as he complied, stripping off his shoes and clothes and setting them aside. The cross gleamed against his bare chest.

"Your eyes are the color of gingerbread," she told him. "We'll make gingerbread men later and frost them. I'd like to do some creative things with that frosting."

His cock was already semi-erect, his thigh muscles flexing as he sat down in the position she'd ordered. "You making me hungrier, Mistress. But not so much for that."

She smiled and plucked the flowers off of her body, sending a blessing to each Goddess face he'd named before sitting up and distributing them in the bowls of water. As she rose to her feet, she felt the strength of the Goddess rise with her. Reborn.

His eyes caressed her body, top to toe, making all of it tingle with the desire to mate, to be closer, touch, rub, stroke and caress every part of herself against every part of him.

But denial, building the anticipation, was the Bruce Willis anti-hero of sex. It made sure the world was saved, good prevailed and the ending was unforgettable. Bastion had told her that, during one of his rare visits to Progeny. He'd been taking a break from a scene, purposefully prolonging it so his submissives would think too much arousal could cause insanity. And that wasn't necessarily a bad thing.

She moved behind Rev. "Back straight." He wasn't slouching, but the order brought his shoulders back further, his chest out and head up. She pressed her mound against the back of his neck as she caressed his shoulders, his skull and jaw.

All hers.

She came to his front and straddled him, closing her legs around his waist, bringing their sexes against one another, his rigid cock pressed to her damp cunt. "This is a Shakti-Shiva pose," she whispered. "When we're joined, the energy is a closed circle. Afterwards, when we spoon in my bed, I'll have you press up against me, behind me, and our chakras will align. That energy will take us into sleep together."

"Where you can dream of me." He had remembered.

"Yes."

He touched the soft skin at the corner of her eye. "No bad dreams. No more, Mistress. I won't let them come."

She pressed her face into his hand. She held that connection as she lifted herself, reached between them and guided him into her, ready and hard, her body slick and willing. They came together close, a firm lock, and that circle closed. Complete and passionate.

"What will you dream of, Rev?" Her voice held the strain of arousal. She would draw the climax out for both of them. Or maybe she wouldn't plan anything. The Goddesses who'd been called to the circle would take them where They willed, into a cycle of arousal and bliss until they were limp with it and slept, spooned together the way she'd described.

"I'll dream of being everything you need me to be, Mistress. And then I'll wake up and make it happen."

She began to move, their souls locked in sensation, in pleasure and need. In love.

"You already are, Rev. You already have."

CHAPTER TWENTY-THREE

The weather for Jasmine and Joss's handfasting was sunny and not too hot, so they could set up their circle under the park's live oaks, rather than in the gazebo they'd reserved for rain. Poles draped with garlands of fresh flowers marked the circle, connected by floating ribbons of gauze in their chosen colors of purple and white. The altar and platform on which it rested had been built by Joss and his father.

After the ceremony, the platform would become a deck around the front steps to Joss and Jasmine's little house, a reminder of this day, every day they came home to one another.

About sixty friends and family would be present. As they arrived, the ones from different faiths showed their curiosity about their surroundings, the trappings of a ceremony different from what they knew.

Most of the curiosity was open-minded, though Jasmine's grandmother had been thin-lipped when she arrived and was escorted by Joss to the front row. Vera wasn't at all surprised that Rev, helping to set out the chairs, found his way to her.

She didn't hear their conversation, but she didn't need to do so. He'd leaned toward the grandmother as they talked together, and in time he coaxed forth a smile. At one point, he'd nodded toward Vera. She expected he'd told Jasmine's grandmother that he and Vera were together.

The grandmother had fingered the silver cross he wore. When she turned it over, she would see that inscription. *By faith alone...*

When more of Jasmine's immediate family arrived, Rev exited the chair, making room for them. He checked with Joss's best man to confirm the needed preparations were done, then he moved to a live oak and leaned against it. More than one female stole a look in his direction. On a normal day, he attracted attention. In his gray suit, he looked even more irresistible.

All mine, ladies. But enjoy the view.

He was as oblivious to it as always, his focus on making sure no one needed anything he could provide. When Vera told the friends who'd been chosen to cast the circle and call quarters to take their places, a signal that it was time for the ceremony to begin, his attention went where it had returned countless times since they'd arrived together. Back to her.

The ritual dress she wore when officiating as a Wiccan priestess had a scoop-neck, black beaded bodice, angel wing sleeves and an ankle-length flowing skirt. She'd worn slip-ons easy to discard when the ceremony began, to be in direct contact with the earth. Her pentacle and Isis pendants gleamed against her chest. Precious stones threaded onto her silver hoop earrings represented love, commitment, protection, insight, wisdom and patience. Important for every relationship, but especially a marriage.

She stepped onto the platform, in front of the altar, and faced the assembled. "Welcome," she said, as people quieted. "Will you lift your hand if you are familiar with a Wiccan or pagan handfasting ceremony?"

About half of the audience members responded, and Vera gestured to them. "Joss and Jasmine have told me to explain things as we go along, but if anything remains confusing, feel free to talk to these attendees afterward. And offer your own experiences. Faith is a beautiful thing to share."

She swept her gaze over the four quarter callers. "I will ask Jasmine and Joss to join me at the altar now, before we start the circle casting. The circle creates a sacred space for Jasmine and Joss's commitment to one another."

Joss and Jasmine had been mingling with the guests, and a ripple of laughter went through the group as she skipped ebulliently over to her groom and seized his hand, twirling under his arm. As the two came up the middle aisle between the chairs, Joss's eyes were on Jasmine, full of love and wonder. He'd looked at her that way from the first time they'd met. In his presence, Jasmine's sunlight personality was even more vibrant as well.

Joss's dark suit and tie suited his unruly brown hair and gleaming beard, framing his blue eyes and strong features. Jasmine was in an ivory-colored dress, a crocheted overlay over a silk sheath, with fringe at the bottom and on the short sleeves. Her blonde hair was coiled on her head and decorated with flowers. She wore a pewter pentacle where each point of the star was formed by two women with elongated bodies and lifted arms, their clasped hands creating the apex.

Vera smiled at the couple. She noted a handful of park visitors watching at a respectful distance. Many people were drawn to a celebration of love. It gave her hope for humanity.

"The ceremony isn't long," Vera told the assembled, "but should you need to leave the circle, we ask that you imagine opening and closing a door as you do so, to contain the energy we will build here."

Because they were here to support Joss and Jasmine, the audience projected a current of happiness and love Vera could use for the ceremony. As she began, she was also aware of Rev's attention. She'd never done this ceremony with a man present who was hers. It would give it an extra blessing of power and intent.

When the circle was cast and quarters called, she called on the power of the Lord and Lady inside the bride and groom to bless the space and strengthen it.

"Life tests us all," she told the young couple. "But your love for one another, your faith, your belief in powers greater than yourself, in the truth inside each of us, creates an energy. You can let it help you move together through those tests, as individuals willingly joined as a couple."

Picking up the scarf on the altar, she wrapped it around their wrists and clasped hands. The blue cloth had been embroidered with the bride and groom's initials by Jasmine's mother, and blessed on Jasmine's altar. For nine days she'd kept it in a glass bowl with crystals nested in the folds. Each day, she'd waved incense over it, a specific fragrance infused with the properties that supported a successful handfasting between lovers.

"You met, and that was a beginning," Vera said. "This is another beginning, an agreement to an even deeper level of commitment. Many of the mysteries you'll explore as you share a life together will be known only to the two of you, beyond words to explain to any other. You will share souls in ways no one else will, and so what you have faithfully committed to one another, that journey and commitment, will not be under the influence of anything else other than your own hearts. Do you agree?"

"We agree." Their hands tightened on one another.

"Joss, do you promise to love Jasmine with an open heart, generosity, and put nothing else above her, because your Love for one another *is* part of the Divine. They are one and the same, and should be honored and cherished as such."

"Yes. I do." His shyness dropped away, his back straightening and grip tightening. He showed her the man he wanted to be for her. Jasmine's eyes glistened.

When Vera asked Jasmine the same, the girl nodded and spoke in a choked voice. "I do. I love you so much, Joss. Thank you."

As the emotional response echoed through the audience, smiles were exchanged and the tissues came out. Vera felt the touch of tears herself.

Though many things had happened in the past few weeks to reinforce it, Vera was still gathering every scrap of evidence to reinforce her confidence and joy in what the world could be and often was. Today she'd get an extra helping of that proof.

"Good. Then here before the Lord and Lady, the spirits of Earth, Air, Fire and Water, Joss and Jasmine have committed to one another's well-being and happiness for the rest of their lives. Blessings upon them. Will you, as their friends and family, also commit to helping them on this journey together as husband and wife? To support that love? Say 'we will' if you agree."

"We will," the group replied. The grandmother was holding the cross she wore around her own neck in one thin hand. When she nodded, Vera bowed in acknowledgement. The Crone was the most powerful face of the Goddess.

"Good. Let us honor the Quarters and the Lord and Lady, and open this circle."

The attendees' heads and bodies turned in each direction as the respective quarter caller bid that element a thanks and the farewell blessing, "Go if you must, stay if you will." When they were done and Vera declared the circle open, she unwrapped the scarf and handed it to Joss. "Your wife's mother created this. I give it to you to conclude this ceremony. In the eyes of the Divine, of your family and friends, you are married."

Joss and Jasmine came together for a lingering kiss, their hands tight upon one another. Cheers and applause erupted. When they drew apart, Vera hugged the couple to her, then stepped aside to let friends and family congratulate them.

Rev was no longer alone at the tree. She saw Ros, Skye, Abby and Cyn, as well as Lawrence, Mick, and Tiger. Neil had been called down range the day before; otherwise he would have been here as well. They had come at her request. Not for the wedding, but for something different.

While the semi-circle they formed around Rev might have been unplanned, the positioning held meaning for her.

She crossed the ground between them, nodding to Ros and the other women before meeting Rev's bemused gaze. It told her they hadn't explained to him why they'd arrived near the end of the ceremony, evidence they weren't here for the wedding.

"Do you remember when I told you that each man—Lawrence, Neil, Tiger and Mick—went through a ritual of acceptance, where these Mistresses formally made them part of our family?" Her gaze passed over the men present, noting from their body language, the flickers in their gazes, how the words called the powerful memories to them.

"I do," Rev said. Anticipation vibrated through him, touching her with its electric current. "Are you telling me that's what you want, Mistress?"

After he'd placed those Goddess symbols upon her and offered to serve her, something had shifted. She didn't need to be fully healed, or have everything figured out about what had happened that terrible day, to be certain of what she wanted and needed from him. It wouldn't dictate what mattered to her.

"It is. But you have to tell me that's what you want."

He clasped her hands. "It's an honor I want with all my heart."

When she looked at the others, she was glad for their presence.

She couldn't help but feel a wave of sadness, though, thinking of how parents, siblings and grandparents being here to witness it had added to the joy of Joss and Jasmine's commitment to one another.

Rev caressed her wrist with his thumb. "The spirit of your born family, of what they should be, is here."

From the beginning of their relationship, she hadn't had to explain much to him about the most important things to her. It was especially true now. The wedding energy that saturated the air had their hearts open to one another.

"Before you do what you plan, I need to say this, in front of the family you found and that found you." His serious gaze held hers. "I would like to love you, Mistress. With everything that I am now, and everything that I may become. May I have your permission to do that?"

Despite the emotional power the words brought, she managed a steady reply. "You're already doing that. *Without* my permission, I might add."

"Couldn't help that. You made it impossible to do otherwise."

She sighed. "Blaming your Mistress. There will be penance for that."

"With you, penance is the first whiff of cotton candy and popcorn at the fair, when you walking toward the gate." He exchanged a look with the other three men, all of them knowing just what he meant. And in that look, she saw confirmation that he'd been accepted as one of them.

Then Rev wrapped both his hands around one of hers. "You know what I've thought about, almost every day since I met you? That if ever you would do me the honor of being my wife as well as my Mistress, I want that. I want to have children together, however God wants to give us that.

"I not asking you to offer me anything you don't want to give, Veracity," he said. "Whatever you can give, I'll take. Though I'll probably always ask for a little more than that, because when it comes to how I feel about you, the wanting and needing never stop."

Her heart thudded in her ears. She saw smiles from Abby and Skye, approval from Cyn. And Ros, the most cautious member of their group on these decisions, because she was the head of their family, and because she'd seen at least one member choose disastrously, had wet eyes, a blessing all its own.

She took a breath. "Do you remember what I told you about the Great Rite, Rev?"

"It a sexual rite, bringing down energy through a coupling between a priest and priestess."

"Yes. I would like to do that, direct it toward our commitment to one another, to strengthen and guide it."

He looked at the women. "With them present."

"Yes. As the four quarters of the Circle, holding it in place. And to give their blessing to the union."

"In our family, it's a way of saying you belong to her, but you also belong to us." Ros drew his attention. "You're ours to care for, as Mistresses. And as family."

The wedding guests had departed for the planned reception, so Rev's gaze stole to the empty chairs, the pillars threaded with gauze ribbon and flowers. "Pretty as this is.. you not thinking of doing it here. Out in the open."

"This is New Orleans. Why not?" Cyn deadpanned, then grinned. "Rev, you just went pale as a vampire."

"Do I have to belong to her, too?" Rev asked Vera.

A chuckle rippled through the group. Vera laid a reassuring hand on his arm. "I wanted to ask you here, because if you aren't comfortable with the idea, but wish to commit to me in the spirit of that ceremony, we can do a symbolic Great Rite, in this lovely setting. If you wish to do the other, we'll move to a more private location. It's your choice, and I whole-heartedly accept either direction. Or you can tell me you want to wait and think about it. You've said you want to be with me. That's enough for today. Truly."

Rev looked at each of the men, then the Mistresses. Then his attention came back to her. Her heart ached with a surfeit of emotion, because she saw the answer in his gaze, even before he spoke.

"I'd like to become yours and your family's, Veracity. I'll do it the way you wish, because I want to serve you with no reservations. I trust your care, as much as I want you to trust mine. Let me become yours, Mistress, in every way you want to claim me."

They took him to Ros's home in the Garden District. The cream-colored historic house had salmon shutters and multiple levels. He wasn't in the right head space to absorb too many of those details, but inside, the formal dining room grabbed his attention right off.

A mat, cut to the large table's oblong shape, had been laid upon it to protect the wood, and it was scattered with flower petals. A sheer blue cloth covered the side bar, a silver chalice and knife with a gold handle resting upon it. There was also a flogger, its ribbonlike tails arranged in a flourish.

A decanter of wine, a plate of crescent-shaped cookies and a bowl of the sugared pecans he liked were grouped with several bottles of essential oils. Incense gave the air a fire and sea water scent.

"Lawrence, Mick and Tiger prepared the space," Cyn noted. "Neil sent the pecans."

The men were absent now, but like Neil, they'd all made their presence known with the preparations, proof of their support for Vera's choice. The look in his Mistress's eyes as she surveyed the extra effort they'd made for her said how much it moved her. He was glad for it.

Before the men had departed, he'd had a chance to speak to Lawrence. "I should have asked you more about this ritual," Rev had said.

The former SEAL's attention had touched on his own Mistress before a smile wreathed his handsome features. "Wouldn't have done you any good. This wasn't what they did for me. It's been different for each of us. It depends on what your Mistress wants, and knows you need."

At some point, he and Vera might stand in front of a preacher or a priestess like her, or both. They'd make their vows and become married in the eyes of the law and all the faces of Divinity, but this was that first step. Like an engagement, it was significant. So he let go of any lingering worries over it, because they didn't matter.

"Go to the upstairs guest bathroom," Vera told him. "Take a thorough shower. As you clean yourself, do that breathing exercise we did together. Think about all parts of yourself, inside and out, that join with me when we come together. When you're done, there's a robe on the back of the door. Wear that and nothing else. You come out with a clear head and soul, waiting to be bound to your Mistress."

She took his hand and put her own on his face, her beautiful breasts against his chest, her hip and thigh brushing his. The eyes that looked upon him were his Mistress's, but something else, too, as if what she planned to call down into them was already there, waiting. He felt it in himself, a simmering energy.

"Don't rush," she told him. "You'll feel when it's time to come back here. Skye is going to go upstairs with you and tell you more about the ritual. While you shower, she'll be in Ros's home office across the hall, if you need anything."

"I don't want a Mistress to wait on me."

"It's not like that. Tonight, you are cared for and watched over by all of them. A reminder of what this is about. Understand?"

"Not fully, but I think it will come clear to me as we go along. I can feel that, here." He put his hand on his chest, and she covered it.

He could also feel from the watching women what she described. Their care was a protective circle around him already. When he followed Skye, he looked over his shoulder and saw Abby, Ros and Cyn draw closer to Vera and take her hands. He wondered what preparations she'd be making.

He asked Skye, and she used one of her recorded voices, a Southern accented female, to respond. "She'll bathe and be anointed with oils, so she can get her mind aligned with the Goddess she'll be calling down within her. Much the same as you're doing now, calling upon God to be with you in this bonding and commitment, this energy raising toward that intent."

So it was similar to the wedding. But when they reached the bathroom door and Skye took a few minutes to explain the steps of the ritual, the mechanics that would help it go more smoothly, there were some significant and distracting differences. However, Rev only asked a few questions, sensing that letting the mystery unfold was important.

They were interrupted briefly by a rasping meow. He glanced down the hall in time to meet a three-legged black cat's interested stare, before the creature hopped nimbly into what he assumed was Ros's master bedroom.

"Freak," Skye said. "He rules the house and had to check you out. Any more questions?"

He shook his head. Nodding, Skye put a hand on his arm and signed the next part. She did it slow, so he could follow it. If he needed anything, she'd be right across the hall.

There was only one thing he could think of needing right now. One woman. His Mistress had asked him to prepare to serve her, to commit to her. Before God. That was what he would do.

In the bathroom, he found male toiletries laid out for him to shower and shave. Probably also handled by the men. As he used them, Rev felt their presence like an outer circle around the inner one. He thought they'd like that comparison.

Before he put on the robe, his skin warm and damp, he knelt on the bathroom rug and bowed his head to pray. Opening himself up to all of it meant letting in the trials they'd recently gone through with his family. He and Veracity had already endured a real-life example of how extreme the challenges to their love could be.

She still wanted him. And he surely wanted her, as she was. Time could take the luster off of the new and shiny parts of a relationship, but those parts didn't matter to him. It was her core, the look in her eyes, what he felt in his soul at her touch. What he felt in his soul, which he believed would always have depths that mystified him, and held and expanded his own.

He put all of himself into what he'd learned about prayer and devotion to God, what she'd taught him about breathing and drawing energy into him, connecting to her spiritually and sexually. As he did that, desire and need intertwined and anticipation surged. It was time to be with her.

He rose and looked in the mirror. A soul was connected to all other souls, but when he desired to be connected to one in particular, to call that soul his mate, it was an important moment.

He put on the robe and opened the door. Skye was on Ros's computer, but when the door opened, she closed it down and came to him. She was so different from Vera, wearing chunky jewelry and a split-sleeved top of melted colors over faded jeans, her blond hair spiky on one side and shaved on the other so he could see an ear cuff shaped like a dragon.

She smelled of lemon cake, and her moon-shaped face was what he imagined a fairy's might look like. However, her dark eyes had a pure Mistress's look, coursing from his face down to his toes and back up again. He waited, knowing he should. She assessed him, physically and mentally, and the warmth and approval in her expression when she was done told him he was good.

As they descended the stairs, he heard music. Women were chanting, their voices rising and falling. The song was coming from the speakers in Ros's living room. When he reached the dining room, the wall of energy coming from the space made him pause. As did what he saw there.

Ros and Cyn were on either side of Vera, who stood at the foot of the table. She'd been veiled with the transparent blue cloth that had draped the side bar. He could see her lips against the sheer fabric, and the curves of her body beneath it. The cloth was all that she was wearing.

Abby stood at the head of the table. At her nod, Skye pantomimed opening a door.

"The circle is opened for the Lord, to join his Lady within it," Abby said, her voice rising above the recorded musical chant. As Rev stepped in, coming to stand before Vera, Skye closed the "door," sealing the energy into the circle.

"Quarters have been called and the circle is set," Abby continued. She was reading from the paper given to her by Veracity. But the sensual purr of her voice contained joy and love, plus those Mistress elements he recognized, reinforced by her look toward him. The women were channeling the things of the Goddess that a Mistress would know and feel.

"The elements, the spirits, have come to witness this Rite, the meaning it will embed in the man and woman who have opened themselves to be vessels for the Lord and Lady."

Cyn and Ros came to him, and Cyn slipped the tie of his robe. Ros took it from him, her nails grazing his shoulders. "You will now give your Mistress the Five-Fold kiss," she said. "Remove her veil."

Rev stepped closer to Veracity, and gingerly pinched a fold of the cloth to draw it off of her. Cyn took it from him.

Veracity stood before him, naked and beautiful, open to him. Her eyes rested in the embrace of his, her mouth soft. While Skye had told him how each part of the ritual was done, she'd also told him he could follow what his heart suggested to him. The words and actions that happened would be what was meant to be said and done.

So when he knelt, his first words were natural as breathing. They'd brought her to him in the beginning. "I dream of kneeling to you, Mistress," he said. "Today and every day of my life."

Though he knew the Lord cared nothing for a silver tongue, Rev concentrated on saying the words proper, to show an additional effort for his Mistress, to prove what she meant to him.

"Blessed be your feet and knees, which I plan to kiss every morning when you give me the honor of being the one to wake you, to the sunrise of a new day together."

He bent and pressed his mouth to both places. Energy coursed through her, nerves and pleasure both. He glanced up and laid his hands on her legs, behind her knees, letting her feel his support. "I here with you, Mistress. I'm nervous, too. And caught up in wonder."

She wet her lips, her gaze clinging to him. "Go on," she murmured.

He pressed his lips just above her sex, inhaling that musk. He was aroused, and finding her in a state of desire just made him harder. "Blessed be your womb, which represents the life that all women give, that God gave to my mother and yours, so that I could have you in my life and have the chance to serve you. And if life stirs there that we have created and God has blessed, I will serve you both."

Her hand fell on his shoulder and gripped, hard. Then he straightened up from his knees, putting his mouth on the sweet valley between her breasts. Her hand moved with him, staying upon him. "Blessed be your breasts, where I can rest my head when I serve you well, and beneath which beats the strong, beautiful and fragile heart I'll do anything to protect. You gave it to me freely, and I'll cherish it, in all I do."

He stood at his full height and looked down into her uptilted face, the light-filled silver eyes, their fringe of dark lashes, the smooth skin of her cheeks, the fullness of her mouth. Her lips parted, evidence of the emotions he saw and felt in all of her.

"I..." He stared at her, losing his place. As she waited for him to find it, he felt certain the universe was turning around them right now. "I kiss your mouth, but the gift and privilege of it, of all of it, has me overcome. I ask that you tell me I'm worthy of it, that I've earned the right."

Her gaze filled with tears. She understood. He was asking her once more, perhaps for the final time, to make it a clean slate between them, to show she'd forgiven him fully, in every corner of herself.

She framed his face with her hands, fingers slipping against his skin. "Parts of me are battered, Rev. But I trust you to protect them as they heal and grow strong again, leaving behind fear or anxiety. I trust you. I love you. You are worthy and have earned my love and my forgiveness. I want you to belong to and serve me, and have no other earthly Mistress but me."

"I want that, too," he told her, and put his mouth on hers. Her lips were flavored with the salt of those few tears, and he wiped them away before he returned his arms to his sides and stood before her, waiting for the next part.

"So there are no doubts," Ros said, "we will echo what our sister has said. You are forgiven, and we have faith in your love for your Mistress."

"Yes," Abby murmured and Skye nodded.

Cyn met his gaze. "No doubts, Rev. Yes."

He swallowed, that overcome feeling doubling.

Then tripling, as Vera knelt. He wasn't sure how he felt about it, but it was part of the ritual, so he stood still.

Vera's lips were soft on the top of his foot. "I honor your feet, which stand firm on this earth while you walk in the Lord's ways. I honor your knees, which kneel to us both, in the service of Love. I also rejoice in the pleasure that gives me, to have you serve me as your Mistress."

Then she moved to his cock, thick and jutting before him. "A celebration of the virility of the Lord, brought to the service of the Lady," she murmured. Veracity kissed the shaft, her hand circling it, and licked away the hint of semen at the tip. "Blessed be your cock, which responds to the pleasure I command from it, serving me in the ways I desire."

She rose and put her lips on his chest. Since her hand was there, too, he was sure she felt the pounding beneath it. "I say the same for your heart, one of the purest and best I know. I have no doubt of the man who carries it."

She lifted up on her toes, his hands going to her waist to help as she touched her mouth with lingering care to his and gazed into his eyes. "Blessed be your mouth, which always speaks love and truth to me. I am letting go of the fear that it won't be there tomorrow. I feel all you are to me here, and know, whatever can come at us, we will find our way as man and woman, Mistress and sub, guided by Love in all its names."

Her gaze shifted to the women and came back to him.

"Each Mistress will leave her mark on you, reinforcing that you belong to me, and to this wider circle, your care as important to them as any in our family. Will you accept this?"

"I will." He looked at each in turn. "And I thank you. I will be the same for each of you. You my family now, too."

The approval in his Mistress's face was weighted with strong emotions. As he spoke, he saw those feelings echoed in the expressions of the others.

Abby moved to the side table and picked up one of the bottles. "Cypress oil," she said. "A blessing and consecration oil. An Earth oil, also a reminder of death, in that an ending is a beginning. Tonight you become something different. Stronger and more powerful together. Able to handle the impossible. Believing nothing is impossible. Just a challenge to be met together, and that Love will heal all wounds inflicted by those challenges."

She laid a line of the oil along one strip of the flogger, then stepped back to the Northern quarter as Skye took her place and picked up another bottle. "Lotus, sacred oil to ancient peoples, used for blessing and healing. It offers happiness and good fortune."

When Cyn came to raise the next bottle, she tossed them a look of erotic mischief. "Tuberose, also known as Mistress of the Night. An aphrodisiac, because healing and communication come through a passionate and healthy sex life."

Ros took her place for the last one. "Rose oil," she said. "Which strengthens, protects and honors love of all kinds. Which is what every one of us here, and the men who serve us, will do for the love you offer one another."

Her gaze fixed upon Rev. "Once we have each marked you, the flogger will be our gift, to keep and use in the household you and Vera share."

Now Skye and Cyn flanked Veracity. As she stepped back, they helped her take a seat on the table. They'd brought cushions, so she could lie back upon them. As she kept her gaze upon him, she spread her long brown legs. The sensual beauty of the pose tightened his heart and increased the throbbing ache in his cock. When they laid the veil upon her upper body and face again, her eyes were as vivid and piercing to him through its mesh as if there was no barrier between them at all.

Abby made a subtle gesture, reminding him of the next step. He moved between Veracity's thighs, Cyn's palm on his chest and back telling him where to stop. His cock was mere inches from his Mistress's sweet wet folds. As Abby took the flogger from the table and stood behind him, Ros replaced her at the head of the table.

"Stand fast," she said.

"Yes, Mistress." When the flogger fell against his back, the significance of it, of why it was happening, why he was here, came home with the first strike. The tips were knotted, so there was pain. The right kind.

The scents that had anointed the strands reached his nose. He'd ask his Mistress to do this ritual upon him on the anniversary of this commitment, as a reminder of it, to renew it, to make evident his willingness year to year to respect everything it required of him. Everything she required of him.

He didn't count the strokes. That didn't matter. He would stand here for hours if that was what she wanted. By the time Abby relinquished the flogger to Skye and Skye finished, his skin was burning. Then Cyn took over.

Their group sadist took that manageable pain and ramped it up three levels with a different stroke and force. Rev kept his gaze on his Mistress, lying on the table, watching him from behind the veil, the inside of her spread thighs brushing the outside of his. Everything under his skin was coiled and ready for her. The mounting pain only made his cock stiffer, straining for what was so close, the ability to plunge inside, join with her.

He wanted to touch her, hold her. He'd suffer any pain for that.

It was Ros's turn. While she wasn't as forceful as Cyn, his skin was sensitive enough now it shuddered at the slap of every individual strip and knot, his buttocks and thigh muscles tightening to keep him in place.

Thwack. Thwack. Thwack. She hit all those places, including his shoulders.

A pause. Veracity's eyes glittered with silver light as Ros moved to the side table and picked up the one unused bottle there. When she returned to stand behind him, he discovered it wasn't an oil, but a lotion. She smoothed it over his back, his buttocks and upper thighs with a firm, caressing hand that appreciated him without taking anything away from his Mistress or his commitment to her.

He wasn't surprised he could read that from her. With Veracity, he'd learned touch had its own language, like the gestures Skye preferred to use.

He smelled cocoa in the blend, witch hazel. It cooled the sting of the flogger without taking it away, which he liked. He wanted to keep feeling it.

He was being cared for and directed by five Mistresses. There was no earthly—or maybe even heavenly—way he could hide his carnal reaction, but what kept him in such a state of need was Vera's gaze upon him. Watching him stand for her. Waiting upon her command to finally serve her the way every cell within him wanted to do.

Ros put the bottle back on the side table and lifted the chalice. Cyn picked up the athame. She came to Rev, offering it to him, while Ros placed the chalice in Veracity's hand. As Veracity lifted her hand to take it, the veil shimmered over her. She spoke the next words.

"By putting the athame into the chalice, the Lord and Lady's Love is symbolically confirmed, fulfilled and honored."

Rev put the knife blade in the chalice, touching the tip to the bottom. He and Veracity held it that way for several long seconds, his hand so close to hers, holding the cup. Then Cyn and Ros reclaimed the ritual items and put them back on the side table.

Had he preferred the symbolic version of the Great Rite, he knew that would have been the pinnacle of the ceremony. But now all four women moved to their places at the quarters. Ros at Earth, the North. Skye at Water, the West. Cyn at Fire, the South. And Abby at East, the Air. His thundering heart, the energy pulsing through the room, told him the time had come.

Veracity removed the cloth veiling her, once again revealing her chestnut brown skin, her dark hair in a cloud around her face. The light in her eyes was no longer shadowed, and he saw the Goddess there.

"Removing this veil symbolizes the opening of my heart, mind and soul for our Joining, and for our life together." Her tone had been firm and clear at the wedding. The sureness was still there, but he heard the woman, too, in trembling emotional notes. "Give me your wrists," his Mistress said.

When he did, she tied the veil around them, tucking in the ends. Her lashes lifted. "I have waited a long time for you, Karman Leone," she said.

"I sorry I couldn't be here sooner."

"I think you came just when you should." Her lips curved. "Now you will come into me, and the Lord and Lady, if They bless and wish to do so, will come down in us and be part of this union."

As he'd suspected, feeling it, living it, helped him understand this part even better. They would be vessels for divine purpose, as well as for their own hearts.

As above, so below. Like the picture in her bedroom said.

The Lord made Himself known in the works of his creations, and had seen fit to give them a direct line back to Him, if they just quieted everything else to see it, hear it. Yes, she was right. It had happened all just as it should, when it should.

"You're beautiful, Veracity. I see all that you is, and I glad to be yours. Grateful, and full of love. I also want to be inside you. Right now, if I'm not being too demanding about it."

"Your demand is you and the Lord being what male energy is supposed to be in a moment like this." Her smile was female and mysterious. And sexy as he'd ever seen. "It's all part of it. Just as me wanting you inside me, here and now, no matter if the world was collapsing around us, is what the Lady and I want."

As he put his knee up on the mat and rose above her, she lifted her legs and clasped them around him. He had no self-consciousness about the other women. They were supposed to witness him honoring and pleasuring his Mistress.

He'd waited for her, too. Known she was there.

When he entered her, a groan of utter bliss tore from his lips. She tightened her legs around him, encouraging him. This moment wasn't about special breathing or that kind of deliberate thought. The energy driving them would dictate the pace, the urgency.

Rev slid his arm beneath her, needing her even closer, needing her hips to tilt and take him deeper. She cried out her pleasure, her hands moving to his shoulders, nails digging in, her cheek brushing his as he put his face down to hers.

The energy wrapped around them, taking them higher, farther inside one another. Divine energy. Whether he called it God or she called it the Lord and Lady, it was there to bless and carry them, to give them this memory throughout their path together. They had the blessings not only of her family, present here and in spirit, but of the Divine.

Gifts that couldn't be measured. Just like the woman he held in his arms, who gave him all of herself, even as she demanded the same from him.

Neither of them was aware when Skye opened that "door" and the women slipped away, leaving the circle to them as their commitment, their love for one another, took them to a release that put them near Heaven.

So close to it that, when they finally floated down to earth, Rev thought angels were guiding them. They held onto one another as long as they wished, a quiet moment in the universe they could also hold onto, for whatever lay ahead for them.

God didn't make promises of an easy path. But when He saw fit to give a soul somebody to share it with, a woman like this, a man couldn't be anything but grateful.

CHAPTER 24

Three Months Later

*B*efore he'd met Veracity, Rev thought a normal climax was a powerful, overwhelming thing. But over the past few months, Veracity had continued to teach him ways to prolong a release endlessly. He could float along in a state where his body vibrated like a tuning fork and his mind swam in waves of pleasure.

And when he was at that point, his Mistress would give him tasks to do. Help her weed her vegetable garden, paint her shed. Give her a "platonic" foot massage while she mused over new fantasies she had about him, and then asked him to tell her his.

She was respectful of his need to be in a different mindset for Sunday services, but this Sunday, after those services were over, she'd brought him home and gotten him worked up in just that kind of way before they went to Progeny for the evening. She drove.

She'd finally let him drive the Aston Martin a few times, but there was no question he was in an impaired state, one he didn't want to have to explain to a police officer if they were stopped for erratic driving.

She'd made it worse by playing her hand over his thigh and straining cock until they reached the club.

Now here he was, in a private room, on his hands and knees, wrists held in cuffs connected by a short chain. Veracity teased his neck with her fingertips and breath as she dipped down to whisper in his ear.

"Who do you serve, Rev? In this room?"

"You, Mistress."

She moved in front of him. She'd chosen to wear what she'd worn to church earlier in the day. Yes, she did respect his need to keep his mind on God during church, but if she ever wore this outfit again for a service, he'd have to work extra hard for that focus.

His Mistress, like God, appreciated effort and sacrifice.

The lavender skirt, silk gray blouse with a hint of white lace at the cleavage, the gloves...Lord above, watching her don the gloves did odd things to him, and when she ran them over his skin like she did now, the feel of the silky cloth made him shudder.

Her hat had a curling feather and that little net veil in front. This one reached her chin. When she'd let him kiss her, she'd kept it in between, so the rough mesh and softness of her lips both had been against his mouth.

She removed the hat, pulling the pin free. Her hair was styled in waves today, pinned against her head, a few soft curls wisping around her face.

She slid the hat along his back, the felt and feather tickling him. Then she set it aside, unzipped the skirt and shimmied out of it, leaving her in a slip. She opened her blouse but left it on, so it framed her high breasts and the snow-white bra that held the mouthwatering sight of them.

Her shin brushed his shoulders and head as she swung a leg over and straddled him, facing his backside. The dampness of her cunt marked him. She wasn't wearing any panties, which made him wonder if she'd been wearing any during the services.

He might have to resort to some medieval methods to keep his focus on God. Like a hair shirt. Lined with thorns.

When he shared that, she chuckled, a throaty sound. "This is the modern era, Rev. Plenty of devices can make your cock behave. You remember that first night at Progeny, the cage you saw around a man's cock? Chastity devices like that become very painful if your cock tries to rise up and draw your attention away from where it needs to be. It will curb that inclination with prejudice. And some of those devices come with a padlock only I can remove, once you've properly served God and are free to serve your Mistress."

Lord help him. She'd warned him the more he learned of this world, the more intriguing he might find what had initially dismayed or unsettled him.

She pricked him with her hat pin. Here, there. Along his upper thigh. He clamped down on the very strong urge to jump as she applied it to his shaft, his exposed testicles.

Her thighs rubbed the lace of the garters against his side. She bent, her mouth on his balls, lips sucking at the base of his shaft. She moved one hand up his thigh, nails scraping, while the hat pin pressed deeper against one testicle. She'd removed the glove from that hand.

Now the sharp pin edge dragged across the perineum, followed by her damp mouth. He was shuddering with the effort to stay still, not knowing where that pricking sensation would come next. He kept pulling in his breath the way she'd taught, and Lord above, the feeling was intense.

At last, when his body was quivering, jerking like he was about to have a seizure, she rose. "Drop to your elbows, Rev. Knees spread, ass up."

The position made his cock and balls feel even more exposed. Since he couldn't see her behind him, he was braced for the pin stick. Instead, she rolled his testicles in her firm grasp and rubbed his shaft. He suppressed a groan as she kept doing it, until even all the methods she'd taught him were about to be useless. He'd have to beg her to stop, so he could hold back the climax until she said he could have one. She knew he didn't like to do that.

But mercifully—and the word didn't exactly mean that when applied to a Mistress—she stopped and came around to his front at last. She was sucking on the finger he expected she'd passed over the head of his cock to collect the small amount of thick fluid that had spurted from it.

She squatted, her slip smoothed tidily beneath her, and caressed his shoulder, his mouth, his brow. "Do you ever think of having me the way an animal would do it, Rev? From behind, your body covering me?"

"Sometimes, Mistress. Yes." Especially now that she'd mentioned it. She liked that Shakti-Shiva pose, her straddling him in an upright position. Or, if they were in bed, she enjoyed having him upon her. It never felt like she held any less control, even as she celebrated his masculinity and strength that allowed him to bring them both pleasure in that position.

"How often? Often enough it makes you even harder to imagine it now?"

"Yes ma'am."

A little hum came from between her moist lips. Her hand dropped to the cuffs. They were locked with small padlocks, unable to be removed except with the key she had hanging around her neck, strung on the chain with her pentacle.

She rarely did that, put him in restraints he couldn't remove himself. Him obeying the hold she dictated was proof of his devotion to her, his willingness to submit.

He didn't care much for restraints he couldn't take off, but he'd found he did sometimes need that.

Like when the more administrative things the church demanded kicked his ass and made his head hurt, trying to read the documents that needed to be reviewed. Mrs. Byrd was helping him as much as she could, but at those times, he longingly thought of just being a janitor who could sing at church and do spontaneous ministering.

But God didn't ask of a man what he couldn't give, and right now he was doing what he was meant to do. When he was with Veracity, everything steadied. If it didn't, she knew how to make it steady.

He didn't ask for that from her. He much preferred to serve her in all things, but his Mistress decided what she would give, and she was as generous as the Lord Himself. And as strict when needed, to ease his heart, and calm his agitated mind.

That was one of the reasons they were here tonight, and she was pushing him so hard. They'd been sentenced this week, Witford and Tisha. Aggravated kidnapping. Eleven years each, eligible for parole in five. They could have received a much harsher sentence, but Veracity had used her connections to ask for leniency.

He also hadn't asked for that, knowing he had no right to do so. But she'd done it anyway. It humbled him, that she'd done that for those who'd wronged her so deeply. She'd sat with him in the courtroom on sentencing day, the first time she'd seen them since it had happened. When Tisha turned around and saw her next to Rev, her face had frozen, but she'd looked defeated. Older. Veracity had stared at her, expressionless. Rev held her cold hand in his, warming it.

Rev hadn't wanted to come, but had known he should. For Teena Joy. This was her sister, her nephew. He held onto that thought throughout it all.

When it was over, and he'd left the courtroom, Veracity's hand in the crook of his elbow, he thought he would be okay. But then he found himself coming to a full stop in the parking lot, his body rigid with things he couldn't explain.

Veracity turned to him and he reached out to her, grateful for letting him hold her, and for her holding him.

When she eased back, she searched his face, seeing the things he had no words to express. "We're going to the club this weekend," she'd said. "After church."

His mind was brought firmly back into the present as Veracity shed the rest of her clothes. Blouse, slip, then garter belt and bra. All with her back to him. His gaze touched the tattoo on her shoulder, the black cat curved around the pentacle. The symbol of her faith, like the cross was for him.

His gaze slid down. While he always appreciated the sight of her gorgeous breasts, her backside had enough temptation to keep his mind occupied. He lingered on the heart shape of it, the lengths of her thighs.

Then she raised her arms to lift her unpinned hair off her neck, her chin bending toward her shoulder. His mouth went dry with the beauty of the pose, his head spinning at the miracle of knowing he belonged to her. And she to him.

She looked over her shoulder, a long measuring moment. Then she knelt, her back still facing him. "Come to me, Rev."

He rose on his knees. It was just a few short movements to get there. He laid his hands reverently on her hips, the chain between the cuffs stretched across the curve of her ass. When he looked down, the head of his cock brushed her wet sex, and she shuddered.

"Mistress?"

"You have my permission, Rev. Come into me slow and easy."

He would never do otherwise, unless she had a different direction for him. He eased in, the feel of it drawing forth another deep groan. The angle was tight, her muscles gripping him. She lifted her head up and back, her throat arching. Her breath drew in as he slid in, and in, and all the way home, his pelvis pressed against her buttocks.

"Cover me, Rev. Touch me as you desire."

He guided the chain over her head and braced both hands on the floor beneath her. She went to her elbows, and he suppressed another reverent oath as her breasts filled his hands. He fondled the nipples, pinched and tugged on them how she liked as he pulled back and then slid in deep again.

Her hair fell forward, and he buried his face in it and the back of her neck, breath hot as he set his teeth there, bit, and earned a cry from her. Her hips pushed back against him, telling him the pace she wanted, the demand she wanted to feel. He could give her that. When she unleashed this part of him, hungry and male, and wanting to take everything she would give, he could lose himself in her. Lose control. It had worried him the first couple times, but now he understood it was a form of service as well.

His Mistress wanted all versions of him. Just as he wanted the same from her.

"Now, Rev," she said softly.

All that energy he'd channeled and banked for hours before this, overflowed the river of arousal for her that never ended. The current was strong through them both, unable to be resisted a moment longer. She let herself go at the same time he did. She covered one of his hands as their lower bodies worked together. Her breast quivered in his palm, nipple stabbing into it as their movements pushed them forward, jerked them back, and then forward again.

His brain emptied out as his cock did, every worry of the week, the pain of the sentencing, all of it. She'd flogged him earlier, too, giving him a different kind of pain. She brought the one they'd used on him that night and had replenished the oils on it, a reminder of their connection to others, to those who would never betray them, never abandon them.

Just as they would never do that to one another.

When they finished, he had his arm tight across her chest, palm curved over her shoulder, his other hand braced on the floor below it because of the length of the chain connecting the cuffs. She had one hand hooked over his forearm, the other holding that chain, fingers tangled in the links.

They breathed deep and heavy together. She'd shed a few tears, and so had he. The release of that energy had brought its own catharsis.

Nothing needed to be said. They had one another, which made everything else bearable.

He eased out of her when she was ready, lifting his hands over her head and sitting back on his heels. She unlocked the padlocks and freed him from the cuffs, caressing his wrists. But before that, while her hands were still on them, he lifted his touch to her face to kiss her. He held there, a good long time.

When he at last rose, he went to the washroom, bringing back a damp towel to help clean her, then himself. After tidying up the room, he knelt, and she allowed him the pleasure of watching her put herself back together.

Veracity didn't put on her clothes the way anyone he knew did. Each piece was donned with care to project a particular look, and she created it like an artist. At least that was how he felt about it.

She chose to leave off the hat. Turning toward him, she put her hands on her hips. "I know you're getting comfortable with this world, Rev Leone, but you're not walking through the club naked for other Mistresses to ogle. You better get dressed. But leave off the shirt."

"It okay for them to ogle my chest?"

"Yes. Because I like to savor their envy."

He grinned. "Yes'm."

After he was dressed, she came to him, caressing his bare chest and side with her tantalizing touch. Even after sex, she was capable of restarting his engine and beginning a whole new journey in that direction. "Want to go hang with the others for a little while?" she asked.

"If that's what you want, then yes."

"There's a reason I choose to ask a question rather than issue a command, Rev. Your opinion is important to me."

He knew that, but for most things, it was one and the same for him. So he gave her the honest answer. "I do want that, Veracity. I like being around them, and I like how they look after you. I want that feeling, and I think you need it, which is all I need to want it, if that make sense to you."

Her finger tapped his chest. "It does. It makes all the sense in the world."

～

The honest response pleased Vera. But then most everything about Rev did. "Thank you, Rev."

He kissed her hand and held it to his cheek. As he did, Vera put her other hand on his jaw. She could see his ragged edges. He still wasn't a hundred percent, but he was working on it, and their session had helped. "I know you don't want me to worry about you," she said, "but I will do it when you need it, and you will let me. I can reinforce that order by shoving my hat pin in places you don't want to think about."

His chuckle made her laugh, too. When they reentered the public play areas and dance floor of the club, the music, communal energy and limitless erotic stimuli only added to the pleasure of what they'd just shared. Icing on the cake, to her way of thinking, and she was ready to lick it off her fingers. Or him.

She cut across the dance floor, turning under his arm and doing a little hip shaking with him. He was known here now, as her submissive. They received an enthusiastic reception and were drawn into a line dance, Rev holding his own with some dance moves that had female subs and Dommes alike eying the ripple of upper body muscles and flex of denim covered ass.

Another male sub matched his moves, shoulder to shoulder. Dex preferred men, but he knew Rev didn't, so it was a friendly competition that ended with a high five as the dance ended and Rev turned back to her.

Though he seemed fine, Vera had kept her eye on his post-session state. Rev's dancing had started out a little less gracefully than his norm, but getting playful with it had helped. They freestyle gyrated and twirled their way to the VIP staircase on the other side.

The others were already in the lounge. Neil was absent, so Abby and Ros sat together. Lawrence perched on the broad top of the booth on Abby's opposite side, his leg pressed against her as she leaned into him. The two SEALs put out a similar energy, so Abby could draw on that feeling to ease the pang of missing her man and any anxieties.

Rev noticed Abby and Lawrence's proximity. "When Neil is gone, does Ros..."

"Share Lawrence? Yes and no. She and Neil have an agreement that she only plays with a sub with him present, but when he's gone, she can join in on Ros's sessions, and sometimes Skye and Tiger's. Not so much hands-on, but participating in ways that ease her Mistress craving."

"Not with Mick and Cyn?"

Vera grinned. "Not Abby's preferred play style. Attila the Hun would be triggered by a session with those two."

Skye and Cyn sat together, Mick on the outside of the booth next to Cyn. Tiger was on a high bar stool behind the booth, close enough Skye could rest a hand on him as the group talked, because her body was turned toward his. His knees were splayed in his worn jeans, his tattooed arms crossed over his large chest.

Mick brought over two chairs, one for himself and one for Rev, so each man could sit next to his Mistress at the ends of the booth, while giving all the women a space in it.

Vera had barely gotten settled, Rev clasping the hand she rested on his knee, when a woman came hurrying over. She had earnest brown eyes and a bouncy blond ponytail bound with a pink bow. Her short denim skirt was paired with a white T-shirt with My Precious Pony on it. Canvas sneakers and white ankle socks completed the look.

"Rev, hi!" she said with girlish enthusiasm. "Would you be willing to sing..."

"Catalina," Vera said.

Her quelling tone stopped the submissive short, snapping her gaze to Rev's Mistress. "Apparently, you've forgotten protocol."

Rev had parted his lips to speak, but Vera's hand constricted on his knee. Her attention never left Catalina. "If you desire something from my submissive, you speak to me. Don't you?"

The hapless woman found herself pinned by the stares of four Dommes. Tiger, who had the softest heart for the female submissives, gave her a sympathetic look. Lawrence and Mick remained impassive, though it took effort. None of them liked to see women punished, even if the women craved it in ways they recognized in themselves.

"Of course, Mistress. I apologize. I...uh..."

Unsurprisingly, her Master had picked up on her distress. He strode across the lounge to join her, putting a possessive hand on her shoulder. "Is there a problem, Catalina?"

"Yes, Sir. I asked Mistress Vera's sub for something without asking her permission first."

"Did you apologize?"

"I did."

Master Bruno glanced at Vera. "Do you accept the apology, Mistress Vera?"

"I do. But you might reinforce the lesson to help her feel better about the faux pas. And ensure it's not repeated."

"Gladly."

Vera shifted her gaze back to Catalina. "What did you want to ask him?"

Rev had come here enough with her to understand the situation, so he remained quiet, willing to follow her lead.

"I wanted to know if Rev is going upstairs tonight. He told me next time I was here he'd sing something for me. For us." She blushed even deeper. "If his Mistress was okay with it."

"I'm glad *he* remembered that part." Vera glanced at Rev, who managed to hold back a smile, supporting her stern look. "When I feel it's the right time for it, I'll have him come and tell you."

Catalina apologized again, then withdrew, her Master giving her ponytail a tug before he led her away with his firm grip still on her shoulder.

"It's okay, Mistress," Rev told her. "It wasn't much to ask."

She slid her hand along his lower back, into the waistband of the jeans to tease the upper rise of his buttocks. "I know you want to give whenever something is asked, but you're still spinning from our session, even if you're not aware of it. I know when the vessel is almost empty. Give it time to refill. Then you'll be able to give her what she's wanting, without that weight upon you."

He might not be aware of the further easing of his shoulders, but the subconscious relief told her the decision had been correct. Rev was a sub who would give until he had nothing left. Learning that his Mistress could say no on his behalf, leaning on that, and being okay with it, was another step in the journey a Domme and sub took together. She was glad the opportunity had presented itself.

As an added perk, Master Bruno would owe her for the excuse to discipline his pretty sub. It might have even been his intent, because there was less tolerance for childish impulsiveness in the VIP lounge than in the section of the club dedicated to Daddy Dom play. Catalina had been too in character to rein herself back.

"Watch out for groupies, Rev," Cyn said. "Next thing you know, they'll be throwing panties at you."

Vera pressed her lips together at Rev's sidelong look, which held the reminder of her rock star fantasy.

"Does anyone *wear* panties at Progeny?" Skye asked, using her Ryan Reynolds voice.

"I'm wearing mine," Lawrence noted.

"The red lace with the bows on the side?" Mick asked. "You know those drive me wild."

"Catalina look different from last time we saw her," Rev noted to Vera.

That had been several weeks ago. She hadn't been playing that night, just hanging out in the club coffee shop with friends, wearing fashionable jeans and a shirt with a wide neckline that slipped off her shoulder, revealing a blue teddy bear tattoo.

Vera explained the Daddy Dom relationship to him. "I guess that makes sense for some," he said, after taking a few minutes to digest it. "Hard to be an adult all the time, especially when the world all the time be demanding it."

With Catalina, that was an understatement. She was an assistant district attorney.

"What does Master Bruno do?" Rev asked. "If he's okay with people knowing."

"He's an oil worker. When he's not out on a rig in the Gulf, he volunteers for the raptor center, helping rehab the injured ones. He and Catalina have played together for about a year."

"Are they...exclusive?"

"No. He's gone too much for that, and Catalina needs what Progeny provides more often. So she has about two or three Daddy Doms. He's her favorite, though, so when he's here, she's with him."

"It don't bother him, her being with others?"

"No. Think of it like a friendship. You don't mind if a good friend has other friends, because you know each friend may provide your friend something different. And you're not in competition with one another, not if the friendships are good, open-hearted ones. You're just glad your friend finds what they need, and that you can be part of that."

That said, she thought if Bruno's schedule ever changed, he might decide he did want that exclusive claim. And Catalina would be totally on board with that.

"Brandy, you a fine girl," Rev hummed. "What a good wife you would be..."

She smiled, not at all surprised he'd picked up on her thought and reflected it in the 1970s classic song.

The waitress had brought another round of drinks, and Ros was taking a sip of Abby's virgin daquiri. Declaring it good, she teasingly tried to swipe it, and Abby slid it away with a mock glare. Skye was showing Cyn something on her phone, signing one-handed as she did. Tiger peered over her shoulder, his brow raised, and winced. He threw a warning glance at Mick. "Brace yourself, man," he said. "They're surfing the Stockroom."

Mick leaned in, pressing against Cyn's shoulder, ignoring the elbow she threw to his midriff. Instead, he rested a hand on the curve of her neck and shoulder, his thumb caressing her. "That is anatomically impossible."

"We should test it out to be sure," she said. His steel-blue eyes went even darker as Cyn stroked his brown clipped beard and firm lips. "I think you agree."

"I prefer to leave you guessing."

"I never guess. Not with you."

He pressed a smile against her lips and nipped her with a flash of sharp teeth.

"Eww, get a room," Skye's recorded voice was the whine of a petulant eight-year-old. Tiger chuckled.

Vera noted Abby had closed her eyes, and Ros had an arm around her. She was stroking Abby's shoulder and upper arm in a soothing manner. When Vera mouthed, "Is she okay?" she wasn't surprised everyone caught it, and glanced in the same direction. When Abby was with them, they stayed attuned to sudden changes in her head

410

space.

Ros signed with one hand. "We'll head out soon."

"You know I can tell when you're doing that. Going away, going back, going away." Abby's eyes opened and she sent Rev a rueful smile. "Don't worry," she told him. "My normal. Gotta go now. Word salad time and no steak to go with it."

Rev and Vera moved out of the booth so Ros and she could slide out. Lawrence offered his arm to both ladies and nodded to the other men, a silent, *got this covered* look. Ros put her free arm around Vera, and Vera looped hers around Abby, including Lawrence in the hug she gave them both. "I'm so glad you joined us tonight. Me and Rev can come by and stay the night if you like."

"No. I'm good. Just need to get home." Abby's gaze was moving in that way it did, not settling on one particular thing, and not making eye contact, but she managed to shoot Vera a smile. "Almost med time. Then bed time. Med time, bed time. Neil's home soon. I hope."

Lawrence gave Vera a nod, suggesting that would be the case. Though the former SEAL claimed he didn't get classified details, he always seemed to know when a mission was drawing to a close.

Vera sent her usual prayer to the Universe, that Neil came home unscathed to the beautiful woman he loved—and who loved him just as vehemently, enough to insist he continue to do the work he needed to do to be fully Neil.

"Who wants to know what Bastion is doing tonight?" Cyn asked, after Ros, Abby and Lawrence headed for the stairs.

"What or who?" Tiger asked.

Cyn bounced her eyebrows at him. "He's showing our new account manager around his preferred club digs. Apparently Ren's a switch."

"How did Bastion find that out?" Vera asked.

"He added a line on the HR form you have new hires fill out," Skye responded without batting an eye, using her crisp Helen Mirren voice. "W-9, social security number, are you into the BDSM scene?"

"Cyn put you up to that, didn't she?" Vera made a fired gun motion toward the woman in question.

"Skye is my give-Vera-an-aneurysm apprentice," Cyn said, unruffled. "She's coming along well. I plan on introducing her to Emperor Palpatine soon."

Vera shot Rev a severe look when he chuckled. "Don't encourage her. Ever. That's an order."

"Hey." Tiger drew their attention to the far side of the club. Vera let out a sigh of relief as Neil came through the foyer entrance into the club, no more than a few steps before Ros, Abby and Lawrence reached it. He had to have come right from the plane, because he looked tired and dusty, but his eyes were alive with purpose as he sought the woman he'd come for.

Abby was in his embrace in a heartbeat, and he held her close, his head buried in her neck as her arms twined around his broad shoulders.

"Must have been a hard one," Tiger said, reading the signs.

"She'll help him with that, like she always does." It was Cyn who said that, and Mick nodded in agreement,

"Yeah. Just being where he is right now, he's halfway to okay already."

Cyn glanced at Mick, then put her hand over his on her shoulder, showing she wasn't unmoved by his subtle admission, or Neil and Abby's unexpected reunion.

When she turned back to the rest of them, though, she offered a typical Cyn crack. "Kind of rude, Neil making Lawrence wait for his own hug and kiss."

"It's a good thing you know MMA stuff," Skye observed, still in the Mirren voice. "Otherwise someone would punch you in the face daily."

"And most the time it would be one of us," Vera added.

"Ros does it at least once a week, during our sparring," Cyn said. "I still can't figure out how. I should be able to wipe the mat with her."

"Ninety percent of her fight skills are here," Vera said, tapping her forehead. "Yours are here." She moved the touch down. "Heart and gut. Still good, but different."

"She's right," Mick agreed. "I keep telling you to work on that."

"I keep telling you that if I want your opinion, I'll give it to you, but you don't listen to that, either."

Lawrence and Ros returned to the table. Neil and Abby had disappeared, headed for home. When Vera glanced at Rev, she could tell he had something on his mind.

"I'd like to sing," he murmured. "Something for you, while you with your family."

"Okay." She stroked his face. "I'd like that."

He rose but leaned down to kiss her, drawing back to give her a long look. His expression showed wonder, gratitude, and love, and she wasn't ashamed to say she literally basked in it, no matter that Cyn made goo-goo eyes at her after he headed off. Vera did throw a balled-up napkin at her, though.

When she told them Rev wanted to give them a song, the others enthusiastically followed her up to the Breathing Room. Once there, she saw Sy and Trey had joined him on stage. They'd seen him earlier and probably had been hoping he'd want to play a couple songs before or after their own scheduled sessions with a Domme. The Breathing Room was a great way for them to practice and perform at the same time.

Bruno and Catalina were here and she knew she'd give Rev the go ahead to take a request from her, at the proper time. But right now his attention was on Vera, and she wasn't going to allow anything to change that focus. Especially when he said he wanted to sing something specifically for her.

As she settled at a table with the others, Rev turned squarely toward her, making it clear that was his intent. Then Trey did a hand over hand up the keyboard, giving him the stream of notes for the song's intro. When Rev began to sing, her heart melted.

"Maybe I'm Amazed," by Paul McCartney.

Sy came in on the drums, the instruments building with the strength of Rev's voice. He spoke of his awe over how she pulled him out of time, how he needed her, what he felt for her, how she helped him sing his song. She felt the overlap, as she did in all his songs, that meeting of earth and the heavens.

She and God were the two things Rev needed most, and he would never hide that from her, never play games, never take away his love when she needed it most.

She saw the others watching her, and him, the final piece in place. Not that she'd ever been incomplete or not part of their group without a man, but that spot had been open and waiting, and she'd craved the right man to fill it.

She'd relied on herself and built her own foundation. Then Ros and the others had given her the home resting upon it. Because of that, tonight she could believe the man she wanted most was going to share that home with her.

It had taken a long time for her to believe in it, in a way that wouldn't get knocked off its pedestal every time life shook it.

It was said the Lord giveth and the Lord taketh away, but she didn't believe that was always true. There was one thing that, once the soul embraced and understood its full nature, became inseparable from the soul. It could never be taken away.

Love.

"Thank you," she whispered. Her heart was speaking to the women she loved and their men, to every step in this journey, every soul that contributed to it and made it what it was. Made her who she was.

Most of all, she said it to Rev, getting lost in his brown eyes, his half smile, and the gift of his voice, the message and promise it offered to her, now and always.

"Thank you all."

WANT MORE? If you've read all five of the Mistresses of the Board Room books, how about a **FREE** gateway-to-series **full length novel** from another one of Joey's contemporary series?

They call her the Ice Queen. At the exclusive BDSM club known as The Zone, Mistress Marguerite is a legend. Tyler Winterman is her male counterpart, one of the club's most powerful Masters. Though he respects the hell out of Dommes, he's convinced Marguerite is a "switch," her soul aching to submit to the right Master.

Uncovering the truth will strip their souls, revealing needs deeper than either expected. But Tyler will risk body and soul to give his troubled angel everything she needs.

CLICK HERE TO READ NOW
ICE QUEEN

BookFunnel link for additional download option (book not free on Nook)

ABOUT THE AUTHOR

Having penned over fifty acclaimed BDSM contemporary and paranormal titles, which includes six award-winning series, *Joey W. Hill* has been awarded the RT Book Reviews Career Achievement Award for Erotic Romance. A submissive herself, Hill brings authenticity to her intensely emotional love stories.

She is grateful for the support of a wonderful and enthusiastic readership, which allows her to live on her beloved Carolina coast with her even more beloved husband and menagerie of animals.

- On the Web: https://storywitch.com
- Twitter: https://twitter.com/JoeyWHill
- Facebook: https://facebook.com/JoeyWHillAuthor
- Facebook Fan Forum: https://facebook.com/groups/ JWHMembersOnly
- MeWe: https://mewe.com/i/joeywhill
- GoodReads: https://www.goodreads.com/author/show/ 103359.Joey_W_Hill
- BookBub: https://bookbub.com/authors/joey-w-hill
- Amazon: https://amazon.com/Joey-W-Hill/e/B001JSCIW0

ALSO BY JOEY W. HILL

Mirror of My Soul

Mistress of Redemption

Rough Canvas

Branded Sanctuary

Divine Solace

Worth The Wait

Truly Helpless

In His Arms

Ignition Sequence

Naughty Bits Series

Naughty Bits

Naughty Wishes

Vampire Queen Series

Vampire Queen's Servant

Mark of the Vampire Queen

Vampire's Claim

Beloved Vampire

Vampire Mistress *(VQS: Club Atlantis)*

Vampire Trinity *(VQS: Club Atlantis)*

Vampire Instinct

Bound by the Vampire Queen

Taken by a Vampire

The Scientific Method

Nightfall

Elusive Hero

Night's Templar

Vampire's Soul

Vampire's Embrace

Vampire Master *(VQS: Club Atlantis)*

Vampire Guardian *(VQS: Club Atlantis)*

Vampire's Choice

Non-Series Titles

Chance of a Lifetime

Choice of Masters

If Wishes Were Horses

Medusa's Heart

Make Her Dreams Come True

Snow Angel (short story)

Submissive Angel

Threads of Faith

Unrestrained

Virtual Reality